Praise for ALL HONOURABL[illegible]N

'Lyall is sure to dispel wi[illegible]er has much charm' – *Th*[illegible]

'A delight of [illegible]*orset Evening Echo*

'Beguiling . . . eleg[illegible]phere, with plenty of high adventure and fair play' – *South Wales Argus*

'Splendid period thriller . . . Cleverly plotted and nicely written, it deserves to be a big hit' – *Coventry Evening Telegraph*

'Early days of the British Secret Service are recreated in thrilling detail' – *Nottingham Evening Post*

Praise for FLIGHT FROM HONOUR

'A great read . . . one of this year's unputdownable thrillers' – *Sunday Telegraph*

'Wry observations on spies and spying . . . action-packed adventure' – *Hampstead and Highgate Express*

'Gripping . . . a very well-crafted period piece' – *Times Literary Supplement*

About the author

'For style without affectation, ruthlessness without the usual mindlessness, Lyall is likely to be your man' – *The Observer*

When Gavin Lyall's first book, *The Wrong Side of the Sky*, was published in 1961, P.G. Wodehouse wrote: 'Terrific! What better novels of suspense than this are written, lead me to them.' After six more adventure novels including *Midnight Plus One*, winner of the Crime Writers' Association Silver Dagger, Lyall created Major Harry Maxim, Whitehall trouble-shooter (played on TV by Charles Dance) in *The Secret Servant*, *The Conduct of Harry Maxim*, *The Crocus List* and *Uncle Target*. His most recent novels, *Spy's Honour* and *Flight from Honour* both feature Captain Matthew Ranklin. Gavin Lyall lives in London and is married to Katharine Whitehorn.

Also by Gavin Lyall

The Wrong Side of the Sky
The Most Dangerous Game
Midnight Plus One
Shooting Script
Venus With Pistol
Blame the Dead
Judas Country
Spy's Honour
Flight From Honour

The Harry Maxim novels

The Secret Servant
The Conduct of Major Maxim
The Crocus List
Uncle Target

All Honourable Men

Gavin Lyall

CORONET BOOKS
Hodder and Stoughton

First published in Great Britain in 1997 by Hodder & Stoughton
A division of Hodder Headline PLC

Coronet edition 1998

10 9 8 7 6 5 4 3 2 1

A CIP catalogue record for this title
is available from the British Library.

ISBN 0 340 70855 7

Printed and bound in Great Britain by
Clays Ltd, St Ives plc

Hodder and Stoughton
A Division of Hodder Headline PLC
338 Euston Road
London NW1 3BH

1

On Tuesday nights the hotel had a violinist and a pianist in the parlour. This was odd because in every other way it was the sort of hotel where, if you asked for an extra blanket, you got told instead how warm a night it was. But the best musicians did not play in Gloucester Road hotels, and Lajos Göttlich had heard their small repertoire too often already, so he escaped to the dimly gas-lit lobby. To go out meant spending money, but he might manage to borrow an evening paper off the receptionist.

However, the receptionist was listening to some tale being spun by the out-of-work Irish chauffeur who had been there only a week (and had asked for "Danny Boy" on his first evening; he had got "In a Monastery Garden" for his impertinence). Lajos heard the receptionist say: "A *Rolls-Royce?*" so he paused, half-hidden behind an aspidistra plant, and listened.

"Can you drive one?" the receptionist was asking.

"I can drive anything," the Irishman said confidently. "Anyways, I *did* drive this one. Quite a nice motor-car, I'm thinking."

"Gosh." The receptionist imagined himself being able to describe a Rolls-Royce as "quite nice". "And will he buy it?"

"If he listens to me. And if he don't listen to me, why'd he hire me, then?"

"Oh, absolutely. Are you going to stay on here, now?"

"I'd not be knowing jest yet. Mind, I wouldn't be saying no if he wanted me to move into the Savoy with him, close and convenient." The Irishman cackled. He had a lean, dark piratical look – an old face on a younger loose-limbed body – and averaging the ages Lajos had reckoned he was little over thirty. But you had to be young to understand all these new mechanical toys that obsessed the world: motor-cars, air-ships, aeroplanes.

The Irishman – was his name Jarman? Gorman? Lajos wished he could remember – caught sight of him and waved cheerily. "And a very good evening to ye, Mr Göttlich."

"He's found a position," the receptionist said.

"Excellent! May I offer my congratulations?"

"Ye can do more'n that: ye can come out and have a drink wid me."

Gorman – he was pretty sure it was Gorman – was obviously going to be so insistent that Lajos could seem reluctant. "It is rather cold, is it not?"

" 'Tis a lovely spring evening and I'll not hear a word against it. Be getting yer coat, then."

"If you wish." A man who lived at the Savoy and sent a new-hired chauffeur to pick out a Rolls-Royce for him . . . Lajos would have walked naked through a snowstorm to hear more.

* * *

Mr Carstairs was not an impressive man, but Lajos had long ago learnt not to judge a man's bank balance by his physique. Shortish – shorter than himself – a bit tubby, fair-haired and with a boyish, optimistic face (the rich, Lajos had observed, did things their own way, wearing young faces on old bodies). At home in his Savoy suite, Carstairs wore just waistcoat and trousers of very dark grey, with an old-fashioned wing collar and one of the dullest neckties in London. But the gold watch-chain across his stomach could have anchored a battle-ship.

They introduced themselves and Carstairs waved at a silver tray. "Help yourself to some coffee, it should still be hot. If not, I can—"

"I am sure it will be fine." The room was big and warm and, being at the back of the hotel, quiet. A small writing-table by one window was piled with company reports and suchlike; today's *Financial Times* lay on the floor.

Carstairs had been lighting a pipe. Now he asked abruptly: "How did you hear of me?"

"As I said in my letter, friends in the City mentioned that you had recently returned from South Africa—"

"Just over a week ago."

"—and that you had been asking about investment opportunities in oil."

"I was." Carstairs sat back in his chair, puffed his pipe and looked critically at Lajos. But he hadn't the face for strong expressions: everything came out boyishly innocent. "And are you looking for an opportunity to make some money out of me?"

"I certainly hope not to be the loser by our acquaintance," Lajos said, unperturbed. "And I am not here on a charitable mission. But may I start with a warning?"

Carstairs nodded.

"You are too late. You should have begun ten years ago. Better still, twenty. Now, oil has become too big a business. With the invention of the motor-car, with navies building warships that run on oil, it is now a game of nations, of empires. Even the Rothschilds, so I understand, are pulling back."

"Hm. Are you saying there's no more oil to find?"

"No, no. Of course there is oil still to be found, but – are you a mining engineer, Mr Carstairs?"

"No, I made my little packet finding engineers who knew what they were doing and backing them – and managing them when they needed it." He smiled. "Which was a bit more often than they expected."

Lajos nodded approval. "That is a rarer talent than most people understand. And you like being your own boss?"

Carstairs puffed contentedly. "I'm spoiled that way."

"Then you are looking for someone who can find, or has found, oil – and does not know what to do next?"

"Something like that."

Lajos seemed about to go on, then paused. Finally he said: "One more warning, Mr Carstairs: oil needs both patience and reliable finance. Do you understand how much it can cost to drill one well in the deserts of the East? At *least* £100,000."

But Carstairs came through that test without batting an eyelid.

"And that is before you have paid all the *baksheesh* to the local sheikhs and government officials, before you must build a pipeline to get the oil out, perhaps also a refinery, charter ships . . . Shall I tell you what so often happens then, Mr Carstairs?"

"Go ahead."

"You run out of money. Somehow, when you see a fortune within reach, the banks become reluctant. They have heard rumours, perhaps your concession is not legally so perfect, they fear a war in that area, shipping rates are going up . . . Ah, such rumours! And then, like the handsome prince in the fairy-story, there comes one of the big companies – Shell or Standard or Anglo-Persian – who saves you. That is, they buy you out for a fraction of what you have spent. And they live happily ever after."

Carstairs took his pipe out of his mouth and squinted at Lajos. "Are you trying to scare me off?"

"No, I only want that you do not say you were not warned."

"Then what do you advise?"

"*Start* by thinking you will sell out to the big companies. Go only so far, spend only so much, to prove there is oil – and then sell. As long as they know you are not hungry, that you do not *need* to sell, then they will become hungry – and a big, hungry oil company is a wonderful sight. Even better, you may have a pack of them, bidding like wolves against each other for your well.

"But they will not buy just rumours, a concession to drill. They are offered a hundred every day. So you must spend some money to prove your strike."

Carstairs got up and walked to the window, trailing thoughtful smoke-puffs. He stared down at the wind-scuffed brown Thames and a small steam-tug, foaming at the bows yet making almost no headway against the combined ebb and current.

"That sounds like good advice. Worth something in itself." He swung around. "So what I'm looking for is someone with a good, likely concession to drill in – where? Mesopotamia? Persia?"

"Not Persia: Anglo-Persian is too powerful there. And Mesopotamia only if you trust the new Turkish Government . . . but I think first of the little sheikhdoms on the Persian Gulf."

"That's still part of the Turkish Empire, isn't it?"

Lajos's Eastern European background showed in a fluid rocking movement of his hand. "It is a long way from Constantinople. And a long time since the Turks were powerful enough to beat on the gates of Vienna. Yes, I think the Gulf is the most likely place, and I have a little connection there. I must find out – discreetly of course – what is the true situation."

* * *

The map was a beautiful map – even as reproduced by the blueprint process, which made it look slightly smudged and, of course, blue. Every sand-dune seemed to be shown by delicate hatching, and the stylised shoreline, where desert met the waters of the Persian Gulf, appeared to ripple with the gentle surf. It was a work of art.

Perhaps a mining engineer would have preferred a work of geology, but the oil concession was clearly marked as a rectangle of red ink, exact position and area noted. It even had a little oil derrick drawn in.

"Artistic licence," Lajos explained with a smile. "However, the true licence from Sheikh Mubarak is also here – witnessed, you observe, by a British vice-consul."

Carstairs passed the document to his solicitor Mr Jay, an aristocratic-looking young man, younger than Lajos had expected, but wearing a proper founded-1803 suit and a true legal air of sceptical puzzlement. "Signed in October 1912," he observed. "Eighteen months ago. What progress has been made in that time, Mr Göttlich?"

"As I told Mr Carstairs, drilling equipment, the latest Parker Rotary patent machinery, has been landed in Kuwait and is now being erected." Lajos dealt Jay a full hand of overseas cables and copies of letters. "Drilling should, I understand, start within the month."

Carstairs crinkled his brow in a boyish frown. "Then why should Mr Divine pick this moment to sell out?"

Lajos gave a sad, exaggerated shrug. "A complete collapse of his health, I am sorry to say. His doctors have ordered him to Switzerland. Between ourselves, gentlemen," his voice grew confidential, "I fear his sickness has much to do with the slowness of developing this concession: it needs a younger, more energetic man to make things move along. Also one who has not lost badly on the French market. But that is rumour, please do not repeat it."

Mr Jay coughed dryly. It wasn't the true Saharan cough of a seasoned solicitor, but it was a good junior version. "The motives for Mr Divine's selling are not legally germane. What concerns me is (a) whether Mr Divine is the true owner of the shares – which the company register appears to show him to be, and (b) whether Mr Göttlich has the right, as trustee, to sell them on his behalf. Which this document –" he routed among the piles of paperwork scattered across the hotel room's coffee-table "– appears to show that he is."

The slight exasperation on Carstairs' face dared Lajos to get annoyed. "Why do you always say *appears?* Do you suggest because I am not an Englishman that I—"

"Calm down, Mr Göttlich," Carstairs soothed. "I never yet met a legal gentleman who'd say it was wet if he was swimming, just it *appears* to be."

But this only seemed to annoy Jay in turn. "Nor can I say," he said coldly, "that there is a single grain of sand in this part of Arabia, a single drop of oil under it, nor a nut or bolt of drilling machinery preparing to seek it out. Only that it *appears* that you would have a good case against Mr Göttlich if this transpired not to be so."

Carstairs was just starting to soothe the lawyer when there was a knock on the door and he let out a bellowed welcome instead. Gorman, dressed in a grey chauffeur's livery and polished black leggings, came half-in. He touched his peaked cap. "Jest wondering, sor, if ye'd be wanting the motor in the next hour, or should I be getting an early lunch?"

"Hang on a moment, Gorman, I may want you to witness my signature and then pop down to my bank and pick something up in a short while. Help yourself to some coffee and find a seat somewhere."

"That's kindness itself, sor." As Gorman bent over the coffee tray he gave Lajos an enormous wink.

"Where were we?" Carstairs resumed. "Oh yes, I was calming you down, Mr Jay. Consider yourself calmed. Anyway, I shall be going out in a week or so to see what I've bought into, and meanwhile Mr Göttlich isn't likely to head for Switzerland for *his* health, so we'll just have to wait and see what *appears* – all right?"

"I am very pleased you say that," Lajos announced. "And if these were my own shares, I would most happily wait until you had seen the concession for yourself. But Mr Divine is seeking a quick sale, so . . . May I remind you that the German Hamburg-Amerika Line also sails to the Gulf these days?"

"Does it? Didn't know the Germans were interested in that area."

"Most certainly. You may have heard they are also building a railway from Constantinople to Baghdad – perhaps further. I believe they would like it to go to Kuwait. But the British have a certain *understanding* with Sheikh Mubarak – in return for protecting him from his own Turkish masters."

"Does that understanding have anything to do with oil?"

Lajos smiled confidentially. "Who knows how the impassive British Foreign Office thinks? But if we may return to more prosaic matters . . ."

"Like the price?"

* * *

"Carstairs," Ranklin grumbled. "*Carstairs*. Nobody's called *Carstairs* except in schoolboy spy stories." He finished signing the name. "And doesn't a false name invalidate the whole deal?"

"I doubt it'll ever be questioned," Mr Burroughs said sunnily. "Least of all by Göttlich-Divine. Did you suspect—"

"Since Göttlich means divine, I did rather."

"Anyway, the £14,000 is real enough; he's not going to want to give that back – the company owes more than that to the American drill-makers. Thank you for saving us a few thou', by the way. You obviously drove a hard bargain."

"We'll take yer thanks in cash," O'Gilroy suggested.

Mr Burroughs was momentarily flummoxed, unused to hearing men in chauffeur's kit say things like that. Then he smiled uneasily and began sorting the paperwork. In fact, he was uneasy with the three agents anyway. It might have been the unease people feel when meeting actors off-stage but still in their greasepaint and costumes, only it wasn't. And they knew it but said nothing.

"So," Burroughs went on quickly, "thank you for a most satisfactory conclusion: Albemarle and Dover Trust now owns a controlling interest in Oriental Pearl Oil and Pipeline."

"Is there really any oil out there then?" Lieutenant J asked. He was stretched almost horizontal, feet on the table and defying his suit, which wanted to sit up in a proper legal manner.

Burroughs hesitated and glanced at Fazackerley of the Foreign Office, who moved his eyebrows in a diplomatic but otherwise meaningless way. "Oh well, you can hardly be gossips in your, ah, profession . . . The answer is that there quite likely is, but the concession isn't in Kuwait any longer. The British Government helped Sheikh Mubarak define his boundaries last year in an agreement with the Turks, and the concession now falls just outside them. So the Sheikh's signature is no longer worth anything as regards that patch of sand."

"So?" Lieutenant J prompted, and Burroughs realised he had to go on.

"However, there certainly seems to be oil in Kuwait – I believe it's oozing out of the ground in places, so perhaps even the experts can't be wrong – and Oriental Pearl also owns the lease on a stretch of foreshore. Göttlich insisted the company bought it from himself; he used to run a pearl-diving business there, he knows Kuwait well. And that bit of foreshore is the only suitable place for an oil pipeline terminal and dock."

"Ah. I noticed mention of a stretch of beach," Ranklin said, standing up. "I didn't know its importance." He went into the bedroom to start packing.

"So," O'Gilroy said thoughtfully, "if'n the boundaries hadn't been spelled out, mebbe Mr Göttlich'd be a rich man? – and honest with it?"

"Possibly. Only possibly." Burroughs finished stuffing papers into his attaché case and snapped it shut. "We know Mr Divine or Göttlich of old and he isn't a real crook. None of this was planned. He's the sort of man who meets a setback, feels the world's done him down and he's got a right to do someone else down. Men like that seldom get rich. Well, thank you gentlemen. Thank you," he called to Ranklin, "Mr, ah . . . Carstairs. Are you coming, Fazackerley?"

"I'll catch you up downstairs." When Burroughs had gone, he went to the bedroom door. "Are you ready to leave, Captain?"

"Nearly. Ring for a porter, would you? And a taxi – at the River entrance, I think. Just in case. And you'll settle the bill, will you?"

"Umm, er, of course." Fazackerley was there to do such things but, after all, he *was* the Foreign Office and they merely Secret Service. So he frowned at Lieutenant J's brandy-and-soda. "I imagine you chaps normally pay for your own drinks?"

"No, no, quite wrong," J said complacently. "Us spies never do that. But do tell, what's the FO doing being so chummy with the oil biz?"

"Excuse me, I'd better ring for that porter."

2

The Secret Service Bureau lived in a jumble of attic rooms in the roof of Whitehall Court and the Commander, who headed the Bureau, lived in one of the bigger rooms. He was a stocky man with a face like Mr Punch, who vastly enjoyed the job, had surrounded himself with ship models, gadgets and a collection of pistols, dubbed himself "Chief" and signed papers "C".

That morning he was being visited by Lord Erith, a meticulous hawk-faced man who was rumoured to have turned down honours, ministries, governorships – whatever you cared to think of – to stay in some minor post in the Royal Household where he had the ear of the Monarch and thus everyone else. Mind, rumour also had it that Erith's influence was waning under the new King, but he was still high on the hill.

The Commander owed him a continuing debt since it was Erith who had chaired a sub-committee in 1909 which had taken the secret decision to set up the Bureau. Not secret from anyone who mattered, of course, just from the voters and Parliament. And even that perhaps mainly from embarrassment, since most people – popular novelists particularly – assumed Britain had had a world-wide and omniscient Secret Service for ages.

Moreover, as long as Erith approved of the Bureau he had invented, and was still listened to by the King, the Secret Service was reasonably safe from the bigger and older predators of Whitehall. So the Commander felt he should be fairly open about his problems.

"I'm still looking for a permanent second-in-command," he

was saying. "Preferably Navy. The Navy's always had a more world-wide outlook and a Naval officer has to *know* something, just to keep his ship off the rocks; the Army can get by with merely showing leadership. So if you have influence at the Admiralty . . ."

"Alas, young Winston seems beyond influence, but . . . Who's doing the job at present?"

"My *acting* second's a Gunner. Chap we call, in our secretive way, Captain R. But he doesn't want the job permanently."

Erith looked politely puzzled. "Surely, if he volunteered, he must—"

"He didn't exactly volunteer. I rather helped." The Commander took his pipe out of his mouth and inspected it for plumbing problems while he considered how much to tell. "He'd had to resign his commission through bankruptcy and gone to fight for the Greeks against the Turks in Macedonia. So—"

"Odd, isn't it," Erith digressed, "in a country that prides itself on its patriotism, how *respectable* it is to go off to war for someone else? Waterloo veterans fighting for Bolivar, our officers running the Egyptian Army—"

"Don't forget Cochrane," the Commander said cheerfully. "He commanded the Chilean, Brazilian and Greek Navies – in succession – after we cashiered him. Wound up buried in the Abbey, too, and he wouldn't have got that by staying at home."

"You were telling me about your acting number two."

"Yes . . . I thought I'd made a mistake there, since it turned out it wasn't this chap's fault. It was his brother playing silly-buggers on the stock market with the family money, then shooting himself and leaving our chap to foot the bill. So he isn't really a *natural* cad, and I more or less had to blackmail him into working here. We pay his family's debts as long as he does. But it's worked out well enough."

Erith had very good control of his expression, but he allowed himself a blink. "And he isn't a little . . . bitter about this?"

"Oh, of course he is. And by now he's learnt to be suspicious and mistrusting, too. I don't want men who've gone through life wrapped in cotton wool."

"Quite, quite so . . . Only, I still wonder . . . if you might do better to pick people who are, well . . ."

"More the clean-cut dashing types who volunteer to Save the Empire in spy stories?" the Commander suggested. "Anyone who thinks like that belongs in a bin. God save me from a man who really *wants* to be a spy."

"I think I'll spare His Majesty that viewpoint. Next thing we know, you'll be recruiting these Irish blackguards for their skill in outwitting us." He looked at the secret, clamped-shut smile on the Commander's face and a horrible thought began to grow. "You don't mean to tell me—"

"Just the one. Oddly enough, it was Captain R who found him on a mission to Cork – they'd served together in the South African War. Now he's turned out to be one of the most effective agents we've got. In his own way."

"I shall most *certainly* spare His Majesty that titbit." Erith looked around the room, at the sloped attic ceiling, at what showed of his shoes beneath the spats. He was obviously gathering courage to ask something . . . "As regards your agents' methods . . . Often, I suppose, women can be surprisingly well informed . . . If you see what I mean."

The Commander didn't.

"That is to say," Erith went on, "do you encourage your people to contract *liaisons* to extract information?"

So *that's* what he was driving at. Erith, whose private life could probably bear the closest inspection, seemed never to have grown out of a schoolboy voyeurism. Now he wanted detailed tales of spies seducing the mistresses of foreign diplomats. Oh Lord.

"I rather leave that to their personal inclinations. And talents."

Erith looked disappointed, almost rebuffed, and the Commander didn't want that. He trawled his memory. "Of course, one of our chaps seems *very* close to the daughter of Reynard Sherring, the American private banker."

Erith went on looking disappointed. The Commander said: "International banking has very good information. It's a good source."

"I dare say, but—"

"We got something of great interest to the Admiralty that way."

"—but do you mean they're *really* close?"

The Commander's patience snapped. "They're probably fucking each other blind, for all I know." There, that was what you wanted to hear, wasn't it? "All I care about is that we got a tip on an oil matter in the Gulf . . . Anyway, she's a widow, so it's perfectly respectable."

"Fascinating," Erith murmured. "Ah – does she know what your chap actually does when he isn't . . . When he's working?"

"I have to assume so. But –" he shrugged his heavy shoulders "– it's all a profit and loss account with invisible figures. You just hope you're getting invisibly rich."

"Quite so . . . So you're involved in the Oil Question. I presume you know of Winston's plans – do they concern you?"

"So far, only marginally. I've a feeling it won't stop there."

"No, I fear not." A small fastidious frown flickered across his brow. Conniving, even fighting, for the silk and spice trade had a certain *something* . . . Something that oil didn't have, anyway. He sighed. "But I can say that you are . . . would 'fully aware' cover it? Excellent." He stood up, quite unconsciously brushing invisible spy-dust off his perfectly-fitting frock coat. "Then I thank you for letting me intrude. I can presume to say that His Majesty will be well satisfied if he hears nothing of your continued progress."

The Commander escorted him out through the sound-proof door and the outer office. This was furnished with unmatched but comfortable-looking chairs, small tables with ashtrays, a scatter of newspapers and magazines. It might have been any small club – and Whitehall Court was full of them – devoted to owning a certain make of motor-car or shooting a particular breed of animal. Three men stood in a huddle by a window.

They glanced at Lord Erith, showed no hint of recognition, and went on talking.

He was disconcerted; surely they *must* recognise who I am, he thought. Then he remembered that they would be carefully trained not to show any reaction, and went his way content.

The huddle was still in session when the Commander came back. O'Gilroy had been able to change out of chauffeur's uniform in Ranklin's – actually the Bureau's – flat downstairs, but Lieutenant J still wore his funereal City solicitor clothes. The Commander asked: "Is it all wrapped up, then? Succesfully?"

They let Ranklin, as senior, answer: "As far as we're concerned, yes, sir."

"Come in and tell me about it."

* * *

"So," the Commander summarised, "we assume Mr Göttlich/Divine is really off to Switzerland by now."

"I think Budapest's more likely, but yes in principle," Ranklin agreed.

"Have you both moved out of your respective hotels?"

Ranklin nodded, looking regretful. He had felt he could get accustomed to the Savoy. O'Gilroy, recalling the aspidistra'd tedium of the Gloucester Road, lowered at him.

"And you're sure the Foreign Office paid all your bills?"

"With no more than a murmur about alcoholic beverages," Lieutenant J said. Then, affecting the innocent air of the young new boy, he added: "You wouldn't believe how generous they get in the company of the oil business, sir."

The Commander shoved his pipe into the narrow gap between the tips of his nose and chin and glared. But that did no good; the three looked back calmly, and he knew they would quietly snoop and ponder until they had their answers. Dammit, that was their job.

So he sat back in his chair, struck a match, and said: "All right, tell me what you think you know."

Again they looked at Ranklin to answer for them. He said politely: "What we guess will happen is the Oriental Pearl's new owners will sell off its assets – such as the foreshore lease in Kuwait – seemingly to try and satisfy the creditors and keep out the receivers. But they'll fail, and let the company go down. Which is hard luck on the other shareholders, but what would have happened anyway. And the obvious people to sell the lease to is Anglo-Persian Oil, who are already in the Gulf area."

Lieutenant J took up the story. "And by a singular coincidence, the registered office address of Albemarle and Dover Trust Co. is that of a director of Anglo-Persian. I'm afraid I got carried away when I was playing solicitor, and looked up a bit more than I was supposed to in company registers and so on. You know how it is, sir." He smiled winningly.

Ranklin resumed: "We can see why Anglo-Persian used back-door methods to get the concession. Göttlich would have got greedy if he knew they were interested, and the Turks might have remembered they really own Kuwait if they'd heard of Anglo-Persian buying in there. But we are slightly puzzled at why Anglo-Persian can't stage its own swindles without asking the help of the Foreign Office and ourselves."

"And even more puzzled," J said, "why the FO gave that help – unless they're most frightfully chummy with Anglo-Persian."

"Like," O'Gilroy topped it off, "they, or the Government, was going to buy Anglo-Persian. Jest so's the Navy'd have some oil of its own."

"Stop," the Commander said. "Stop where you are." He glowered at his table-desk with his pipe sending up war-dance signals. Finally he said: "Young Winston's going to put this to Parliament as soon as he reckons he can persuade them. But it'll cost a hell of a lot and he'll have a hell of a job, and the whole thing could go smash if somebody gossips about it beforehand. *Especially* to a friend in the City, no matter how close." He had shifted his glower to Ranklin for that.

Ranklin gave a nod and smiled placidly back. In fact, all three were smiling.

"Smug buggers," the Commander muttered. "Go on, get out. Not you, Ranklin, I want a word."

When the other two had gone, the Commander relaxed and grinned. "And you think the Foreign Office ended up happy?"

"As happy as that chap Fazackerley ever seems to get. Was that what it was all about?"

"Mostly. If we can get them turning to us in their hour of need . . . well, it may stop them trying to strangle us in our cot." Normally, the Foreign Office resented the upstart Bureau, and not entirely without reason. Ambassadors disliked sharing their job with spies, particularly when the spies got caught and undid years of diplomacy with a single blaring headline.

"But we'll see what happens next time," the Commander added. "Meanwhile, thank your girl-friend for the tip that Göttlich was trying to unload his shares; I assume that's where you got it? Did I hear that she – at least her father – is interested in getting involved with the French on a new Turkish loan?"

"Did you, sir?" Ranklin said coolly. But the Commander, thanks to his second wife, was himself in the world of yachts and Rolls-Royces, so he could well have City friends of his own.

"I'm sure I heard something . . . But that being the case, you'd better become our Turkish expert."

"For Heaven's sake, I've only been to Constantinople, and that for just a few days as a tourist years ago."

"And you fought against them in Macedonia, didn't you?"

"Pitching shells onto people's heads at four thousand yards doesn't give you a great insight into their national character."

"Every little helps," the Commander said. "You're still the closest to a Turkish specialist that we've got."

And that, Ranklin had to accept, was true. In the tiny Bureau, you were well-versed if you knew one fact about a foreign country, while knowing two made you an expert. So in the next days he took to noting every reference to the Ottoman Turkish Empire in the newspapers, and even read several books on the Eastern Question, although without finding out exactly what the question was, let alone the answer.

He had the time to spare, particularly in the gloomy March evenings. O'Gilroy had gone back to their *pension* in Paris and Corinna was either on her way to Constantinople or already there, indeed involved in a possible Turkish loan. Their last meeting had been one of the strangest episodes of his life.

3

The Commander had got one thing wrong: "Mrs Finn", *née* Corinna Sherring, was not a widow. The San Francisco fire of 1906 (which did *not* involve an earthquake, as any resident without earthquake insurance could tell you) destroyed so many public records of births and marriages that it became, retrospectively, where most of America's confidence tricksters had been born or married. But what (a kindly judge asked himself) could a millionaire's daughter gain from falsely declaring she had lost both husband and his birth certificate in the flames when no inheritance was involved? The judge's wife might have pointed out that society – particularly in Europe – allowed widows far more licence than unmarried girls, but more likely she'd have kept such knowledge to herself. Anyway, the judge hadn't asked her.

Corinna had not, in the eyes of society, abused her freedom. She did not steal others' husbands, however obvious the offers from the husbands (and occasionally their wives). She had simply set out to enjoy the full life she had heard whispered about at her Swiss finishing school. And if anybody said she could only do that because her father was very rich, she readily agreed and pointed out that, since he *was* rich, she'd be silly to pass up the chance.

Her interest in making as well as spending money was a different matter. For as long as she could remember she'd been intrigued by what her father actually *did*, and when her brother Andrew showed no interest at all, he nurtured her curiosity into a fascination with the world where money was not pennies and dollars in your purse but something as invisible as the breeze, as powerful as the typhoon – and as vital as the trade winds.

Meanwhile, her mother, long deserted by her husband and now apparently by her daughter as well, took to drinking even more heavily. It was, Corinna now realised, terribly unfair that the effect was so obvious when she didn't understand the cause. And when she understood that the cause was her father, she had to cope with hating him for that whilst loving and admiring him for the rest. She found she could manage that. But it left her very, very wary of marriage.

Perhaps she felt safe with Ranklin just because they had no future together. And she could be honest with him – even about the late, fictitious Mr Finn – because they had swapped hostages and she knew, and kept, his own more dangerous secret. With him, she didn't have to face the forever.

She had summoned Ranklin to meet her at the end of a grey March afternoon in an upstairs room of a Bond Street gallery, one of those places dealing in *beaux arts* which could be anything from probably Venetian crystal to an attributed Gainsborough via a restored Hepplewhite commode. She was talking to one of the staff "experts" (salesmen), who had manoeuvred her near to a comfortable chair and obviously wanted her to sit down and give him a turn at dominating. He had Ranklin's sympathy.

Corinna – several inches taller than Ranklin – had literally a head start when it came to dominating, and her clothes did the rest. She bought mainly from someone called Poiret in Paris, so while the rest of Bond Street tottered along in pastel hobble skirts and small feathery headgear she wore a loose kimono-like coat of purple-red and a black matador's hat.

Most women would have become invisible inside such clothes; Corinna got away with it because of her vivid and rather actressy exaggeration of eyes, mouth and black hair. She saw Ranklin and blazed a wide grin at him. Standing too close, the "expert" recoiled from the muzzle blast.

"Hello there. You know Constantinople, don't you?"

"I've been there."

"What d'you think of this, then?"

"This" was an oil painting placed on a display easel to catch what little light came from the window over the street. Ranklin couldn't see if it were signed by an artist he should admire, but with its minarets and Byzantine domes and small boats it was unmistakeably Constantinople.

"It is," he pronounced, "unmistakeably Constantinople. At sunset," he added.

"Ignorant yahoo," Corinna said. "That *could* be by Vanmour, painter to the French Embassy in Constantinople in the eighteenth century. You didn't even know embassies had artists in those days, did you?" She spoke with the confidence of very new-found knowledge.

The "expert" said hastily: "I'll leave you to discuss it then, madam, sir." He bowed slightly and vanished downstairs.

"I know nothing about art," Ranklin said, "but they sell those by the yard in the souvenir shops of the European quarter. Why the interest?"

"I've got to go there."

Ranklin looked at the picture again. "Well, if you add the smell of someone brewing coffee with sewer water and the sound of a street fight in Greek and French, staring at it might help. *Got* to? – why?"

She finally sat down. Untypically, she made quite a procedure of it, propping up her dainty umbrella and carefully placing a large piece of hand baggage that she insisted was just a "purse". "Oh, business, more or less."

She was keeping something back, but Ranklin knew enough just to nod. Perhaps she realised the impression she'd given, so started to drown it in explanation. "The Turks are looking for a big long-term loan – again. Their Finance Minister's been running around Europe all winter trying to raise one. The City here won't touch the idea, the Germans aren't lending money to anyone at the moment, so the French are his best bet, they've lent so much in the past they're riding a tiger. And their people are out there talking right now.

"We've got a new Ambassador in Constantinople, Henry Morgenthau. A Democrat." She considered, then perhaps remembered the poor man might have been born that way, and went on: "He used to be a Wall Street lawyer. And the Turks apparently asked him Could America help out? It seems the answer was mostly No, but there's one guy, Cornelius Billings from Chicago, who's been a pretty good client of ours over the years, and he got interested and went out there in his yacht—"

"In this weather?" The Eastern Mediterranean wasn't the Bay of Biscay, but Ranklin had imagined American millionaires as strictly summer sailors.

She got a little austere. "It isn't a bath-tub toy. It's over a thousand gross tons, three turbines and does sixteen—" She caught his expression of polite uninterest. "Anyhow, it's bigger than ours. So: he went to Constantinople, he listened to them, and cabled Pop saying he was getting interested. Pop's pretty wary of the Turkish market but doesn't like to say No to an old client, so he's sending me, so I can take the blame if Billings starts saying we've let him down. It won't be the first time." She sounded philosophical about it, then added: "And Billings may be right and there's some good business to be picked up there. The Turks certainly need the money. According to Billings, the Balkan wars literally ran them out of cash so the Government can't pay its wage bill. I mean, *think* of that: you do a week's work but don't get paid at the end of it."

Scandalised by the thought, she stood up and strode to frown out of the window. Ranklin was less moved. He didn't pretend to know Turkey, but he had met Eastern fatalism. And there, if you hadn't been paid, well, "It is written." Anyway, most of your income wouldn't be from your salary but bribes – *baksheesh*. And what could you do about it? Certainly not take a stand on principle. Sometimes he thought that her world, with its vastly complex deals measured in eighths of one per cent, only worked because of its simplicity: you kept your word or you were an outcast, and probably a bankrupt. He knew about *that* side of it.

But he also knew a little of the world where making a promise was infringing the prerogative of God.

"And?" he prompted.

"The French are making a foreign treaty out of this loan, all sorts of concessions and rights, and it's taking time. As Americans we aren't interested in that, so there might be room for a simple cash-down deal to tide the Turks over. That's what banks like us can still do. We'll never have the capital the big joint-stock banks have nowadays. But we don't have their dozens of directors and thousands of small depositors, either. We can travel light and fast."

"That sounds most noble. What's the problem?"

"Is anything likely to happen in Turkey to make them default on our loan? Another war, anything like that. Just in the next – say – six months."

"Ah."

"I don't expect you to know, just find out." Simple: the British Secret Service Bureau should dig and delve for an American private bank. But, as the Commander had guessed, this was one of the strata of their relationship.

Ranklin took it calmly. "I think a European war'll happen because something somewhere takes us by surprise – and Turkey's such an obvious place, with all the Great Powers wanting part of their Empire, that it *won't* be the place. If that's any help."

"You don't get a fire at the firemen's ball, huh? It's a good argument – but I'd like a little more."

"And what do we get out of it?"

Her smile suggested she was about to make a naughty joke out of that, but then didn't. "It's no secret that Britain's looking for a reliable, controllable source of oil – right?" Then she told him about Lajos Göttlich.

When the resident "expert" poked his head up to top-step level, he saw them both leaning propped against the window-sill, staring at the floor a few yards away. They made a puzzling pair. He was used to elegant women accompanied by short, fat men whose wallets were tall and handsome, but knowing who Corinna was made Ranklin a conundrum.

Corinna glanced his way, fired off a grin and called: "We're still talking it over. Thank you."

Roused from his thoughts, Rankiin looked at the picture of Constantinople and said carefully: "I know you have problems with men in the City who aren't used to talking finance with a woman, but in Turkey . . . they prefer women seldom seen and never heard. Are you going all by yourself?"

"No-o . . ." She swivelled slightly to look out of the window. "No, but I've got a connection with the French financial delegation there. Edouard D'Erlon, of D'Erlon Frères, one of the Paris private banks. We've done business with them. He's the son of the firm. He's also a director of the Imperial Ottoman Bank. That's the biggest bank in Turkey. Now French-controlled."

The staccato sentences were like the vibrations of an imminent earthquake. He had barely time to brace himself before it struck.

She stood and faced him. "Pop wants me to marry him, and I think I'm going to have to."

All Ranklin's experience as a spy clicked into play. From his expression, she could have been telling him about this wonderful little dressmaker she'd found.

Then, from being clipped and hesitant, she suddenly became voluble. "Ethan, he's Pop's main New York partner, had a heart attack last month. He's got a new young wife (so it serves the old goat right) and he's talking of retiring to breed horses. That's got Pop thinking of mortality and dynasty and what happens to the House of Sherring. He's given up on hoping Andrew will join the bank, so he wants to breed an heir from me. And he reckons Edouard's the right stallion, good banking blood on both sides, see? And later, maybe some sort of merger. That sort of thing's coming anyway. It's the only way the private banks can survive. The world's getting too rich." She smiled wanly. "Hadn't you noticed?

"If I was a man I could walk out on Pop and with my experience any bank would take me on, maybe offer me a partnership straight off, let me owe them for it. But as a woman, people only deal with me because I'm Pop's daughter. So I *need* him, I need the House of Sherring, if I'm going to stay in the game.

"So it's the money, in a silly kind of way. I'll always have enough for myself, unless Pop goes completely bust, but when I marry Edouard, Pop'll settle enough on me so I can buy my own partnership, properly, carry on as I am. Better than I am. That's the deal. It's unfair and Pop knows it and he's got me over a barrel."

During all this, Ranklin had more or less got his feelings formed up and ready for inspection. He had, he told himself, always known it couldn't last. Only he'd thought it would end tomorrow, never today. "What's this chap Edouard like?"

"Oh, perfectly civilised, pleasant company, lousy taste in *objets d'art* but that's French bankers for you, a bit younger than you, a bit taller—"

"Sounds like a bargain. We always knew we weren't permanent. I mean – what future have you got with a captain of . . . whatever I'm a captain of, these days?"

Deceived by the quietness of their tone, the "expert" reappeared, smiling and salesmanlike. Neither of them noticed.

"You're being noble," Corinna said accusingly. "You're being self-sacrificing."

"I'm being sensible and rational."

"God, how I *hate* self-sacrificing, sensible men. They're so *righteous*, so *unfair!*"

"I'm just facing up to things," Ranklin protested. "There really isn't any way we could make a proper marriage—"

"*And that's another thing!* You never even asked me to marry you! Oh no, you were quite happy just *using* me whenever it took you fancy. Well, let me tell you—"

The "expert" almost fell down the stairs before a stray thunderbolt hit him.

"For God's sake, *using* you? What d'you mean? As I recall—"

"I wouldn't marry you if the alternative was the Spanish Inquisition."

"Isn't that just what I was saying? It would be—"

"I'm going to marry Edouard. And I had a plan, but I'm not so sure I'll bother with it, now."

"That's fine. I think you *should* marry Edouard. It's the sensible thing."

"Don't you even want to hear my plan?"

"Only if you want to tell me." Ranklin was being so upright that you could have moored the British Empire to him.

"I don't think I'll do it now, but what I was *going* to do was, just before I marry – I can time this – you get me pregnant, so there's a fifty-fifty chance the heir to Sherrings and maybe D'Erlons too will be *our* son. How about that?"

Ranklin gaped, horrified, appalled. In all his years as a soldier, then as a spy, he had learnt a lot about what men can do to each other. But *women* . . .

All his training fell away. "You can't . . . I mean . . . that is *unthinkable!*"

She grinned, happy that at last she'd shaken him out of his reasonableness. "Nonsense, this isn't cricket, nothing so serious. It would just be playing their game with our own twist."

"My God, I need a drink," Ranklin said weakly.

"Yes, you do look a bit that way. We'd better get you one."

As they went down the stairs, Ranklin said grimly: "On the North-West Frontier, the Pathan women come out and dispatch wounded British soldiers, slowly. Kipling has a poem about it."

"No kidding? Usually he gets his women wrong."

4

Ranklin was sitting in the flat at the end of a gloomy, misty day – but a windless one, more like autumn than March – when the voicepipe shrilled and the hall porter reported that a Mr Tilsey, "a friend of Major Kell's", was asking to be shown up. Kell headed their sister, spy-catching, service (and didn't call himself silly things like "Chief" or "K"), so Tilsey must be one of his men.

"Ship him up," he ordered, and went to the decanters on the sideboard to see what he had to offer.

Tilsey turned out to be a thin man of roughly Ranklin's age, with sandy hair and moustache and generally looking military. Which he was, of course. He would be invisible in a respectable London street or Government building, but little use for keeping watch on foul opium dens in dockland. However, any spy who wanted to frequent foul opium dens was welcome to get on with it unwatched.

They exchanged greetings, Tilsey accepted an Irish whiskey and water, and stood warming himself in front of the fire. "Have you heard of a chap called Gunther van der Brock? He's—"

"One of the Continental secrets-for-sale boys, otherwise a cigar wholesaler in Amsterdam."

"That's the chap."

"—only it's a whole firm and I believe they pass that name around, so it may not be our lad."

"Just under six feet, stout, dark hair, big moustache, spectacles, last seen wearing a light grey town suit and a dark green cloak," Tilsey recited.

"He's the one I know. Is he over here?"

"You know him? Good. Yes, he got into town around teatime. He's staying at the Metropole in Northumberland Avenue, quite openly using his own name. Van der Brock, anyway."

Good for them picking him up so quickly, Ranklin thought. And presumably following his every footstep – or rather, since Kell was even more understaffed than the Bureau, getting Scotland Yard's Special Branch to do so. "He's probably the best of that ilk, deals in only the top-quality secrets. But here, he'd bloody well better be selling, not buying. What's he been up to?"

Tilsey sighed. "We hoped he might have come to see your people, but obviously not. We lost him in Whitehall."

"In *Whitehall?*" They'd managed to lose a large man in a green cloak in one of London's widest streets, well lit and probably not too busy?

Tilsey put on a lopsided smile. "Perhaps you haven't looked out of the window recently."

Ranklin walked over, twitched aside the curtains and stared blankly. He rubbed the glass, then realised it was London that had gone blank. Fog.

There should have been trees, lights, a skyline; there was nothing. Down below should be street lamps: there might be a slight glow, that was all. The building felt it had become an island, and those in the street must feel they had fallen overboard in mid-ocean.

"I see what you mean." He walked back to the fire with an instinctive shiver.

"We were out of touch for nearly two hours," Tilsey resumed. "He got back to his hotel just half an hour ago. Of course, he *may* just have been wandering around, lost, himself. But . . ."

Ranklin shared his doubts. Gunther must know London well enough, he wouldn't be in Whitehall by accident. And that put him within yards of every important Government department, even the Prime Minister.

They sank into armchairs and thoughtful gloom. Reaching for any hope, Ranklin said: "Of course, he wouldn't be too likely to be visiting an informant in a Government office, out of hours and dressed that memorably. He'd choose a crowded tea-shop or railway buffet . . . sorry."

Tilsey was nodding politely; he must have thought all that already. "The only other places we know he visited were St Martin's post office – he picked up a *poste restante* letter there – and a cigar shop in Trafalgar Square. He was in there about twenty minutes, but perhaps just to give himself a business alibi. Then we lost him near the Admiralty."

"Perhaps Whitehall was a blind and the cigar shop was what mattered . . ." Ranklin's imagination raced ahead: important men went to cigar shops, and they didn't buy in a hurry, they stopped to chat. A cigar shop as an intelligence exchange? – no, a whole raft of them, all such shops in central London, secret messages rolled up inside Havanas . . . It was far better than the popular myth that every German waiter belonged to a great spy ring.

He coughed apologetically. "Daydreaming . . . But how can we help?"

"As I say, we hoped he might have visited you chaps, but . . . However, since you know him, would you care to bump into him 'accidentally'? – if we can suggest a venue?"

"I'm happy to – but he won't think it's an accident," Ranklin said firmly. "It'd tell him he's being watched. And he doesn't let slip information, he sells it."

"Major Kell will have to decide whether it's worth that. But if he approves, it may have to be early tomorrow: van der Brock's only booked in for one night. May I telephone you in, say, half an hour?"

"Of course." And Tilsey left to search in the fog for the New War Office, luckily only the width of the street away. Ranklin wondered if he should try and locate the Commander and ask for his approval, but decided it was too delicate a matter for the telephone and eavesdropping operators. And dammit, if he was acting deputy, he could authorise himself.

Tilsey rang up after twenty-five minutes. "Would you feel like breakfast at the Metropole tomorrow at eight?"

* * *

After his stay at the Savoy, Ranklin's hotel standards were high, and the Metropole didn't match up – except for size. At breakfast time, the vast pillared dining-room had a funereal air. Not the jolly scandal-swap when the deceased has been planted, but the brittle, respectful hush of the gathering beforehand.

Ranklin persuaded a waiter to lead the way to where Gunther – still wearing a distinctive and foreign-looking light grey suit – was buttering toast and reading the *Financial Times*. He looked up, spread his arms in welcome and spattered crumbs from under his heavy moustache.

"Captain! A wonderful surprise! Sit down, sit down. Coffee?" The waiter found another cup. "You have not yet eaten?" Ranklin asked for bacon and eggs. "If I had a magic carpet, I would every day breakfast in England. Except, I do not understand *porridge*."

"It's Scottish. A Presbyterian form of the confessional: after eating it, you can behave any way you like."

Gunther chuckled, adding more crumbs to the atmosphere. "And your Chief is well? Good. And Mr O'Gilroy? I thought of him only this morning. This weather hurts my side," and he touched his right ribs. That dated from their first meeting when Gunther wanted to kill them and had rashly got into a bayonet duel with O'Gilroy. However, once he had convalesced, they had become . . .

. . . not friends. Yet more than business associates. Looking idly around the room – not full, at this time of year – Ranklin thought smugly *They don't know*. Here we sit, two men from the world of international espionage, and nobody here knows. Such thoughts were one of the few compensations of the job; it was like belonging to a secret family: you can't choose your relatives, but they were still family . . .

The waiter brought Gunther a plate of bacon, eggs and everything else, assuring Ranklin that his would be along in a moment. Then, professionally looking at neither of them, asked: "Are you gentlemen together?"

"On my room bill, of course," Gunther said expansively. A clue? Since he watched the pennies, had he already concluded a good piece of business? But buying or selling?

He held his knife and fork poised, deciding which part of the crowded plate to clear first, and asked before his mouth got full: "And is this just a sociable meeting?"

"When one hears that a master dealer has set up his stall in town, naturally one hurries to view his stock." Then Ranklin realised he had to go on, since Gunther's cheeks were bulging. "We were just a little hurt that you hadn't let us know you were coming."

Gunther swallowed. "Others have more money." Of course he would claim he was selling, that was no crime. And the ministries were certainly richer than the Bureau. And Gunther had been in business longer than the Bureau: he must still have other clients in London.

Gunther added: "I have an Italian naval code," before restocking his mouth.

"Yes? When are they due to change it?" Gunther wouldn't cheat by selling the same information twice: the code to you, then the fact that you'd got it to the Italians. But he'd sell a code that was about to be abandoned. It was a fine line, and a funny-peculiar one, but he trod it religiously in a world where heresy was a capital offence.

Gunther grinned, shrugged, and suggested: "The Schlieffen Plan? Do you know the latest amendments of that?"

"If you can prove it really isn't just a staff exercise," Ranklin said, "we might swap it for something about the Spanish Royal Family." Then his bacon and eggs arrived and the conversation became just nods and grunts, finely tuned to mean "Everybody knows that" or "You're joking". Ranklin was now convinced that Gunther hadn't anything serious to offer and was mainly trying to find out what the Bureau knew or – just as important – wanted to know.

So when they had finished, and called for a fresh pot of coffee, Ranklin asked bluntly: "So what are you doing here now?"

Gunther's eyebrows rose from his thick spectacles in mock surprise. "Selling cigars, it is my business. Have one." He opened a silver pocket case. From their looks, they might have served to take away the taste of an over-hot curry, but not just after breakfast. Gunther lit one himself.

The hotel didn't exactly allow smoking at breakfast, but it didn't want to alienate what few clients it had in the low season. Anyway, the only others left in the room were foreign tourists waiting hopefully for the fog to clear. So Ranklin lit a cigarette.

"And how about the Eastern Question?"

"Ach – only you English could have such a phrase, that can mean everything or nothing. No, I have nothing from there. But Serbia, I hope soon to have some most interesting news from Belgrade. You must remember to call me . . ." The conversation wound down slowly until, at half past nine, Gunther heaved himself to his feet. "Now, you will excuse me, I am going home today and first I must observe the English custom and 'have a breath of fresh air'." He chuckled as he gestured at the world beyond the windows.

"I'll come out with you."

Gunther had brought his cape downstairs with him and they stood on the front steps looking out on nothingness the colour of dirty washing-up water. But not silence: Northumberland Avenue was a cacophony of honking horns, clattering hooves and jingling harness. Lamps glowed, crawled past attached to the dim shapes of cabs and taxies, and vanished. On the pavement, pedestrians moved hesitantly, unbalanced, staying close to the walls and peering at the hotel name to locate themselves. One man was standing under the glow of a street lamp a few feet away, trying to read a guide-book map.

"A true London fog," Gunther said, as if he were viewing the Taj Mahal. Then he turned to shake hands. "You have come far – in only a year, is it? When I hear of you – I hear very little, I assure you – I think 'I knew him when he had just begun.' "

"You tried to kill us."

"I did not see you as a future customer. Also – I think violence is not a proper part of our trade. I gave you a bad example, and I hear . . . But probably I am wrong." His spectacles gleamed cheerily as the yellow lamplight caught the droplets forming on them. "Au revoir."

Ranklin took a couple of steps, then paused, professionally interested to see if he could spot the Special Branch man who should be following. Gunther had paused, too, wiping his spectacles under the lamplight.

The man with the guide-book turned, put a pistol to Gunther's face and fired. The back of Gunther's head burst and his hat fell off soggily. The man ran, disappearing in three steps.

Ranklin caught Gunther before he hit the pavement, but he was too heavy. Suddenly there was another man, helping ease him down, then blowing a fierce shriek on a whistle, but Gunther didn't react to the sudden close noise. His eyes were already wide and unmoving in a bloody, sooty mask of gunsmoke. Ranklin felt for the pulse in the thick neck, then stood up.

Already the doorman was gawping, pedestrians were stopping. Ranklin said loudly: "Get him inside, get a doctor, an ambulance. *Quick!*" And having stirred them into useless babble and motion, vanished himself.

* * *

Ranklin blundered his way back to Whitehall Court, numb, shivering with shock and simple disbelief. Life could seem so strong. A growing plant could crack through stone; men clung to life with the ghastliest of wounds. So how could it be so fragile? You snapped off a flower head, unthinking. A man turned away and died, from just two little bullets.

* * *

They met in a small room in a Pall Mall club, a good place for a private meeting on virtually neutral ground. The rest of the time, it seemed to be the unread part of the library: sets of thick books that must represent lifetimes of patient work. Had *they* died happy?

He found himself explaining for the umpteenth time: "If I had stayed, the Branch officer would have hung on to me, at least as a witness. I was quite prepared to explain myself, as I did later to Detective Sergeant Dix—" He nodded to a solid, placid and heavily moustached man being self-effacing on the outskirts of the seated group. "But not there and then, not in public."

"But also," the man from the Home Office said, "it seems that you made no attempt to catch the assassin."

"He'd vanished in the fog. I had no more chance of grabbing him than the Branch officer had," Ranklin pointed out.

"The officer was supposed to be following van der Brock, not protecting him," Sir Basil Thomson said. On looks alone, his long face kept a funeral parlour and his nose a pub; in fact, he headed the Yard's Criminal Investigation Department and Special Branch – effectively, all its plain-clothes detectives.

The Home Office man frowned. He was young and trying – too hard – to keep his end up in grand and mysterious company. He was also the only one who was going to have to write a report; Sir Basil, the Commander and Major Kell of the counter-espionage service were all their own bosses.

He said: "Nobody seems to have thought to be armed – except the assassin."

"It has never been Government policy that policemen in Britain should normally wear sidearms," Sir Basil said. "I cannot, of course, speak for the Secret Service." His past experience of the Bureau, particularly an occasion when they had certainly been armed, had left him officially Deeply Concerned and privately Bloody Furious.

"Sorry," Ranklin said, "I hadn't got a gun, either. Not that I'd have started blazing away in that fog anyway."

"Delighted to hear it," Sir Basil said coldly.

"And we don't even have a proper description of the man, just –" the Home Office man turned a copy of the *Evening*

Standard on the table to read from the front page "– 'about five feet six tall, long dark overcoat, face obscured by a scarf'."

"Like most sensible people out in that fog," Kell observed.

The Commander grunted and said: "Professional," and everyone but the Home Office nodded sagely. He blinked at them and tried another tack: "Then was this van der Brock known to have had any enemies?"

Now everyone smiled; the Commander even chuckled, but left the answer to Kell, who said: "He was a notorious seller of state secrets, so at one time or another every Power in Europe had reason to want him dead. However, I believe he was so even-handed that each Power expected he'd be selling to them next week, so let him live. Until today."

"Probably your lads who did him in," the Commander said cheerfully. "*We* shall miss him."

"We shan't, that's for certain," Kell said. "But I'm afraid it still wasn't us."

The Commander grinned at the Home Office. "Well, that narrows it down for you. Only Germany, France, Austria-Hungary, Russia and a few others to suspect."

Sir Basil's voice had become grave. "All highly amusing, gentlemen, but his death doesn't fall to your charge. He's *my* unsolved murder – and likely to be a highly publicised one, if the press get any inkling of his true job. They're already aroused by the way he was killed, assassination-style." He tapped the *Evening Standard*.

"Can't you stifle those bloody editors?" the Commander asked. "I mean, ask for their responsible co-operation? It's my Bureau which will suffer from this: other dealers getting wary of us, perhaps even blaming us for the murder. So, believe me, we'd very much like to see this solved. Only," he added, "I don't think it's solvable."

The Home Office consulted his notes. "I believe there was something about him picking up a *poste restante* letter . . ."

Sir Basil craned his skinny neck to summon the detective sergeant into action. Dix coughed and said: "We didn't find anything that looked like such a letter on him, sir. One theory is that it might have been an introduction that he could show at the door of one of the ministries in Whitehall. And he left it there or destroyed it after his visit."

The Home Office added this all up. "Then he could have visited a ministry last night, when you'd lost him in the fog?"

Sir Basil nodded and put on a slight smile. "There is, in fact, other evidence that he did."

Everybody looked at him, puzzled. Then Ranklin said: "Money. I bet he had a lot of money on him."

"Over £200 in gold and bank notes. How big a secret does that suggest to you gentlemen?"

"Then," the Home Office said, "surely all you have to do is ask around the ministries to find out which—"

"We have already asked the most likely – and they say they will, reluctantly, check. Whether anyone will admit they spent tax-payers' money on such people . . . Would you?"

There was a silence. Then Ranklin asked: "Are you letting the newspapers know any of this?"

"We haven't done so, not yet."

Feigning hesitancy about telling Sir Basil how to run the Yard, Ranklin said: "Publishing the fact that he'd sold us a secret might nullify that secret's value."

The Commander nodded firmly. "Quite right. If – as a nation – we've gained something from his visit, let's for God's sake keep it, whatever it is." He looked around, collecting agreement. "But does this mean he was killed for revenge?"

"Not necessarily," Kell said. "It could still have been prevention – if he was killed by a foreign power. They needn't know he'd already passed the secret on."

There was another silence – a rather uneasy one on Sir Basil's part, Ranklin thought. Perhaps he was torn between wishing it *were* a foreign power – what could he be expected to do against that? – and fearing public outrage that foreigners could do such things in London.

Rather too casually, Kell asked the Commander: "Will you know eventually who it was?"

"Oh yes. In a few weeks or months it'll seep out on the

grapevine. No proof, of course, but we'll *know*." But they were just showing off in front of the young Home Office. Gratifyingly, he gazed at them with horrified awe.

A slight wind had worked up around tea-time, thinning the fog. And although the wind had gone and there were now millions of coal fires adding their mite to the air, you could now see for ten or fifteen yards. The Commander paused on the steps of the club, perhaps calculating whether it was bad enough to excuse not going home. He could, rumour had it, always find somewhere to spend the night.

"Any private theories about Brock?" he grunted.

Ranklin, who had spent half the day trying to have a theory, shook his head. "None, sir."

"Well, as I say, it'll come out in the end."

"I could do with it being a bit sooner. The *Standard* quoted the waiter as hearing me called 'Captain' and quite a good description of me."

"We don't have to be *invisible* in this business."

"I'm thinking of Gunther's own firm. They'll be reading every last comma for hints as to what happened, they might recognise me and then think I was leading Gunther into a trap."

"Aren't you being overly imaginative?"

"They're competent," Ranklin said, "and they're widespread. That's why we have dealings with them."

"What d'you want to do about it, then?"

But Ranklin, rashly, hadn't thought that far. "Er . . . nothing dramatic, I suppose . . . But if we do come across any answer, I'd like approval to pass it on to Gunther's partners."

"You aren't developing a sense of *justice*, are you?" The Commander eyed him closely. "It would be entirely inappropriate in your work. Now, for me, it would be rather suitable. They could say 'He's a swine, but a *just* swine.' I'd like that. But I'm Chief of this Bureau and you're not, and *my* sense of justice is all we need."

"As evidence of our good faith?" Ranklin suggested. "For good future relations?"

The Commander was still looking at him. "Umm. Well, perhaps . . . Did you like this van der Brock?" he asked casually.

"Like him? I don't think so, particularly . . . He was more like . . . family. One of us."

That was just the sort of answer the Commander's temper had been waiting for. "No he bloody well wasn't! Only *we* are us."

5

The fog cleared the next day and more typical March winds blew in. The railway companies found out where their trains were and began moving them to where they ought to be. Scotland Yard made no visible progress on the Gunther case and wished the popular papers would shut up about it. Ranklin surreptitiously opened a file on the case and kept it in the Registry – a single, albeit locked, bookcase – misleadingly labelled "Historical/Biblical Espionage". The Commander believed he'd invented spying and wasn't interested in history.

So Ranklin wasn't worried that he'd found the file when he was called into the inner office. The Commander fluttered a message at him. "They want you at a meeting at the Admiralty – or rather, they want me or our Turkish expert."

"Who's 'they', sir?"

"It sounds like a conference of the powers: the Foreign Office and the India Office, as well. That's why I'm not going myself." He grinned. "They may have wheeled out the big guns to bully me into something and they can't if I'm not there. So just say what an interesting idea and you're sorry you can't take a final decision yourself."

"The India Office?" That Office handled, as one would expect, Indian affairs, and Ranklin hadn't thought of it as being interested in Turkey. But, old-maidishly, India could imagine enemies at very long range. Until now, it had usually been Russia, but with her more-or-less an ally, perhaps the Turkish Empire – stretching to the Gulf of Persia – had been promoted to bogeyman.

"Yes, them. The only other clue is that they expect you to be *au fait* with the Baghdad Railway. What d'you know about it?"

Ranklin shuffled his thoughts. "It adds on to the existing line from Constantinople into central Turkey. They're building an extension through the mountains on the south coast and down across Syria to Baghdad. And probably further, to Basra and perhaps the Persian Gulf—"

" 'They' being?" the Commander prompted, smiling.

"Some German company—"

"Right. Hold those two thoughts in mind: a German company and the Persian Gulf, and you'll see what's exercising minds at the Foreign Office. Sir Aylmer Corbin's going to be at the meeting."

"Ah." Corbin headed the anti-German faction in the Foreign Office, seeing the shadow of a *Pickelhaube* helmet darkening the map of Europe. Asia Minor too, it now seemed. "Do you know who else will be there?"

The Commander consulted the message. "Hapgood from the India Office. You don't know him? He's a very . . . *worthy* chap. Most able."

Or, decoded, Hapgood did not come from one of the great landed families. Presumably not even from one of the great university families, who made up in brains what they lacked in acres. Well, bully for Hapgood making it to the India Office. Poor isolated sod.

"I believe he's one of a select few who understand the rupee."

To Ranklin the rupee was just currency. "Understands it?"

"Perhaps he can make it do tricks. Climb a rope and disappear."

"I'd think anyone in the City can do that with mere pounds," Ranklin said with some feeling.

"I don't know who else. The meeting's at three o'clock so you've time to swot up the latest on the Railway." The Commander struck a match, lit the message, and moved the match to his loaded pipe as he watched the paper burn out in an ashtray. He disliked paperwork, which was a good thing in espionage; on the other hand, he set fire to a lot of wasterpaper baskets.

* * *

The alcove in the Admiralty entrance hall hadn't been built for a life-size statue, so a rather small version of Nelson watched Ranklin hand over his hat and coat. Then he was led up a stone staircase, along a corridor with a vaulted roof like a tunnel, and into a room that seemed more like a study than an office.

A well-heaped fire blazed in the grate, being poked constantly by a man in vice-admiral's uniform sitting on a corner of the leather-and-brass club fender. Three other men in civilian clothes sat in a collection of chairs, the one in the best leather arm-chair being Sir Aylmer Corbin of the Foreign Office.

Ranklin couldn't remember ever having been introduced to Corbin; from a certain moment Corbin knew him, but the moment itself had passed unnoticed, at least by Ranklin. It was the way things worked in Whitehall: once you realised a man was important or useful, you *knew* him and be damned to introductions.

Now Corbin bobbed up to shake Ranklin's hand. He was a smallish man with pale eyes and a thin, stretched face like a featherless baby bird's. His movements had a birdlike briskness, too. "Ah, Captain Ranklin from the Bureau. You may not know Vice-Admiral Berrigan, our host here? And Hapgood from the India Office? And you've met Fazackerley."

Ranklin smiled and nodded to them and sat in the empty chair. The Admiral stayed seated on the club fender, poker in hand, and with one leg – perhaps a false one – stuck out stiffly. His expression was one of curiosity, an expression that said: "I thought you'd be grubbier." Ranklin was getting used to it around Whitehall. Hapgood, the rupee expert from not-*quite*-the-right-family, just sat smiling, a large fair young man looking like the hero of a school story. You were sure that whatever he had done to get his nose broken at some past time must have been an honourable something. Or perhaps Ranklin felt an instinctive sympathy for him as the other social outsider here.

No matter whose office it was, Corbin was clearly in charge. He launched straight in: "Captain, as your Bureau's Turkish expert, you're doubtless up to date on the progress of the Baghdad Railway and its recent problem?"

"I've no inside knowledge on this at all." Ranklin decided to be frank. "So this is just culled from the newspapers. The biggest problem seems to be breaking through the Taurus Mountains in southern Turkey, having to build long tunnels and bridges and so on. On top of that, work seems to have stopped because a local bandit has kidnapped a couple of German railway engineers and beaten off a rescue attempt by a Turkish Army detachment that was supposed to be guarding them."

"Reasonably accurate. However, the 'bandit' which the newspapers variously describe as a sheikh or pasha is actually a local chieftain figure who ranks as a bey and is named Miskal. A gentleman of advanced years and at least part-Arab extraction. Now, do you know who I mean by the Dowager Viscountess Kelso?"

"I don't think I've heard of her."

"Or Harriet Mayhew, as she started life?"

"That rings a bell. Wasn't she the woman who—?"

"Whatever it was, the answer's almost certainly Yes. I think she was one of those women who read too much Byron too early . . . sometimes I think there was hardly a carpet in the Middle East without some runaway Englishwoman sprawled invitingly across it, and mostly the fault of that damned poet . . . Anyway, she seems to have made a fairly disastrous early marriage to a diplomatist posted out there, kicked over the traces and ran off with some desert sheikh. Didn't stick with him, of course; seems to have done the round of sheikhs' tents more regularly than the milkman."

Admiral Berrigan chuckled gently. All senior sailors develop some foible, and with a perfectly-cut uniform that had never been near the sea, a non-regulation cravat and pearl pin, he had clearly chosen dandyism. It made a change from drink or religion.

Corbin smiled briefly and went on: "Then – her charms fading, I dare say, and thinking about providing for her old age

– she married the fourth Viscount Kelso. He was a widower by then, good deal older than her, and they settled down in Italy – she couldn't come back to Britain by then, of course. Even the Marlborough House set wouldn't have touched her . . . He didn't last long. One likes to think," he went suddenly pious, "that he died happy. Satiated, anyway.

"Of course, there was a frightful row with the family over his will. In the end, I think, she had to threaten to publish her memoirs . . . Anyway, they let her keep the villa on Lake Maggiore and a reasonable remittance – provided she stayed abroad. And that would be the end of the story, *except* that in her desert-carpet days she had a fling with Miskal Bey when he was a young officer in an Arab regiment. And our Foreign Secretary, in his wisdom and his quite sincere desire to get the Baghdad Railway off the agenda of Anglo-German disputes, has asked her to use whatever influence she still has with Miskal to get the Railway engineers freed. Nobody knows whether she still has such influence: the point is to show willing on our side. And the Germans have accepted gratefully."

"The Turks also?"

"Since the prisoners are German nationals, the Turks seem to be giving the Railway pretty much free rein."

"Tell me, who do you regard as actually running Turkey nowadays?"

Corbin cocked his head and looked at him with a birdy, beady eye. "Isn't that the sort of the question we should be asking *you*?"

Ranklin smiled blandly. "Certainly – once our Bureau is as large and well-funded as the Diplomatic Service."

Corbin considered this. "Perhaps we'll neither of us live to see that . . . ah, *happy* day . . . Then, to answer your question: officially, the Committee of the Young Turks – number and composition a secret, but according to our Embassy in Constantinople, dominated by Jews and Freemasons." He paused, then smiled wryly. "Which seems, one has to admit, rather unlikely for a Muslim country. Perhaps we should remember, charitably, that our Ambassador there is rather new . . . However, of this Committee, a handful seem to be taking over, as one would expect: Talaat, Enver, Djavid, the ones who get their names in the papers. And I dare say it'll eventually boil down to one strong man, it usually does. Or another revolution, of course . . . May we get back to Lady Kelso?"

Ranklin nodded. "How old is she by now?"

Corbin blinked at this lapse in taste, but perhaps decided that Lady Kelso's reputation wouldn't suffer too much damage. "In the region of sixty, I believe . . . And in undertaking this mission, she becomes effectively a nominee of the Foreign Office, so it is quite logical that we should provide a Diplomatic Service escort . . . Perhaps you follow my drift?"

"Ah . . . yes, I think so."

"Excellent." He took out his watch and glanced at it. "I must apologise, I'm keeping some tedious but self-important visitor waiting. But I think we've covered the broad picture. My colleagues will fill in the details for you." They shook hands and he scuttled away.

Bewildered, Ranklin looked around the remaining three. But nobody else seemed surprised at Corbin's disappearance. Fazackerley, still looking young but anxious beyond his years as he had at the Savoy, re-arranged a sheaf of papers, peeked over his spectacles, and took up the thread. "Returning to the Railway itself for the moment . . . The mountains there aren't especially high, no more than ten thousand feet, but they are, it seems, very steep and jagged. And the winter weather must have made things very difficult. So while everyone seems to know just where Miskal Bey and his captives are – apparently in an old hilltop monastery – it would still take an army to dislodge him. Particularly since someone seems to have sold him repeating rifles."

"Pity they didn't make it Maxim guns," Admiral Berrigan muttered.

A little frown, as if he'd seen someone pass the port the wrong way, crossed Fazackerley's face. "So if we might return to policy matters . . ."

"Difficult," Hapgood suggested.

Fazackerley nodded briefly. "Traditionally, Britain has never really *liked* the Baghdad Railway. The possible threat to India—"

"Dammit," Berrigan whacked the poker into the fire, "it's far more of a threat to our oil in Persia, and . . . anywhere else."

There was a pause while nobody mentioned Kuwait.

"Quite so," Fazackerley agreed. "And while we all applaud the Foreign Secretary's desire to reassure Germany, it still might be that the national interest would not suffer from a prolonged delay in completing the Railway. If you follow me."

Young he might be, but Fazackerley had learned the Foreign Office's elliptical manner well. And suddenly Ranklin saw why Corbin had left: he was going to be asked to sabotage the Railway – somehow – and there are some things a man of honour cannot bear to hear himself saying.

But then there was a discreet knock on the door, the Admiral called: "Come!" and a messenger came in with a tray of tea things. Berrigan said: "Ah, tea," in a ritual way, and heaved himself onto his stiff leg to do the pouring. The messenger checked the coal scuttle, then the windows and said: "I expect you've seen enough of today, haven't you, sir?" and pulled the heavy red curtains across a view of the forecourt. He turned on a couple more desk lamps, asked if there was anything more and went out.

The ceremony left the room feeling even more warm and grandly cosy, and while Fazackerley and the Admiral took it in their stride, Hapgood clearly relished it. Similar rituals would be going on all over Whitehall – in rooms of a certain rank and above – but Ranklin felt unsettled; the drawing of the curtains against the outside world had been too symbolic. He and the Bureau belonged on the outside.

Setting aside his cup, Fazackerley glanced over his spectacles. "If we might return to the kidnapped engineers? – What the newspapers do *not* know, and we've only just learned, is that a fortnight ago this Miskal sent a message to the builders demanding a ransom equivalent to £20,000 in gold coin. So, if this is paid, tunnelling could be restarted very soon.

"Corbin told you the Turks were giving the Railway pretty well a free hand. However, one faction of the Committee regards paying the ransom as giving in to brigandry and prefers to let the engineers take their chances. In addition, neither the Railway-builders, the Deutsche Bank nor the German Foreign Office – which is deeply if not openly involved – can agree who should put up the money and take the risk of defying the Turks.

"But it seems that an agreement has now been reached in Berlin. They still hope Lady Kelso will get the men freed without it costing them a penny – but if she doesn't, they're ready to pay up. Without the relevant faction in the Turkish Government knowing, of course. And for that reason the money will have to be moved covertly. You still follow me?"

Ranklin nodded.

"Good. Now, Hapgood has a little scheme which I'll let him explain himself."

Hapgood sat up straighter, cleared his throat, and launched into his Big Moment. "What I thought was, if we can slip you into the affair as Lady Kelso's escort, you could then intercept this ransom payment and replace a fair part of it with – let's say – lead. So when Miskal Bey comes to count it, he'll think the Germans have cheated him, become even more obstreperous, and the tunnelling – and hence the whole Railway – will be delayed yet further."

And, after quick looks at the other two, he sat back smiling. Ranklin was doing his best not to gape; all his sympathy for Hapgood the outsider had vanished. Dazed, he instinctively looked to the Admiral, who should have some experience of making realistic plans. But Berrigan was studying the fire with deep concern. And Fazackerley was showing just as great an interest in his own finger-nails.

"I see," Ranklin said slowly. "But . . . just suppose Lady Kelso manages to get the engineers set free and the ransom doesn't come into it?"

"We regard that as rather unlikely," Fazackerley said, still intent on his nails. "Particularly with a man of your ingenuity at hand."

In short, his first task might be to sabotage Lady Kelso.

"Does the Foreign Secretary know about the ransom demand?"

"Sir Edward sees everything that comes in from diplomatic sources."

So they'd learnt of the ransom from some back-door source . . . Gunther? he wondered. And whose office would he have come to: the FO, India or the Admiralty?

"Bound to be problems," Berrigan said, waving the poker in slow circles, "but that's what you chaps are trained for, isn't it?"

And in his way, the old bastard was right – if I'd had any training worth the name, Ranklin thought sourly. He said: "Naturally I can't commit the Bureau myself, that'll be up to my . . . Chief. But I'll put the whole thing to him as fairly as I can."

"We quite understand," Fazackerley said. "And in the light of other matters, we hope you'll emphasise the importance of this."

"And its urgency," Berrigan said. "The Germans are in a hurry, so we can't afford to dawdle."

Fazackerley nodded. "Now, as to details . . ."

* * *

The Commander listened to the story without interrupting, or not often. When Ranklin had finished, he said thoughtfully: "I've expected to be asked to do something about that blasted Railway for the last couple of years . . . And they're quite right, of course; it isn't just Foreign Office jingoism. We trapped ourselves when we decided to change the Navy from coal to oil and the only place we could find our own source was in the Gulf. So we're bound to protect it when we see the Germans driving a railway down to that part of the world. Their intentions may be entirely peaceful – in peace. But come a war, they'll use every weapon they can, and that Railway's one of them."

"Then you want to take this on?"

"I don't think we have a choice. I've been saying that we're here to do dark-alley jobs like this, that this is how we can co-exist with the Foreign Office – and now they've taken me at my word. I don't think we can say No."

"The FO may be right," Ranklin said, "but the the idea of interfering with the ransom is sheer lunacy. The Germans aren't going to carry a load of gold coin into brigand country in a shopping basket. It'll be shut up in safes or strongboxes, under armed guard probably."

"You'd better make a quick study of safe-cracking before you go. But yes, I agree . . . You say that idea came from Hapgood? Perhaps, with his background, he's trying a little *too* hard."

Comments like that about Hapgood made Ranklin feel a little awkward. He must have worked far harder than Corbin or Fazackerley to get where he was, he deserved every credit and so forth . . . and yet, damn it, this involved people's *lives*. Come to that, he wondered, why did the Foreign Office let the India Office in at all if it was the threat to the Navy's oil, not to India, that mattered?

He set that thought aside and said: "None of this seems to be sanctioned by any of the ministers involved."

The Commander eyed him curiously. "You have a latent streak of democracy that you should keep an eye on . . . Ministers don't soil their hands and minds with the likes of us. My chosen interpretation of the situation is that Sir Edward wants the Railway delayed, and that sending the Kelso woman is just an empty gesture of goodwill. So his civil servants are doing their proper job of ensuring that the Railway *is* delayed, and not bothering him with the details."

"Such as the problem of the ransom. And us."

"Exactly. And if my interpretation is wrong, it doesn't matter because it isn't politicians we have to please; they could be gone next week. Civil servants last longer and it's the Corbins we have to live with – if we want this Bureau to survive. So just think of the Royal Navy running out of puff in mid-ocean, and remember that *anything* you can do to bugger up this Railway puts us in profit . . . Now, how much d'you know about railways? D'you think it would really be better just to dynamite it? – anonymously, of course."

Ranklin shook his head slowly. "In South Africa, the Boers kept on cutting our lines, tearing up rails, derailing trains – but our chaps usually had things working again in a day or two. I learnt that once a railway's in place, it's a pretty tough thing. Stopping it being built at all seems a better way."

"Then just go along, and if a chance to do evil crops up, seize it. Perhaps Lady Kelso will introduce you to this brigand and you can bribe him to kidnap a few more Germans." He thought for a while, chewing on his pipe and rattling a matchbox. "Did they say how they found out about this secret stuff, the ransom and so on?"

"Gunther van der Brock."

"Did they say that or are you guessing?"

"I'm guessing. But the timing fits, and the story's from the German end, not the Turkish. And I remember that when I tried Gunther on the Eastern Question, he shied away from it. Normally he'd at least have discussed it, to see what we're after."

The Commander's chomping on his pipe got positively carnivorous. "So van der Brock was selling us a German secret, which suggests the Germans were behind his murder. So won't they be watching to see if we interfere?"

"It sounds possible."

The Commander grinned again. "D'you still want to go?"

Ranklin shrugged. "If it was ever worth doing, it still is. But if I get caught working under a diplomatic alias, then it'll look as if we're doing the sweetness-and-light bit with one hand and knifing them with the other."

"The FO will disown you, say you're an impostor. And the Prime Minister will say we *have* no Secret Service, so you must just be some patriotic but barmy officer acting on your own."

"That may fool our journalists and their readers," Ranklin persisted, "but the Germans won't believe a word of it. It could make the international situation worse."

"The FO must have considered that."

"Perhaps. I just wonder if the FO has considered what a European war could mean in this age."

Ranklin was one of the few Britons who thought he did know, had learnt fighting for the Greeks in the 1912 Balkan war – and, the Commander felt, it was about time he bloody well forgot it. "You shouldn't let your adventures in Macedonia colour your whole view of warfare."

But Ranklin also thought the Commander saw such a war as largely a naval event; perhaps as most Britons did. Fleets pounding each other to pieces in a few glorious hours, not men cowering for weeks in the mud, with their feet and lungs rotting. And where stray shells might kill a passing herring, not women and children, nor grind down the houses, factories, roads, all the complex heart of twentieth-century civilisation.

But the Commander had heard all that before and wasn't about to hear it again. "You cannot be an agent and fool yourself that you're working for some abstraction, like clergymen serving God or lawyers saying they're doing it for Justice and Truth and not the money. An agent works for his country – that's all. And there's no doubt that buggering up this Railway is in our national interest. Also there's a long distance between a piddling little agent like you getting caught and starting a European war, so don't put on airs. Just do the job and concentrate on not getting caught. Now –" briskly "– what d'you need for that?"

"I'd like . . ." Ranklin husked, then began again more firmly: "I want O'Gilroy with me, and a good alias. Something that fits with being a well-born hanger-on to the Diplomatic Service."

The Commander lumbered to his feet. "Ah. Now there, I stumbled across something the other . . . Kilmartin . . . Kilmarnock . . . *Kilmallock*." He took a copy of *Who's Who* from a shelf and dropped it with a thump in front of Ranklin. "Look up Kilmallock in that. He's an Irish peer, I forget the family name. You'll find he had two sons; I know the elder's in America – what's the younger called?"

"The Hon. Patrick Fergus Snaipe," Ranklin read.

"Right. He's about your age, isn't he? He turned out an imbecile and he's hidden away in some looney bin in an Irish bog. Perfect: his existence is verifiable, but the rest is a dark family secret. So he could just as well be in the Diplomatic as in a bin."

"And his Irish valet?"

"If you can talk O'Gilroy into being a manservant again. *And* your girl-friend's already out in Constantinople, isn't she?" The Commander's grin was sly rather than savage. "If we can't out-think 'em, perhaps for once we can outnumber 'em."

6

No king could have worn his Coronation robes with more dignity than Mr Peters did his grubby apron, and Ranklin knew he had come to the right man. It was comforting to know that such men still existed in a world now so dominated by factory production and its good-enough standards. With unhurried precision, the locksmith unfolded and read through the letter of introduction. "Ah, yes. Mr Spencer –" that was Ranklin's normal alias, but it was wearing thin for use in the field "– of course. I assume you'd like this back." He returned the letter. "And you want me to teach you to be a top-notch safe-cracker in the next hour."

Ranklin tried a deprecating smile. "I'd like that, but I realise that, even for a man of your exceptional talents . . ." His voice faded and died. Peters recognised oil, and knew that it clogged the works.

"And what make of safe would it be?"

"I'm afraid we don't know. But probably German."

Peters nodded. "Most likely to be a combination lock, then. Will you be able to use heavy tools or explosives?"

"Nothing that leaves a mark. It has to be an undetected entry."

There was a long silence, then Peters sighed. "Well, I can show you a few safes, explain the principles of the discs and the tumbler gate, point out the differences between different makes, but . . . I won't try to tell you your business, but I suggest you concentrate on the owner of the safe. Open him, and maybe the safe'll follow. Apart from that . . . Are you a regular church-goer, Mr Spencer?"

Surprised, Ranklin said: "Er . . . I'm afraid not."
"Start today."

* * *

Terence Gorman,
Pension Chaligny,
Paris 12e

Dear Gorman,

You have been recommended to me by James Spencer Esq. as a loyal, sober and discreet manservant. I trust that Spencer did not exaggerate your qualities because I am offering you the opportunity to attend to my needs on a mission for His Majesty's Secretary of State for Foreign Affairs which will take me to Constantinople and perhaps further into the Turkish Empire.

You will be engaged under the usual conditions at a wage of one sovereign a week, paid at the end of the week, but I am prepared to advance you a week's wage upon your acceptance.

I assume that you will take this handsome chance to better yourself, and will present yourself clad in a fitting manner, and with your accoutrements suitably packed for immediate railway travel, at the Gare de l'Est at 2 in the afternoon on Tuesday next.

Yrs
The Hon. Patrick Snaipe

* * *

Ranklin came into the Commander's room just as another paper was burning out in the ashtray.

"You're off to Constantinople tonight? – tomorrow?"

"I've just got to pick up a diplomatic passport."

"Thought you'd like to know: Scotland Yard's pretty sure it knows who killed your chum van der Brock. A man suspected of being a professional assassin, name of – Bugger! I've forgotten." He glared at the smouldering remains in the ashtray. "Doesn't matter, he escaped abroad the same day and they can't prove it anyway."

"What does matter is who hired him."

"Possibly . . . I don't want you wasting time on it, anyway. Give my regards to O'Gilroy."

* * *

Fazackerley handed across the diplomatic passport with the cheering comment: "You understand that this confers only as much immunity as you can squeeze out of it? You can expect virtually no backing from us if you get yourself into any sort of trouble. If that happens, we'll say that you misrepresented yourself as an old friend of Lady Kelso's and we gave you the same sort of temporary protection we're giving her, and we're sorry we didn't know what a fearful rotter you really were."

Ranklin nodded appreciatively. As alibis went, it should stretch to cover the Foreign Office if things went wrong. Just the Secret Service Bureau up to its slimy tricks again.

He unfolded the document and was impressed despite himself. It might have little backing, but the least sensitive border guard could scarce forbear to cringe before the dignified imperialism of that passport.

He checked the Snaipe personal details, then sprinkled the paper with drops of coffee, rubbed them in with a fingertip and began crumpling its edges. "Don't want it to look as if I've only joined the Service today," he explained.

Fazackerley smiled. Hapgood prompted him: "You were going to mention travel arrangements."

"Oh yes. The German Embassy said you'll be met in Strasbourg tomorrow evening. It seems they've managed to borrow a . . . well, not quite a private train, but a couple of coaches from the Emperor Wilhelm's one. It sounds as if the whole thing has Very High approval." He frowned a little at that, and Ranklin himself wasn't overjoyed. If the German Emperor was taking an interest, the details were likely to be carefully scrutinised, and he was one of the details.

"What do they want private carriages for?"

Fazackerley shook his head. "Something about having to collect people at different places in southern Germany, including Lady Kelso . . . I didn't cross-examine them, we want it to seem just a minor administrative chore for us."

Ranklin approved of that. Then Hapgood suggested: "Or perhaps they want something safe and private to carry a ransom in gold? That could be a useful opportunity. Anyway, worth watching out for." He smiled, in an encouraging team-spirit way, then took a paper from an inside pocket. "I've made a few calculations that might prove useful. I was working in sovereigns, but since gold is valued by weight, this should apply, roughly, to any coinage. Twenty thousand sovereigns should actually fit, without any other packing such as canvas bags, into a box only a foot square. However, they're unlikely to, because they weigh approximately three hundred and sixty pounds."

"Two mule-loads," Ranklin said absently.

"I beg your pardon?"

"You reckon about two hundred pounds to a mule-load."

"Fascinating," Fazackerley said. "Your Army experience, no doubt. Still, it might be relevant, since I imagine the final stages of this journey will be by horse or mule. And are you otherwise all prepared?"

"I think so." Already the world of Whitehall offices was becoming unreal, fading into translucence as Ranklin's mind reached out on the journey ahead. He pocketed the passport and stood up. "It's going to be crack-of-dawn stuff from Dover tomorrow, so I'm getting down there tonight. Just one more thing: our Embassy in Constantinople – are they expecting the Hon. Patrick Snaipe?"

Fazackerley stood also. "They're expecting a genuine honorary attaché, so keep up the front; a pity if *they* unmasked you. Still, they should be too panic-stricken at entertaining the notorious Lady Kelso to notice you much. Good luck."

* * *

A model of servile sobriety, O'Gilroy raised his bowler and asked: "Would it be the Honourable Patrick Snaipe I'm addressing, sir?"

Just as important as each of them playing their parts was the relationship between them – almost a third character in itself. And no time like the present to get started. So Ranklin acted surprised. "Yes? Ah, yes. You must be Gorman, of course. Er . . ." He directed a rather vacuous scrutiny at O'Gilroy, who was wearing the traditional manservant's "pepper-and-salt" suit under a long dark overcoat. "Yes. Yes, you'll do. See to my baggage, will you? Just the two suitcases, they've got my initials on them."

"Certainly, sir – only ye haven't said where we're going."

"Haven't I? Oh, Strasbourg. Yes, definitely Strasbourg. Well, get on with it, man. Find a porter."

"There was one other thing, sir . . ."

"What? What other thing?"

"In yer letter, ye mentioned a week's wages in advance. One golden sovereign."

"Ah yes. As regards that . . ." Ranklin leant a little closer and said: "Balls."

"Very good, sir."

The compartment's ashtrays were full, so O'Gilroy lowered the window just long enough to pitch his cigarette butt into the grimy, windy afternoon. "So we jest find a strong-box full of gold, change half of it for lead, and run away laughing?" He shook his head in wonder. "Does that Foreign Office get all its fellers from mad-houses, like yeself?" He thought a little more. "Mind, do we get to keep the gold if'n we *do* get our hands on it?"

"Sorry, I never thought to ask. The thing to remember is putting some blight on the Railway – in any way we can find."

"Mebbe we should start a union."

Neither the time of year nor time of day made the train popular, so they had a first-class smoker to themselves and could step out of character while Ranklin explained their purpose.

"Oh – did you hear about Gunther van der Brock getting killed?"

"I did that." O'Gilroy's face turned grim. "And a whisper around the parish that somehow we'd been mixed up in it. I been keeping me head down on that front."

Ranklin nodded gloomily, though it was no worse than he'd feared. "He *may* have sold the Railway plot to the FO, and it *may* have been the Germans who had him killed – so they *may* be suspicious of anybody like us turning up on this trip."

"Thank ye for telling me. What was ye thinking of doing about it?"

Ranklin shrugged. "Just keeping an eye open for it . . . Are you armed?"

"I am."

"I'm sorry; but that had better go out of the window before we cross the frontier. I don't think a manservant would carry a pistol, and we have to assume they're going to search our baggage at some point."

"And yeself?"

"Going into brigand country, I think the Hon. Patrick would bring a pistol. You can always borrow it if needs be."

"Yer usual popgun," O'Gilroy said sourly. He loved anything mechanical and new, and nothing more than his Browning semi-automatic pistol. Ranklin had simply pocketed a Bulldog revolver, such as any gentleman might sport unsuspiciously. O'Gilroy despised it, but really, so did Ranklin. As a Gunner, he didn't think anything that fired less than a 13-pound shell was serious.

"And we're going all the way to Constantinople?"

"And beyond. We stick with Lady Kelso."

O'Gilroy lit another cigarette. "Then ye'd best be giving me one of yer lectures, 'fore we meet up with anybody."

A *lecture?* Ranklin felt he should haul a lantern-slide projector out of his hand-baggage, cough and ask if he could be heard at the back. But some précis of whatever country they were heading for had become a necessary routine. O'Gilroy's self-assurance made it too easy to forget how much basic education – and educated conversation – he had missed by being born in an Irish back street.

On the other hand, he had no fashionable opinions and prejudices to unlearn.

Ranklin coughed (he couldn't help himself) and began: "I've only spent a few days in Constantinople years ago, so this is very much school-room stuff . . . The Turkish Empire's a big place. Theoretically it covers most of North Africa and the Levant as far east as the Persian Gulf. So it's got a very mixed bag of inhabitants: Arabs, Kurds, Armenians, a lot of Greeks and God-knows-what-else. And the average Turk doesn't think much of any of them.

"Until a few years ago, it was officially run by a Sultan. Real old-school sort: corrupt, murderous, looted the treasury and so on. Then he got shunted aside by a thing called the Committee for Union and Progress – they seem to be mostly Army officers and usually known as the Young Turks. But as someone said: 'They've got hold of the dog's collar, but has anyone told its fleas?'

"So we'll probably find the fleas still in charge: the bureaucrats. I'll give you one example I came across of just how weak the central government is: it can only collect five per cent of taxes itself. It has to farm out collecting the other ninety-five to the governors of provinces and districts. Gives them a figure, and anything they collect above that, they keep. Plus the bribes, the *baksheesh*, for doing their jobs . . . well, you can see why most of them *buy* their positions. And why a railway linking things up better appeals to the Government," he added.

"Things are a bit different in Pera, that's the part of Constantinople we'll be in. That's run by Europeans: they have their own hotels, clubs, shops, houses of course, newspapers – and courts. And all have virtually diplomatic immunity: a European can't be tried by a Turkish court, a Turkish official can't even enter the house of a European without his permission."

O'Gilroy let smoke trickle slowly from his nostrils. "How in hell's it keep going?"

"European loans – mostly French. And European help. All the Powers want some part of the Empire only daren't take it because of the other Powers, so they all help instead: we're reorganising their Navy, the Germans their Army and building this Railway, the French lending money—"

"Wasn't ye fighting the Turks yerself a coupla years ago?"

Ranklin nodded. "On behalf of the Greeks."

"Was they any good? – the Turks?"

"Traditionally, they're a warrior race. But terribly badly equipped: most of them hadn't even got boots." And after a few weeks in the mountains, his Greek Gunners were no better off, so it was a real prize to find a Turkish officer, dead or prisoner (in practice, the difference was that he felt he should look the other way while his men stripped a live officer of his boots).

"And at yer own game – as gunners?"

"They'd got the latest German seven-point-sevens – they'd spent their money on those, not boots – and they used them pretty well. To start with. We heard their artillery commander was a German, but that might have been just a Greek rumour put about to explain why he was any good. We just knew him as 'the Tornado'; I think it was one of those silly newspaper nicknames . . .

"Then one day, after we'd had a counter-battery duel –" was he getting too technical? "– guns shooting at guns, trying to knock each other's pieces off the board – their control seemed to fall to pieces. They weren't shooting to any plan . . ." It was odd how, behind the apparently random confusion of modern war, you might still sense a pattern that was an enemy mind, isolate a personality and feel you were duelling with *him*.

"*I* said we must have killed their gunner commander, or knocked him out, anyway. My brigadier didn't agree, he was . . ." He shrugged.

"Did it matter?"

"We'd have advanced quicker if we'd known they wouldn't react because their gunnery control had collapsed."

O'Gilroy had been about to make a glib comment, then

realised Ranklin was talking about a level of soldiering he would never know. "Did ye ever find out?"

"No, I was pulled home soon after that. But their gunnery was supposed to have saved Constantinople from the Bulgarians a few weeks later, so they must have got themselves sorted out by then."

Then he shook his head. "All a bit once-upon-a-time by now. Cut along to the dining carriage and see if you can rustle up some tea."

* * *

It was near nine o'clock when they chugged into the frontier station of Deutsche-Avricourt and changed to a German train and railway time, an inconvenient fifty five minutes ahead. And although Ranklin and O'Gilroy were nodded through Customs, thanks to the diplomatic passport, they still had to wait for less significant souls. Luckily the buffet was open.

"*Un cognac, s'il vous plaît.*" Ranklin tossed a sovereign on the table. "*Et une bière*. This is exceptional," he warned "Gorman". "Normally you buy your own alcoholic drinks. And only when you're off duty, mind."

O'Gilroy nodded, then asked: "Did I hear that Mrs Finn will be in Constantinople?"

"Most likely."

"Will ye be calling on the lady?"

"I don't think she'd ever have met Patrick Snaipe before." Corinna had little enough time for any diplomatists, let alone ones who were *en poste* by birth rather than merit. "But I think it's quite likely we'll bump into her, so I'll probably send you round with a note as soon as we know where she is. I did think of sending her a telegram, but what could it say if she isn't supposed to know me?"

O'Gilroy nodded, looked around and hunched his shoulders into a posture of deference. This frontier was a metaphorical one as well: from here on, they must both play their characters full-time, except in moments of certain privacy. "Ah – might I be so bold as to ask what part of the Ould Counthry ye come from, sir?"

"South Limerick."

"Of course, sir. Then perhaps ye'd be knowing Mr Tobias Gallagher? – a noted farming man in those parts . . ."

"Please tell me more." So for ten minutes O'Gilroy recalled some of the notables he had encountered during his time as a chauffeur at one of the Big Houses, and whom a real, and sane, Patrick Snaipe would know. The one thing neither of them was bothered about was Ranklin's lack of accent: most of the Irish nobility learned the King's English at their nanny's knee.

Gradually, there and on the train as they headed across Alsace-Lorraine, German territory since 1870, Ranklin evolved the character of Snaipe. He couldn't be a complete fool – he had been over-playing, he realised, at the Gare de l'Est – or even the Diplomatic Service wouldn't have touched him. More importantly, people wouldn't bother to talk to him. But he must not be curious. This should both head off suspicion and account for his having achieved virtually nothing in his forty-odd years.

The first impression he gave in Strasbourg would be vital. Then, if he later forgot himself and said something perceptive, it should be dismissed as an aberration. Perhaps affable bone-idleness was the key. And for that, he could recall more than one brother officer to model himself on.

7

They reached Strasbourg just after midnight, the station empty, windy and cold. There was an instant scurry and babble as the other passengers sought their luggage and a warm bed as soon as possible, but Ranklin held back.

"Should I see to the bags, sir?" O'Gilroy asked.

"No rush. I think the best thing is just to stand here and look lost."

So they did that for a while. Twice an official in the double-breasted military overcoat of the Prussian Railways strode past, seemingly looking for someone important. By the third time he had lowered his standards and stopped to demand if Ranklin were the Honourable Snaipe.

"Yes, that's me," Ranklin said.

The official – he looked rather like the late Prince Bismarck, but it was a popular look – gave him one hard stare to make sure he wasn't being trifled with, then barked for action. Porters appeared out of the steamy gloom and went off with O'Gilroy to the baggage van, while Ranklin was led across to the most distant platform, and then further still. In the marshalling yard, among the rows of dark, engineless trains, a lone carriage stood leaking light from curtained windows.

They tramped across the tracks towards it, the official mounted at one end and rapped on a door. A moment later, Ranklin was invited up.

The layout of the carriage was simple, although Ranklin didn't take it all in immediately. Starting from that end there were two rooms, each the full width of the carriage – about nine feet – and over a dozen long. Thereafter, it became more normal, with a row of four sizeable sleeping compartments off a side corridor, and a toilet in the vestibule at the far end.

He was led through the first room, lit only enough for him to avoid a long dining table and its chairs, and into the second. It wasn't warm, but it looked it: shaded gas mantles glowed from the pillars between the dark blue-curtained windows, reflecting off polished and inlaid woodwork, gilt fittings and etched glasswork.

Amid this plum-cake richness, the only occupant came as a relief because he looked like a cut-out photograph, all black and white. The black was the overcoat and its collar, suit, Homburg hat and slight moustache on the white face above a white scarf. Although he had been seated, he was wearing all this in the compartment temperature. "Good evening. I am Dr Dahlmann, a director of Deutsche Bank." He bowed slightly and held out a hand.

"*Nett, Sie kennen zu lernen, Herr Doktor. Mein Name ist Pat Snaipe, sehr untergeordnet Mädchen für alles vom der Foreign Office.*" German isn't a language for self-deprecation, but Dahlmann's brief smile suggested he appreciated it. Or he was sympathising with the FO for having such a "dogsbody" on its hands, but that suited Ranklin just as well.

Thereafter they spoke German, which betrayed nothing, since even Snaipe's dilettante education would have covered that. Dahlmann gestured to a chair. "Sit down, please. I suggest you keep your overcoat on: our service carriage with the boiler has been detached. We will find it tomorrow."

Ranklin sat and couldn't help just gazing around. The floor was covered with a thick, richly patterned carpet, probably Turkish. The easy chair he was sitting in was one of half a dozen, all upholstered with floral embroidery, and the walls were padded with lilac-coloured buttoned velvet. But the false ceiling was the real glory. It was totally covered with painted panels of figures set among clouds or fairy-tale landscapes, a mixture of Wagner and classical Greece but with a few non-denominational cherubs thrown in. Each panel was framed by thick, gilded rococo swirls.

In a sympathetic surge of fantasy Ranklin saw this as the

original parent of all railway carriages, whose descendants had grown weedy, drab and functional.

Dahlmann had been watching with a tight, proud little smile; it wasn't his carriage, but it was his Kaiser's. Then he remembered he was the host. "Would you like a drink? – and something to eat?" He looked around, but could only find the brandy decanter he'd been nibbling at himself.

Ranklin saw a sudden opening. "Why don't we wait until my servant gets here? – he'll find whatever there is."

"You have brought a servant?"

"Of course."

"But if you are going into the mountains of Turkey with Lady Kelso—"

"Even more important, surely," Ranklin said cheerily. "I mean, the hotel staffs in such places probably aren't up to much."

Faced with that, Dahlmann didn't know where to begin, so didn't. He was only a little taller than Ranklin, probably in his fifties, with a squarish face, high cheekbones and a thin nose – and the whole held in constant tension. He was literally tight-lipped, and it gave him a prissy look, as if he were disapproving of your tuppenny overdraft. But if the Deutsche knew what it was doing, there must be more to Dr Dahlmann than first impressions showed.

He finished the subject of O'Gilroy with a warning: "I am afraid you will have to share a sleeping compartment tonight with your servant . . ."

"Oh well, rigours of foreign service, eh?" Ranklin said undaunted. Just then a clatter and a sudden draught showed that O'Gilroy, porters and baggage had arrived. Dahlmann directed that the bags went in the last-but-one compartment.

A couple of minutes later, O'Gilroy appeared. Ranklin introduced them – no handshakes, of course – then said: "Now, be a good fellow and scout about and see if you can raise anything to eat and drink. Try any cupboards next door." In other words, snoop into every cranny you can while you've got an excuse, but O'Gilroy didn't need telling. "There should be a second carriage attached, but it's gone off somewhere. Does it," he asked Dahlmann, to hold him in place, "have a kitchen, too?"

"Naturally. And also a boiler and generator –" he nodded at some dead table lamps which Ranklin hadn't realised were electric "– and baggage space and a cabin for the staff. Your servant must move in there tomorrow."

"Splendid. And what's the plan, then?" Snaipe could show that much curiosity.

"Tomorrow, perhaps later tonight – we must find a train to be attached to, or an engine – we go south to Basle, then to Friedrichshafen, to meet the ferry of Lady Kelso who comes from Romanshorn. Then, I do not know for sure yet. The telegraph . . ." He nodded at the outside world, where others must be taking decisions. Nods, brief and sharp, were part of Dahlmann's vocabulary, gestures were not.

O'Gilroy came back with a stone jar of pickled herring and half a coffee cake. "And there's drinks of all sorts, sir. I can't be reading the labels, but from the smell I can do yez a whisky."

"Whisky would be splendid," Ranklin murmured, deciding against herring at one in the morning. "Oh, and we're going to have to share a compartment tonight. I trust you don't snore."

"Living single, nobody's ever told me, sir," O'Gilroy said mournfully.

O'Gilroy insisted on clearing up all the cups, glasses and so forth and washing them in the toilet hand-basin – which gave him the run of the whole carriage while Ranklin and Dahlmann chatted between long silences. The banker wasn't probing and Snaipe wasn't the inquisitive type, so not much got said. Ranklin and O'Gilroy went to bed about half past one.

The walls of sleeping compartments can be deceptively thin – though these seemed more solid than usual – and they kept their voices down.

"Dahlmann's in the one next to the room ye was in," O'Gilroy reported,"and some railway feller between this and that, then the last one's empty. There's no papers in the dining room 'cept some railway maps in German, but there's a small safe. Locked. Ye can't say easy how big a safe is from the outside, but I wouldn't be thinking it could hold that much gold. Ye said 'bout a foot square?"

"The India Office did." They sat on the bottom bunk measuring small cubes in the air like modest anglers talking about the ones that got away.

O'Gilroy shook his head. "Not that big."

"Maybe it's in the detached carriage. Or it'll come aboard later. Has the safe got a combination lock?"

"It has. How much did ye learn about them?"

"Little enough. But if I get a chance, I'll try my luck." But even if the gold were there, what could he do about it? He hadn't got any lead to substitute: he reckoned he'd need at least a tenth of the total weight, which meant explaining away over thirty pounds of lead if his baggage got searched.

Still, it would be progress of a sort to find the gold was actually on the train.

* * *

Some time in the night – call it three in morning since the middle of the night is always three in the morning – Ranklin heard somebody clump down the corridor and start banging around in the next compartment. He had just dozed off again when, at another three in the morning, an engine or train backed into them with a jolt, paused for an interval of shouting, and jerked them – temporarily – into motion.

He lost count of the threes in the morning after that, but at the last one he realised they were rumbling along steadily if not fast. When he next woke they were stopped again, light was seeping past the blind and O'Gilroy was offering him a cup of coffee.

"We're at somewhere called Basil, sir. I think it's in Switzerland."

"Uh? Oh, Basle. Yes, I think it's in Switzerland, too, but only just. Hold on, I'll come down."

He scrambled down the ladder from the top bunk and tweaked aside the blind. They were in another marshalling yard and there was a drizzle with lumps in it that could have been half-hearted snow. He shivered. "Give me my dressing-gown."

"Ye'd be warmer if ye got dressed properly, sir," O'Gilroy said censoriously, but passing the gown. "'Tis past nine o'clock."

"So?" Ranklin felt that Snaipe wouldn't be an early riser. Anyway, what was the hurry? – they were where they wanted to be, and comfortably helpless. All decisions were out of their hands. He took a swallow of coffee; it wasn't more than warm, but surprisingly good. "Is there anything to eat?"

"They had some stuff sent in from the station. All cold, supposed to be cold, I mean, sir." O'Gilroy refused to get used to the Continental idea of starting the day without hot food.

In fact, Ranklin got dressed rather quicker than he'd originally planned, having remembered he'd lose less blood if he shaved while the carriage was stopped. The hot tap wasn't working, of course, but O'Gilroy conjured a pitcher of luke-warm water from somewhere.

Well before he reached the dining compartment at the far end he could hear a difference of opinion going on. It turned out to be two men in different coloured railway uniforms stabbing forefingers at a map, displaying sheaves of paper and conversing as if they were a hundred yards apart. It so much reminded Ranklin of a tactical discussion between infantry and cavalry that he felt quite at home.

The exchange faded to mere argument at the far end of the table while he helped himself from the jug of coffee, platters of cold meat and cheese and a basket of varicoloured bread at the near end. And looked around, casually, for the safe O'Gilroy had spotted last night.

At last he realised he was standing right by it, a black-and-gold cube whose outside was no more than twelve inches on a side, sitting on the floor under a small vertical bookcase and almost certainly too small for the gold. Probably it was a permanent fixture for when this was part of the Kaiser's train and there were state documents to lock away. He went back to eat in the saloon and gaze out of the window at what was still a Swiss marshalling yard in the drizzle.

He had never particularly liked Switzerland, being unable to quite shed the English feeling that it was the duty of foreigners to be colourful, lively and unreliable, at all of which the Swiss failed miserably. But they were only here, he assumed, because at this point Swizerland spread across the natural frontier of the Rhine and trapped a few square miles of Germany as North Basle. Not that frontiers meant much in this part of the world anyway; nobody had asked for his passport and probably wouldn't as long as he stayed aboard.

Perhaps it would have been different if they *had* been carrying £20,000 in gold coin; surely Customs would have been mildly interested. But then they'd probably have gone a different route, staying inside Germany.

He had just lit a cigarette when a sudden clattering and clumping heralded a procession of Dahlmann, a tall man with a black-grey beard, and three porters struggling in the narrow doorways with luggage. They went straight through into the corridor. Apparently released by this arrival, the two railway officials appeared outside the window, voices back at full strength and backed by flag-waving and the toot of a guard's horn. Soon after, they were jerked into motion.

Dahlmann came back and collapsed into a chair. "The motor-car," he said firmly, "is a wonderful invention. It does not run on rails. It can go when it wants and stop when it wants. And pass other motor-cars in safety." He gave Ranklin a prim smile before tightening his face up again. "Now we are to be attached to an *Eil-Zug* that will take us to Singen. It is the best we can do."

"Wonderful," Ranklin murmured. *Eil-Zug*, with the international deceitfulness of all railways, meant "fast train" without telling you there were two faster types and only one slower.

Then the bearded man came back and they stood up for Dahlmann's introductions. "Zurga, may I introduce the

Honourable Patrick Snaipe of His Britannic Majesty's Diplomatic Service? Zurga Bey, of His Imperial Majesty's Consular Service."

They shook hands. Zurga was considerably taller and leaner than them, wearing a thick, tweedy German knickerbocker suit that didn't make him look in the least German.

"Zurga Bey is coming with us to Constantinople," Dahlmann explained, "and then to the south with you and Lady Kelso. He knows Miskal Bey, I think?"

"By repute only."

It was time to plant a first impression of Snaipe on Zurga. So, while Ranklin knew just who Miskal was – though hardly anything about him – he looked hopefully blank.

Dahlmann saw this and said: "The man who kidnapped the railwaymen. The whole reason we are—"

"Oh, the Pasha."

This genuinely annoyed Dahlmann, but Zurga was only amused. "The newspapers think everyone in Turkey is a pasha. In truth, a pasha is a general or a governor, a bey is a colonel or the *vali* of a district, after that everyone is *effendi*." Such rank-consciousness was perhaps inevitable in such a bureaucratic country.

"Miskal is Bey because he was a colonel, once," Zurga went on. "Now he has only the authority of *kaimakam*. Chief of a village. He is an Arab –" that was no compliment "– and supporter of Sultan Abdul Ahmet, so naturally the Committee could not trust him, and made him to retire. There are many like him, just important in one little bit of country."

Except that little bit of country is the one you need to blast a rail tunnel through.

During this, the carriage had been shunted back and forth, but now it seemed to be picking up speed steadily. The marshalling yard narrowed and vanished, trees replaced houses and glimpses of the Rhine appeared between them. It was about the width of the Thames at London and full with fast brown water flecked with white, like teeth; beyond it, the wooded hills looked pallid in the drizzle.

The Wurttemberg State Railways official came in, dabbing rain from his wide blonde moustache and announced that they were on their way to Friedrichshafen via Singen, on time. Dahlmann offered him coffee, he accepted and sat down in a permanent manner.

This rather put a stopper on the conversation until Zurga switched to English on the quite blatant assumption that the railwayman wouldn't understand. "Do you come all the way into the mountains?" His English was nowhere as good as his German, which had been fluent, better than Ranklin's.

"Oh yes. Wherever Lady Kelso goes, I tag along."

"It will be cold. Still snow, I think. Do you have good clothes?"

"Warm ones? I expect so. I told my man to pack whatever I'd need."

Ranklin wondered if he'd overdone the casual Snaipeishness, since Zurga began to study him carefully. He could only gaze blandly back. Behind the short wiry beard, Zurga had a big sharp nose in a triangular face, rather like an Italian cat and typically Turkish so far. But the face was flatter, the eyes wider spaced, almost Eastern. But despite a reputation for being nasty to minority races, the Turks had more mixed blood than they usually acknowledged, and they had originally come from further east anyway. In Ranklin's memory the beard was odd, usually worn only by older men and *mullahs*.

And unlike Ranklin and Dahlmann, who both wore their overcoats firmly buttoned up – they were too few in that big compartment to add anything to the temperature – Zurga seemed happy lounging back in his knickerbocker suit with even the jacket unbuttoned.

"You're a Consul, are you?" Ranklin asked. "Jolly good. Are you stationed in Basle?"

"No. I am in Frankfurt. But I was travelling in the Black Forest when the message was to meet this train."

"Ah. Nice country, there." Their route up the Rhine was skimming the west and southern edges of the Forest.

"And do you know the Lady Kelso a long time?" Zurga asked.

"Never met her," Ranklin said cheerfully. "Have you?"

"I have seen her, in Constantinople, many years before now. It was said of her . . ." He hesitated.

Perhaps heading him off, Dahlmann leaned forward. "You must help me, Mr Snaipe, so that I do not make mistakes. How should I call the lady?"

This was one area where Snaipe, as an "Hon" himself, could afford to get it right. "Strictly, she's the Dowager Viscountess Kelso, but she most likely prefers to be –" what was her Christian name? Oh, yes – "Harriet, Lady Kelso. To distinguish her from her stepson's wife, who's plain Lady Kelso."

Dahlmann mouthed "Harriet, Lady Kelso," a couple of times in a whisper.

"But," Ranklin added, "since the Christian name is just to avoid confusion, 'Lady Kelso' will do. Unless we get the other one on the train as well."

"And I call her My Lady?"

Ranklin winced. "No, not unless you're a servant. Just Lady Kelso to start with, then Madam."

This didn't seem grand enough for Dahlmann. "Are you quite certain?"

"Oh, yes." So Dahlmann whispered "Madam" a few times to see if he could aggrandise it.

"Mind, she may say 'Call me Harriet', so—"

"I shall call her Lady Kelso," Dahlmann said firmly, pulling his overcoat tighter about his shoulders. It occurred to Ranklin that the banker was probably more comfortable dealing with ladies who had morals but no titles rather than the vice versa sort.

During all of this, Zurga had listened with careful interest. Being as rank-conscious as any Turk, he would want to get it right, too. Now he leaned back and said: "So this woman can be a Viscountess but also an adulteress? – almost a whore?"

That was going a bit far for Dahlmann. "Please, Zurga Bey, I beg you not to say such things. The lady will be with us in a few hours."

Ranklin said: "She wasn't born in the gutter, you know, not

if she married a diplomatist. The nobility can afford to marry chorus-girls – often do, actually – but not diplomatists. Anyway, as I see it, she's coming along just because she was an adulteress, no other reason."

"In Turkey—" But Zurga stopped there. In Turkey, adulteresses lost more than a place in decent society.

* * *

This was timber country: stacks of cut logs lay beside the track, and at almost every station there was a yard full of planks, a carpeting of damp sawdust and the smell of cut wood seeping in whenever the outside door was opened. Between stations, the forests of mingled pines and larches came in waves, surging right up to the track, then ebbing around a clearing, a handful of fields, or a sudden sight of the Rhine. In places the larches were matted so thickly with creepers that it became a dark green arras, blotting out the gloomy forest depths.

Nearly four hours after leaving Basle they were abandoned at Singen junction and, as Ranklin and O'Gilroy watched from the platform, a shunting engine pushed a similarly painted carriage up behind and men started coupling it. The rear of the new carriage had double baggage doors and was windowless, the front half had a scatter of vari-sized windows and nice warm steam wisping from two stubby chimneys. A man in the white apron, hat and bad-tempered look of a true chef sneered at them from a doorway.

The baggage compartment doors were fastened by a big padlock. Ranklin murmured: "There's probably a door on the inside, so if you *can* get a look . . ."

"Surely. Where'd this one come from?"

The only other line from the junction – Ranklin had borrowed a look at a railway map – was from the north. "It could have come from Strasbourg by the quicker, shorter route. If it's got the gold, they may not have wanted to take it through Swiss territory."

"Mebbe 'twas picking it up and they didn't want us to see."

"From the middle of the Black Forest? It doesn't seem likely."

Dahlmann appeared, probably from the local telegraph office, and urged them: "*Komm schnell!* We are going to move."

Ranklin glanced at either end of the train. "Er – I think we'll need an engine, first."

Dahlmann took another look and hurried away again.

"What d'ye make of the Turkish feller?" O'Gilroy asked.

"Zurga? I just don't know. His German's good, but I'd have expected more of a merchant type – and Turkey's got plenty of those – as a consul."

"Did ye see his hands? He's not been sitting at any desk, he's been doing some real work."

"He *says* he's been in the Black Forest. It's not exactly mountain country but it can be quite rocky. If he'd been climbing, that would roughen up his hands."

"This weather?" O'Gilroy grunted, then added: "His baggage is all locked. And the labels been cleaned off."

"Ah, you had a snoop. Thank you, but don't take any risks."

"Best done while I can. Looks like we're going to be crawling with staff from now on."

Dahlmann appeared again. "The engine is coming. When we move, we will have lunch in half an hour. Meanwhile, your luggage will be put in the baggage compartment."

"Thank you." Ranklin nodded the problem on to O'Gilroy.

"Right away, sir. Ah –" he turned deferentially to Dahlmann "– if ye could have the baggage doors opened, I could bring it along the platform, sir. Easier than hauling it all through the train."

That was so sensible that it took Dahlmann a moment to think how to refuse it. "Er, no, we may move very soon. Just make sure it is ready, the other servants will help."

So the baggage compartment was strictly *verboten*. O'Gilroy just bowed his head and walked quickly away.

8

It was nearly half past three when they reached Friedrichshafen, and also just after lunch. This had been a proper affair of silver cutlery and hock glasses directed by the *Chef de Train*, another Bismarck copy in (of course) Prussian blue uniform and medals. He had made it clear that the formality was because *he* had standards, not because he thought bankers and foreigners did.

They paused at the main station to pick up two railway officials from a welcoming party, then chugged on half a mile down a spur leading to the dockside itself and yet more officials. With all this official attention, it was getting to be a secret mission in a spotlight – but Ranklin was realising that, for Berlin, it wasn't a secret mission at all. They might well want European sympathy in dealing with a Turkish brigand, and any secrets – such as what was in the baggage compartment – could be well hidden in the extra-dark shadows a spotlight throws.

Just before it ran into the lake, the spur line ended at a complete but toytown-sized harbour. There was a station with a short platform, already occupied by a two-coach local train, so again they ended up in a goods siding, but a tiny one with just odd wagons parked. A few more had strayed, via a turntable, onto the quayside itself where two little cranes could lift cargo directly onto moored steamers. There was even a traditional half-timbered Customs house along the landward side of the quay.

The drizzle had stopped, but been replaced by a water-honed wind, and across the lake behind the low grey clouds and lower grey hills of Switzerland the sun was already setting. Dahlmann went off with the officials to be busy, and Zurga took one breath of outside air and said: "I am going to stay warm." Ranklin suspected he simply wasn't going to rouse himself for an adulteress, Dowager Viscountess though she was, but staying warm was finally possible: the return of the service coach had re-connected a heating system. Ranklin himself wasn't anxious to be out of doors, but felt the honour of the Foreign Office demanded it.

So he and O'Gilroy paced along the quay. Although the little harbour was obviously kept busy – they could see a steamer that had left only shortly before – nobody else was fool enough to hang about in that wind. They had the quay to themselves and one inevitable dockside loafer in a flat cap.

"Is this the place they make the Zeppelins?" O'Gilroy asked.

"It is, and we show absolutely *no* interest in that."

"Surely. Jest hoping to see one. But too much wind, I'm thinking."

"How are your new quarters?"

"Jayzus!" O'Gilroy said fervently. "Ye wouldn't keep a pig in them, 'cept I think they did. Mind," he added grudgingly, "the carriage is clever for what it is. Jest too much space for baggage."

"When the Kaiser travels, it'll all be used. Can you get at it?"

"Not easy. There's a proper locked door and one of the fellers, sort of train guard and mebbe t'other sort as well, he's got a seat right alongside it. I'll try later: if ye dress for dinner, ye'll find ye haven't got any neck-ties. Give me a bollocking and send me to get 'em double quick. Mebbe that'll stampede them to let me in."

"Good idea."

Dahlmann strode – except that with his short legs it was more of a scurry – up with the news that the ship perhaps a mile away, and already sparkling with lights in the dusk, was the one from Romanshorn. "In ten or fifteen minutes she is here. Ah . . . you will not get lost, I hope?"

Ranklin suppressed a smile. "Oh, I don't expect so. It seems quite a small town."

Dahlmann hurried off again and Ranklin did a standing dance to keep his feet from frostbite.

O'Gilroy said approvingly: "Ye've got him thinking Patrick Snaipe's a pure fool, anyhow."

And indeed, Ranklin felt happy that he was getting across his new persona convincingly – although he'd have to start all over again with Lady Kelso. So he may have forgotten that however well he played at being Patrick Snaipe, he still matched perfectly a description of Captain Matthew Ranklin.

As the steamer hooted its arrival, the dockside suddenly spawned a flood of porters, waving greeters, outgoing passengers and a row of horse-drawn cabs. Ranklin and O'Gilroy strolled along to where the gangway was being readied and Dahlmann reappeared, relieved to see they weren't lost.

About a couple of dozen passengers disembarked, and Lady Kelso was obvious as the one lone woman in a crowd of businessmen and families. Dahlmann stepped forward, swept off his hat and bowed, a gesture that would have gone better without the jostling of other disembarking passengers. Uniformed town and railway officials crowded in to be introduced next, so Ranklin hung back and watched.

The first impression was that here was a genuine dowager viscountess, with all the fore-and-aft opulence of King Edward's time – in miniature. She was one woman who was shorter than Ranklin: even at a distance, he had a perfect eye for that. And despite the way she glided like the figurehead of a ship, the face between the wide hat and the muffling fur collar was startlingly petite, soft and feminine. Age had been kind to her: Ranklin knew she was about sixty, but her face didn't sag, no matter what her corset was coping with. For a woman whose reputation if not life had been made in the evenings, she had a morning look: bright, fresh and – since God enjoys a joke – innocent.

Finally it was his turn. He raised his hat: "Patrick Snaipe of the Diplomatic, Lady Kelso. Your official escort."

She smiled. "How sweet of them. And do you know Turkey well?"

"Hardly at all," Ranklin said cheerfully.

"Well, between us we should manage." She smiled inquiringly past him at O'Gilroy.

Ranklin was deliberately slow catching on; first impressions, again. "Oh, and that's Gorman, my man."

Very properly, she didn't offer any handshake, just: "Good evening, Gorman."

O'Gilroy dipped his head. "Good evening, M'Lady."

Dahlmann and the officials closed in again. "I have arranged that your baggage is brought to the train, My – Lady Kelso. It is only two hundred metres, but if you wish a cab—?"

"Of course not. Oh, Dr Zimmer." He was shaped like a snowman, a round head on a round body, with sleek black hair and thick spectacles. He wore an overcoat with a turned-up fur collar and carried an attaché case.

He bowed over her hand and said: "I must hurry, alas, Madam. I am most honoured to have met you. And the very best of luck in your travels." He disappeared into the churning crowd.

"An admirer I seemed to acquire coming through Zurich," she explained. "Now, have we really got a private train? How gorgeous. All the way to Constantinople? How clever of you." Dahlmann preened himself; whatever his private feelings about Lady Kelso, nobody else in the party had called him *clever*.

Walking along the quayside, she turned to Ranklin again. "And the Foreign Office has sent you to keep me out of trouble . . . well, at least you don't seem to be one of those tall sunbronzed Englishmen who wander the unexplored world making such a nuisance of themselves."

"Er, no. I'm not," Ranklin said, wondering if he should sound regretful.

By now it was almost dark. Lights and lamps were coming on around the Customs house and station building as the little procession, porters bringing up the rear, picked its way across the tracks to the welcoming glow of the private carriages.

Ranklin and O'Gilroy stayed outside to let Dahlmann, Lady Kelso, officials and porters jam the corridor, and O'Gilroy observed quietly: "We've lost the engine again."

"Probably just gone to collect more coal or water." But Ranklin was beginning to feel the cold. "Damn it, I'm getting in the other end."

He stumped off down beside the carriage to climb up at the dining-saloon end. That meant going through the shadow of a couple of wagons – the light from the private coach came out well above his head – and he had to watch where he was putting his feet. So he wasn't watching a large figure slip out from between the wagons, but he felt something ram into his ribs.

Ranklin froze.

The pistol, it could only be that, wriggled against him and the man said: "*Komm mit mir.*"

"You aren't going to shoot me here," Ranklin said in German. But it was one of those silly things you say when you don't know whether he will or not.

"I have orders."

So Ranklin moved on. They went past the blind service carriage, past more goods wagons and beyond the station buildings, heading up the tracks into darkness.

He *is* going to shoot me, Ranklin realised. There I was, being so clever at persuading them I was Snaipe, and all the time they were working out how to get rid of me. Just an armed-robbery-gone-wrong, or a simple disappearance, and the Wilhelmstrasse full of remorse and regret but no Diplomatic Incident.

Little I'll care.

But I don't *want* to die now – it's so inconvenient, so much unfinished. It leaves my family in a mess, I haven't sorted things out with Corinna, this job incomplete . . . I have to try something. Only . . . what?

Then they reached a level crossing and turned off into the sparsely-lit streets of the old town. This puzzled Ranklin more than it cheered him. It probably meant a more complicated plan, maybe an interrogation ending with him "accidentally" drowned in the harbour . . .

Abruptly he was pushed in through a side door of a half-timbered building that had the smell and distant babble of a beer hall. Ahead of him was a dim-lit uneven wooden staircase and he was shoved up it. And into a wide, low-ceilinged room with its furniture pushed back against the walls, except for a single table and chair in the middle. Sitting there was the snowman-shaped Dr Zimmer of Zurich.

He looked up and said in fluent but accented English: "You are Captain Ranklin of the English Secret Service Bureau?"

9

Ranklin tried to look outraged. "I'm Patrick Snaipe, attached to the Diplomatic Service, and I most strongly—"

"Yes, yes, of course. But I will proceed as if you were Captain Ranklin. You are accused of helping arrange the murder of a man known – to you – as Gunther van der Brock."

A great relief flooded Ranklin: the Germans hadn't uncovered him, only Gunther's people, and they knew him anyway. He might still get murdered, but he had his professional pride back. "I've no idea what you're talking about, and I've most certainly never arranged the death of any—"

"You are here in Germany to accompany Lady Kelso, who goes to Turkey to help release two engineers on the Baghdad Railway held hostage for ransom. Do you want more details? About Miskal Bey defeating Turkish soldiers with his new rifles?"

"Who are you?"

"You may go on calling me Dr Zimmer. But I am a partner of Gunther. Will you now stop pretending?"

Ranklin looked around. The room was big, probably used for parties and meetings, and bare – for any room in Bavaria. The walls held only a scattering of religious prints, mountain views, photographs and official notices, a clock and several empty flower baskets. It was lit by a single electric bulb hung from the ceiling that was anything but bare: its shade looked like a harvest festival with tassels on, letting only a glow of orange-pink light leak out. From below came, incongruously, the friendly early-evening mumble of the beer hall. "Is this a trial, then?"

Zimmer gave a tiny shrug. "Perhaps, but not like your

English trials. It is . . . an inquiry, before Hunke takes you out for execution."

"It seems I've been found guilty already."

Zimmer said indifferently: "I could have had Hunke shoot you in the rail-yard. Instead, I am being fair. You can try to explain yourself."

Good God, the bastard really *means* this, Ranklin realised. Any feeling of relief was gone now. He was going to be taken out and shot like . . . like a spy. He swallowed and asked: "May I sit down?"

Zimmer nodded; Hunke brought over a chair, then himself sat against the wall square to Ranklin, dangling the pistol between his knees. His knubbly face seemed solemn and phlegmatic under his wide flat cap – he may have been the dockside loafer glimpsed earlier – but quite capable of obeying nasty orders.

Ranklin said: "Gunther didn't come to see the Bureau in London, he saw somebody else. I don't know who. I called on him at breakfast because we'd heard he was in town—"

"Who told you?"

"The police spotted him at the port. Gunther didn't tell me anything, we said good-bye outside the hotel, then a man waiting put a pistol in his face and killed him. I saw that myself."

Zimmer had his attaché case open on the table, spilling a collection of papers, and was checking Ranklin's account against a newspaper cutting. "Did you try to catch the man?"

"No, he'd vanished in the fog. It must mention the fog. Anyway, I might have thought twice about chasing an armed man who killed that freely. And that's all."

Zimmer seemed to be considering this judiciously. "Are you sure he had seen someone in your Government?"

"As you said, I wouldn't be here in Germany if he hadn't, would I? And the English money the police found on him."

"Money?" Zimmer frowned and consulted the cutting again.

"Two hundred pounds. No, they were trying to keep that out of the newspapers."

Outside the door a board creaked and Hunke lunged silently to his feet; for a big man, he moved very smoothly. He tiptoed to the door and listened, keeping his pistol pointed warningly towards Ranklin. There was silence, except for the murmur from beneath, then heavy, unsuspicious footsteps came down the stairs, past the door and on down until they blended into the noise below. Hunke shrugged and sat down again.

Zimmer picked up the thread: "So you say you did not arrange his death?"

"Of course not. We wouldn't kill the golden goose."

"Pardon?"

"We got information from him. We wanted – still want – to go on getting it from his firm – you. Why should we suddenly want to kill him?"

"To protect the secrets he had given you, so that he would not sell them to anyone else."

That was a new idea for Ranklin. He'd been standing too close to the event, not seeing enough of how it might look to others. "We wouldn't do that. We trusted Gunther, we wouldn't have had dealings with him if we hadn't trusted him."

"But this time, you said, you did *not* have dealings with him."

And what was the answer to *that?* Zimmer went on calmly: "You see, I know what the famous English Secret Service thinks of us. You believe, because you are patriots working only for your country, that you are superior to us who work for any country, and also for money. We do not matter – is it not so?"

"No," Ranklin said. It was difficult to think in big general terms when faced with the specifically gigantic thought that Hunke was about to take him out and kill him. "No. That might be how generals and cabinet ministers think, if they didn't despise all of us, their own spies as much as any others."

Again the small, almost indifferent, shrug. "Perhaps. Perhaps now I do not think you killed Gunther, or want him killed. But that does not matter. Like a soldier – and I think you are also a soldier? – then you must die, not for what you have done, but for what your country has."

"But you don't *know* it was my country! It could be the *Germans* who found out what Gunther had sold!" He was ashamed to hear the desperation in his voice, then he thought The hell with shame, this is my *life*.

Zimmer shook his head and smiled sadly. "I said you do not understand. You think you belong to a small Bureau. Probably you say you have not enough men, not enough money, so you *think* you are small. But not really, because you belong to *England*, and that is big. So a defeat does not mean so much, it is not the end of everything – and one day, probably, you will take revenge. But we are truly small, and belong to nobody, and a single defeat will destroy us if it is known that we do not act, and quickly. So it is more important to show we will take revenge, than that we take the right revenge. Do you understand that?"

"That saving your honour justifies any mistake?" But hadn't it always?

Somebody tried the handle of the door, then gave a heavy knock. A voice called: "How can I bring in your drinks if you won't open the door?"

Zimmer and Hunke swapped surprised looks. "*Did you—?*" Zimmer hissed, and Hunke shook his head.

The voice outside was impatient. "Open up!"

Hunke pocketed the pistol and opened the door. The landlord – presumably – waddled in with a tray of beer-mugs, and doled them onto the table beside Zimmer's case.

Zimmer asked: "Who ordered these?"

"The other man. The Englishman."

Zimmer instinctively looked at the door – at O'Gilroy sauntering in with a friendly grin and going straight up beside Hunke. Going so close you couldn't see his hand behind Hunke's back.

"There's your change." The landlord slapped it on the table and waddled out, muttering about locked doors and secret societies . . .

O'Gilroy patted Hunke's pockets and whisked the pistol away. Hunke stood very still, knowing exactly what was poking into his back.

Then O'Gilroy stepped away quickly. "All under control," and by now his smile was lopsided and nastier. "D'ye want me to shoot them in any partic'lar order?"

Ranklin got carefully to his feet, unsure about his knees. "Give me my pistol." Even to himself, his voice sounded unnatural.

O'Gilroy snapped open Hunke's gun – it was a big military-calibre revolver – to check that it was loaded, then passed over Ranklin's smaller weapon. The simple feel of it in the hand flowed straight to his knees, stiffening them. His hand clenched and he almost shot a dent in the wall.

Then he walked back and held the gun a few inches from Zimmer's face. "I told you, I saw Gunther killed. The man put a pistol to his face – just like this – and fired. It blew the back of his head off. His brains fell into his hat. I saw it."

Zimmer had his head twisted back and away, in a rictus of terror, as if a few inches' distance could make any difference. Life so strong, life so fragile: just an ounce or two of pressure on a trigger . . .

Ranklin relaxed his finger, took a deep breath and straightened up. "All the honour in the damned world . . ." His voice cracked, dry-mouthed. He took a couple of gulps of beer and said in a more normal tone: "Ah, that's better. Try it yourself. Now I think we'd all better sit down again, there's still one or two points to clear up."

So, except for O'Gilroy, they all sat. Gradually the atmosphere simmered down – at least for Ranklin. What Zimmer felt didn't worry him.

He said: "I'm trying to think how Gunther might have handled this. And I think he wouldn't have done anything until he was sure he knew the truth. In the end, that's what your firm's reputation was based on, not honour and revenge. He wouldn't have destroyed the firm by starting a feud with my Bureau, one killing the other like two Sicilian families. And he certainly wouldn't have betrayed me to the Germans, which comes to the same thing. So think about that. Don't just give me a quick answer because there's a gun pointing your way."

In the dim light Zimmer looked pale and sweaty, and he

hadn't dared reach for a beer-mug with his shaking hands. But his words were braver than his voice: "I will promise anything, talking to a pistol."

"Yes," Ranklin said. "I know something about that." He looked around, thinking, and then said slowly: "We could kill you both here and now – not for revenge or anything, but just the way I would a poisonous snake, to stop it killing me, now or in the future. Only we've got a train to catch and no time to make a tidy job of hiding two bodies.

"So I've no interest in saving your firm's reputation, revenge for the sake of revenge sort of thing; that's your problem. But I do want to know why Gunther was killed, and I'll help by passing you anything I find out. That's a promise. I won't ask any promises from you because, as you say, we've got the guns. But think it over."

Zimmer nodded. Ranklin stood up and said to O'Gilroy: "I think you can give the gentleman his pistol back, now."

O'Gilroy's reluctance wasn't wholly pretence. But he jerked open the gun – it was self-ejecting – and pocketed the cartridges before kicking it across the floor into a corner. Then he took back Ranklin's pistol and backed watchfully behind him towards the door.

Zimmer called: "One more matter . . ."

"Yes?"

"You owe us £200." He didn't stand up; that might have shown the wetness down the front of his trousers. But he had got back his business sense.

Ranklin paused, then said: "I suppose we do. But, given your recent attitude, don't you think it might be a mistake for me to pay you now? Let's say I'll take it up when I get back to London – alive."

They walked back to the railway tracks. Ranklin said: "Thank you for the rescue."

"My pleasure. Sorry I took so long. Had to go back for yer popgun when I'd seen where he'd taken ye. D'ye think ye convinced them?"

"I don't know, but I doubt it." He shivered; he was only realising how much he'd sweated now the night air was drying it on him.

"Any ideas how they found us?" O'Gilroy was casually flipping Hunke's cartridges away among the tracks.

"I suppose Zimmer attached himself to Lady Kelso, it's public knowledge that she's joining the expedition, and sent Hunke on ahead to scout and make arrangements. They must have guessed they'd find one of our people slipped in with her."

He wasn't happy that they'd guessed right so easily. What was to stop the Germans guessing right, too? Perhaps they just didn't expect the British to be sabotaging a venture they had suggested themselves.

Dahlmann and Zurga were sitting in the saloon. The banker demanded: "Where have you been?"

"I, er . . ." Ranklin was unprepared; he had been dwelling on the more vivid past. "I went looking for the engine, then thought I'd have a quick glance at the town . . ."

"With your servant?"

"No, he came to find me. Are we in a hurry?" There still hadn't been an engine attached.

"The locomotive is getting water, it will be back at any moment . . . You *could* have been late," he growled.

"But I'm not, so all's well," Ranklin said, perhaps overdoing the infuriating cheerfulness; he still wasn't feeling quite himself, let alone Patrick Snaipe.

Heading for his sleeper, Dahlmann called: "Tonight, of course, we shall dress for dinner."

"Of course."

* * *

This, Ranklin thought, was more like life on an Imperial private train. The dining compartment was warm, the electric table lamps glowed steadily, the white-gloved waiters moved dexterously in the narrow space, smoothly replacing plates and pouring more wine. The train rocked but only gently, since they were now on a more main line north to Ulm, and barely any sound filtered through the padded walls.

Also, it was rather nice to be alive.

One snag was that O'Gilroy's ploy to get into the baggage compartment to rescue his black ties hadn't worked: the guard had simply brought the bags out to him. Still, they would be on the train for at least two more days.

Perhaps because he now had a viscountess to cater for, their private Bismarck had let rip with a dinner of clear soup and dumplings, some lake fish bought in Friedrichshafen, then goose. And all backed by a crescendo of German wines, starting with a cobweb-light *Kabinett* and ending in pure treacle with the pudding. Even Zurga had an occasional and appreciative sip. But not many Turks were strict Muslims when it came to drink and it must be particularly tricky in Germany: once you'd taken alcohol and pork off the menu, the table looked pretty bare.

Yet it was Zurga and Lady Kelso who looked most at home in that setting. He with his short beard and a suit of tails so old it must have been inherited, she rigidly upright in a low-cut gown of pink silk terraced with lace and her hair – of that extreme fairness that can go white almost unnoticed – piled high into a modest tiara. Together, they brought the elegance of candlelight and the Congress of Vienna to this modern world of the telephone and motor-car.

However, it was quite clear that they were *not* together, Zurga replying with cold courtesy whenever she tried to pull him into conversation.

Dahlmann, who simply looked like a banker dressed up, made a little speech of welcome. "Our two great countries have had certain differences over the building of the Baghdad Railway. But we believe that Lady Kelso joining us, at the request of your Foreign Minister, shows such diplomatic problems are now all solved. I think it is most important that we are such an international group: German, English, Turkish, all going forward together to solve the Railway's other problems. I speak for the Deutsche Bank and the Railway also when I say Welcome, Lady Kelso."

It was graceful of him, if a trifle disingenuous, and Ranklin clapped, then they all drank a toast. And Lady Kelso said she was very happy to be here and hoped she'd be of some help – and where, incidentally, were they going next?

"We go first to Munich where Dr Streibl of the Railway company will join us. There we will be attached to the Orient Express for the rest of our journey."

"How splendid," Lady Kelso smiled. "It's ages since I went on the Express – and in a private carriage, too. I feel like the consort of an emperor – or sultan." And Zurga glowered. He must disapprove of sultans, so it was hardly tactful of her. It may, however, have been deliberate. "Why," she went on to Dahlmann, "doesn't your Bank have a private train? It must be rich enough and you seem to travel a lot."

Dahlmann, perhaps misunderstanding the word "consort" and uneasy with it, now became truly shocked. "It would not be economical. It would be very bad for a German bank to waste money on such luxuries. We are not American bankers."

"Very right and proper," she soothed, wafting herself with her fan – it was years since Ranklin had seen such natural, expressive use of a fan. They seemed to have died out in England. "Then we should be grateful to your Emperor. He must think we're jolly important."

"In Germany we are most proud of the Baghdad Railway. Because, of course," he explained quickly, "it is so helpful to the Turkish political economy."

By now the conversation was slipping from German to English and back, each tending to speak their own language and leaving Zurga doing quick gear-changes. Lady Kelso tried once more to involve him: "Tell me, how is your Government progressing with the modernising of your Empire?"

It was a polite question, and Zurga kicked it straight out of bounds. "I am sorry you do not have time to keep informed of Turkish affairs now you have left our country."

But she didn't kick quite so easily. The fan fluttered. "Oh dear, how true, how true. I just sit by Lake Maggiore reading week-old copies of *The Times*. But I do read them. And all I seem to learn is that you've spent another loan on new battleships and things." The fan snapped shut.

"We have enemies," Zurga protested, unexpectedly on the defensive. "How do you English spend your money if three countries wanted to capture London – as Russia, Greece and Bulgaria all want Constantinople? If the people of London had heard the sound of enemy guns, so close only a year ago?"

Ranklin could imagine the distant rumble spilling over the hills and down through the streets of Pera, and yearned for a Turkish view of that battle. But Snaipe, alas, wouldn't even have heard of it.

But Lady Kelso had had enough of battles, anyway. "Now someone really must tell me more about this wonderful Railway I'm supposed to be helping. I do recall it was the talk of Constantinople, but that was was over ten years ago."

There was a pause and Dahlmann thrust himself into it: "The Baghdad Railway," he announced firmly. "When it was begun, we understood it could be . . . *ein Zank'apfel*—"

"Bone of contention?" Ranklin offered.

"Yes. For Russia, England, France . . . So we said it should be truly international. But your English financiers were not interested, the French Government did not want to give money to German builders, so it is now almost all financed by money raised on the German bond market."

"By your Bank?" Lady Kelso asked.

"That is correct."

"But didn't I read that the French are giving a new loan to Turkey?"

"That is not certain. I have some business to do with it in Constantinople." So Dahlmann might be meeting Corinna and her damned French boy-friend. Ranklin was frankly jealous – but of Lady Kelso: in a few minutes she'd got something out of Dahlmann that he hadn't got in twenty-four hours.

Dahlmann added: "And the loan will not go to help the Railway."

"Ah, for other things." She didn't say "battleships". Zurga could hear her plain as day *not* saying "battleships".

He said: "It is important that the Railway will join up Aleppo, Mosul, Baghdad to Constantinople. It will bring civilisation, and also quick justice to the bandits in the desert – to bandits *anywhere*. It is a shame it was not built when you were travelling in those provinces, Lady Kelso. You would have found it more comfortable."

"Really? Of course, I was younger then, but I recall being *extremely* comfortable in those parts." The fan moved languidly, like dreamy reminiscence.

10

It was another of those three-in-the-morning times when Ranklin woke to silence. Or nearly so: they had stopped, but there was the distant rattle and hoot of other trains moving. He tried to decide if he were going to get to sleep again and realised he was too dry-mouthed. He should have allowed for the heating and, like a Decent Englishman, slept with the window part open.

Anyway, the effort of deciding had woken him thoroughly so he got up, lit a cigarette and put on his dressing-gown. Then, to spread the smoke more fairly, he went out into the corridor. He was surprised to see light under the door of the saloon and, when he investigated, Lady Kelso.

At first glance, he thought she'd changed into another, blue, evening gown. It certainly had all the frills, lace and fuzzy bits, though was less likely to give her a chest cold, but finally he decided it was a species of dressing-gown. Her fair hair hung loose, well past her shoulders, and she had been puzzling through a German newspaper with a lorgnette.

"Good morning. No, please go on smoking, I don't mind." And as Ranklin reached to twitch aside the window curtains: "I think we've got to Munich. And here, I imagine, we stay until the Orient Express comes through at about midday."

The view from the window was, in its way, familiar. "Get to travel on the Kaiser's train and see the marshalling yards of South Germany." He turned back. "I was looking for something to drink – just bottled water. Can I try and find you anything?"

"Go ahead and ring the bell," she said firmly. "I've spent too much of my life *not* getting what I want because it'll inconvenience the servants or the horses. Camels," she reflected, "are just perfect. They hate you so much already, you don't mind making them do some work."

What they got was one of the waiters, already half-dressed so he must have been on duty but hadn't expected to do any. Ranklin asked for *Mineralwasser*, and Lady Kelso suddenly decided she'd have a cognac – "Maybe *that'll* help me sleep."

While they waited, he asked casually: "Have you been in Constantinople recently?"

"Not for over ten years, since before the Young Turks (I'm supposed to call them The Committee, aren't I?) took over." She sighed. "I expect I'll find it changed . . . The old Sultan's court was as corrupt as buzzard meat, but they were *gentlemen*. Now, I suppose it's all run by people like Zurga Bey."

"I got the impression that you and he don't see eye to eye on everything."

"That's very perceptive of you, Mr Snaipe." It was said with a straight face.

"Do you think he feels you're . . . sort of . . . associated with the past, the old Sultan's regime?"

Now she let her smile show. "If so, he certainly isn't very perceptive. No, it's *my* past that troubles him. He thinks I'm no better than a whore. Nothing shocks a Turk more than the idea of a woman choosing her own life and not coming to a bad end. And probably worse than that, it's who my past was with: the Arabs. I bet Zurga Bey's one of those Turks who names his dog 'Arab'. A lot of them do, you know."

The waiter brought in a tray with their drinks. Lady Kelso took a sip of her brandy, then loaded the glass up with water.

Ranklin said: "Zurga seemed . . . sincere enough. About reform, and the Railway . . ."

"I'm sure he is. And the old Sultan was quite as sincere about the Railway and for the same reason: to keep the Arabs under his thumb. The story going the rounds was that he'd talked the Kaiser into building it during the visit of . . . it must have been '98. As much as one emperor needs to talk another into any daft grand dream. So now Dr Dahlmann and his Bank have to scurry about to make the dream come true."

"Daft?" Ranklin queried.

"Well, of course. It may be sensible within Turkey itself, linking the north to the south, but then going on down to Mosul and Baghdad, that's ridiculous. It's desert. For all the trade they do, they only need a few camel caravans such as they've had for thousands of years. I suppose it might help a few pilgrims part way to Mecca, but for the rest . . ."

Then she cocked her head at Ranklin and waved the lorgnette; it didn't work quite as well as the fan. "Mind you, I *have* read articles that say the Railway's a bad idea for Britain, that it's a threat to India and our oil-field in Persia . . . Do you hear talk like that in the Foreign Office?"

"The Foreign Secretary himself asked you to come and help get the Railway building going again, didn't he?"

She frowned delicately – as all her expressions with her small features had to be. "Well . . . No. What I was actually *asked* to do was appeal to Miskal to let those two engineers go, just out of common decency. Now I find that thousands of workmen are standing idle waiting for me to wave my fairy wand and start up the whole thing again, all its bridges and tunnels and trains and things . . . It's . . . it's *terrifying*."

"I don't think anyone expects you to work miracles," Ranklin soothed. "It's just the way they see it. I don't suppose they'd give a hoot about the lives of two engineers if it *wasn't* holding up the Railway."

"Then if they don't care, why do they *let* it hold up the Railway?"

Ranklin found his mind bare of answers. "Ah . . . perhaps because it's been reported in the papers . . . the chaps' families . . . the other engineers . . ." He was having no trouble at all in sounding like Snaipe.

So now it was her turn to sound soothing. "Never mind. Perhaps we'll find out as we go along." She sipped her brandy-and-water. Then, casually: "What do they say of me in England these days?"

"I . . . ah . . ." Nobody Ranklin knew said anything of her. But Snaipe, as a minor aristocrat, should know more.

"I haven't heard anyone say anything unkind . . ."

"Not even when they knew you were going to be my escort?"

"I wouldn't discuss Foreign Office matters even with my family," Ranklin said, finding inspiration in false virtue.

"Of course not." But she sounded a little disappointed. "Do you think that if I bring this off, Sir Edward will invite me back to London? – if only to say thank you?"

Thus giving her an *entrée* to English society? It seemed highly unlikely. As far as Ranklin could tell, Sir Edward cared as little for society as he could get away with; his passion was angling, which was hardly sociable.

"Things have changed a bit with the new King. He seems to be rather more a family man . . . Of course, King Edward's friends are still around, but not so much at Court. It's a more . . . ah, a *quieter* place now, I believe . . ." For God's sake, read between my lines, woman: blatant adultery is just Not On these days.

"If I were still just Harriet Mayhew, or even Mrs Fenby –" (that had been her first, diplomatist, husband) "– I could just go back and brazen it out, find my own level. But being Lady Kelso now, it . . . it isn't so easy. I've rather trapped myself. I seem to have swapped my old self for a passport that's valid only so long as I never try to use it. It's really so silly: I was never particularly happy in England, but it's where I was born, and I would like to die there."

* * *

Breakfast had been under way for some time before Ranklin got there; luckily the *chef de train* was feeling indulgent, and there was still a good spread of cold meats and cheeses, bread and jam, with eggs to order.

Daylight hadn't improved the view of the marshalling yards, and although there was plenty of blue sky, it had a temporary, windswept look. Just as Ranklin was thinking of taking his last coffee into the saloon, Dahlmann bustled through from the outside world. He was well wrapped up, so it was probably as cold as it looked.

"Dr Streibl's train is here soon," he said over his shoulder, bustling on.

Ranklin followed. "That completes our merry band then, what? Next stop Constantinople and all that." He sat down in the saloon; Zurga and Lady Kelso were already there. "And then to the mountains . . . I say, what are we going to do when we get there? I mean, what's the actual jolly old plan?"

There was a sudden pause, but no rush to tell him. Zurga looked at Dahlmann, who had stopped at the door to the corridor. "What do you mean, Mr Snaipe?"

"Well, we go to Miskal's mountain stronghold – d'you know the place, Lady Kelso?"

She shook her head. "When I knew Miskal he was in the Army, in Syria. But I've been through that part of Turkey, the old caravan route up across the Cilician Gates."

"Yes, well . . . But I mean, what then? Do you and I roll up at his front door and ask politely that he lets his prisoners go? Or what?"

Dahlmann said nothing, but he took off his overcoat and hat and laid them carefully over a chair.

Lady Kelso looked at him, then Ranklin. "Obviously you want me to approach the dear man first, but really, Mr Snaipe, I don't think there's any need for you to come along. It makes the whole thing rather *official*, don't you feel?"

She was letting him down lightly. He frowned. "Ah. Yes. But the whole point . . . What the Foreign Office sent me for . . . Well, I mean, I'm supposed to look after you and you don't really need that *until* we get to . . . wherever . . ." Her expression, as pretty, polite and just as inflexible as a china figurine's, told him he would get nowhere. Not now, anyway. He changed tack somewhat: "But what's this chap doing in the mountains anyway, if he's an Arab? I thought deserts, tents . . ."

"His people were Syrian mountain Arabs – I think," Lady Kelso said. "I've no idea how he got to *these* mountains."

"He was exiled to there," Zurga explained. "The Committee

did not want him to be a leader among his own people, to make trouble like so many Arabs, so they gave him an Armenian village that had become . . . empty." Ranklin held onto a bland expression, though he guessed just how an Armenian village in Turkey could suddenly become "empty". From Lady Kelso's fixed smile, she guessed, too – perhaps in more detail.

"Of course," Zurga went on, "his family was permitted to go with him, and I think more than his family . . . I think many of his people went also. He became, not officially, the *kaimakam* of the village." He seemed to debate with himself, but in the end added: "I think it was not a good idea."

So now, Ranklin assumed, instead of a village full of troublesome Armenians *without* repeating rifles, the Committee had created a village full of troublesome Arabs with same.

Lady Kelso murmured: "Perhaps the Committee hoped the climate would kill them off quietly. They don't know the weather in the Syrian mountains."

Last night, Zurga would have had an indignant answer. This morning, perhaps he had realised they had a long journey still ahead, because he just gave a brief smile and shrug.

Ranklin asked: "And the jolly old monastery, is that part of the village?"

Zurga glanced at Dahlmann, but got no help. "I do not know the country there, but I think the village is in the mountains and the monastery – it is a ruin – is more near to the Railway. Where the Railway must go."

"Ah." Ranklin nodded, as if all were explained. "And what are *you* going to be doing?"

Lady Kelso seemed interested in knowing that, too. Zurga said: "I am asked – if Lady Kelso does not succeed – to speak to him as once a soldier of the Ottoman Empire. And perhaps to warn that the Committee will become . . ."

He didn't want to specify, and was saved by Dahlmann being hasty and apologetic: "Forgive me, Lady Kelso, but we must allow for the possibility that you will fail. So we must be ready with other things."

Ranklin was watching, and her polite smile was Dresden

china again. Then she looked at him. "Does that answer all your questions, Mr Snaipe?"

No, of course it didn't. But Snaipe probably wouldn't have persisted. "Oh yes . . . Well, mostly . . . Plenty of time, though . . ."

"Splendid." And one sweep of her lorgnette closed the conversation. Dahlmann, relieved, gathered up his coat and headed for his compartment. Zurga lingered a while longer, then picked up his coffee cup and went in the opposite direction, into the dining-saloon.

Lady Kelso put down her lorgnette and magazine and said briskly: "Balderdash."

"I beg your pardon?"

"What Zurga says he's going to say to Miskal. He must know that's absurd. A man like Miskal won't take any lectures from a jumped-up Stambouli who's sold his soul to us infidels – and that's how Miskal will see him. He'll have captured those two because they're foreigners wanting to carve up his land, so *he's* being defender of the Faith – and that's what matters to the Arabs, not being patriotic to some Ottoman Turk idea of Empire."

Ranklin frowned. Put like that, Zurga's task did look pretty hopeless. "Then why d'you think he's here?"

"Heaven knows if you don't." She cocked her face to give him a cool look. "I do think the Foreign Office might have given you a better brief." She might not be a lady who always knew what she wanted – considering what she'd got, one certainly hoped not – but Ranklin couldn't see her as a hapless plaything either.

However, that wasn't what bothered him most. Granted that they'd prefer her to talk the prisoners free and save themselves £20,000, what happened if Miskal Bey said "Nice to see you again, old girl – but where's my ransom money?" – and she knew nothing about it? They must surely tell her before she met him. Perhaps they were sizing her up first, guessing how she'd take it.

Wanting a little peace and quiet to think things over,

he patted his pockets, muttered: "Seem to have left my cigarettes . . ." and went along to his own sleeper.

He got his first sight of Dr Streibl from the window of that compartment. A tall man, his half-unbuttoned overcoat flapping in the wind, was marching across the tracks of the yard towards them. He carried a wide-brimmed hat in his hand, showing a sun-tanned bald head with long grey strands of hair fluttering around his ears, and the sure-footed way he matched his stride to the tracks without looking down marked him as a true railwayman. Outdistanced behind him came a single porter with – by the standards of the rest of them – a meagre load of luggage.

Ranklin heard him come aboard and decided it was safe to re-appear. He came into the saloon at the tail-end of Dahlmann's introductions: "Ah, and here is the Honourable Patrick Snaipe of the English Diplomatic Service. Herr Doktor Martin Streibl of Phillip Holzmann Gesellschaft from Frankfurt."

"Rumpled" was the word for Streibl: his clothes, his hair and even his face, with ears and bulbous nose exaggerated like a cartoon drawing. His tie was askew and too much bulged his pockets. Nor could he keep his attention on Ranklin or any of them: just on the carriage itself. After a hearty handshake, he went back to peering at the paintings on the ceiling, tapping the walls, poking the carpet with his rather unshiny boot.

Feeling responsible and perhaps a little vexed, Dahlmann said unnecessarily: "Perhaps you have not seen this train before?"

"Hm? *Nein, nie . . . bemerkenswert* . . . I am sorry." But he couldn't keep his eyes on mere humans, murmuring: "*Außerordentlich . . . erstaunlich . . .*"

Lady Kelso had her mouth pursed to stop herself laughing aloud, and went on being chirrupy when more coffee had been brought around and Dahlmann had led Streibl away for a private chat. "So now all we're waiting for is the Orient Express, and Eastward Ho! I don't suppose we'll have any international problems, not in these carriages."

Ranklin was glad someone had brought that up. After Budapest the line ran through Serbia and then Bulgaria, both of which had been at war with Turkey a year ago. And Serbia's recent past – turbulent or murderous, depending on how close you stood – had given them a rare mistrust of any foreigners.

Zurga gave a fatalistic little shrug. "We hope not."

When they were rolling through Munich's stolid surburbs, Dahlmann appeared back in the saloon. "Lady Kelso, gentlemen: we are now attached to the Orient Express but it is most strictly agreed that we must remain separate. There is no connecting door, and I must ask you not to board their carriages when we stop at stations. Thank you. Now, Dr Streibl has brought me some important news that has come from Turkey. If you will please . . ."

So they trooped in to join Streibl in the dining compartment and sit, conference-like, around the bare table. A subdued Lady Kelso caught Ranklin's eye and made a little moue of mock apprehension.

Dahlmann hunched himself as chairman at the head of the table; at least he didn't stand up. "This is an unfortunate development." He looked around to make sure they were well braced. "The railway camp in the south has had a message from Miskal Bey. He demands, as payment to release our officials, a ransom in gold coin of 400,000 marks."

Dear me, what a wicked deceitful old banker you are: you knew that all along, Ranklin thought. But it was a relief to stop pretending not to know it – for both of them, probably. He adjusted Snaipe's expression to a baffled frown.

But if Lady Kelso hadn't naturally been sitting bolt upright, she would have done so now. "*That* doesn't sound like Miskal. He's a gentleman, not a *bandit*."

Dahlmann's voice had a hint of satisfaction. "I am afraid – unless the message is quite misunderstood – that he *has* done this."

"I could understand him shooting your people, for trespassing. Or putting out their eyes and sending them back as a warning. But not holding them to *ransom* – that's just not him."

"Perhaps you understood him wrongly," Dahlmann suggested rashly.

She stared at him as if he were a new and unnecessary discovery in the insect world. "And just how well do *you* know him?"

Dahlmann mumbled that he hadn't met Miskal.

"I knew him *rather well*."

Dahlmann looked for support and didn't get it. Zurga avoided his eye, Streibl seemed honestly devoted to the painted ceiling. "Perhaps . . . we may hope when we arrive, it is all a mistake. But please, at this moment, may we pretend it is true? And my Bank must decide if paying it is advisable." His confidence crept back with the sound of his own voice. "My thought now is to hope that you, Madam, can persuade the Bey to release the men without payment. But if you do not succeed, and Zurga Bey cannot also persuade him, then I think I must recommend payment.

"But naturally, I welcome all your opinions . . . Lady Kelso, do you have any more . . .?"

Her voice was gentle but distinctly cool. "You already know my opinion, Dr Dahlmann . . . But if you want me to *pretend* Miskal has made a ransom demand, I'm not sure there's any point in my going there at all. If what he wants is 400,000 marks, he's not going to settle for me fluttering my eyelashes at him."

Oh *Lord*. Ranklin saw the whole scheme collapsing gently around him. Because if she decided to get off at the next stop and go home, he had no choice but to go too.

But Dahlmann was just as taken aback. "Oh, no, Madam, I beg you to do as Sir Edward Grey himself has asked you to. As you agreed."

"To save you 400,000 marks?"

"Naturally, the gold is important. But it is not everything—" He was floundering. Yet, though he couldn't admit it, he'd had plenty of time to foresee such an obvious snag. Poor staff work, Ranklin disapproved.

Zurga rode calmly to the rescue. "But to pay the money will not change Miskal Bey's mind. Only you can do that, Lady Kelso. And end the matter in peace – for his people as well as the Railway."

She was cool to any idea coming from Zurga, however sensible. And, Ranklin guessed, she probably didn't trust a word he said. But in a sudden change of mood, she smiled. "Very well, you've persuaded me, Zurga Bey. But if I don't succeed, then my opinion doesn't count for anything. You must do whatever you think best."

Dahlmann couldn't have been more relieved than Ranklin, but at least he could show it. "Thank you, Lady Kelso. And you also, Zurga Bey. Do you have anything more to say?"

Perhaps Lady Kelso's change of mood was catching, because Zurga's politeness seemed more than formal. "I much regret I still do not agree with Lady Kelso about Miskal Bey, though I do not know him. But, like her, if I fail I cannot tell you what you should then do. But also I must tell you that some of the Committee, the Government, will not want you to pay money to a man *they* think –" and he looked carefully at Lady Kelso "– is a bandit. So if you must pay, it must be most secret."

It was a nice speech, seemingly not too rehearsed, and it put their little play back on track after Lady Kelso's surprise derailment. And the story was now as Gunther had been selling it nearly a week ago.

Dahlmann said gravely: "Thank you, Zurga Bey. That is an important matter – secrecy. Now: I have already the opinion of Dr Streibl." He seemed to remember Ranklin, and asked politely: "Mr Snaipe – do you feel you can say what your Foreign Office might recommend?"

Ranklin said: "Four hundred thousand seems a bit of an odd figure – was it the result of bargaining or does it translate into something easier in Turkish money?"

"An interesting observation. No, not in Turkish money, but the demand is for half a million francs, to be paid in new

French gold coins. As you all know, such coins are the most common in Turkey, but at the Deutsche Bank we do not have so many, not new, so we must get it from the French Imperial Ottoman Bank in Constantinople. We will tell the French it is for wages and supplies. So I must beg you not to mention this to anyone – and especially, Mr Snaipe, your colleagues in the British Embassy."

"Oh, absolutely our little secret," Ranklin said. "As long as the French Bank isn't going to be surprised at you suddenly wanting that much in coin . . ."

Dr Streibl abruptly came down to earth to say: "In Turkey almost all payment is in coin, only a few in Constantinople use the banks. And in summer we have perhaps thirty thousand workers building the Railway who must be paid, and also fed from food bought locally. Nobody is surprised that we need a lot of coin."

Ranklin doubted the average Turkish worker saw any *gold* coin, not unless he got paid yearly, but he had another thought to raise: "One other thing occurs to me: with half a million gold francs, old Miskal Bey's going to be able to buy a sight more repeating rifles, if he's a mind to."

"But that," Dahlmann said smoothly, "is why we must hope Lady Kelso – or Zurga Bey – will manage to change his mind."

The meeting dispersed slowly back to the saloon and sleeping compartments in a sober mood. The thing that struck Ranklin was that if the gold was coming from a French bank in Constantinople (and why should Dahlmann mention that at all if it weren't true?) then it wasn't already aboard this train.

So what, if anything, was?

11

In the service carriage, O'Gilroy was coming to realise he had to hit someone. The train staff had not made him welcome. They hadn't expected anyone to bring a manservant, and when he took the fifth bunk in the sleeping compartment, it left only one spare for everyone to dump his kit on (their boss, who seemed to be called Herr "Fernrick", shared another compartment with the chef, and good luck to him. In O'Gilroy's experience all chefs were mad, bad-tempered, and had access to knives).

Only Albrecht, who tended the boiler and anything else mechanical, spoke English, and O'Gilroy had virtually no German. But this allowed them to make jokes about him in front of his face and that had kept them reasonably sunny for the first twenty-four hours. But in the bustle of preparing lunch while he lay on his bunk and smoked, the insults got plainer and demands to get out of the way less reasonable.

So he was going to have to hit someone. The old manly ritual. Knock one of them down, helpless, to show he was as good as they. Ten years ago, the thought would have cheered him. Or rather, he wouldn't have *had* the thought, just lashed out from instinct. Now, at least he'd be working to a plan.

Of course, if they all ganged up on him, he'd be beaten to a pulp. But he didn't think that would happen. It would mean broken bones and bloody faces and how would that look when serving dinner? The row could go all the way up to the Kaiser.

It wouldn't be enough to pick on the smallest of them, which let one of the waiters off the hook. Nor Albrecht, partly because of the English, but also because he seemed the butt of jokes himself, being a Bavarian among Prussians. Which left the second waiter or, preferably, the guard. He was beefy enough, and if his face got marked, he wasn't on public display.

The moment came after lunch. He had volunteered to help with the washing up, and they had seen to it that he got well splashed with greasy water. He was back in the compartment routing out a clean shirt when the guard jostled him and snapped for him to step aside.

"Fuck off," O'Gilroy said over his shoulder.

That didn't need translating. He felt everyone in the compartment go still.

The guard's *What*-did-you-say? didn't need translation, either.

"Tell him," O'Gilroy said to Albrecht, "to learn some manners or bring his mother along to protect him. *Tell him!*"

Albrecht did, hesitatingly. There was a moment's pause, then O'Gilroy felt the guard's hand clamp on his shoulder and spun around, trying for a head-butt, realised he couldn't make it and followed up with a left-hand punch whacking into the guard's stomach. As he folded forward, O'Gilroy yanked him up by his lapels and rushed him against the door, slamming it shut and knocking a waiter aside.

"Bugger around wid me and I'll break every fucking bone in yer body!" he spat. "*Verständen?*"

The guard hung there, pop-eyed and gurgling for breath. Then the door tried to open behind him. O'Gilroy pushed him away, a cannon off the waiter and onto a bunk. The door opened and Herr Fernrick stood there, moustache bristling, eyes glaring.

Everyone except the guard snapped to attention, and O'Gilroy realised he had, too. The scene had an old, familiar feel to it.

Fernrick started to speak.

"Tell him," O'Gilroy instructed Albrecht, "that I started it and I apologise."

Albrecht began, but Fernrick shut him up. He looked at O'Gilroy. "Thank you, but I understand enough English . . . This place is too small for trouble, too small for trouble-makers.

Do you understand? If anything more happens, I will report you to your master."

He switched back to German to say what must have been much the same except longer and with a mention of the Kaiser. Then he slammed out.

As they relaxed with a collective sigh, O'Gilroy made a vulgar gesture at the closed door. And someone laughed. Then someone handed him his shirt off the floor, another gave him a cigarette.

It's only in schoolboy stories that the man you've beaten shakes your hand and becomes your friend for life. Quite likely the guard had become his enemy for life, but what mattered was that the rest now accepted him. Just like in a new barrack room. Which wasn't surprising, since he was now certain they were all soldiers.

* * *

With the party complete and now hooked up to a proper train – and one of the fastest in the world – the journey took on a new sense of purpose. Indeed, they let most of their own purposes drift into limbo and the journey take over. As they were bustled across the last of Bavaria and through Salzburg into Austria, they picked their favourite chairs and invented their own time-spending routines – just as a visitor to a strange city will quickly adopt a certain table at a certain café as his own. They were all used to long passive journeys by train and ship; it was what most travel was about.

And the longer they travelled, the more the view from the train windows became unreal, just exquisitely-painted stage scenery of snowy peaks, the onion domes of Orthodox churches, wayside shrines. It needed no caring, no interpretation; turn one's eyes to a book or magazine and it was gone. A stop became like the end of a balloon journey, an unwelcome bump back into reality.

They were due into Vienna soon after eight in the evening and Dahlmann announced that dinner would begin immediately they left. So they had to dress first, and Ranklin summoned O'Gilroy to "help" by sitting and smoking a cigarette.

O'Gilroy mentioned that the staff were all soldiers – "Except the chef, probly. He's just barmy like them all."

Ranklin considered. "I suppose it's not surprising. I believe a lot of the Kaiser's staff are soldiers; he likes having them around him. What have they been doing? Close-order drill in the corridor?"

O'Gilroy told briefly about the fight and Herr Fernrick's intervention—

"*Who?*"

"The chief butler, Swiss Admiral, that's his name."

"I think you mean *Fähnrich*. It means senior n.c.o. Colour sergeant."

O'Gilroy nodded slowly, letting smoke trickle from his nose. "Ah. Then I wasn't so clever as I thought. They're not hiding it, jest not saying it neither . . . Give me some money: I'll rate better with cigarettes and a bottle of me own to share round."

Ranklin gave him a sovereign. "Where do they hide the bottles?"

"In the coal for the boiler. Herr Fernrick don't inspect that."

In so many things, armies are all the same.

For many Orient Express travellers, Vienna was the end of the line; from here, it was downhill socially to Budapest, Belgrade and Sofia, and a month too early for visiting Constantinople. So the train loitered while baggage was unloaded and most of the remaining passengers got out to buy cigarettes and newspapers, smoke, chatter, try to peek into the Kaiser's carriages, and generally get in the way.

Ranklin saw O'Gilroy scurrying off to shop as he stepped down. Dahlmann and a group of bankers or Embassy officials were already in conference in one patch of lamplight. Their chef was doing a deal in chicken and fish with the Express's kitchen. A young man in evening dress accosted him.

"Patrick Snaipe? I'm Redpath, from the Embassy. Just popped along to see how things were going with you and Lady Kelso."

"Very civil of you. Come aboard and meet her."

They eased past the guard, who had deserted the baggage compartment to protect the main carriage from riff-raff, and Ranklin introduced Redpath to Lady Kelso. She gave the lad five minutes of undiluted charm while Ranklin stood by and had philosophic thoughts. Such as: small men tend to be temperamentally quite different from big, tall men, but small women are femininity more concentrated. How about that for a theory? Perhaps there was something in the Viennese air; there was a Dr Freud here who was having some pretty daft ideas about people, so he'd read.

Then he thought of something more important and interrupted: "I say, can you send a cable for me?"

"Of course, just the sort of thing I'm here for." So Ranklin wrote out a cryptic message to "Uncle Charles" at a London club address. If the Commander read it properly, he would know that Gunther's firm was responsible for Ranklin's untimely end, if he met one. There was some small satisfaction in arranging revenge ahead of one's death.

The dull, and doubtless soggy, Hungarian plain of the Danube slipped past in the night. Even the stop at Budapest barely rumpled Ranklin's sleep and they clattered across the iron bridge into Serbia and Belgrade while still at breakfast.

Now they had not only left Europe's drawing-rooms, but gone through its back door and into the ramshackle outhouses of the Balkans. Dahlmann collected their passports, warned them to stay put, and hurried off. Ranklin saw him ally himself to one of the train staff and start haggling with Serb officials. Alongside the severe well-fitting Orient Express uniform they looked scruffy down-and-outs.

And that, really, was the whole story: the Express travelled across Europe in a private metaphorical tunnel lined and protected by sheer wealth. Only if you got off might you become fair prey; as long as you stayed aboard you were untouchable. The argument, obviously, was about whether the private carriages belonged in the same tunnel – although these certainly weren't the first such to be attached to the Express.

Ranklin reckoned himself and O'Gilroy to be fireproof behind the diplomatic passport; anyway, Britain wasn't a player on this bit of the chessboard. But Zurga . . . He realised the Turk was keeping to his sleeper.

The discussion outside ended and Dahlmann came back on board to announce: "We may proceed, but a Serbian officer must ride with us through Serbia to Nis." He tossed the passports onto a table and hurried through, presumably to warn Zurga.

Moving unhastily but smoothly, Ranklin scooped up the passports, handed Lady Kelso hers, Streibl his, took his own and was left with a handful of solely German ones for Dahlmann, the staff and one must be for Zurga. So they were smuggling him through the Balkans as a German citizen. Which was sensible, but placed Zurga even further in the Baghdad Railway camp.

A Serb officer in a high-crowned peakless cap and a worn great-coat down to the ankles of his semi-polished boots came in, saluted with a slight bow, said a few inscrutable words of Serbo-Croat and sat in a corner. Dahlmann came back and picked up the passports, looked at them, at Ranklin – who was deep in a book – and finally said nothing.

With Belgrade, they had seen the last of the Danube and the wide plains. Soon they had turned up the valley of the Morava, winding gently but tighter into the hills that would become mountains and last the next twenty-four hours. Gradually the sodden fields beside the river were left behind and drifts of snow, worn like the land itself, appeared on the hillsides. Both landscape and snow got fresher as they climbed away from cultivation. Early March is no time to admire what mankind does to the land.

They stretched an untalkative luncheon until they slowed into Nis, a market town with buffalo-carts and peasants in baggy white trousers trudging the muddy streets. The Serb saluted, bowed, said another something and got off – and it was as if an aged and disapproving grand-parent had gone to bed. Streibl made a weak joke about the Serb commandeering a buffalo for his return to Belgrade and they roared with laughter. Ranklin decided he *would* have a cognac, and Streibl joined him.

"What about poor Zurga Bey?" Lady Kelso said suddenly. "He hasn't had anything to eat since breakfast. Have them bring him something as soon as we're moving."

Dahlmann protested that it would upset the kitchen, the servants—

"Fiddlesticks," said Lady Kelso. "If they won't do it, I'll cook him something myself." And Ranklin and Streibl backed her up.

Perhaps Dahlmann was trapped between the correctness of not wanting to offend the Kaiser's staff, and seeing his group united for the first time by an irresistible party spirit. In any event, while Ranklin fetched Zurga from his sleeper Dahlmann said God-knows-what to Herr Fernrick, and a meal of soup and warmed-up chicken was produced. Fernrick's revenge came in insisting his own men were off duty and making O'Gilroy serve the damned foreigners.

Lady Kelso stayed in the dining-saloon with Zurga, and Ranklin found himself next door talking to Streibl. With that atmosphere and the cognac, the railwayman talked happily – breaking off to point out interesting or faulty construction details beside the line – but always railways, railways, railways.

"Ships discovered the world, but only railways can make it tame, civilised. When a ship passes, in a few minutes there is no sign. The sea is not changed. But the railway changes the land forever. Think of America, when it was a land of savages and wild animals, if I could have worked on those great railways . . ." His eyes glowed behind his thick glasses.

In fact he had worked on the German *Mittel-Afrika* scheme, making a railway of the old slave route inland from Dar-es-Salaam. They laid the first rails directly into the surf from lighters, dumped a locomotive atop them – and they had a few metres of a railway that would build itself across 700 miles to

Lake Tanganyika. Through jungle and swamp and rock, beri-beri, malaria and sleeping-sickness. Through drought where they needed one water-carrier for every workman, and then more to lubricate the rock-drills. Or water that was plentiful, but so full of minerals that it encrusted and jammed the works of the engines. And all, apparently, on a diet of dried mud barbel. Ranklin hadn't a notion of what dried mud barbel was, but the mere sound of it . . .

He sucked on his pipe, nodded, and let himself be swept along with Streibl's rambling odyssey. The man was a visionary, but his visions were of steel, his dreams held together with greasy nuts and bolts.

"Beyond there –" he gestured towards the front of the train "– is half the world. From Constantinople, one day we can go by train to Arabia, Persia, India, China. From Berlin to Peking – can you think of that? To join the West to the East, to trade with the people of half the world." Then he suddenly grew sombre and his gaze turned fierce. "And one old man with some rifles is in our way. Can he stop such an idea? Can he be *permitted* to stop it?"

"Oh, no," Ranklin agreed, since some answer seemed called for. "And, of course, the engineers themselves, their families. . ."

"Yes, of course," Streibl said, as if he'd forgotten and were trying to catch up.

"And how long have you worked on the Baghdad Railway?"

"I do the first survey on some sections – ach! they are always changing the line so as not to go too near the frontier and offend the Russians or too near the coast so battleships could bombard it – then I go to Africa again, then to work at head office . . . *Politik*," he muttered. "It is good to be out again."

"And are you coming along because you know Miskal Bey?"

"No, I never hear of him before . . . I am just to help if . . . if there are problems . . ."

The sudden vagueness warned Ranklin to veer the conversation back to the view from the window. But he felt he was beginning to understand something of Streibl. Like many good regimental officers, he loved the day-to-day detail of his work –

but his visions were unreal because they were just enlargements of that. He lacked a political dimension and, like those officers, would never make a good general.

Which, if the Army was anything to go by, wouldn't stop him actually becoming a general at all.

* * *

In the service carriage, O'Gilroy was welcomed back from his table-waiting with friendly banter. He accepted a swig from somebody's bottle of schnappes and, translated via Albrecht, assured them that he hadn't been raped by Lady Kelso or buggered by "That Turk" – but pleased them by suggesting that both had been close escapes. Like all soldiers, they saw the outside world in simple, unsubtle colours – exactly as outsiders saw soldiering.

It seemed that Herr Fernrick (O'Gilroy still thought of him as that) had given them a talk whilst he had been acting waiter, on the Dreadful Dangers of Constantinople if they didn't stick together, on *never* accosting a woman, assuming all Turks were cheats, sticking to beer – and the address of a reasonable Austrian-run brothel. It was the lecture all sergeants gave on a troopship or a posting to a new town, but O'Gilroy listened with an expression of gratefulness as Albrecht passed it on.

It was now openly admitted that they were soldiers, and it suddenly occurred to someone to ask why O'Gilroy hadn't done any service.

"I did," he told Albrecht. "Ten years."

Immediate interest; had he been in action?

"Surely. In the South African War."

That brought growls, and he remembered that Germany had backed the Boers, had supplied them with Mauser rifles and Krupp artillery. But now he was started, he plodded on . . .

. . . towards God-knows-where for God-knows-why, in the heat of the sun and the dust of the column, and saw the growly expressions fade because he was talking about any soldiering anywhere . . . But then the sound they hadn't heard yet, of bullets going past, first as a whuffle and soon as a crack with the range shortening. Until the one that made no sound at all because it stopped in his thigh.

He told of being left by the column to wait for the medical cart, of being picked up instead by an artillery battery, dumped atop an ammunition wagon, and so found himself shut up in the siege of Ladysmith while his own battalion was shot to pieces outside. And then, mostly recovered, being conscripted by the artillery lieutenant to fill a gap in a gun crew—

"What number?" Albrecht asked.

"Five, handling the ammunition. Later, sometimes four, loading," O'Gilroy said calmly. He routed in the biscuit-tin lid of cigarette ends saved from the saloon ashtrays, and found one of Ranklin's English ones with a few puffs left in it. He lit it and went on . . .

. . . about the siege which saw them eating horsemeat soup and rat but somehow left the senior officers with enough to welcome the final relieving force with a banquet (his listeners understood *that*, all right). But mostly about the young Gunner lieutenant who had spotted his love of mechanical things and explained just how everything on a gun worked and why, preaching what the beautiful weapons could do, properly handled. He described all that, but not the officer himself. They might have recognised the young Ranklin.

* * *

Changing for dinner gave time for the party spirit to evaporate somewhat, and the uncertainties they would face in Constantinople and beyond to loom. But it was still their last dinner as a group and – apart from a fear that Dahlmann would make a speech – they all set out to enjoy it.

Moreover, Lady Kelso and Zurga had reached at least the pretence of mutual respect. Both knew life in the Turkish Empire far better than the rest ever would – but that, of course, was the problem. They shared knowledge but their experiences were poles apart.

Ranklin was glad Lady Kelso had waited until the coffee stage before saying: "I expect I shall find many changes in Turkey after all these years . . ."

There was a moment of held breath as they waited to see how Zurga exploited this opening. But he nodded and said: "I think – I hope – the Railway is a symbol of such change. The Empire cannot last unless it becomes modern. Without it, the Powers of Europe and particularly – forgive me, Mr Snaipe – Britain and France, will pick the bones of Turkey bare."

Ranklin privately agreed, but felt Snaipe should protest mildly. "Oh, I say . . ."

"But we should deserve it. Sultan Ahmed *did* deserve it. The Empire was corrupt, shameful, with the sultans. Just jewels, women, palaces – and the reports of spies; when they took his palace they found rooms full of such reports. And of course the *valis* and *kaimakams* were also little sultans in their districts.

"It was the Army that saved Turkey. Even the Sultan – he let the Navy rot – could see that he must strengthen the Army or our enemies would eat us away, bite by bite. So he went to our German friends – and brought his own doom on himself. He forgot that to clean one wall of a palace makes the rest look more dirty. It was the Army that saw the dirt. So it was the Army that overthrew him, that brought back the Constitution to the people of Turkey."

"Yes, I'm sure the Sultan had to go," Lady Kelso said. "But, under the Committee, is it Turkey for the Turks or for everybody in the Empire? – Arab, Armenian, Kurd . . ."

This was another moment when the rest of them held their breath. But Zurga just smiled. "It is an Empire – perhaps like your British Empire. Is that for Britons or does every peasant in India and Africa have also your wonderful Parliament?"

She shook her head and smiled ruefully. Zurga pressed on gently: "And would they understand a Parliament if they had it? Would your Arab friends know?"

"Oh, they'd understand the House of Lords, all right. Miskal could walk straight in there now and not be noticed bar his clothing."

And once again the fuse flared up close to the gunpowder barrel. And once again Zurga snuffed it out by chuckling with the rest. "So you have still your sultans, I think. But yes, you will find many changes, I hope. But not all: we have had only a few years. There are still corrupt *valis* and *kaimakams*. There is inefficiency and waste and justice is often for sale. After a century of sleeping, it takes time to awake."

"And when you do wake up, Turkey will be in Europe, will it?"

"Not all. We must have the Railway, the telephone, the motor-car. And money also. We need these things. But we must also say 'Enough, beyond this, you must not meddle.' Because we must also remain Turkey, a nation of Islam. Without God, Turkey does not exist."

Was Dahlmann trying to hide his affront? And was Lady Kelso staring past them, past the walls of the carriage and perhaps of time and seeing her old romantic Turkey fading in a harsh new dawn?

Zurga smiled again and said politely: "But of course, you were not concerned with the politics, with the hope of change."

She came back to the here-and-now with a thump. "I'm a woman, Zurga Bey. Who cared what I thought?"

He had no answer to that. Yet, as he tried to straddle two worlds and perhaps found himself torn between them, here was a European who had submitted easily to the East and then, seemingly as easily, stepped back again. Zurga could believe he understood European women and, separately, the few respectable Turkish ones he could respectably meet. But not Lady Kelso. However much, in his mind, he labelled her a whore of Arabs and an infidel (and Ranklin was sure he did both) he'd know that wasn't understanding. And hate both his need to understand a woman and inability to do it.

12

By morning they were clear of the mountains and rolling, reasonably fast, along the valley of the Maritsa, expecting to reach Constantinople by teatime. But they were still in Bulgaria and Zurga stayed in his sleeper.

As always on a long journey, with the end in sight everybody wanted it over with *now* and their mood was impatient, yesterday's party spirit long gone. Dahlmann had a long, private, and probably pointless, conference with Streibl. Ranklin drifted about lighting his pipe, letting it go out and lighting a cigarette instead. Lady Kelso abandoned her magazines to watch out of the window, as if doing so would hurry them forward.

Perhaps Herr Fernrick was still nursing yesterday's grievance because lunch was very much an eating-up-what's-left-in-the-larder affair. Halfway through, they crossed the Turkish frontier, and Zurga re-appeared. The sight of Turkish soil obviously cheered him; to Ranklin, it was simply soil – no trees, not much grass, just as if a grey-brown blanket, patched with snow, had been spread over a collection of rocks. A few wild dogs appeared and ran alongside.

"In Constantinople there are now no dogs," Zurga said.

"Really?"

"They caught all the wild dogs and put them on an island which has no water."

Frankly, Ranklin didn't much care: the snarling street packs hadn't been his favourite memory of the city. But as Snaipe he felt he should say: "Oh, I say. Dash it all . . ." And Zurga looked quietly satisfied.

Perhaps two hours before Constantinople, with all but Zurga

in the saloon, the train's wheels suddenly locked and they screeched and jolted to a halt. They were in a shallow cutting, with banks on either side just higher than the train so you couldn't see what lay beyond. After half a minute there was some distant shouting and then, unmistakeably, a shot.

The effect rippled through the saloon. Lady Kelso sat up straight and pressed her nose to the window; Streibl also peered out. More agitated, Dahlmann looked back towards the second coach. Ranklin sat still: their position was too perfect, caught in a defile with no view. This must be an ambush.

Zurga strode through, jacketless and with shirt sleeves rolled up, his face set and swearing to himself, heading for the rear of the train. He paused to warn Lady Kelso to get away from the window: "Broken glass can be as bad as a bullet sometimes."

"Thank you." She gave him a brilliant smile and stood up. "I feel quite safe with you coping." He went on and a sharp barking-match in German began somewhere around the kitchen.

Lady Kelso selected a chair well away from any windows and re-opened her magazine. Streibl went on bobbing around, trying for a better view, and there didn't seem any point in trying to stop him. Ranklin got up.

"Where are you going?" Dahlmann demanded.

"Er . . . to get my diplomatic passport."

"This does not seem to me a diplomatic situation."

In his sleeper, Ranklin dug out his revolver and pocketed it. As an open-air weapon it was useless, it wouldn't reach accurately to the top of the banks. But if it came to a barney in the carriage itself . . .

Then he went on forward to the little vestibule with its outside doors, where they linked to the rest of the train. He opened the right-hand door and leaned out cautiously, although he was pretty sure he wouldn't be conspicuous: human nature would have dozens of heads poking out right along the train.

Zurga strode past, heading forwards and shouting in Turkish. He waved Ranklin back inside; Ranklin obeyed briefly, then leant out again. From the kitchen carriage, one of the staff ran up the bank carrying a rifle, paused to peek over the top, then threw himself flat and brought the rifle to his shoulder. A second followed, more lithely, dark hair fluttering – and damn it all, it was O'Gilroy.

Well, of *course* it was. If there was a spare rifle, a mere language problem wouldn't have stopped him talking his way to it.

Ranklin knew there must be a similar group on top of the opposite bank. But now, for the moment, the situation froze in place – and Ranklin with it. There was a knife-edged plains wind flattening the ochre-grey tufts of coarse grass, and little smut-stained patches of snow lingered in every shadowed pocket of the banks.

After a moment more, he went back to his sleeper, put on his overcoat and found his binoculars. They were naval, really too powerful to use except with a steady rest, and a giveaway that he was a long-distance soldier if anybody guessed he was a soldier at all. Back in the doorway, he propped himself against the side and tried to focus on a group at the front of the train.

Two or three were passengers, being hustled back aboard by the train staff. And Zurga distinctive in shirt sleeves, standing with legs spread and hands on his hips obviously laying down some law to a group of drab, ragged men with rifles. Through the shifting group and spurts of steam from the engine, Ranklin could just make out some obstruction on the line beyond. Logs, maybe, though God knows where they came from on this treeless plain.

Then a machine-gun fired. Just one quick rattle, perhaps ten rounds, and from the other side of the train. In the moment Ranklin's binoculars had wavered, the group around Zurga had dived into crouching positions beside the train wheels. Only Zurga stayed upright, and he then vanished, apparently into the train. Ranklin hurried across to the other door.

At the top of that bank, three of the German staff knelt or sat around a Maxim gun on a heavy tripod. They were quite still and looked very competent. Ranklin swivelled the binoculars to see Zurga marching – barely a hint of scrambling – up the bank to stand, arms akimbo again, and bellow in German – extremely fluent German, in its own way; ". . . *dumm Sohnes von Huren* . . ." and similar phrases.

A shudder passed through the group around the Maxim, as if a sudden wind had blown in their faces. Zurga marched down the bank and vanished again.

Five minutes later, Ranklin came back into the saloon. "The excitement seems to be over," he reported. "Zurga Bey appears to have persuaded them to dismantle the block on the line and he's on his way back."

"Of course he did. He's a very capable man," Lady Kelso said calmly, laying the magazine in her lap. She looked at Dahlmann. "And so are the *servants*, it seems. I didn't know we had a Maxim gun on board."

Dahlmann smiled cautiously. "This line can be dangerous – as events have shown."

"You seem to have thought of everything." She picked up the magazine again.

The machine-gun crew on the bank were dismounting the weapon, folding the ammunition belt back into its box, lumbering down the bank with the unwieldy tripod. Herr Fernrick knelt with a rifle, covering them. Then he blew a whistle to call in the far-side picket and walked down the bank himself.

They heard Zurga clump aboard at the end of the corridor, but he stayed there, perhaps showing himself at the open door, until they were well under way. They passed the group of half-a-dozen ambushers; most of their feet were bundles of rags. Two of them, rifles slung, were starting to carry one of their logs up the bank – saving it, perhaps, for a less defended train. Another pointed his rifle in the air and fired a last defiant shot.

Then the cutting dwindled down and Ranklin saw a little group of horses and a cart a hundred yards out on the lumpy plain. That explained not only how the bandits travelled but what the machine-gun had threatened.

Zurga came in, face grim and shoulders hunched with cold.

He was aiming for the rear carriage, but Dahlmann and Lady Kelso waylaid him.

"That was very brave of you," she said. "Who were they? – brigands?"

"Of a kind. Most of them had been soldiers. Or deserters, who had not been paid for a year. Unfortunately, there are many such, since the war." His expression got grimmer.

"But our machine-gun scared them off," Dahlmann said confidently.

"That machine-gun nearly ruined everything! The sight of it was enough, they know what it can do. Did you want them chased *into* the train, hiding and shooting among the passengers?"

Dahlmann's assurance had evaporated. "I will talk to them."

"*I* will talk to them. Now!"

The banker's face wasn't used to sending any but the subtlest of signals, but now it was trying to transmit warnings, alarm, near-panic. And some of it got through. Zurga said: "First I should put a coat on. It is very cold." He turned about and headed for his sleeper.

Dahlmann, relieved but discomfited and looking for the office cat to kick, said to Ranklin: "So: you did not need your diplomatic passport after all."

"So I didn't."

"I noticed Gorman," Lady Kelso said, "out there playing soldiers with a will."

"You were warned not to look out. Yes, he's an old soldier. You can never cure that, it seems."

But after that, everybody was even less ready to settle down again. Streibl recalled native uprisings against the railway in East Africa, Dahlmann muttered some comments about Turkish discipline, and Zurga went about looking grim with angry shame. Abruptly, all this changed to an about-to-arrive scurry, and they besieged Dahlmann with questions that they had meant to ask earlier. So he called a final conference around the big table.

"Lady Kelso," he read from a list, "is invited to stay at the English Embassy. Dr Streibl and Mr Snaipe will go to the Pera Palace hotel. I am sure you will be met at the station. Zurga Bey – I think you have your own arrangements? As I have."

"When and how do we leave for the south?" Lady Kelso asked.

"As soon as we have collected the gold coinage. The railway will take you to Eregli and then to the work camp. From there, I am afraid, you must go by horse or mule into the mountains. I understand it is more than a day's journey."

Lady Kelso nodded cheerfully.

Streibl woke up again: "If you do not have them now, buy warm clothes here in Constantinople for the mountains. Down there there is nothing to buy."

"No dressing for dinner, what?" Ranklin said.

Dahlmann said: "I understand it is not the custom on the back of a mule, Mr Snaipe."

"And you aren't coming that far, is that right?"

"I am not ashamed to be pleased that I am not, Mr Snaipe. My duties to the Bank will keep me in Constantinople."

When the meeting ended, a pent-up rush of staff bringing baggage was released. O'Gilroy was helping willingly, hoping for a last-minute look at what the luggage compartment held – apart from that machine-gun. But the narrowness of the carriage was against him: it was too easy for the single guard to block his view. He trailed back to help Ranklin pack; he might not be all that good, but he had had more experience than any spoiled officer.

He had barely got started when Lady Kelso knocked and put her head round the door. "I do beg your pardon, but I wonder if you could lend me Gorman for just a moment? The lock of one of my bags . . ."

"Of course."

"Close the door, please, Gorman," she told O'Gilroy, "and sit down."

Women like Lady Kelso were mysterious, mythical figures to O'Gilroy, reminding him of some dark references his mother used to make. He sat on the bunk bed as far from her as he could.

"There's no lock problem," she smiled briskly. "That was just my little ruse. I wanted to ask you . . . But first, have you been with Mr Snaipe long?"

"Sort of off-and-on, M'Lady."

"Would you agree he's – Oh dear, this really is rather difficult – perhaps not one of the world's great thinkers?"

Despite his fright, O'Gilroy twitched a smile. "Perhaps not, M'Lady."

"But an honest patriot?"

"Oh, surely that, M'Lady."

"And you yourself were a soldier, I believe."

Instinctively, although O'Gilroy's instincts were well controlled by now, he straightened his back. "I was that. South African war 'n all."

"How splendid. And whatever else I may be, I'm an Englishwoman through and through . . . so I'm worried about all this business."

A puzzled frown. "All what, M'Lady?"

"You do know about it, don't you? What it seems to boil down to is that I'll be helping the Germans complete a railway that I'm far from sure is in Britain's best interests."

A volcano of thoughts erupted in O'Gilroy's mind. She was having patriotic doubts: good – so far. But suppose she got the notion of doing a little sabotage on her own? Then there'd be the most God-awful muddle. Yet she obviously didn't believe Ranklin, as the Hon. Patrick Snaipe, was capable of doing anything original himself . . .

With a sudden cold professionalism, he wondered if they could pull off a coup and somehow leave her to take the blame, keeping their characters intact. He shelved the idea only because it wasn't the most urgent. Right now, he must keep her as a possible ally yet dissuade her from acting on her own.

"I thought the Foreign Minister, Ma'am, Sir Edward, he'd asked ye jest to talk to this feller with the prisoners. If ye do that much, nobody's going to blame ye if—"

"Oh, never mind about *blame*," she said testily. "I'm bothered that Sir Edward himself might . . . well, let's say he may have been poorly advised. He must have a lot on his plate." She cocked her head. "I wouldn't say this to Mr Snaipe, so this is *utterly* between us two, but I've found in my travels that our Diplomatic Service, and the Foreign Office back home, don't *always* get things right."

O'Gilroy was trying to look as if this idea, while wholly new and startling, wasn't entirely unbelievable.

"In fact," she added, "when I think of my first husband . . . No, never mind that." She suddenly sat up straight. "Or do you feel I'm trying to involve you in things that shouldn't concern you?"

"No, no, M'Lady, it's not that. But – if I might be making a suggestion . . .?"

"That's just what I'm asking for."

"I was jest thinking, M'Lady –" he frowned, as if unfamiliar with deviousness "– that if ye waited until yer talking to the feller – Miskal, is it? – ye'd be talking a lingo me and the Hon. Patrick don't know at all, so if ye said Go right on keeping the prisoners and let the Germans fart in their beer (begging yer pardon, M'Lady) then who'd be knowing?"

Her smile was a sunrise. "What a *splendid* idea. I'm most indebted to you. And I don't think you need mention our little chat to Mr Snaipe. It might . . . *confuse* him."

"Never a word, M'Lady."

"Thank you so much. You're a most intelligent man, Gorman." She hesitated, perhaps trying to make up her mind, then deciding what could she lose? "What do you make of Zurga Bey? D'you think he could be a spy?"

"Er—" O'Gilroy was taken aback. He would far rather she did not go around wondering if people were spies. "I couldn't be saying . . . Jest who would he be spying on, M'Lady?"

"Oh, any and all of us. In Turkey you get spies everywhere. It's their way of life, everybody wants to know what their rivals are doing. Even Europeans down on their luck do it, spying on other Europeans for the Government – and I'm sure *that* hasn't changed with this Committee. So be careful who you say anything to."

Relieved, he realised she was talking about *informers*, not real spies. "Thank ye, M'Lady, I'll be remembering that . . . But about Zurga, I can tell ye one thing: he's a soldier, an officer. Or was, not long past."

She sat back with a delighted expression. "Ah yes – and you'd be able to tell, of course. Thank you again. Now I'd better let you get on with your work . . ."

Ranklin had just about finished the packing, but he lit a cigarette and let O'Gilroy – who would clearly rather have faced an army of brigands than the notorious Lady Kelso – do the rest and pass on the news.

When he had finished, Ranklin was looking pale. "My God, she isn't going to do anything on her own, is she?"

"I think I talked her out of it. And was telling her Zurga's really an officer."

Ranklin nodded. "The way he handled those bandits? – and spoke to the machine-gun crew? Yes, I'd guess he was in Germany learning German Army methods, and his Turkish masters probably added him to this mission to look after their interests. And the Railway company doesn't want to be seen as high-handed foreigners if things get exciting, so they welcomed him . . . Probably they welcome a British contingent to share the blame, too," he added.

"I thought if Lady Kelso don't get the prisoners released, they jest hand over the gold."

"Yes, but paying kidnappers keeps them in business. I suggested Miskal might use the ransom to buy more guns, and nobody took me seriously. But it's so obvious a point, they must have thought of it." He paused for thought. "It might be that getting the engineers back is just the first step. And the second will be making quite sure Miskal can't try the same thing again."

O'Gilroy considered this for himself, then: "D'ye reckon that machine-gun's coming all the way with us, then?"

"I doubt they brought it just to scare off brigands. You haven't got a look inside the baggage compartment? – then it could be full of Maxims for all we know. Though I wouldn't choose them for tackling a mountain stronghold." Machine-guns were for defence in open country, not lugging – dismounted and unfireable – around rocky slopes.

O'Gilroy shrugged. "All packed, yer Honourable sir. And ye've only one clean collar for a dress shirt left, so hope the hotel laundry knows its stuff."

"Fine." Ranklin got up to look out of the window. The train was curving gently around the coast, past isolated wooden houses and slumped stone huts, through a gap in the old Byzantine city wall, towards the low rocky headland of Stamboul. "When we get off the train, the Embassy will probably be meeting Lady Kelso, and I imagine I'll get caught up in that. But nobody'll care about you. I want you to hang around the station and see what happens to whatever's in the baggage compartment."

O'Gilroy thought about this. "Could be they'll move it out to some goods yard before they unload."

"The only goods yard is right alongside the station itself – look." Ranklin unfolded the map in his Baedeker. Squeezed between the sea and Seraglio Point, the station had no room for elaborate marshalling yards. "I don't say you'll get right up to it – they're probably wary of thieves – but you might see something."

O'Gilroy saw the sense of it, but it was still a tall order for his first move in an utterly strange city. "D'ye have any Turkish money?"

"Sorry, not yet, but they take French gold and silver, if you've still got any."

"And give me yer gun."

Ranklin frowned, but passed it over. Then he ripped the map out of the Baedeker and passed that over, too. He wasn't sure how good O'Gilroy was at map-reading, but it might help. "Get a cab when you're through. We're at the Pera Palace hotel, everybody knows it."

The train slowed yet further as they came in sight of Stamboul, uneven steps of wooden buildings that climbed gently to climax in the stalks of minarets and great buds of domes that glowed pink and gold in the setting sun.

"Keep this memory," Ranklin advised. "Once you're among it, it won't feel the way it looks now."

13

Despite being the end of the line for the Orient Express, Stamboul station was surprisingly unpretentious: no great arched glass roof, just individual canopies over each platform. Since they couldn't get through Customs until the porters had unloaded their luggage, nobody could rush and the platform turned into a social occasion. Relatives fell into each others' arms, friends shook hands, hotel agents tried to find who had booked with them and tout for more. And both the British and German Embassies had guessed the private coaches would be at the front of the train, so arrived through the crowd at a diplomatic scamper.

"Harriet, Lady Kelso?" Very correct. "I'm Howard Jarvey, Second Counsellor at the Embassy." He was tall and slightly stooped, with a head that was lean and, when he raised his top hat, virtually bald. Yet he had a dark moustache that Ranklin couldn't keep his eyes off; it looked dead, like a moustache on a skull.

Jarvey turned to him, forcing Ranklin to raise his eyeline a few inches. "The Honourable Patrick Snaipe? Splendid. Did you have a good journey? – we heard there'd been some trouble . . ."

"Just brigands," Lady Kelso dismissed them as she might have done a mosquito.

"Really?" Jarvis was a little surprised to have the topic ended so quickly. "Ah . . . the Ambassador's having a little dinner tonight, if you feel up to it—"

"How sweet of him. I'd be delighted."

"Splendid. And you, too, Snaipe." No "Mr": he was on the diplomatic ladder here, and the bottom rung of it. "No need to call on the Ambassador formally, it isn't as if you're joining our little family. Seven-thirty, the Embassy's very near the Pera Palace. I'm afraid we can't offer you a lift now, the Embassy motor-car's . . ." But Ranklin never learnt what, since Jarvey had escorted Lady Kelso out of ear-shot.

The crowd was thinning and Ranklin became aware of O'Gilroy at his elbow, whispering: "I need ye and the passport to get me off'n the platform."

Ranklin had forgotten that, but his diplomatic status eased them through the Customs hall and he left O'Gilroy outside as if finding them a cab.

In fact, O'Gilroy had great difficulty in not finding several cabs, along with porters, guides, half a dozen boarding-house touts, several things to eat or drink, and some offers he could only guess at. Any idea of standing there and taking stock of his new surroundings vanished. He could only stride off purposefully, like trying to out-run a cloud of midges on a beach.

The Customs exit was at the side of the station. After a hundred yards or so, he had worked his way round to the front, end-on to where all the lines – only four of them – terminated. The crowd there seemed more concerned with its own purposes, and he found a table on the outskirts of the station buffet and sat down.

The first thing he saw was a shop sign – probably. But it wasn't that he couldn't read the words, the very *letters* meant nothing. In the twilight a few electric lamps had wavered on, but far more oil lamps were flaring up, lighting alien faces in strange clothes, jabbering incomprehensibly. And behind that, the jingle, clatter and yells – the Turks shouted in deliberately low-pitched voices – of horse-drawn traffic, and behind *that* the rumble of unseen ships' sirens. Shapeless, rowdy and menacing, the world tried to engulf him. He clutched the familiar pistol in his pocket for reassurance—

A waiter stood looking at him impatiently. O'Gilroy managed to croak: "*Café*, please," and the waiter nodded and went away. He had spoken to this world, and it understood! He leaned back, nestling in a surge of confidence, lit a cigarette and set to watching the crowd more calmly. Almost all were men: the very occasional women wore black from head to foot, held a fold of cloth across their faces and generally looked as unmysterious as a bag of washing. But even allowing for it being a cold evening, the men were barely less drab, except that most wore the scarlet flowerpot of a fez. So much for the "colourful East".

But they were still *different*, and in so many aspects of clothing, mannerism, movement, that he stood no chance of blending into any crowd. He needed something to do, besides sit and look. So after he had drunk what they seemed to think was coffee he moved on.

On the opposite side of the station from where he'd first come out, a dark road lined with warehouses ran parallel to the lines of the goods yard. There was nowhere to loiter inconspicuously, so the most O'Gilroy could do was confirm that there was a gate into the yard – there was, and it was guarded – then see if the road led anywhere else. It dissolved into a tangle of alleyways with the loom of bare trees and a barracks-like building beyond, so he turned back.

It would be an outrageous compliment to call the road surfaces here cobblestones: they were just vari-sized rocks hammered into the half-dry mud. The idea of pavements hadn't occurred to anyone yet, so he had to squeeze himself against a wall as a procession of three ox-carts lumbered by. They were empty, but with enough men on the driving seats to form a work-party and as they passed he heard a snatch of conversation – and was sure it was German.

He saw them turn into the yard gateway and walked back to the front of the station. There he bought a four-day-old London newspaper and a handful of postcards, then found another café. Now he could pick one not obviously overlooking the goods yard road since a convoy of ox-carts would be slow and highly visible. Here also they had the idea that coffee meant a thimbleful of sandy sour treacle, so perhaps it was a common Turkish delusion. He dried the tabletop with his sleeve and began to write postcards.

* * *

The immediate lobby of the Pera Palace hotel – built by the *Wagons-Lit* Company specifically to house its Orient Express passengers – was quite small and a little austere.

"Has my man Gorman got here yet?" Ranklin asked, and was told, of course, No.

"Silly ass," he grumbled. "Went looking for some bit of baggage he'd misplaced . . . Get someone to unpack for me, would you? I've got to tog up for dinner at the Embassy, but right now I want a cup of tea. You do make a decent cup of tea, I trust?"

And having established Snaipe's character yet again, he drifted up a few steps and turned into the public rooms, where things got more palatial. High-ceilinged, chandeliered and most overlooking a park and the ships gliding up the Golden Horn, the idea was obviously to give you the feeling that you were experiencing Constantinople without getting your shoes muddy or your back stabbed. The furniture and decor blended Eastern patterns with European comfort without satisfying either the discriminating eye or backside, but got high marks for trying.

There he had to order tea, even though he'd have preferred coffee, and face up to the fact that he could run into Corinna at any moment. He felt . . . That was the trouble: he didn't know and had, so far, avoided trying to find out.

Ranklin took the mature and reasonable view that the world was crowded with women who adored him. To start with, those whom he had left behind must obviously still yearn for him, while those who had given him the push would now be bitterly regretting it. And others who, once they got to know him . . . So all he had to do was get over what he felt for Corinna.

Then just what did he feel for her? He had known from the start that it was hopeless to fall in love with her – but neither had he fallen in hopeless love with her. Hopeless love was a special condition that suited some people very well, being very stable and requiring minimal effort. Men who locked up their private lives in cabinets marked Hopeless Love had the energy to go out and build empires.

Ergo, he was not in any sort of love with Corinna. Therefore it only remained to get over . . . let's say, his *annoyance* that she was going to marry this ghastly French banker. He just wished . . . But set aside what he wished: there was the practical problem that they could bump into each other – she was probably staying at this hotel – and she might address him as Ranklin. She should know better, but to be fair (reluctantly) to her, she wasn't a trained agent. Not even British, among her other faults.

He could ask at the desk who *was* staying here – that would be unsuspicious – but he daren't pretend that Snaipe would know her. If O'Gilroy were back, he could be sent with a discreet note . . . He wondered how he was getting on.

* * *

The Army had used similar wagons in South Africa and O'Gilroy knew that oxen were creatures with just one speed. The wagon-drivers made plenty of noise, but mostly to warn other traffic that they were coming through, unhurried but virtually unstoppable. Now that the wagons were loaded (and with tarpaulins tied over the top, to baffle snoopers) the work-party ambled alongside. There were about a dozen of them, half Turk and half German, with Albrecht and the guard from the train staff among them. Because of that, O'Gilroy stayed well back, stopping to admire the view or consult his map to keep from catching up.

They were now, he reckoned, halfway across the Galata Bridge, low, wide and long, that led to the Pera side. Anyway, in front lay a hillside sparkling with lights brighter and more numerous than the area they had left. And the crowd on the bridge seemed to overflow onto the water. Lights, on small steamers, ferries, sailing ships and rowing-boats, weaved their way to, apparently, one massive impending collision. Yet somehow a clamour of hoots, clangs and shouts kept them apart. Or perhaps drowned the sounds of drowning, for all he could tell.

One other thing he remembered from the war was that oxen might not be fast but they kept going indefinitely. So these buggers might have begun a hike of thirty or forty miles . . . Him, too?

* * *

It could have been a diplomatic drawing-room almost anywhere in the world and identifiable as British only by the royal portrait on an end wall. But its rather cluttered elegance was a comfortable contrast to the outside of the building which, apart from the size of the windows, had the style of a prison block, right down to a high wall and gatehouse. Ranklin had bowed over the hands of His Excellency the Ambassador and his wife, who claimed to be delighted, grinned at Lady Kelso, the guest of honour, and been whisked away by Jarvey, looking even more Death-like in white tie and tails.

"I'd like you to meet David Lunn, one of our secretaries. I'm sure he'll look after you."

Lunn was young, almost as short as Ranklin and had a puppyish enthusiasm that wouldn't last long in the Diplomatic. "You came in the Kaiser's private carriages *and* got held up by bandits, didn't you?" He was openly envious. "Did you get involved?"

"Er, not really. They held up the front of the train and we were at the back. And it turned out that we had a Maxim gun on board and that scared them off."

That brought a hush of interest. "Most fortunate," Jarvey murmured. "Er – who manned this gun?"

"The kitchen staff." Since that sounded a bit stupid even for Snaipe, he added: "My manservant – he's been a soldier – reckoned the whole carriage staff were soldiers. And the

Turkish gentleman travelling with us, Zurga Bey, is probably an officer. Do you know him?"

They swapped glances but got no profit from it. "No help, Turks only having one name," Jarvey said. "Do you know if this Maxim gun is being taken south with you?"

"No idea at all, I'm afraid."

Lunn said happily: "Perhaps they're planning to blow old Miskal Bey out of his stronghold. He'll probably cut and run at the first shot if it's the first machine-gun he's met."

As Snaipe, Ranklin couldn't point out that Miskal Bey had been a soldier and Lunn bloody obviously hadn't. But Jarvey was more cautious: "Perhaps, perhaps . . . And when do you leave for the south?"

"When I'm told," Ranklin said. "Dr Dahlmann of the Deutsche Bank seems to be in charge – so far. I don't think he's actually coming with us, but I got the idea there was a certain amount of hurry involved."

"Quite probably. I understand they're badly delayed on the Railway by all this."

Reluctant to let the conversation wander off from the exciting new toy, Lunn said: "I wonder if the Committee knows about this machine-gun."

"I imagine," Jarvey said, "that every beggar in the street knows about it by now. Excuse me, I'd better get back to H.E. . . ." He drifted off to collect the next guest from His Excellency.

Ranklin sipped his sherry and glanced around. There were about ten people in the room by now, so probably they were heading for a dozen or fourteen. And, of course, with men badly outnumbering women; most Turks simply never brought their wives out, and some Europeans would be bachelors or travelling alone.

"You're quite new to the Service, aren't you?" Lunn was saying with exaggerated casualness.

"Oh, the paint's hardly dry on me."

Lunn grinned. "You haven't got your name in the List yet, I noticed."

Noticed be damned. The moment they'd heard he was coming they'd rushed to look him up and try to read between the lines. The Army would have done exactly the same, so he should have foreseen this.

"I think I'm only a sort of honorary attachment. I don't know if I get onto the List or not – Tell me, how is life here?"

Lunn was easily sidetracked into showing off his new-found knowledge. "Actually, you know, Turkey's a particularly difficult posting. Most people don't realise how *different* it is. A bit like Japan, I believe: a totally strange culture and religion, but with an overlay of European civilisation . . ." Ranklin kept his expression fascinated while he let his eyes and mind wander. An obvious Turk had just come in – alone, of course – which made eight men as against Lady Kelso and three Embassy/British community women . . . and another woman just coming in, late and apologetic . . .

Corinna.

Naturally.

* * *

Once off the bridge, the ox-carts turned right, along the Galata quay where it appeared that serious steamers and trading schooners moored to unload. And since ships bring their own international environment with them, the warehouses, chandlery shops and cafés opposite them were familiar and welcoming. Most of the signs were in English, too, or at least French.

Then two men stepped forward, one holding up his hand, and O'Gilroy recognised the imposing figure of Herr Fernrick. The carts stopped, the work crew closed up about them, so this was their destination. They had come, O'Gilroy reckoned, less than half a mile and that was a relief, too, given the potential range of oxen. It was time to choose yet another café.

* * *

Naturally a single, respectable woman like Corinna had a value beyond rubies on the English-speaking dinner-party round, so Ranklin should have expected her there. And talking of rubies, she had those, too: indeed, she must have chosen the dress to match her necklace, and its slightly dated look as a kindness to that company. But she still made the other women – perhaps excepting Lady Kelso – look part of the furnishings. Watching her toss back her head in a burst of free laughter, vivid, magnificent yet pliable, Ranklin ached at her unattainability – and knowing that with a single mistake she could wreck him.

She swept a smile around the room, froze on him, almost grinned, and looked quickly away. He breathed out and gulped his drink. But they were still fated, by Jarvey's diligence as a diplomatist, to meet eventually.

". . . and finally, may I present the Honourable Patrick Snaipe, one of our honorary attachés who's escorting Lady Kelso? Mrs Finn, who represents her father, Reynard Sherring, in financial matters that are quite above my head."

"Patrick Snaipe," she repeated, committing it to memory. She held out her gloved hand. "So you're travelling with Lady Kelso? What an *interesting* assignment."

"Er, yes. Fascinating. We came down in a party led by Dr Dahlmann of the Deutsche B—"

Jarvey interruped: "I think Mrs Finn probably wants to get away from banking for the—"

"No, no," she assured him. "So Dr Dahlmann – I've never met him – is he here for the loan negotiations or the Railway?"

"Both, I think, but I believe he's staying in Constantinople for the negotiations while we go on south."

"Fascinating. If you don't know that part of the world, you must attach yourself to Bertrand Lacan – 'Beirut Bertie' as the English here call him. He's just got back from Paris, probably getting told what to say at the loan negotiations, but he's quite an expert on the south and Arab matters . . ." Then she let Jarvey haul her off to more distinguished company.

"That's our Bertie, over there." Lunn indicated a man aged about fifty, modestly stout, with a round, pleasantly relaxed face wearing his eyes permanently half-closed. He also had a sun-tan that was unique in a room full of correct diplomatic pallor.

* * *

In between a small white-painted liner and a drab little tramp steamer lay a flight of stone steps leading down to water level. Not far down, since in these tideless waters the quaysides were not high. And poking above the side O'Gilroy could see the brass funnel of a big launch, letting off lazy wisps of smoke into the dim lamplight. Rather too dim for the task of dragging heavy boxes – two men to a box – off the carts and down the steps, but Herr Fernrick seemed to prefer it that way.

For all that, such activity on this quay was obviously normal and attracted no attention except from a couple of uniformed men who had strolled up, been shown some documents and handed a little something, and strolled off. That also seemed normal.

Since he would be recognised if seen, O'Gilroy had chosen not the nearest café but one almost fifty yards off. It had a better-dressed, more European clientele than the cafés back across the bridge, but the view was poor. He could just see that the boxes were of fresh bright wood, in many shapes and sizes, and varying weights. There were always two men to a box, but they obviously had more trouble with some than others.

Then one of the men lost his footing on the shadowed, slimy stones, a box crashed down, and half the work-party threw themselves flat.

* * *

Ranklin was placed midway along the dinner table between the seemingly inevitable Lunn and the wife of a British resident – a lawyer, he gathered. A string quartet in what might have been Albanian costume played in a corner.

Luckily the wife wasn't at all interested in Snaipe's diplomatic past: what fascinated her was the brigands and the Kaiser's carriages – such as did Lady Kelso really sleep in the Kaiser's bed?

"Er, no, we didn't have the Kaiser's actual *Schlafwagen*—"

"And when the brigands attacked you, is it true that she offered herself to them?"

"Good Lord, no. They didn't get within a hundred yards of our carriages."

Obviously disappointed, the wife gazed at Lady Kelso, seated next to the Ambassador. "I do think it's *noble* of H.E. to entertain a woman with such a reputation. Does she usually wear Turkish – no, it was *Arabian* – dress?"

"She didn't on the train and I doubt she does in Italy."

"I've heard that when she was here as a diplomatist's wife, that was how she made her *assignations*. All wrapped up like that, even your own husband wouldn't recognise you, everyone assumes you're just a servant carrying a message. That's how Turkish wives do it today. In the streets of Constantinople, one feels one is absolutely *surrounded* by infidelities."

"Really? That must make shopping trips much more interesting."

Across the table, between a vase of flowers and a lump of Embassy silver, he caught Beirut Bertie's lazy smile.

So did the wife. "Now, M'sieu Lacan, you know all about Turkish and Arab customs, isn't that so?"

"Not those customs, alas, dear lady. Only dull matters such as the proper conduct of blood feuds."

"Come now, I'm sure a Frenchman wouldn't waste *all* his time on the laws of feuding."

"Ah, but my time belongs to my Government."

Ranklin asked: "Are you also a diplomatist, M'sieu Lacan?"

The wife said: "Beirut Bertie – that's what we call him and he has to pretend he doesn't know – has worked for everybody out here."

"True, but it began with the *Diplomatique* – as it now seems fated to end. All my life I have sought only simple luxury. Early on, I was seduced by childhood books of life in the East: I pictured myself reclining on cushions, sucking sherbet – have you ever sucked sherbet, Mr Snaipe? It is quite disgusting – and surrounded by poorly-clad dancing-girls. I was, I admit," he sighed, "a rather advanced child. But when I found no dancing-girls in the *Diplomatique*, I moved to work for the Imperial Ottoman Bank. And alas, they had no dancing-girls either, so I went to the Anatolie – the Railway company when it was French owned – and can you guess what I found?"

"No dancing-girls?"

"You have great insight, Mr Snaipe. All the luxuries I have found in the East have been brought from Paris or London. Including the dancing-girls. So – why argue with fate? – I came back to the *Diplomatique*."

"Where he does nobody-knows-what, mostly in Beirut and Damascus and Baghdad," the wife said. "but *I* think he's a spy."

Bertie made an elegant gesture of hopelessness. "You see, Mr Snaipe? – how my search for a life of humble luxury makes me a misunderstood outcast of good society?"

* * *

When a trained soldier throws himself flat, others don't stand about asking questions, and O'Gilroy almost vanished under his table. Certainly he spilled his coffee. But nothing else happened. The Germans picked themselves up and wiped themselves down, while the Turks in the work-party watched in astonishment. Then Herr Fernrick moved in, bollocking the man who'd slipped while his companion – presumably speaking Turkish – reassured the others.

The waiter came up and suggested, in French, that O'Gilroy would want another coffee. But apart from feeling such coffee was better spilt than drunk, he wanted something stronger now. A little bad French and good will narrowed the decision down to a *raki*, whatever that was.

On the quayside, work restarted, slower and more cautiously, and O'Gilroy looked around to see if anyone else in the front of the café had noticed. Then, because Herr Fernrick was also glaring round to see if he'd attracted attention, went back to his postcards. But his hand was trembling. He had, guessing the weight of that box, been altogether too close to a hundred pounds of explosive nearly going off.

14

When the ladies had withdrawn, the men remained standing for a few moments, waiting politely to see who wanted a private word with whom. Bertie murmured to Ranklin: "In small, isolated communities, do you not find that female conversation seldom rises above the waist? As a topic, Lady Kelso must be a Godsend."

"Have you run across her before?"

"No. But her trail . . . stories, memories, they live on in the desert . . . It is a bit like meeting a living myth . . ." His face went serious, and he looked away.

The male guest of honour, Izzad Bey from the *Porte*, roughly the Turkish Foreign Office, had now moved up alongside H.E. the Ambassador and they were also, and openly, discussing Lady Kelso.

"But," Izzad was saying, "her *liaison* with Miskal Bey must be twenty, at least twenty-five years ago now."

"Then you don't put her chance of success very high?"

"The time is not the problem. Perhaps she will get to meet Miskal Bey again. But no matter how good her arguments may be – to be merciful, to let the engineers free – how can he *appear* to be influenced by a woman? Rather than risk that, he may even harden his resolve to keep them as prisoners."

"Might be counter-productive, you think?"

"It is just possible."

"Hmmmm." It was half a hum, half grunt. "Well . . . we aren't *sending* her, we only offered her as a possible mediator. And your Government and Wangenheim – the German Ambassador here," he explained to Ranklin, "accepted the offer, so . . ."

Izzad smiled. "And if the Railway is not restarted soon, perhaps you will not weep too much."

"Oh, I think the recent discussions have settled everybody's position on the Railway quite amicably."

"Or swept them under the carpet. The very best Turkish carpet, of course."

"But probably you've got enough on your plate with the new loan negotiations. Am I allowed to ask how they're going, now that you've got M'sieu Lacan back from Paris? Talking to Mrs Finn tonight, she didn't seem too happy. But I thought she was only out here as fiancée of . . . who is it?"

"D'Erlon," Bertie supplied. "Edouard d'Erlon. But no, the lady is here very much in her own right – or her father's. She most certainly understands finance."

"Really? We're quite beset by *influential* women tonight. They seem to be taking charge. Perhaps my successor will be wearing skirts. Although I wonder if she'll appreciate a good cigar." And he puffed luxuriously.

They all laughed. Then Bertie went on: "But I fear she has some trouble appreciating the problems of finance in this country. As does her countryman, Mr Billings."

"Finds it difficult to see how you translate your passion for Arab interests into eighths of one per cent, eh? I can't blame her for that."

Bertie smiled politely, but this was obviously a delicate subject. "But doubtless matters will arrange themselves. Indeed, tonight I am invited on board Mr Billings' yacht for a 'pow-wow' when I leave here."

"Gosh!" Lunn couldn't stay silent. "You're going, of course?"

"How can I resist? I have been aboard far too few millionaires' yachts in my poor life. Also I understand that Dr Dahlmann of the Deutsche Bank will be there."

"You travelled down with Dahlmann, didn't you?" Jarvey said to Ranklin, quickly but casually.

Ranklin nodded. "Seemed a nice enough chap . . . A bit bankerish, if you know what I mean."

They smiled sympathetically. Bertie said: "Really? Then

would you do me the honour of introducing me, Mr Snaipe? I'm sure Mr Billings would want me to bring you."

Ranklin looked at the Ambassador. "I'd be delighted, but perhaps . . .?"

"Oh, you go along, Snaipe. Unless *you're* jaded by millionaires' yachts."

* * *

The box now being carried was the thirty-eighth and must be the last, O'Gilroy realised: the rest of the work-party was putting on its coats and lighting cigarettes, and in a minute or two the launch would move off. Obviously he couldn't follow, but he might at least get an idea of which way it was heading. He looked around.

The quayside itself was no use, quite apart from blundering into the work-party; the ships moored along it blocked most of the view. He might have done best to sprint back to the bridge, but that was too far. So he had to get high, higher than the decks of the moored ships, to see which way the lights of the launch turned. And it must be showing lights: to go without in those waters would be like crossing Piccadilly with your eyes shut.

Then he remembered that behind the café the city rose steeply; he had passed alleys and side-streets that were just flights of steps. He sauntered out of the café, turned left and found only an alley too narrow to give any useful view. So he reversed, towards the now-loitering work-party. He pulled his bowler hat down, turned his collar up, and walked with a stoop, *not* looking to see if he was being noticed.

And there was a street of steps, narrow and dark but as good as he'd find, and with a lowish building at one corner, so if he could get high enough to see over that . . . He started climbing.

Used as he was to cities and their sudden boundaries, the change was still startling. In a few yards he went from brightness and the smell of the sea to darkness and the stink of humanity – of far too much humanity. He kept his eyes on the ground: the smell wouldn't break his ankles, but the steps might; they were perhaps two feet apart but even the "flat" bits sloped, and were built of irregular, misshapen stones.

When he thought he might be high enough, he stopped and looked back. Not quite, just a few more steps . . . about where a couple of figures were standing and casually muttering, dimly outlined against the glow from an uncurtained window. O'Gilroy started wheezing heavily, to excuse his slow progress and pauses.

He passed the two men, noting only Turkish dress and fezzes, and stopped a little higher to look back. Now he could see most of the launch, moored stern-on to the quay to fit between the bigger ships. It had a canopy over most of its near-fifty-foot length and the funnel was pouring smoke as it worked up the energy to leave. A few minutes more and he'd have seen all he could . . . but he wished those bloody Turks would move on.

Then one of the bloody Turks did. He tramped softly up past O'Gilroy – and stopped, a few steps higher. Nobody had said a word, or done anything quickly, but suddenly O'Gilroy was surrounded and his situation felt very different. His heart went into double time and he edged against the wall as he glanced back at the launch. It was moving, clanging its bell as it poked cautiously out into the slow swirl of lights in the bay. It vanished under the stern of a moored steamer, but that was just the angle of O'Gilroy's view, not a turn. He waited until it re-appeared, still heading straight out, then looked around at the Turk above him.

Who was leaning against the wall and watching. Watching O'Gilroy? But they had been here first, they *had* to be watching the launch, picking this place for the same reason he had . . . However, they were certainly watching him now. He gripped the pistol in his pocket, wishing it were his own proper grown-up one . . .

The launch kept going. If it wanted to turn, surely it had room now, but it kept straight on for the faint lights of the far shore. The figure below relaxed and began to turn round, but O'Gilroy stared on at the lights of the launch, now beset by so many other lights . . . He heard a movement behind him.

All pretence gone, he launched himself across the steps,

skidded, but ended with his back against the opposite wall, both Turks as much in front of him as he could manage. They stopped, then moved to close on him from above and below. He pulled the gun from his pocket.

But what would a gunshot do in this blasted town? Bring an avalanche of police or pass unnoticed? Then the lower Turk made a move that could only be drawing a knife, and ended any choice. He fired high past the man, into the far wall.

That stopped them. There was a moment of ringing silence, then from one of the houses a woman screamed. She couldn't have seen anything, perhaps she felt it had been been a dull day so far, but it changed things. The lower Turk moved back and up past O'Gilroy, snarling something – then they both ran.

They went upwards into the dark unknown, O'Gilroy went down, towards the quayside lights that now seemed as warm and familiar as his own bed, stuffing the gun into his pocket. People were gathering at the bottom of the street, the work-party among them.

O'Gilroy reached the quay gibbering and gesticulating with fright. He'd been attacked, fetch the police, the British consul, the army, fetch his *mother* – then recognised Albrecht in the crowd and grabbed him like a brother, pointing and gabbling.

* * *

Izzad Bey, as the senior male guest, led the way to rejoin the ladies, the Ambassador properly hanging back as rearguard. As the non-diplomatic guests trailed out, Jarvey said to Ranklin: "If you're going to this yacht later, we'd be interested in anything Bertie says about the loan and Arab rights."

"Of course . . . but are they connected?"

The Ambassador chuckled. "*He'll* connect 'em. Gone a bit native, wouldn't you say, Howard?"

"Arab native, anyway. Seems fascinated by them. And don't believe that guff he hands out about seeking a life of luxury: he's never off the back of a camel and I wouldn't call that luxury."

They began strolling towards the door. The Ambassador

blew cigar smoke, frowned, then asked: "Just what did the Office in London actually tell you to *do*, Snaipe?"

"Just to stick by Lady Kelso, sir. Give her such protection as I could."

"Hm. But you don't know that country at all, I think? And she must know it well, better than any of us, I dare say." He turned to Jarvey. "Do you think Snaipe should hire an armed guard of men, Howard?"

Jarvey said sombrely: "They *might* prove of some use."

The idea appalled Ranklin, and he fumbled for excuses. "Won't we be mostly surrounded by Germans with their own Turkish Army guards?"

Jarvey said: "I don't think you'll find those guards going up into the mountains with you, not after what happened to them last time. A body of men you've hired yourself *might* prove more loyal – if they're properly led." His doubts were clearly whether Snaipe could lead a cat to cream.

Ranklin said tentatively: "I'd rather go along with what Lady Kelso wants, sir. Either she's still got some personal influence with Miskal or she hasn't. I think an armed guard might simply be . . ." He shrugged, and if they wanted to interpret that as "a mistake", fine; what he actually meant was "bloody stupid".

The Ambassador crunched out his cigar in an ashtray offered by a servant. "Perhaps . . . But in any case, your best plan may be to let Lady Kelso do her act, and then, whether she's successful or not, get her *away*. Drag her by the hair if necessary. I'd rather have her complaining you've spoiled her *coiffure* than the newspapers saying we let her get murdered by that brigand. Don't you think, Howard?"

Jarvey doubted Snaipe's ability to do even that much. "Frankly, sir, and with all due respect to Snaipe, I wish the Office had sent Lady Kelso all on her own. This way loads us with a responsibility we can't guarantee to fulfil."

"Oh, I wouldn't go that far, Howard. *Masculinité oblige*, don't you think?"

* * *

One of O'Gilroy's great strengths as a liar was his ability to believe – for the moment, anyway – that he was telling the truth. The Turkish policeman spoke no English, and since O'Gilroy was keeping his meagre store of French to himself, questions and answers had to go through the man who had been superintending the work-party along with Herr Fernrick. O'Gilroy assumed he came from the German Embassy.

"He says," the man said, "that Constantinople . . . I think you say 'bullies'? . . . they almost never use guns."

"They used one on *me*. Ye heard it yeself, didn't ye?" He shivered at the memory. And all the time Ranklin's pistol was pressing against his thigh, well hidden by his overcoat. But why should the police search the victim? And double that for a Turkish policeman and a privileged European.

"But you were not hurt?"

"Thanks to the grace of Mary, Mother of God, I was not."

The Embassy man didn't translate that, just shook his head. The policeman asked another question.

"And where were you going in that street?"

"From God-knows-where to more of the same. I was lost. I reckoned if'n I was going down hill I'd be finding the quay and mebbe the bridge and know where I was. And I suddenly think Mebbe there's someone following me and I looks and mebbe there is, so I take a turn or two and they're still there behind me and God knows now I really *am* lost and so I'm hurrying, Jayzus, I'd've been *running* if they knew how to make proper streets in this town, and then I see the lights here and mebbe they see them and reckon it's their last chancst to get me and one of them yells and one of them shoots and I come down that street mebbe faster'n the bullet, for all I know."

Another of O'Gilroy's strengths was the apparently random wordiness of his lies.

The policeman was either convinced or overwhelmed, although he'd written hardly any of this down. They were seated at a table in a café – not, thank God, the one O'Gilroy had watched from, but the one nearer where the launch had moored: Herr Fernrick, Albrecht, the train guard, the policeman, a couple of Turks – maybe they were something to do with the Embassy, too – and the man asking the questions. Now he had one of his own, not from the policeman: "You did not . . . meet them? They were not waiting in that street?"

You mean watching what you were doing loading that launch?

"Jayzus, mebbe I passed them way back, but I told ye, they was *following* me. Was a lucky thing ye fellers being here, mebbe they'd've followed me right out here, otherwise. Was ye jest passing or having a drink or something?"

Go on, you bugger, let's hear a lie from *you*, for a change. But the Embassy man just asked: "Did you see what they looked like?"

"I told ye, they was *following* me. And have ye seen those alleys back there? – a bat'd be walking in those." O'Gilroy shrugged. "I think mebbe they had those flowerpot hats on."

The Embassy man had a conversation with the policeman, perhaps wanting him to ask why O'Gilroy was roaming the streets (O'Gilroy had a story to explain that), but the policeman had obviously heard enough. He finally stood up, not rudely, but decisively.

"How would I be getting a cab in this town?" O'Gilroy asked.

The Embassy man came close to asking a question, then sighed and said: "I will show you."

"Will he know where the Pera Palace is? Can I be trusting him? How much does it cost?" It was best, he felt, to keep the man smothered with words. And on top of his regret at not being able to tell his story about why he was on the streets, he had suddenly realised that he *hadn't been behaving illegally at all.* Apart from shooting a hole in a wall, and that had been justifiable self-defence. He started to feel quite self-righteous. A bit disconcerted, too.

* * *

Bertie, Corinna and Ranklin shared a cab from the Embassy down to the Galata quayside.

"Just who," Ranklin asked, "is this Mr Billings I'll be imposing on?"

"To me," Corinna said, "he's a client of my father's bank. To the Turks he's a rich man who might put together a loan for them. To the United States he's a Chicagoan turned more-or-less New Yorker, and head of Union Carbide. To you, he's a good host with a nice line in comfortable steam yachts."

From the dimness in his corner of the cab, Bertie chuckled. "I pass."

* * *

O'Gilroy talked his way into the Pera Palace hotel and then, using some of his surplus self-righteousness, into Ranklin's room (of *course* he had to arrange his master's things for him, he'd never hear the last of it, God alone knew how the man had got dressed for the Embassy without him . . .).

Once inside, he locked the door, then sat down and muttered to himself a report of his evening, trying to discard the lies and avoid turning guesses into facts. When he was satisfied, he actually did a bit of re-arranging of Ranklin's clothes, made up a bundle of laundry, found where Ranklin had hidden his spare ammunition and reloaded the fired chamber of the Bulldog revolver.

What to do with the spent cartridge? – that wasn't something to be left in a wastebasket. In the end, he pocketed it, planning to throw it in the water tomorrow. And after that . . . His own room was a cubby-hole in the attic, no better nor worse than most servants' bedrooms, but definitely not within reach of a bath. However, nobody in the place would recognise him yet, so he half-undressed, put on Ranklin's expensive dressing-gown and strolled along to the guests' one at the end of the corridor.

15

A man in a private naval uniform met them on the quayside, helped Corinna down and led the way to a white-painted motor-launch waiting near the bridge. From within its cabin, Ranklin couldn't see where they were going nor where they'd got to except that it must be Billings's *Vanadis* and moored not far off shore. They went up a gentle gangway amidships, turned aft, and almost immediately into a big room or cabin or whatever. Big enough to look low-ceilinged, which it wasn't, and to be lit in pools of light from wall- and reading-lamps.

Billings himself was only a little taller than Ranklin, with a face like a frog. A friendly frog, however, with a wide smile under a large area of clean-shaven upper lip, who seemed pleased to meet them all.

"Mr Snaipe is escorting Lady Kelso on her diplomatic mission," Bertie said as the only explanation for Ranklin.

"Is that so? You should have brought her along. When I get home, Mrs Billings will be most annoyed not to be able to disapprove of me meeting her." He had a growly American accent but spoke reflectively, contrasting with Corinna's crispness. "Now let me introduce you . . ."

There was Dahlmann, whose manner suggested he had hoped for a few Snaipe-free hours, but Ranklin watched Corinna go smiling up to another man and peck his cheek. So this had to be D'Erlon. He was extraordinarily handsome.

Until studied more closely. Then his eyes were too close-set and too pale, his fair hair was too long, his nose should have been more prominent or less so, there was an underlying weakness to his firm chin, and his ready smile seemed untrustworthy.

"—and Monsieur Edouard D'Erlon," Billings was saying, "a partner in D'Erlon Frères and a director of the Imperial Ottoman Bank."

Viewed dispassionately, D'Erlon seemed about Ranklin's age but, of course, taller and wore rimless glasses. His white tie was *definitely* too big and floppy.

Corinna was standing close, waiting for a private word with her fiancé, so Ranklin backed off, accepted a glass of champagne from a waiter and looked about the room. Apart from the royal-blue curtains across the windows, it glowed with warm browns and shades of orange. The walls were panelled in, probably, mahogany to match the furniture that effectively divided the place in two. The far end was arm-chairs, small tables, shelves of leather-bound books. The near end had a round table with chairs that looked too comfortable for dining where Dahlmann and D'Erlon had been sitting. In all, it looked expensive but cosy in a masculine and late-night way.

Bertie had replaced Corinna with D'Erlon and she came smiling up to Ranklin, standing by the sideboard where the drinks were kept.

"And how are you finding Constantinople, Mr Snaipe?" Then she lowered her voice. "Is Conall with you?"

"Oh, fascinating. Utterly fascinating . . . Yes, he's here, too . . . What's going on tonight?"

She turned to survey the room. "A little polite banging of financial heads together by Mr Billings in the hope that *he'll* find out what the hell's going on . . . I was talking to Lady Kelso over dinner. She's quite a woman – Don't you think?"

"Oh, yes. I had two days of her on the train."

"Only now she's living in *exile* in Italy."

"She'd be worse off in Britain, with society cutting her dead."

"I don't think that says a hell of a lot for English society."

"Would it be different with New York society?" And when she didn't answer that, Ranklin went on: "I've been on the outside looking in, too. Not the way she is, but . . ."

"Yes, I know . . . But all because she walked out on a stupid bastard of a husband—"

"Not just that."

"No, maybe – but she's certainly paying for it now. And now your Government's *using* her: what's she going to get out of that?"

Ranklin shrugged. "Thanks – for trying. Nobody seems very hopeful she'll achieve anything."

Corinna looked at him belligerently. "Aren't you along to make sure she *doesn't*?"

"May we pass lightly over why I'm here? We're all part of some great game of nations—"

"*Not* me. Anyhow, she's alone, with nobody behind her. Going into those hills to talk to that bandit. Suppose it goes wrong? Who's going to get her out?"

"I'll do my best. I hope you really believe that."

After the briefest pause, she said: "Yes, I do . . . but you're working pretty much alone, too. Your people won't acknowledge you or send help. But you're used to that, you've accepted it."

"Then what are you suggesting?"

"I don't know. But *something*."

Ranklin shivered. That *something* had sounded like a lighted fuse.

Then Corinna caught Billings's eye and went to sit next to him at the table. The seating divided clearly but not blatantly into the two Americans, the two Frenchmen, and Dahlmann by himself. Ranklin realised that the waiter had quietly vanished; rather than be the only one left standing, he also took a seat, coincidentally between Bertie and Billings but with his chair pushed back to show he didn't really belong. It looked rather as if they were about to start a card game, only there were no cards and no money on the table. There were only glasses, ashtrays and single sheets of paper in front of Corinna and Bertie.

Billings hunched forward to open the proceedings, leaning gradually back as he spoke. "Now Dr Dahlmann's gotten here, I'm hoping maybe we can finally figure out if I can be any use in this loan business . . . Though I'm kind of fuzzy about what chips the Deutsche Bank has in this game."

"My bank has many and wide interests in the Turkish Empire." Dahlmann spoke with quiet authority: this was his world. "And there is also the unissued part of the 1910 loan we and the Viennese banks made to Turkey. They may demand that we complete that."

"Can you remind me how much that is, Dr Dahlmann?" Corinna asked.

"About three million Turkish pounds."

D'Erlon made a gesture that swept the three million aside. "But now we are talking of a loan of over thirty million pounds."

Did I think there was no money on this table? Ranklin wondered.

Dahlmann gave a small, tight smile. "It is still a factor – along with the Baghdad Railway bonds still held by the Imperial Ottoman. Which I think your Government will not let you sell on the Paris market."

Corinna said: "Because they don't want the French investing in a German project." Everyone else must already know that, so she could only have been saying it for Ranklin's benefit.

Billings said: "All this must be important, but it's going to take time to work out. Now, Talaat Bey himself told me that Turkey's broke. Just plain broke. They're scratching for pennies."

"I do believe," Bertie said languidly, "that they have just reduced their soldiers' pay from a *medjidieh*, that is –" he paused for calculation "– perhaps seventy-five of your cents, to under twenty cents – per month."

"Sure. Exactly. So, while you're sorting out the details of your long-term loan, why shouldn't Sherring's and I get together a short-term loan to tide them over? – say five million of their pounds for maybe three months?"

"At what rate?" D'Erlon asked.

"Ten," Corinna said. It was quite remarkable how much she

could get into one syllable: confidence that it was *right*, yet with a hint of flexibility.

"Ten?" Dahlmann queried. And he was a professional, too: in his voice *ten* became preposterous, a fairy-tale.

Billings said: "We could talk about that. But Turkey needs money *fast*, and we can have this on the counter in a week."

"And no strings attached," Corinna said. "No complications about rights of our citizens or concessions to build this and that. Just cash down."

D'Erlon and Bertie looked at each other, then D'Erlon shrugged and said: "If you wish to put it to the Committee . . ."

"Not without you back us," Billings said firmly. "You boys know the people here. But the way I see it, a short-term loan should help you, give you time to get your details just right. And with Turkey broke . . ."

D'Erlon said bluntly: "You were invited by the Turks, Mr Billings. Not by us."

Corinna stared at him. "Are you telling us to keep our filthy dollars to ourselves?"

Bertie interceded quickly and more gently. "Tell me, what would happen in the American Army if your soldiers' pay was reduced suddenly by three-quarters?"

Billings frowned. "Mutiny, I guess."

"Exactly. In France, I am sure, also. But here . . . the soldiers are not being paid anything anyway, so what do such reductions matter?"

There was silence. Billings reached slowly, drank the last of his champagne, and looked at Corinna. "It seems, my dear, there's more ways of being broke than we knew about." He got up and took his empty glass to the sideboard. She gave D'Erlon a thoughtful look, then followed.

Dahlmann, to whom all of this had been music to a deaf adder, said: "May I ask what matters concerning French interests in Nort Africa are to be involved?"

Bertie said casually: "I believe it is accepted that France has a duty as protecting power in Morocco and Tunisia."

"And in Syria?"

Bertie made a delicate balancing gesture. "It is difficult . . ."

"We had heard talk that France might ask for rights for Arabs, even a dual Turkish-Arab state, like Austria-Hungary."

"Truly?" Bertie's face was smooth and bland now. "Most interesting. But there is always talk."

"I am sure it will be simpler if only Morocco and Tunisia are included."

Bertie smiled his lazy smile. D'Erlon, who had been sitting between them looking just blankly handsome, roused himself. "Do you speak for Turkey now, Dr Dahlmann?"

Dahlmann pretended to look around. "They are not here. And if we do not consider their interests tonight, it will take many days of drinking much coffee . . . So: the matter of raising Customs dues . . ."

Ranklin reckoned nobody would miss him, so took his glass back to the sideboard. Billings poured him some more champagne. "I started off thinking your City people were acting timid with this market, Mr Snaipe. Now, maybe I think they're well out of it."

"There's still room for a short-term loan," Corinna said doggedly.

"Sure – if your boy-friend at the Imperial Ottoman agrees. Not if he's working against it behind our backs."

"The moron."

Billings looked even more frog-like with a wide grin. "Woah, woah there. You're talking of the man you love."

"Cretin."

Ranklin hoped his sudden cheerfulness didn't show. Billings consoled Corinna: "You know what I think? – I think I was hauled in just to get the French worried, hurry them to terms. So maybe we shouldn't expect the French – like your Monsieur D'Erlon and Monsieur Lacan – to love us. They want the Turks in a hurry, not themselves." He looked back at the table. "Just who is Monsieur Lacan, anyhow?"

"French *Diplomatique*," Corinna said. "And he's just got back from 'consultations' in Paris, so I guess he's supposed to be slipping in clauses to help French policy while the Imp Ott handles the money side. Although they do say Lacan's always pitching for Arab rights, always in the desert, speaks all the Arab dialects . . ."

Billings nodded. "Does that make him maybe a little senior to your boy-friend?"

"Right now, I can think of *cockroaches* who are senior to my boy-friend. He might have *told* me what he was doing. We could have had a nice simple little deal."

"But perhaps," Ranklin suggested, "a bit too simple for the Eastern mind. I think they like things rather convoluted: that way, everybody can believe they've come out on top."

"Listen to the diplomatist," Billings said. "Sometimes – if you'll pardon me, Mr Snaipe – they know what they're talking about. And there –" a nod at the table "– they're talking more than money. They're building empires . . ." He paused to look like a frog thinking. "What was that about Baghdad Railroad bonds?"

Corinna frowned as she searched her mental files. "The Imperial Ottoman took thirty per cent of the original bond issue back in 1903 . . . They were shamed into it by the old Sultan, but the French Government objected and outlawed selling them in France, so they're still sitting in the vaults here."

Billings winced at the thought of money all alone in the dark. "Worth what?"

"I think around sixteen million francs at par. Say just under three million dollars, and only earning four per cent."

"So maybe your *fiancé* would like to see those bonds stop mouldering and turn into something useful – like sixteen million francs? Or even a good bit less?"

Stony-faced as the Sphinx, Corinna said: "Maybe."

Billings nodded and moved away, not directly towards the table but circling it, like a hunting animal positioning itself down-wind. Just then Bertie got up, stretched, and came over to refill his glass.

"*Ça marche?*" Corinna asked.

"*Il marche*. Slowly, of course . . . But another matter has occurred: it seems that Dr Dahlmann's Bank is drawing half a million of gold francs from the Imperial Ottoman tomorrow and it would be proper to have independent witnesses. Would you care to add your distinguished signature, Mrs Finn? And, of course, that of the Diplomatic Service, Mr Snaipe."

"I'm not counting any half-million francs," Corinna objected.

"Oh, no, no. It is only a matter of taking a glass of tea – or coffee – and agreeing that the event happened. And being shown the most splendid bank itself, quite as noble as any sultan's palace, if you have not already seen it?"

"I've seen it, but I'd recommend it to Mr Snaipe. And okay, I'll come along myself."

"I'll be there," Ranklin agreed. "Unless my Embassy needs me, and they haven't shown much sign of it."

"Excellent. At eleven o'clock? Splendid." Bertie ambled back to the table.

"What on earth was that about?" Corinna wondered. "Do you know?"

Ranklin shrugged. "Is it usual procedure for such handovers?"

"God knows, I never deal in *cash.* I'd expect a few lawyers hanging around; they tend to swarm at the smell of gold. They'll need some porters, too," she added. "Half a million gold francs isn't something you slip in your purse."

A thickening haze of tobacco smoke was spreading from the table and fuzzing the outlines of the room, making it more like a card game than ever. Bertie was chain-smoking, Dahlmann puffing a cigar and D'Erlon waggling a long and, Ranklin felt, rather effeminate cigarette holder.

Bertie picked up his sheet of paper. "May we see what has been agreed? The Turkish Government may create and sell monopolies on playing cards, cigarette papers, alcohol and sugar." He glanced at D'Erlon, then Dahlmann; both nodded. "Also we accept a one per cent rise in Customs dues and establishing *octroi* controls. The Deutsche and the other banks will *not* issue the second part of the 1910 loan—"

"That is for Turkey to say," Dahlmann said calmly.

"Of course, Dr Dahlmann. I was forgetting."

"And," Dahlmann continued, "there are the Baghdad Railway bonds which you have not been able to sell for eleven years . . ."

D'Erlon's nose wrinkled, very briefly, as if he'd remembered a bad smell.

Dahlmann said: "My Bank believes it can help you in that matter. Unfortunately the market value is not so high at present, but I think my directors would agree if I offered only ten per cent under market."

"Why not market?" D'Erlon asked, but he couldn't sound indignant about it.

Dahlmann smiled bleakly. "Because, if you could sell them at any price you would surely have done so in the last eleven years."

Billings said: "Maybe I can bid a little higher, hey?"

There was a stunned moment, then consternation. All three jerked upright as if their puppet-master had sneezed. Then Dahlmann subsided, impassive but probably with his mind whirring, Bertie did his damnedest to look as if he were going back to sleep, and D'Erlon couldn't repress a slow smile as he realised he might be running an auction.

"I've never owned a piece of a Turkish railroad before," Billings went on with an innocent smile. "And maybe some of the boys back at the club would like a share. How much *is* the market value, Dr Dahlmann?"

Stiffly: "I am sorry, I do not have the exact figure."

Standing just behind Billings, Corinna said: "It has to be well under three million dollars."

"You see?" Billings smiled. "Chicken feed."

Bertie said: "And you have such millions, just like that?"

"I came to Constantinople expecting to invest at least that much, Monsieur Lacan. Of course, we'd like to see a prospectus, if you can dig one out. But subject to that, count me as interested, Monsieur D'Erlon. You might say *very* interested."

"I am sure you will find no problems in the prospectus." D'Erlon was now looking positively sunny.

Dahlmann was not looking sunny. "We are trying to make a bigger picture, Mr Billings. To take off the board just one piece—"

Billings smiled again. "Then go right ahead and outbid me." He got up and walked away with Corinna. Ranklin wasn't sure he should go with them, but quite sure he shouldn't stay with the other three. An urgent bluebottle buzzing had started between D'Erlon and Bertie, with occasional references to the rigidly gloomy Dahlmann.

At the sideboard, Corinna was saying quietly, "I think you are being a very naughty man, Mr Billings."

Billings, back to the table, flashed a vast froggy grin. "It shook the bast-boys, didn't it? And wouldn't your father like a piece of a Turkish railroad?"

"He'd bust an artery. Are you serious about buying four per cent bonds?"

Another grin. "It all depends on the price, doesn't it? There might be something in it, short term. Never mind the Baghdad end, I'm not interested in that, it's the stretch they're building now. It hasn't gotten anywhere, so nobody uses it, there's no return on what they're spending. But once they bust through the mountains, they'll have linked up the north and south coasts, and that's got to be worth something in new revenue. So it could push up the price of those bonds."

"I hope you're right. I'll start finding out what the current price is first thing tomorrow. But—"

"Thank you. Anyhow, I don't like being used, Mrs Finn."

"I can understand that. But . . . Mr Billings, I have a feeling this Railroad has troubles it can't even guess at." She was looking straight at Ranklin. "What do *you* think, Mr Snaipe?"

Ranklin tried a vacuous smile. "Just couldn't say . . . but I'm off to see where they're building it in a day or two, perhaps I'll have a better idea when I get back."

Billings nodded, intent now. "Of course, you're going with Lady Kelso – That can't be far from the sea, there?"

"I think where they're tunnelling through the coastal range is about twenty or thirty miles inland."

"Were you thinking of taking this yacht on down for a look?" Corinna asked.

"If I was staying longer . . . But I want to be in London next week . . ." He came to a decision. "If I went back by the Orient Express, would you like to take this boat down there and look for me?"

"M*e*? But I don't . . ." Then Corinna seemed to remember something. "Sure. Sure I'll go – if you trust my judgment of railroads."

"Fine. That's settled, then."

It's odd, Ranklin thought sadly, how seldom people lend *me* their steam yachts.

16

Corinna and Ranklin shared another cab to the Pera Palace. For a long time, she sat silent and Ranklin just watched the lights of the city jolt past. Not as many lights as he'd find in London or Paris, but the European part of Constantinople certainly wasn't all in bed yet.

At last he said: "I wonder why Bertie invited me onto Billings's yacht?"

"No idea." She went back to silence.

"It can't have been to introduce him to Dr Dahlmann, because that was going to happen anyway . . ."

More silence, except for the rumble of wheels and the clop of the horse. Then she sighed and said: "I suppose I can't ask you what the hell you're planning to do to that Railroad?"

"Me? What can one man do about a railway?"

"You *and* Conall. God knows. But knowing you two . . . I wouldn't bet on the Railroad."

"D'you think Mr Billings is serious about buying Baghdad Railway bonds?"

"Could be . . . I don't usually discuss our bank's clients' business with you."

"Yes you do, when you think it might help," Ranklin said blithely. "What I don't see is why Dahlmann cares who owns the bonds. Bondholders just get an income, they don't own the Railway the way shareholders do."

"Bondholders can be a big pain in the backside when things go wrong. Like the company defaults or wants to spend its money a new way . . . I'd guess Dahlmann wants to get those bonds into German hands, for safety's sake."

"Not in the hands of a neutral American?"

"It might be a problem – in a war."

"Well," Ranklin said soothingly, "Billings hasn't committed himself, you think it's a rotten investment anyway – and you're going to be there to see for yourself, aren't you?"

He had the feeling she was eyeing him sceptically through the darkness of the cab. "A remark like that doesn't *exactly* convince me your intentions are wholly honourable. Yes, I'd like to be there, but mostly to provide a back door for Lady Kelso in case you land her in something."

So *that* was why she'd suddenly taken to the idea. Ranklin was startled, though not for the first time, at how strong the bonds of disparate womanhood could be. And how quickly they could grow. It was an uneasy reminder that under his rock-solid masculine world were shifting feminine sands.

Obliquely, he said: "Mr Billings seems a nice chap . . . Seems to take advice from you quite happily."

"It's Pop he really trusts. And maybe as a Chicagoan he likes to show he's more open-minded than the staid old New York crowd. That's why he's here and they aren't."

Then they reached the hotel. There were a couple of messages for Corinna and she stood reading them while the night clerk told Ranklin that his long-lost manservant had turned up and would be waiting dutifully in his room.

The lift was a Jules Verne contraption run by an old man whose control of gravity took so much concentration that Ranklin felt queasy. As much to distract his own feelings as Corinna's, he said: "A good-looking chap, Edouard D'Erlon."

"Yes, isn't he?" Her smile was brief and flat. The lift stopped at her floor. "Well, I guess I'll see you at the Imp Ott Bank in the morning. Good night, Mr Snaipe."

She left him to creak and shudder on up to the smaller rooms above.

As he had more or less expected, "waiting dutifully" to O'Gilroy had meant filling the room with cigarette smoke, then going to sleep in, not on, Ranklin's bed.

Ranklin opened the window and when he turned round again, O'Gilroy was wide awake.

Ranklin took a seat. "Please don't apologise. How did you manage?"

O'Gilroy slid the revolver from under his pillow and passed it over. "I used one shot. Had to," and began telling his story.

"You think that box was full of explosives?"

"When a coupla fellers drop a box and every soldier goes flat, what d'ye think's in it? Turkish Delight? Nor machine-gun ammunition, ye could roll that down a mountain and never—"

Ranklin nodded.

"Could be a lot of the other boxes, too."

"I suppose it doesn't *have* to be anything to do with Miskal – but yes, we have to assume it is. So perhaps they're hoping to blast him out of his stronghold. But if they assume they can get that close, why not just overrun the place?"

"Do we know what this place looks like? Mebbe there's a cliff, like, they could blow down on his head."

"Or blow up his water supply, 'thirst' him out, as it were . . . No, I don't know anything about his stronghold, except that it's an old monastery, so anything might be possible . . . And the launch kept going, straight across the Bosphorus?"

O'Gilroy nodded. So it was almost certainly delivering the boxes to Haydar Pasha station, start of the Baghdad Railway. "And you're sure these other two, the Turks who attacked you, were also watching?"

"Certain sure. Mebbe they was down on the quay before, watching the loading close up. There was a lot of coming and going."

"But we don't know who they are, or working for . . . What can they report about you? Did you say anything?" O'Gilroy shook his head. "Then only your general build and that you wore a bowler hat . . . just for safety, scrap that. Have you got a cap? Then wear it. I give you special dispensation."

"Yer too kind. And what happened to yeself?"

"Nothing urgent – I think. I'll tell you in the morning. But now, if you don't mind, I'd like to get some sleep in my own bed."

"Sure, and I was jest warming it for ye."

* * *

Constantinople got its weather either from Russia or the Mediterranean, according to the wind. But that morning it had got muddled and was offering bright blue sky with a north-east wind like a Tartar sword. After a late breakfast, Ranklin went back to his room to meet O'Gilroy and run through events at the Embassy and on Billings's yacht. Then sent him off to buy a coat suitable for the mountains, directing him back across the Galata Bridge to the Grand Bazaar.

"Anything at all as long as it's warm: leather, sheepskin, looks don't matter." He paused. "I wouldn't be sending you there if they did, but you should have quite a choice."

After he'd gone, Ranklin wished he'd told him to pick up some lead shot, too. If some miracle put them within reach of the gold coin, he'd better be prepared. So he went out early himself, found a gun dealer in the *Grande Rue* where most of the European shops were, and bought a kilo of No. 3 shot. Then he took a cab to the Imperial Ottoman Bank.

The moment he got there, he realised he knew the building already since its bulk dominated the lower slope of Pera: at least seven storeys high and with the south side looking more Indo-Chinese than Turkish with bits of wide roof sticking out three-quarters of the way up. Perhaps the French had got muddled and sent the plans to the wrong address. Ranklin walked up the broad steps at five to eleven and realised he didn't really know who to ask for.

"*M'sieu Lacan?*" he tried, but that meant nothing. Reluctantly, then: "*Ou M'sieu D'Erlon?*"

"*Ah, oui – vous êtes l'Honorable M'sieu Snaipe?*" In Constantinople French that sounded very much like the Orrible Mr Snaipe, but Ranklin agreed and presented his card. He didn't need to: a flunkey was detailed to escort him personally. Up a wide staircase to the main "public" floor which, if not truly grand in the Sultan's-palace sense – a sultan would hardly have chosen so much *brown* marble – was grand enough since it was all some sort of marble: square pillars, counter tops and the Eastern-style grilles instead of balustrades. And with that odd habit banks have of building to show how little they care about money, the core of the place was pure wasted space: an indoor courtyard surrounded by umpteen levels of balconies to a glass roof.

It was also busy: unlike the cathedral calm of a British bank, this looked as Ranklin imagined the Stock Exchange to be: prosperous-looking men stood chatting in groups or sat in niches, many of them wearing fezzes above well-filled European suits or frock coats. Waiters weaved through them carrying silvery trays of coffee cups and tea glasses. And everybody smoked. It seemed an amiable way to do business if that's what they were doing.

The flunkey led him down a quieter corridor away from the busyness, around a few corners, knocked and opened a door, and there was Edouard D'Erlon, smiling, handsome, well-dressed and welcoming. There were also Corinna, looking bored, Dahlmann looking sour and Streibl, who seemed happy since he was probably daydreaming of railways.

* * *

This must *be* the Grand Bazaar, only Ranklin had forgotten to tell him it was entirely roofed over. So at first sight it was a tunnel of murmuring humanity, churning in the dimness, with lamplight winking off cascades of metalwork. On second sight, it was a whole labyrinth of such tunnels, reeking of spices, tanned leather, hot metal and people. It was daunting but it was also much more like the Mysterious East than anything O'Gilroy had yet seen, so after a moment's pause, he stepped inside.

After a few minutes he no longer noticed the noise, a constant babble that echoed from the vaulted roof where a little light, green where it filtered through plants wind-seeded on the roof, came from small glassless windows. He also realised it was divided into districts: a whole tunnel of stalls selling brassware, then one selling carpets, then embroidered silks . . . and all the stalls tucked into arches like miniature versions of London railway bridges. Happily anonymous, he just wandered, weaving around porters under massive loads and men carrying tea glasses on trays with handles like shopping baskets. He smiled and shook his head at imploring stallkeepers – who couldn't follow far from their stalls – confident he'd find what he wanted eventually.

* * *

After the inevitable tea or coffee they had finally got down to business and the whole party – now about a dozen including various Bank employees, one of which wore a uniform and pistol belt – were tramping along a dim-lit corridor somewhere beneath the Bank. Dahlmann plucked Ranklin's coat and hissed: "Why are you here?"

"Er, Beirut Ber – M'sieu Lacan – invited me to come as a witness."

"You should not have agreed. It connects the gold with Lady Kelso's mission."

"Oh, sorry about that," Ranklin said, cheerily vapid.

Dahlmann glowered. "Also, your manservant – did you know he was going about the city alone last night?"

"Really? I sent him out to buy some tobacco and he hadn't got back by the time I had to go to the Embassy . . . Probably got lost. Did *you* find him for me?"

"Ach, no . . . I heard . . ." Dahlmann shouldn't have opened a subject without thinking where it might lead. "Then you did not send him to . . ."

There, he'd done it again. Ranklin helped: "To buy some tobacco? Yes, I told you. He didn't break any laws, did he?"

"No . . . I think . . ." He pulled himself together and in an announcing whisper said: "You must be ready to leave today at three o'clock. Half past two," he amended, allowing for vapidness.

There was a clicking of keys and bolts from the front of the column and they had arrived at a vault of whitewashed stone with a single light bulb dangling from a recent cable in the ceiling and several oil lamps hung around the walls. But they weren't what lit the room: their light was sucked in and glowed back by a tabletop of gold. Among all these moneymen, Ranklin was the only one who should have been impressed, but there was a long moment of reverent silence from everyone.

Then D'Erlon made an elegant if flamboyant gesture and said: "*Bitte, Herr Doktor Dahlmann—*"

Looked at more soberly, the gold didn't really cover the table, which was big and solid, since there was plenty of room for a set of brass scales and a heap of small canvas bags as well. But someone had spent a happy morning arranging eight hundred stacks, each of twenty-five twenty-five-franc pieces so that they covered nearly a square yard to a depth of about three inches. And the result was certainly impressive.

Dahlmann must have begun his career as a mere cashier and hadn't forgotten his dexterity with the stuff of human happiness. He bent down and squinted to make sure the stacks were all of even height, picked one up, flickered through a count, paused to examine a coin or two more closely, then another stack . . .

Around the vault were several hard chairs and one elderly leather-and-gilt one, almost a throne. Probably it was for a Turkish grandee to lounge in while the infidels counted out his wealth, but Corinna got it this time. Ranklin began to feel bored, then decided Snaipe would be childishly fascinated by all this loot, so had to became that instead.

Finally Dahlmann said: "*Sehr gut. Danke*," and stood back.

D'Erlon waved up two helpers who began scooping stacks into bags – five hundred coins to a bag, Ranklin reckoned – then sealing the drawstrings with a dab of wax. D'Erlon reached into a pocket and put half a dozen gold coins on the table. "Just in case we have made a mistake," he smiled.

Dahlmann looked at the coins coldly. "We are bankers. I am sure there is not a mistake." And for once, Ranklin actually felt sorry for D'Erlon.

Already standing close, he picked up one of D'Erlon's coins. It was roughly the same size as a sovereign, and its neat, tiny detail was a wry contrast with the brutal crudity of the dungeon that was the natural home of such things in such quantity. He turned it this way and that to catch the light, then put it down again. "That reminds me: I'd better change some sovereigns into some of these, if this is the usual currency in Turkey. Can I do that upstairs?"

"Of course," D'Erlon said.

Having filled ten of the bags, the helpers jammed them into a robust wooden box little bigger than a cigar box and nailed the lid on top. The hammering echoed like the day of doom in that space, and Corinna winced. D'Erlon was immediately solicitous, suggesting she go back upstairs.

"But if I'm to sign as a witness . . ." she objected.

D'Erlon glanced at Dahlmann, who was obviously going to stay put, and who said: "It is not important to me. I did not suggest witnesses."

"I'll take Mrs Finn upstairs," Ranklin volunteered, and a spare employee was detailed to show them the way.

* * *

Just wandering and looking was one thing, but when you wanted to buy something it all changed: now you were a victim. The coat O'Gilroy was trying on was, unquestionably, a winter coat: leather, and with a fur lining. But it also had embroidery on it that made him feel like a pantomime bandit. Still, it was warm and more-or-less fitted, so he tried asking the price.

If O'Gilroy understood the man, he was talking about the Turkish loan, not the price of a coat. He took it off and frowned at it while wondering what to do next. Damn it, he *needed* a coat.

"May I be of assistance?" He was a middle-aged man, not too thin, with a roundish face and sleepy-cat eyes. French, from the accent.

"That's kindness itself, sir. I was having a bit of trouble understanding the price."

"Ah, here there is no price." The man began to examine the coat critically. "There is just bargaining. Hm." He pulled at a pocket, tore the stitching, and instead of apologising, frowned accusingly at the stallkeeper. There was a quick exchange of Turkish and the coat was tossed aside.

"You want a coat for cold and wet weather? Then it is best to do as the animals themselves do. They wear, you may have noticed, the fur or fleece on the *outside*. Odd, but perhaps they have reason." He took what looked like a bundle of uncleaned sheep-shearings from the seller. "Like this."

He helped O'Gilroy into it. "It may seem a little . . . primitive, but to clean it will make it to leak. Sheep do not wash, I understand." He sniffed. "There may, I should warn you, be a slight danger of rape: possibly you smell most enchanting to other sheep. However . . ." He walked around O'Gilroy, looking critically. "It is comfortable?"

It was certainly warm right down to the knees, and when O'Gilroy found the pockets they were deep and seemed well-stitched. It was definitely *not* as worn in Park Lane, but he wasn't heading there. "Seems jest fine. Er – how much would it be costing?"

This launched a long, but essentially polite, episode of negotiation, reminiscence, an exchange of cigarettes, an offer of tea – delicately refused – and at last an apparent swearing of eternal fealty before the Frenchman said: "Nine francs. I am sorry I did not have time to get it cheaper, but . . ." So O'Gilroy handed over the equivalent of seven shillings and sixpence.

By now he had a good idea who the Frenchman was, and that he knew who O'Gilroy was – was pretending to be, that is. So he said: "Would ye be asking if he'd give me a receipt?"

"A receipt?"

"Ye see, me master give me the money for the coat and he'll be wanting the proof of it."

"Ah, of course."

"And, er . . . mebbe if the receipt said twelve francs? Or fifteen, say? – he'd never be knowing."

One touch of dishonesty not only makes the whole world kin, it may make half of it think it has a hold on the other half.

* * *

"Gold," Corinna said as they reached a daylit floor, "has its uses, but it doesn't make people polite."

"Very philosophical. *Are* you taking the yacht south?"

"Probably. When are you going?"

"It looks like this afternoon."

"By train?"

"I imagine so. It all being for the Railway." They could, he supposed, catch one of the coastal steamers that linked Turkey's ports, but it seemed unlikely.

"So Lady Kelso will be on the opposite side of the mountains: you'll be coming from the north and me on the south. Hm."

When she said no more, he asked a stray employee where he could change some sovereigns and was taken up to the long marble counter. The Bank might be French, but after fifty years in Constantinople it was now thoroughly bureaucratised, so this involved several flights of higher mathematics, half a dozen forms – and coffee.

Leaning on the counter, Ranklin observed: "I expected Beirut Bertie to be here."

"Me too, but Edouard said he'd got a cable calling him back to Beirut. He's leaving later today."

It seemed odd to haul Bertie away from Constantinople and the loan negotiations at this stage – but Ranklin was keeping an open mind about M'sieu Lacan.

So instead, he said: "Everything lovesy-dovesy with Edouard again this morning?"

"What a *revolting* phrase. And mind your own damn business."

"Ah, the effects of gold again."

* * *

"What a strange coincidence!" Bertie said, shaking his head in amazement. "Still, everyone comes to Great Bazaar . . . Do you know, I met your master only last night, at the British Embassy? He seemed charming. But then," because he wanted to give O'Gilroy room to differ, "I am not his servant."

"Ah, sure he's pleasant enough. Jest stupid, is all."

"I am sure you exaggerate . . . Has he been in the Diplomatic long?"

"Not him. Doesn't seem to stick at anything, what I hear. But he's got money, and land in the Ould Counthry, so . . ." O'Gilroy shrugged at the way life was. He was giving, metaphorically, an imitation of a freshly ploughed field, waiting for whatever Bertie wanted to plant.

They were sitting in one of the many small coffee-houses that were mixed in with the Bazaar's stalls – the source, O'Gilroy realised, of all those boys hurrying about with trays of coffee and tea. Such boys provided the only sign of hurry; most of the customers were taking their time, some playing backgammon, others sharing a hubble-bubble pipe, each sucking at his ornate mouthpiece with a contemplative look.

Bertie saw where O'Gilroy was looking and smiled lazily. "Hashish, probably. There are many ways of passing time, one's life, one's troubles . . . I still prefer more European vices." He took a large silver flask from his pocket and filled his half-empty coffee cup, then proffered it. "I beg pardon – would you care to improve yours also? Here I cannot find proper cognac, but this is a passable imitation . . ."

It had a strong brandy smell although it didn't taste much like it. But anything was better than Turkish coffee.

Bertie sat back and lit another cigarette. "Do you take much interest in diplomatic affairs yourself, Mr Gorman?"

O'Gilroy shrugged. "Ye hear a lot of talk . . . Seems pretty much mixed up, most'f the time."

"True, true, the world is very confused. But at least now Britain and France are allies . . . You must be a patriotic man yourself."

"Been a soldier of the Queen," O'Gilroy offered. "And the King, too. Last one, that is."

Bertie nodded and seemed uncertain about how to go on. Meanwhile he called for more coffee. Then he said: "Do you think your master can have much influence with the Ambassador here?"

Surprised, O'Gilroy blinked. "I . . . I wouldn't be thinking so."

Two more cups of coffee arrived and Bertie drank half his in a gulp. "Quick, while the waiter does not see . . ." He topped up their cups from his flask again. "I think your Ambassador here is a most charming man. Charming. But perhaps too much of the right family, the right school, and the world today . . ." He leant forward confidentially. "I tell you, Mr Gorman, I am concerned about the *German* influence here, in Turkey. Britain has so great an Empire to think about, sometimes perhaps . . ."

He seemed so close to saying something, to making some proposition, that O'Gilroy had to listen. But like an expert tightrope walker, Bertie went on teetering without taking the plunge. He just droned on, and his voice receded into the background murmur, the clattery of crockery, the click of backgammon pieces . . . Maybe it was getting cold, too, although O'Gilroy felt clammy . . . was it clammy? It was difficult to tell . . .

Bertie was leaning forward again, looking concerned. "Are you feeling unwell? Finish your coffee and we can get into the fresh air . . . I can get you back to the hotel."

Obediently O'Gilroy emptied his cup – by now pure brandy – and swayed onto his feet. Bertie scooped up the sheepskin coat and supported him out into the crowded tunnel, then guided him. O'Gilroy concentrated on getting one foot in front of the other . . . Damn it! – what a time to get some foreign germ . . .

Then a blast of cold air cut him to the marrow, but he was being helped into a cab and clattered away briskly somewhere, anywhere to outrun the drowsy dullness, to find a fresh live new world . . .

* * *

The Deutsche Bank (or the Embassy or the Railway, they seemed indivisible on this matter) had provided its own porters and another bruiser in a pistol belt to get the boxes of coin into a closed car in the street. They had also put each box into their own canvas sacks, but not with any hope of deceiving passers-by: two strong men carrying something smaller than a shoe box from a bank are unlikely to be delivering cut flowers.

Everything had been signed for prolifically: first by Dahlmann and D'Erlon, then by Corinna, who had read everything carefully, and Ranklin, who signed Snaipe's name to anything, and finally by Streibl and Dahlmann as the Deutsche pretended to pass over running expenses to the Railway. Then Streibl had driven off with the guard to see the boxes onto a launch for Haydar Pasha station and the south.

Dahlmann looked at his watch. "So. Mr Snaipe, you will be ready to travel at half past two, yes? The motor-car will take you to your Embassy for Lady Kelso also, then Dr Streibl will lead you. You will be ready?"

Ranklin agreed distractedly. He had been hoping to share a cab with Corinna, but D'Erlon was all over her – well, his eyes were – and the most he could do was persuade himself that she was taking it coolly. So he went back to the Pera Palace alone. He wasn't worried to find that O'Gilroy was still out.

17

"Just a mixture very similar to laudanum," Bertie was explaining. "Which most likely you have had before as a sleeping draught. It does no damage, I assure you, or I would not have taken it myself. However, over the years, I have built up some resistance to opium – it is the cure to everything in the East – indeed, I believe a true opium-eater can take one hundred grains a day, an amount that would certainly kill an elephant. Quite remarkable. But you have taken perhaps one grain or less . . . Ah, my neck is becoming stiff."

He gabbled something and the Turk (or whatever) who had been trudging O'Gilroy round and round the room, started marching him to and for instead. They had let him be sick, indeed had given him some foul stuff to bring it on, and since they could easily have killed him already if that was what they'd wanted, he'd taken it without a struggle. Now he felt weak, slow-witted and with a headache coming on, but nothing else. Except murderous, of course.

Seated in a chair in the middle of a room in what seemed to be a private house, Bertie went on: "You will be interested in your future." He took out his watch. "I am leaving Constantinople this afternoon. When I have gone, and Lady Kelso's mission has also departed, soon you will be set free. We are, as I said before, allies, and I have no wish to annoy your Bureau too much. I hope you believe that?"

O'Gilroy glowered at him but was forced to keep on walking. "Me master'll be turning the town inside out looking for me, and with the Embassy to help besides—"

"Perhaps, but I much doubt it. I think a man like that will

think that you are a quite normal manservant who has quite normally got drunk. And lost."

There was no chance of O'Gilroy betraying himself by a sudden change of expression: thoughts took far too long to sink into his sodden sponge of a brain. But it slowly seeped through that Bertie still thought Ranklin was the genuine Snaipe and that the Bureau had sneaked an agent in as his servant. He couldn't work out how that helped; it was enough for the moment that Bertie had got *something* wrong.

Bertie had said something more that O'Gilroy had missed, but then came a knock on the door and a woman came in with a tray of coffee pot and big cups. She looked odd to O'Gilroy, yet it took him time to work out that she was unveiled and wore a European skirt and blouse despite her Mediterranean looks of olive skin and bold dark eyes and hair. She gave him a curious look – perhaps it was the closest her strong features could come to impassivity – and set the tray down.

"*Merci beaucoup, Theodora*," Bertie murmured. "*Noir pour le petit pauvre. . .*"

At last O'Gilroy was allowed to sit down and Theodora – was that a Turkish name? – handed him a big cup of real black coffee. The headache apart, he was feeling . . . well, at least better enough to realise it would be a mistake to show it. So he let the cup tremble and slop in his hands.

Bertie drank half his coffee, then went and conferred privately with Theodora. They glanced around the walls, which were hung with rugs instead of pictures, then went out. The Turk stood by the door and watched O'Gilroy impassively. He had a big curved knife shoved into his cummerbund.

* * *

By two o'clock, Ranklin was really worried – the more so as he was limited to doing what Snaipe would have done, which wasn't much. He thought about telephoning the police, but then called the Embassy instead to let them, with their greater clout, do so. He wrote a cryptic note to Corinna, who hadn't come back yet, and a formal letter to O'Gilroy telling him to catch up if he could. There was never any doubt that he himself had to go on: the job came first, and O'Gilroy would know it. It was an odd consolation that they shared that knowledge across a gulf that just might now be as wide as death.

"Gorman's got himself lost, the damned fool," he told Dahlmann, when the German Embassy car arrived. "He might come along later, I've left him some money—"

"Do you not want to stay to be sure he is unharmed?" Dahlmann asked hopefully.

"Oh, no, duty comes first, what?"

The car was a big closed Benz with a roof rack for luggage and hung about with spare tyres and petrol cans, so it was probably used more as the Embassy workhorse than for diplomatic visiting. A few hundred yards up the hill Lady Kelso was waiting at the British Embassy. So was a stormy-looking Jarvey; he herded Ranklin aside.

"Damn it, man," he raged quietly, "it isn't enough that you go off signing God-knows-what at the Imp Ott – yes, we *know* about that – but now you can't even find your own manservant. Just think how it reflects on us, going cap in hand to the Turks saying 'Please, one of our chaps has lost his servant, can you find him for us?' The Ambassador is *most*—"

"He's usually very reliable, so he could have run into trouble." By now, Ranklin was sure of this, but daren't say so.

"Then if you're so worried, you'd best stay here and help find him. Young Lunn can take your place. The Ambassador and I have talked it over and—"

"Be damned to *that*," Ranklin said flatly. "Sir Edward Grey sent me on this mission – *and* briefed me –" he was inventing desperately now; an Ambassador has an awful lot of power in his own bailiwick, despite the speed of the telegraph "– and you'll have to clap me in irons to stop me."

"*Mutiny!*" Jarvey's cry brought the loading of the German car to an interested stop. He toned down to a venomous hiss.

"By God, you can forget any career in the Diplomatic and go back to farming your Irish bog after this. We'll be sending an absolute *stinker* about you to London."

"I'm sure we're both doing what we think is right and proper," Ranklin said stiffly.

Looking very much like a frock-coated cobra, tall, stooped and poisonous, Jarvey glared the big car out of the gate and on its way.

"Mutiny?" Lady Kelso asked cheerfully.

"Just a little disagreement on protocol." Ranklin was trying to wriggle back into the persona of Snaipe, like donning an overcoat while sitting down. "I say, have you heard what that fool of a manservant of mine has done? . . ."

* * *

The room had the dark, crammed look of a bygone European age, but – apart from antimacassars and such – most of the cramming was Eastern. There were carpets and rugs everywhere and half the furniture was heaps of cushions. The few chairs and tables were of elaborately carved wood with the legs in the wrong places, and every surface was scattered with brass bowls, ashtrays and paraffin reading-lamps. A large cast-iron stove sat under a tiled conical flue in one corner. They hadn't let O'Gilroy near the windows, but if the corner of building he could see was part of this house, it was all made of green-painted wood and he was on the first floor.

He was still alone with his guard, who didn't look like the average Turk, being bulky, bearded and wearing some sort of turban rather than fez, a padded and embroidered jacket and baggy white trousers. These were probably clues enough for an old Eastern hand to say "Ah, a Hobgoblin from the Blarney region" but O'Gilroy had regressed to his Army days and saw him as just another bloody native.

The Hobgoblin hadn't displayed a pistol, but had made a point of expertly-casually carving up an orange with his curved knife, and O'Gilroy had got the message. But the man's build would have made him a handful anyway.

So he just sat and smoked and thought through his headache. He had to start with the idea that he had made a mistake. But Bertie had been following him anyway – or been close behind some inconspicuous Hobgoblin who had followed him to the Bazaar – which meant he had been suspect already. So was it Bertie's men who had been watching the launch last night and brought back a description of him? Probably; firing off that pistol had spoiled his pose as a tourist. And there didn't have to have been only two of them: maybe another on the waterfront, studying him as he talked to the Germans afterwards.

But then where had he gone wrong? He reckoned he had played his part cleverly enough in the Bazaar coffee-house, hinting at his own corruptibility, ready to listen as Bertie revealed his own schemings . . .

And *that*, he suddenly saw, had been wrong. He hadn't hit a false note, he'd been playing the wrong tune. Instead of being upright, loyal to his master, touch-me-not, he'd been clever. One hint of cleverness was all Bertie had needed to confirm his suspicions – and here he was.

So now would they really let him go? The French – still assuming Bertie really was working for them – *were* allies, of a sort, and maybe they just wanted him out of the way while they got on with their own plans. But he wasn't going to count on it. He wasn't going to count on anything but his own nastiness from now on.

* * *

Wherever they were going, it didn't seem to be to the crossing to Haydar Pasha station; the car was heading north-east alongside the Bosphorus.

"I can tell you now," Dahlmann told them now, "that you do not go by railway: we said that to deceive anyone who . . . anyone. Instead, you will go in the *Loreley*, the *stationnaire*. You understand?"

Lady Kelso seemed to, Ranklin didn't. "When I come first to Constantinople," Dahlmann explained, "all the Powers had *stationnaires* here. Yachts for the Ambassador, like Herr Billings's yacht, but sailed by the Navy."

"Are we catching her at Therapia, then?" Lady Kelso asked, looking out of the car windows.

"That is correct, Lady Kelso. I hope you do not object to sea travel."

"I'm sure it'll be more comfortable than the train – but how long will it take?"

"Perhaps three days. But by the Railway to the camp on the north of the mountains needs also a long time, more than a day, by horse. And more uncomfortable for you."

He smiled at her but got only a twitch of a smile back. She might be feeling a bit like a secret parcel. And that reminded Ranklin: "So we'll arrive on the south side of the mountains; what about the gold?"

Dahlmann peered at the glass partition that kept the driver in his place but seemed reassured. "Always it was to go in the *Loreley*. The boxes Dr Streibl sent to Haydar Pasha were – how do you say?"

"Dummies?"

"Yes. Dummies."

"Very clever," Ranklin said. "But if you do have to give Miskal this ransom, I assume you'll want him to sign something saying he promises to leave the Railway alone in future?"

After a moment, Dahlmann said: "That is a matter for the Railway."

"Quite an important matter, I'd think." He'd more or less raised this on the train; he was interested to see if they'd followed it up. It seemed not.

Lady Kelso said: "If he gives his word, that's what matters. Not legal agreements."

"Honourable man, is he?"

"Yes . . . In his own way," she conceded.

"Oh, I think that's true of most people," Ranklin said

blithely. "Just odd how often that way turns out to be what they want to do anyhow."

He felt her, sitting next to him on the car's back seat, lean away so that she could stare back at him more intently. He went on smiling innocently straight ahead.

Therapia was perhaps ten miles up the Bosphorus, a one-time fishing-harbour which had become a resort since the nations began building their summer embassies there, away from the heat, smells and infections of Constantinople. The German one was a whole walled compound of white-painted wooden buildings, now shuttered and looking empty, just across the road from the water. Moored a hundred yards off-shore was what must be the *Loreley*.

She had the sleek beauty of all steam yachts, with a clipper bow and overhanging stern, but in her case a rather middle-aged beauty (later, he learnt she had been launched nearly thirty years ago at Glasgow as the *Mohican*). The single funnel was rather tall and thin and she had three masts with sails furled along their booms, so probably she wasn't shy of using some help from the wind. Being Navy, there were two tarpaulined shapes right forward and aft – probably small-calibre quick-firers – and despite being Navy she was painted white with yellow funnel and masts and some gold fiddlededee around her bows.

There was a large steam launch waiting beside a wooden quay and sailors immediately started putting their luggage on board, so perhaps there really was some hurry. When they had got out of the car, Dahlmann announced: "I shall leave you here. Dr Streibl is now your guide."

Nobody said how much they regretted the parting, so he went on awkwardly: "I must wish you much luck in your errand of . . . mercy. Mercy," he repeated, trying to convince himself he'd got it right.

Lady Kelso looked to Ranklin and the Foreign Office for some appropriate and flowery words.

"Jolly good," Ranklin said, and they all shook hands and

climbed down into the launch. Before they even reached the yacht, its funnel had begun to boil black smoke.

* * *

Bertie reappeared after about an hour, along with a second Hobgoblin carrying something that O'Gilroy didn't recognise but did not like at all.

"All is arranged," Bertie smiled. "I am afraid tonight you must spend under my poor roof, and tomorrow you will be free. And so you will not be tempted to flee, and to make life simpler for my servants, I must ask you to wear this . . . rather medieval object." It looked like a hinged dog-collar and chain but made of old and heavy iron. "I believe it is a true antique, at least two hundred years old, so perhaps you will regard wearing it as historical research and do not resist?" O'Gilroy had already decided not to: the two Hobgoblins would get it on him anyway, plus perhaps a broken arm. "Ah, splendid. I can assure you that Ibrahim has just cleaned it, quite possibly spoiling its value . . . I will not ask if it is comfortable, but it is quite becoming. And who knows what famous prisoners of past sultans may have worn it? You may care to feel honoured – but I will understand if you do not. But I forget my manners: Ibrahim I have named, your other guardian is known as Arif the Terrible."

"What's he so terrible at?"

"I hope you will not find out. Now, before I catch my ship, we must have a little talk." He pulled up one of the few chairs and sat facing O'Gilroy. "We all know Lady Kelso will talk to Miskal the famous bandit who was also once her lover. But suppose she does not persuade him to release the engineers? – what will the Railway do then? Remember – we are allies."

O'Gilroy stuck a finger inside the iron collar. "Funny how that keeps slipping me mind."

Bertie smiled his lazy smile. "I assure you . . . But what will the Railway do?"

O'Gilroy tried to shrug but the weight on his shoulders was too much. "No idea."

"Perhaps they would offer money, that seems logical. Was there a hint of that?"

"And me stuck away with the other servants in the guard's van."

Bertie nodded. "But of course." He made as if to get up, then: "And when were you told of this task you must do?"

"I jest came with me master . . ." But O'Gilroy realised he mustn't harp on his "master"; best to keep Ranklin out of it, and out of Bertie's suspicions. "I think . . . when the fellers decided to ask Lady Kelso . . . they naturally wanted to send someone to help . . ."

"But *when* did they decide?"

What on earth was Bertie after? "Ye think the High-and-Mighty tell me things like that?" He could half-admit to being a spy and still be a fairly mere hireling.

And Bertie seemed to accept that. "I am late. *Au revoir*, Mr Gorman, and please give my apologies to your Chief."

He went out with Theodora and Ibrahim, leaving O'Gilroy seated on a chair in the middle of the room, a dozen feet of chain in his lap and a puzzle on his mind. Did Bertie *really* not know about the ransom? Or had he wanted to know if the Bureau knew of it?

And how and when it had learned?

Downstairs, the front door slammed. Watched by Arif, O'Gilroy went on sitting for a while, then decided What the hell? – he was never going to be left alone, so he'd best find out now what wearing this thing did to his movements. To shorten the amount of chain dragging on his neck he hung as much of it as possible on his shoulders and cradled the rest in both arms when he walked. Alternatively, he could just manage with only one hand holding up the weight and the end of the chain dragging on the floor, but it made a grinding clanking noise and was liable to catch on things. He had never thought of a collar and chain being such a handicap even when not locked to a wall. Mind, he couldn't recall thinking about such a thing anyway.

Arif watched – from a distance. He didn't look the

imaginative type, but at least he could envisage O'Gilroy clouting him with a length of chain. So could O'Gilroy: the problem was that it could only be with a short length at close quarters. Anything longer would take time to get started.

He also realised that the most comfortable position would be lying flat, with all the weight of the chain off his neck. So he did that on a heap of fancy cushions and watched the twilight thicken the shadows and dull the brassware around him.

Theodora came in and lit the paraffin lamps, then stood staring down at him. She radiated strong-mindedness and her favourite pose was feet well apart and hands – fists – on hips, as now. "So we have become a pasha? Ha. Do not think I am going to feed you *there*."

* * *

For a long time, Ranklin just sat in his cabin – a good, large one, much bigger than the train sleeper – watching the banks of the Bosphorus go past. It went past at quite a lick, given that these were busy, narrow waters. The Captain had obviously been told not to dawdle.

He had unpacked, but that hadn't taken long since he had brought the minimum along with what he planned to wear in the mountains. So he had nothing to do save watch – and worry. He was *fairly* sure that O'Gilroy wasn't dead – though that might just be his own lack of imagination – and so must be locked up somewhere. But convincing himself of that didn't really help, because although he could guess at why almost anybody here – except maybe Corinna and the British Embassy – might have waylaid O'Gilroy, it was just guessing. There was too much that he didn't know.

There came a knock on the cabin door and he let Lady Kelso in. "I was coming to ask if you'd be changing for dinner," she said, looking at his "travelling" tweed suit.

"My collar. That's about all I can do."

"Me too. I mean, the same sort of thing." She was wearing a plain wool skirt in dark blue and a high-necked white blouse.

He was about to suggest she sat down, but was a little too late. She asked: "Have you brought everything you'll need?"

"I think so. I'm not completely helpless without a servant."

She smiled quickly. "I didn't mean to imply . . . Are you worried about him? – Gorman?"

"I am, yes. He's quite bright, you know, but he doesn't know Constantinople, not at all."

"Ah, I forgot that you do." There was a coolness in that comment that Snaipe wouldn't have recognised but Ranklin did. But he couldn't explain which aspect of Constantinople he was talking about.

She went on: "Are you afraid he's gone off the rails with drink or drugs, something like—?"

"Oh, no, not him."

"Then you fear he's in deep trouble? – you don't think he might even be dead?"

"In trouble, yes . . ." How could he say O'Gilroy was a hard man to kill? Still, it all helped bring him out in worried frowns, and her in sympathy. It occurred to him that she might be here on a mothering mission: after all, he'd overplayed how much he relied on a manservant just to explain why he'd brought one.

And with O'Gilroy out of the running, he might need an ally. And they *were* supposed to be a team, after all.

She asked: "Do you know if Zurga Bey's on board?"

"I understand not. I expect he went on by train last night. Are we going upstairs?"

They found Streibl already in the main-deck saloon, and perhaps his enthusiastic re-welcome was the only sort he knew. "I hope you did not mind that we are so secret about coming by this boat? It is so complicated. Railways and politics should not mix; in Africa it was much more easy . . . I am sorry, do you wish a drink? Or coffee, tea?" He waved at a steward in a high-collared white mess jacket.

"I'd like coffee, please," Lady Kelso said. "We seem to be going at quite a speed already."

"Yes. We must go fast, naturally. The delay to the Railway . . ."

"Has Miskal Bey given you any time limit? Has he threatened the hostages?"

"Ah . . . no. No. But it is most worrying for the Railway."

"And the railwaymen's families," Lady Kelso reminded him tartly.

"Of course, yes."

It occurred to Ranklin that here were two people whose outlooks on life were about as opposite as the North and South poles. Lady Kelso, with her courtesy, could *pretend* an interest in anything, but really cared only for people. For Streibl, unless you could wind it up or stoke it, he wasn't interested. Without the company, stops and incidents of the train, this could be a *long* voyage.

He said: "Of course, I don't know anything about ransoms and hostages, but if I knew there was five hundred thou in gold francs heading my way then I probably wouldn't be too impatient – what? I suppose he does know it's coming?"

"Yes, I am sure he has been told."

Lady Kelso frowned. "It's still putting a *price* on life . . ."

Then the coffee tray arrived and she gave up on Streibl and sat down with it. They were in the aftermost of two deck-houses; the forward one, under the funnel and bridge, seemed to be officers' territory and, with the dining-room and their cabins directly below here, there was an obvious hint that passengers should stay aft and out of the way. The saloon itself was big and had everything to make it comfortable – leather arm-chairs, small tables, ashtrays – but gave the impression of a hotel run by the military so that it was all correct, solid, and of good value but quite without style or homeliness.

Ranklin asked: "And how fast does this ship go?" He was pretty sure Streibl would know the answer. He knew more.

"Twenty-two kilometres per hour . . . ah, twelve knots, I think. The engine is of three cylinders, triple expansion, and I understand that with one hundred and eighty thousand kilos of coal it can . . ."

Ranklin hardly listened. Even if Streibl were worried about the fate of his comrades-in-railway – and, perhaps because they were mere flesh and blood, he didn't seem all that worried – why should Dahlmann and the Railway management feel the same way? Miskal wasn't just putting a price on life, he was putting a damned high price, given that men got killed every day building railways; that might sound callous, but it just happened. Moreover, if the worst came to the worst and Miskal murdered the hostages, he'd label himself a villain in the eyes of the world, the Turkish Government would be forced to act – and the ransom money would be saved.

Perhaps it *was* just the delay; hundreds or thousands of men standing idle was also a high price. But he couldn't help wondering if the worst was somehow worse than they'd been told – and how.

He woke up to hear Streibl saying: ". . . and tomorrow, the Captain thinks maybe there is a storm . . ."

* * *

Towards dinnertime O'Gilroy was herded downstairs and along to the kitchen where Theodora was working at a big cast-iron cooking stove. It was a large, warm place full of copper cookpans, a smaller version of the Irish Big House kitchens O'Gilroy had sat and cadged in when he was genuinely in service as a chauffeur. And as in them, here the cook was Queen, ordering Arif and Ibrahim to pass this or do that and getting unquestioned obedience. She spoke French to them; O'Gilroy knew a little, but had decided not to admit to even that.

"Beg pardon for asking," he said, "but all of this don't seem what I'd heard a Turkish house was like."

"*Turkish?*" she exploded. "This is a French house. And did you think I am *Turk*? I am Greek, you . . . imbecile."

"Sorry about that. And these fellers, too?"

"They're Bedouin. To you, Arab. Do you think M'sieu Lacan would have *Turks* in his house?" She despised him with her dark eyes. "English are bad enough."

"I'm Irish."

Her gesture told him that that wasn't going to help.

They ate – a thick vegetable soup, then lamb and something that looked like rice but wasn't quite – at the big scarred kitchen table. By putting O'Gilroy in a high-backed chair with the chain wrapped around the top bar, they both pinned him down and got most of the weight off his neck, leaving his hands free. But that done, they treated a man in chains as quite unexceptional, not worth comment or glance. That rather depressed him.

At least Theodora offered him real coffee with the sticky-sweet bits that ended the meal. The two Arabs got interested only when he lit one of his cigarettes.

"Tell 'em they can smoke their own, less'n they're going to let me go buy some more."

A quick conversation established that the household was almost out of cigarettes. "Arif," Theodora said, "will buy some. Give him money."

So O'Gilroy gave him a handful of change and Arif went out. Theodora began clearing away.

"Tell me," O'Gilroy said, "wasn't yer people – the Greeks – at war with Turkey jest a year'n so ago?"

"We took back Salonika that is a Greek city always."

"Was ye in Constantinople the while?"

"Of course – but M'sieu Lacan saw that I was not harmed. He protects his people."

"Good for him . . . Did ye ever hear of an Englishman, an officer, was helping yer Greek army with its guns at Salonika?"

She thought, then asked: "The Englishman they called Sheep?"

"Eh?"

"He wore the sheep's coat, so he was called, I think, Colonel Sheep . . . no, the Soldier Sheep . . . no –" she snapped her fingers impatiently "– you would say, the Warrior Sheep."

"The—?" O'Gilroy nearly ruptured himself containing an explosive chuckle; Ranklin had never admitted to *that* nick-name.

"You also know him?"

"I work for him. His name's Ranklin. He's –" No, he'd better not say Ranklin was in Turkey "– he sent me here to work against the Turks. And Germans."

She sat down again and took one of his remaining cigarettes. "He has gone back to the English Army, then? And you are also a soldier – yes?"

"In a manner of speaking, yes."

She considered this. "And did you tell M'sieu Lacan?"

"He didn't give me much chance, jest out with the opium – and here I am."

She nodded approvingly. "He thinks you were a . . . an obstacle."

"And is he really going to let me go?"

"Did he not say so?" Her bold dark eyes challenged him to disbelieve that.

Reluctantly, O'Gilroy set aside the matter of his future. "Have ye heard of a feller Zurga Bey? Turkish soldier – could be a major."

"Colonel, if he is Bey," she said automatically. "No, I do not know him."

"Biggish feller, forty or thereabouts, got a beard—"

"Turkish officers do not wear beards."

O'Gilroy shrugged. "Well . . . he had one. Been in Germany, they had a German passport for him coming through the Balkans, but he's Turkish, right enough."

Despite herself, she was intrigued – by the beard, by the false passport. After all, this was a household apparently devoted to intrigue. "Ottoman names tell so little, just one name often, and it may not be real, a name made by friends –" she snapped her fingers again "– how do you say it?"

"A nickname?"

"Yes, yes . . . The Efficient, the . . . Sword . . ."

"The Terrible?" That got him a dark, sharp glance and he tried to make up ground by recalling the nickname of Ranklin's opponent in the 1912 war. "The Tornado?"

"Yes. There is an officer called the Tornado. I think he was named that at the Military Academy. Kazurga."

"Huh?"

"Kazurga, Tornado." This time she heard her own voice. "You said Zurga . . . Kazurga." She stood up and ground out her cigarette. "Wait."

"Ye think I have a choice?" O'Gilroy muttered.

A few minutes later she came back with a bulging scrap book, leafing through pages pasted with clippings from newspapers. "There." She slapped the book down in front of him. "Is that the man?"

It was a poorish reproduction of a stiff studio portrait, in uniform and, of course, without the beard. O'Gilroy tried mentally pencilling one in. "Could be him . . . nose and eyes seem right . . . What's it say 'bout him?"

She didn't need to refer to the book. "He was the *big hero* –" a sneer "– who saved Constantinople from the Bulgars. Of course," she relented, "Bulgars *are* animals."

"Didn't get wounded, did he?"

This time she picked up the book and mouthed her way through the cuttings. "Yes . . . yes, he was hurt in the fighting for Salonika. By our Greek Army." She nodded approvingly, then shut the book with a snap. "So this Colonel Kazurga, Zurga, has been in Germany but came back with the men of the Railway. And he has also gone south?"

"Haven't seen him since we got here, but I think that's the idea."

"I must tell M'sieu Lacan." She instinctively looked around, wondering how to go about it.

"So Monsieur Lacan's going down there, is he? Not back to Beirut."

"I did not say that!"

O'Gilroy reassured her: "Ye never said a word." He had been too clever again. She could have been grateful enough to kiss his hand, fall on his neck, show him the way out . . . Or, of course, she might be a shrewd professional such as a shrewd professional like Bertie would hire and trust.

She was certainly eyeing him shrewdly now. "And so you think I should say thank you and not care what M'sieu Lacan tells me, that I should let you go free – yes? And you will promise anything, no? Oh, I know men like *you*." She took another of his cigarettes and stood looking down at him.

He said mildly: "Ye said ye were going to let me go, anyways."

For a while she didn't say anything. Then she relented a little: "Tomorrow, I will tell you what must happen. A Dr Zimmer comes to Constantinople—"

"Zimmer?"

"Perhaps it is not his real name, but—"

"Mebbe we met once," O'Gilroy said thoughtfully, very thoughtfully. "In Friedrichshafen, I'm thinking."

"Good, so you know him. Then you go with him, yes?"

"Monsieur Lacan, he said ye was to send me off with Dr Zimmer?"

"Yes. That is good for you, no?"

"That's jest fine with me," O'Gilroy lied.

18

It was not a good night. Normally O'Gilroy had a certain fatalism where time was concerned and could sleep when there was nothing else to be done, but that was before he took to wearing an iron collar. Time after time he wriggled into a position where he felt That's it, all I have to do is stay like this. But after a couple of minutes it wasn't, and he had to start wriggling again.

Above all, the damn thing was *cold*. He knew that scientifically it was the same temperature as its surroundings, just a better conductor of heat away from him, was all. Knowing that didn't stop the bloody thing being cold.

Being alone to fiddle with the chain and padlocks was no help, either. The locks – brand new, probably bought that day – were simple but hefty and even if he had a pick-lock, it would also need to be hefty, just to exert the sheer leverage needed. And rusted though the chain was, it needed another century or so before its quarter-inch thickness became vulnerable. So he spent too much time imagining Dr Zimmer and Hunke arriving in Constantinople, hurrying round here – wherever here was; he guessed they were still in Stamboul, but the carriage ride had been a fuzzy, disjointed time – and carting him off . . . How? By carriage or car? Certainly at pistol-point. And then . . .

Then, whatever happened wouldn't be in Bertie's house, and would be long after he was known to be aboard a ship going south. Nothing to do with him. Neat, that, without O'Gilroy around to contradict.

His one pale hope was that Theodora didn't know *he* knew what was going to happen. Whether she knew herself didn't matter. It only mattered that he had convinced her he was looking forward to Zimmer's arrival and had abandoned thoughts of escape. But lying there in that collar, the other end of the chain padlocked to the iron bedstead, there seemed little to abandon.

* * *

After breakfast, Ranklin dressed as for the mountains and went up to walk on deck. By now they were through and well south of the Dardanelles, but there was still land like a rough-edged grey cloudbank on the eastern horizon. They'd probably be in sight of land most of the trip, since they were following a coastline which had crumbled into a myriad islands and he hoped the Captain would miss them all.

Particularly in bad weather, which was supposed to arrive later in the day. The wind had backed westerly and they were getting an extra nudge from it, having set main- and fore-sails and some jib (if he'd got that right). That gave them a cracking pace, a lot of spray and a heel to port. It felt wrong, a steamer leaning steadily like that.

He walked cautiously along the high side of the deck, breathing deeply and healthily when he thought anyone might be looking, past the forward deckhouse onto the wet foredeck and round to the low, lee side. There, a door in the deckhouse below the bridge was labelled *Kapitans Büro – privat*, which could only be for the benefit and discouragement of passengers, since the crew would know which cabin was whose. Ranklin felt more benefited than discouraged. Nothing like a healthy stroll on deck after breakfast. If only O'Gilroy were here, or accounted for, he'd feel quite cheerful.

By lunchtime the wind had become gusty and the sails had been lowered, but instead of putting the *Loreley* upright this let her roll indiscriminately. Lunch was a very thick stew and pureed vegetables which stuck to the plates no matter what the ship did, which was obviously intended and a bad sign. Nor did any of the officers eat with them, but to Ranklin that was a good sign. The more of them that were busy not bumping into islands, the better.

Streibl ate very little and Ranklin asked solicitously: "Are you a good sailor?"

"*Hein*? I am not a sailor. I am—"

"I mean, do you get seasick?"

"I expect so," Streibl said lugubriously.

Lady Kelso reprimanded Ranklin with her eyebrows and he changed the subject. "Tell me, do you use quite a bit of explosive in digging tunnels and so forth?"

"Naturally."

"*Quite* a bit, I mean?" Ranklin felt he wasn't handling this well; Streibl looked at him oddly. "I mean, quite a *lot*?"

"In the mountains, when work goes well, perhaps one hundred kilos a week. It sounds like a war."

"Gosh," Ranklin said, trying to sound foolishly impressed to give some point to his question.

Soon afterwards, Streibl retreated to his cabin. Lady Kelso and Ranklin went back upstairs to the saloon for coffee.

"What," she asked, "was all that about explosives?"

"Er . . . I heard a vague rumour we might be taking dynamite for Miskal Bey – his stronghold, anyway – as a last resort."

"But if the Railway's got it by the ton, there'd be no need?" she said crisply. "I certainly hope, with a storm coming, that we *aren't* carrying anything like that."

"Oh, most explosives are very stable." Then he added hastily: "So I've been told. We must be carrying ammunition for those guns on the deck anyway. But so do all warships, if you think about it, and they don't blow up in storms."

"I suppose not." She balanced her cup carefully and took a genteel sip. "But we do know we're carrying all that gold coin . . . Have you any idea where?"

"Er . . . hadn't thought about it," Ranklin lied.

"Just suppose," she said calmly, almost dreamily, "you could find out where that was kept and pinched some of it, or just threw it overboard, that would rather spoil their little plans, wouldn't it?" And she gave him a sweet bright smile.

* * *

The morning had passed slowly for O'Gilroy. Inspired by the success of chaining him to the bedstead, they'd now padlocked it around the foot of the cast-iron stove in the first-floor room. That meant Arif didn't have to watch him the whole time and made it even more humiliating as Theodora dusted the room around him, topped up the paraffin lamps and re-lit the stove. But he had to pretend to be hopeful and cheerful, merely bored.

"It will not be long," she assured him. "The train from Vienna comes I think at three o'clock." Then, judging from the sounds on the stairs and below, she went off to the market. He was getting pretty good at knowing where they were – or at least how close – from such sounds.

So when he was re-chained up there after lunch, and reckoned they were all downstairs for the moment, he moved.

From the stove, he had a twelve-foot radius of action plus the length of his arm. He worked quickly and to a plan, holding as much of the chain off the floor as he could to be as silent as possible. First he emptied a brass fruit bowl, then collected all the lamps within reach – four of them – and shook out their paraffin into the bowl. He got well over a pint and wished it were petrol, since paraffin only burned when it was warmed or diffused in something like a wick – or torch. Still, a torch was easy when it wasn't your own house: he wrenched a leg off the chair, wrapped a lace antimacassar around it and soaked it with paraffin. He put the bowl of the rest on the stove to warm up, took the shade off the last lamp and lit the wick.

Then he thought through what should happen next, and as an afterthought sprinkled more paraffin on a small rug nearby. When he heard feet on the stairs, he lit the torch from the lamp and picked up the bowl.

Arif came in first, Theodora close behind, and the flame had their immediate attention. Theodora gave a yell for Ibrahim.

"Fine; more the merrier," O'Gilroy said. "'Tis a wooden house, I'm thinking. Had some good fires with houses like this in this town, so I heard. Wouldn't mind seeing one for meself."

Ibrahim hurried in. O'Gilroy said: "Right, first thing, Theodora unlocks this damn chain. Ye two, stay where y'are."

Arif alone might, just might, have been sensible, but not in the presence of Ibrahim. And vice versa. As it was, both drew their knives and came forward. O'Gilroy stooped and brushed the torch across the rug. It flamed up willingly.

They stopped, looking to Theodora for orders. She didn't say anything. The rug burned merrily and firmly. O'Gilroy splashed paraffin onto the nearest wall-hanging.

Then Theodora spoke in a low, firm voice and the Arabs, reluctantly, sheathed their knives and stepped back. She came forward. "You must let me put out that fire first, or it will—"

For answer, O'Gilroy slopped more paraffin onto the flaming rug.

Looking – to someone better read than O'Gilroy – like Medusa on one of her bad days, Theodora fished the key from her apron pocket and unlocked the neck collar. "M'sieu Lacan will *kill* you," she spat. The collar and chain crashed to the floor.

"Now don't be giving me more reason to burn the man's house down." He still held the torch and bowl close together as he stretched and swivelled his neck with relief. "Jayzus, that's better."

"*Now* I must stop the fire."

"Go ahead, take all the help ye need. Jest keep the boyos out of me way, is all."

Feeling as light as a ballerina, O'Gilroy headed for the door. Ibrahim circled carefully past him to help Theodora, but Arif stood in his way, hand on knife and calculating . . .

"Tell Arif he'll reach hell burning already," O'Gilroy warned.

Theodora called an order – but Arif didn't obey. Being known as "the Terrible" is something you have to live up to.

O'Gilroy tossed half the remaining paraffin onto Arif's beard and front. He jumped back and *hissed* with fury, whipped out the knife and – O'Gilroy was holding the torch like a knife of his own, ready to lunge. The paraffin smell stung Arif's face as it warmed on his chest.

Then he snarled something and stepped aside.

O'Gilroy went smoothly through the door and down the stairs, suddenly realising that his flaming passport to the outside world would expire the moment he stepped beyond the wooden house. He'd be rather conspicuous carrying that torch, too.

He reached the front door, where he was going to have to set down either the bowl or torch; he hadn't planned this far in detail. Arif watched from the head of the stairs.

After a moment, O'Gilroy put down the bowl, opened the door, picked up and emptied the bowl over the door-latch area on the inside and torched it. Then he slammed the flaming door in Arif's face as he bounded down the stairs.

Then he ran.

The road outside was no more than a cobbled mule-track, with a choice of uphill or down. O'Gilroy ran down. That way, he should eventually reach a waterfront and find where he was; it was the dark heart of the city that scared him. He looked back at a corner and saw nobody running after him, but turned it anyway, then refound a downhill slope at the next one. This was a broader and busier street, with stalls in it, so he slowed to a brisk walk.

But the moment he did, the crowd seemed to close around him, as alien and threatening as it had seemed in his first minutes in this city. Any one of those well-wrapped dark figures might be about to thrust with a hidden knife, and him unarmed . . . But then he remembered he had been imprisoned, not robbed, and a couple of minutes later was carrying a tourist dagger, bought from a stall, hidden under his own jacket as he moved more confidently through the mob.

Then the street curved and the horizon opened to water and anchored ships that seemed to glow like the hearth of home. A hundred yards later he came out onto the waterfront just along from the Stamboul end of the Galata Bridge.

Twenty minutes after that he was stepping down from a cab at the Pera Palace beside a big car of unfamiliar make. He'd seen almost no cars of any type in Constantinople, and couldn't resist walking round it (it was a Cadillac) before going inside. A man in chauffeur's uniform was waiting inside the small lobby, which was heaped with luggage. At the desk his welcome was distinctly cool. The clerk had his own ideas on how to treat a servant who had gone AWOL: tell him his room was taken, hand him Ranklin's message, and settle down to enjoy O'Gilroy quailing and blenching as he read it.

He was disappointed. The first thing O'Gilroy took from the envelope was a £5 note which he slapped on the desk. "Gimme gold for this, *if* ye'd be so kind." He read the note. "And ye've got me bags stored somewheres. I'll take 'em."

The clerk was about to grit his teeth and obey when he looked over O'Gilroy's shoulder and his face broke into a fawning smile. "Mrs Finn! So now you are leaving us, we are quite desolated. We *so* much hope you have enjoyed—"

"Yes, yes, sure. The Embassy was supposed to be sending an automobile – Good God! – Conall! Where have *you* been? I got a note from Matt . . . Here, tell me what happened."

Dazed and pop-eyed, the clerk watched as one of the hotel's richest clients hauled an errant manservant into a conspiratorial huddle.

"*Now* tell me."

"I think the phrase is 'unavoidably detained'."

"By what?"

"Mebbe I'd best not say. Jest that if I meet up with Beirut Bertie again, I'm going to carve bits off'n him with a blunt axe."

"Oh. Then he's not just a smooth diplomatist?"

"He has some rough bits."

"Well, you're not likely to meet him: he's off back to Beirut."

O'Gilroy shook his head. "No. He's headed for the Railway, where they're tunnelling and . . . and all."

"Where Matt and Lady Kelso have gone?"

"Did they get off all right, then?"

"As far as I know, yes."

"Did I hear yez going down that way yeself in the yacht?"

"I am, starting right now," Corinna said slowly. "But I am *not* having our Bank, or Mr Billings's boat, tangled up in any of your shenanigans."

"Sure and it'd be a Christian act entirely, jest giving a lift to a poor servant feller that got drunk and missed his train."

"Yes, if you *were* a poor servant. You can take today's train. Or tomorrow's. You'll only be a day or two behind."

O'Gilroy shook his head sombrely. "Then I'd best get into hiding until the train goes . . . and send a telegram to the railway camp, warning the Captain about Bertie – and another problem he don't know he's running into. Him and Lady Kelso besides."

"That'll be read by both the Turkish telegraph people and the Germans at the camp."

"Jayzus, and I niver thought of that."

She clamped her teeth, then opened them to say: "You evil-hearted, blackmailing son of a . . . *All* right. Get your damned bags together."

Ten minutes later they were on their way in the Cadillac.

"When we get on board," Corinna re-asserted herself, "I shall let it be known that I'm giving a ride to a friend who's been robbed of everything and had to borrow a servant's suit, out of pure Christian charity—"

"As ye are indeed."

"Shut up. And because I'm pumping you for British foreign policy information en route."

O'Gilroy nodded approval; Christian charity wasn't really a believable motive.

"I am *not*," Corinna finished, "having them think I'm having an affaire with you." And she was satisfied to have shocked his Irish soul, that was so prim in certain ways.

So for several minutes he was quiet as the car wound its way down the hill, obviously heading for the Galata quayside or thereabouts. Then he said: "Have ye got a fixed time to be getting started?"

"No, just when I get on board."

"Then could ye jest be making a small loop so's I could get a word with a coupla fellers off'n the three o'clock train from Vienna?"

"What fellows?" she asked suspiciously.

"Ah, jest some fellers . . ." O'Gilroy was being elaborately unconcerned ". . . that me and the Captain had a bit of a run-in with at Friedrichshafen . . . Bertie was going to hand me over to them so's they could . . . But the Captain'll want to know how they're involved with him."

"A bit of a run-in?"

"Nobody got shot."

"Yes, but—"

"And nobody'll be getting shot at the station, with the crowd and all. Anyways, I haven't got a gun. Being a poor manservant, like."

"But if *they're* armed, they could force you . . . Damn it, if you *must*, at least take my pistol with you."

She always carried a Colt Navy Model in one of her handbags, and over-riding O'Gilroy's feeble protests, now passed it to him. Then leaned forward to give the chauffeur new directions.

Then she sat back, gradually realising that she had let herself be talked not only into giving O'Gilroy a lift in the yacht but detouring for him to confront two hoodlums and insisting he did it with her own pistol.

No wonder Irish-born politicians seemed to be taking over America.

The Vienna train had come in some time before, but passengers were only now seeping through the Customs hall to begin bargaining for cabs and guides. That made it a cosmopolitan crowd and O'Gilroy was conspicuous only by having no overcoat: both his real one and the sheepskin affair were somewhere back at Bertie's house. He could stand the cold, but Colts must have been thinking of overcoats when they advertised this pistol as a "pocket" weapon.

Then Hunke came out, carrying a small Gladstone bag, and stood irresolutely staring around; he was immediately besieged by touts. O'Gilroy watched, feeling smugly like an old Constantinople hand – but also suddenly doubting why he was here. Had he just wanted to cock a snook at these two? – that was unprofessional. He should be doing some *real* spying as well, not just the pistol kind.

He strolled up. "Can I be offering ye any assistance at all?"

Hunke's eyes widened. Then he switched the bag to his left hand, and looked back for the snowman-shaped Dr Zimmer, coming up behind. He also stopped dead at the sight of O'Gilroy.

"And a very good day to ye, too." O'Gilroy flapped open his jacket to show the pistol butt, then folded his arms so his right hand rested naturally on it. "Jest thought I'd pop down to let ye know things've changed, 'twas all a mistake. Me and Monsieur Lacan, we talked it over and reckoned we was really allies, so . . . Sorry if ye've had a wasted journey."

"M'sieu Lacan is not here?" Zimmer asked, looking around.

"Says he's sorry."

"And he let you go?"

"Here I am," O'Gilroy smiled. "Ye think I escaped? Ye don't know him so well, do ye?"

"I never—" Then Zimmer clenched his mouth shut.

"Anyways, he had urgent business – ye know? But 'fore that, we reckoned we was really on the same side. We talked over what Gunther had told us—" Zimmer expressed . . . well, it was difficult to say what. The point was that he *expressed*, and a proper agent wouldn't have; Zimmer really belonged behind a desk. "So it seems Gunther sold the same information twice, to the both of us."

"No." That was more bewildered than definite.

Trying to keep him off balance, O'Gilroy pressed on: "All 'bout the Railroad . . . And Miskal Bey . . . The ransom . . . all what Gunther picked up from the Germans . . ." And at that item on the list Zimmer's expression relaxed.

"And did M'sieu Lacan send you to here?" Now Zimmer was confident, almost playful. O'Gilroy had shown that he didn't know something important.

"Must've done, else how'd I know? But like I say, I'll be leaving ye to do a bit of sight-seeing, mebbe. Pity to waste the trip."

He turned away. Hunke took a step forward and O'Gilroy spun back, his right hand half out from his jacket. For a moment they just stood there, and if the crowd noticed them, God knows what it thought: there could be no missing the death-rays that crackled between them.

Then O'Gilroy said deliberately: "Best start that sight-seeing: it improves the mind something wonderful, they do say."

Zimmer laid a cautious hand on Hunke's sleeve. O'Gilroy took a couple of steps back, then turned away—

—right into Arif's path. And if he had been The Terrible before, now the look on his face and the bandages on his hands – he must have tried to open that blazing door – showed the only sight likely to improve *his* mind was O'Gilroy's insides.

O'Gilroy didn't pause. He pulled the pistol out and aimed at Arif's belly. Then, as the Arab flinched aside, slashed his head with the pistol, barged past both him and Theodora just behind, and ran for the Cadillac.

"If yer ready to leave this town," he panted, flopping in beside Corinna, "me, too."

19

Throughout the afternoon the sky had crowded with clouds, the sea became flecked with white and the wind started to make serious sounds in the rigging. By his last sight of the sun, Ranklin reckoned the Captain had turned away from the coast and islands to give himself more room for mistakes; he thoroughly approved.

In the saloon the steward had put away all the bottles and glasses and was making sure the tables and chairs were tied to ring-bolts in the floor. But he had issued Lady Kelso with a wide-based mug of coffee and offered to fetch another. Ranklin said he'd wait until the tying-down was finished and, picking his moment in the ship's roll, dropped into a chair.

"No sign of Dr Streibl?" he enquired.

"I'm afraid the poor man's confined himself to quarters."

"But not you."

"I've got quite a strong stomach. I should have, after twenty years of eating Bedouin food and getting around on camels." The steward had disappeared towards the galley and she seemed about to say something.

Ranklin beat her to it: "I was a bit surprised you say that Miskal Bey's a *mountain* Arab. I mean, I think of Arabs as desert types, you know."

"'Arab' is just a race – like English, and at least as varied. You get as many mountain Arabs as desert ones – and most live in towns, anyway: Baghdad, Damascus, Beirut . . . It was the *Arabs* who founded the Islamic Empire and they don't forget it. The Ottoman Turks are Johnny-come-latelies who were hired as mercenary soldiers. Then, over time, the wheel turned." She smiled ruefully.

The steward came back with Ranklin's mug of coffee. Then, just as Lady Kelso was about to get onto the topic of her choice, one of the ship's officers came in from the deck, accompanied by a howl from the weather until he slammed the door on it. He saluted quickly and steadied himself on the back of a chair, dripping water from his sou'wester all over it.

"Please: there is much storm . . . the Herr *Kapitan* asks you do not go on the outside, the deck – Yes?"

"Thank you," Lady Kelso purred.

"Wouldn't dream of it," Ranklin said.

The officer saluted again and handed his way out, letting in another brief howl from the storm.

The steward had gone and this time Ranklin had to let her have her say. "Actually, this wouldn't be a bad time to go looking for that gold coin. Nobody'll expect you to be on deck, nobody else'll be, the Captain's sure to be on the bridge and *I* think it's in his office cabin sort of thing, it's marked *Büro* towards the front on—"

"I saw it, too."

"Good. There's a safe inside—"

"You *looked?*"

Again the sweet smile. "Oh, nobody minds a woman being snoopy, they expect us to do the most frightful things. Do you know anything about breaking into safes?"

"I *say*, hold on, wait just a minute . . . Do you really think we ought to be doing this . . . this sort of thing?"

"I think Sir Edward just sent me as a gesture of goodwill, but he assumed I'd fail. But he didn't know about the ransom, did he? How could he have done? So it seems to me he'd *expect* us to spoil that, if we can. We'd really be doing what he originally wanted: helping delay the Railway."

She'd probably convinced herself that was true, too. Or was thinking of riding into London society as the great patriotic heroine. Or both. Either way, he was left wondering who was supposed to be the spy on this damned mission. Here she was urging him to do something he was planning anyway. If he just said No, he could lose her as a potential ally; if he confessed who he really was, he was putting his life, the whole mission, in her hands. Perhaps he could play the deeply-shocked diplomatist but go ahead with the burglary anyway, without her knowing . . .

Not realising it, he must have pulled a deeply-shocked-diplomatist face because she said: "If you feel you really can't, I'll have a stab at it myself. I can probably talk my way out if I get caught."

He really should stop being surprised how naturally women turned to blackmail. And whether she meant it or not, he had to let it work. "No, no," he said gloomily, "I'll have a go."

"Oh, how *splendid* you are! It looks quite an old safe, and the Captain's probably left the key or the combination in his desk drawer. I didn't have time to look."

"I'll try when we're through with dinner . . . What are you going to be doing?"

She'd got it all thought out. "Persuading everybody that you're still around here. I thought the best way was for me to go into your cabin. If a steward or anybody hears my voice, they'll assume you're there, too." This was delivered with yet another bright innocent smile. "Just chatting about England and the Season, of course."

* * *

Corinna found O'Gilroy planted at the big table in the middle of the *Vanadis*'s saloon, where the almost imperceptible roll of the vessel would be at its least. She had been prowling the yacht – the first chance she'd had – and comparing it with her father's *Kachina*. But all yachts had much the same layout: that was inevitable once you'd put the engine and boiler rooms where they had to be, and the officers' cabins within easy reach of the bridge. This was bigger and more powerful than *Kachina* but coal-fired, which meant a lot of cleaning whenever they coaled, and the decor was too conventional for her taste. Her father had let her decorate *Kachina* in light woods and subtly cheerful colours – except for his "study", which was the usual

Banker's Spanish Main, and his bedroom. He could pick the decor in which he entertained his lady friends for his own damned self.

O'Gilroy pushed the paper he had been writing on aside and staggered to his feet. She waved him back. "I got the wireless operator to send a message to the British Embassy saying you'd been found safe and would they tell the Honourable Snaipe you'll try to catch up – if they know where he is."

"Thank ye. I reckon the Captain'd be worrying."

"I also learnt that the German Embassy yacht, the *Loreley*, left Constantinople yesterday afternoon going full steam. And today the wireless operator picked her up in the Aegean morsing for weather information, which means she's going the same way that we are. So probably Matt and Lady Kelso and your German chums are aboard her."

O'Gilroy was surprised. "Them on a boat, too? . . . What's that mean, then?"

"That they won't reach the south coast, a place called Mersina – where we're going – until the day after tomorrow. But our Captain also reckons we're about four knots faster, and if they run into a storm – it seems there's one down past Smyrna – and have to slow down, we should catch up quite a bit."

"Are we heading for a storm, then?"

Corinna had forgotten how resolutely bad a sailor O'Gilroy was. How he had ever managed to get off Ireland . . . Lying flat and groaning, presumably. "We shouldn't be; he says it'll have blown inland by the time we get there. Just a bit of a sea."

He looked at her with dark suspicion. "Worse'n this?"

They were in a near-flat calm in the almost land-locked Sea of Marmora. "This is *nothing*. This is *normal*." Then she curbed her impatience and tried a bit of distraction: "Apart from nearly shooting each other's heads off – *with my pistol* – did you learn anything from your buddies at the station?"

"Mebbe . . ." O'Gilroy had been trying to work out what he had learnt, or come to suspect. But this was usually Ranklin's job; O'Gilroy contributed mistrust and muscle, and neither was much help here. He needed a fluent mind to help interpret and while Corinna certainly had that, she was still a foreigner. Tied up with the French, too, who seemed to be playing an unexpected part . . .

He'd try to advance step by step. "D'ye recall a feller Gunther van der Brock? Was using another name when ye met him—"

"Of course I remember him. That was the first time I ever had to use my pistol. I ought to charge the Secret Service whenever—"

"Sure, sure . . . Two weeks back, Gunther got himself killed in London. No, 'twasn't us. Only his partners – the fellers at the station – they reckon 'twas our fault. He'd come over to sell us the . . . the story 'bout the Railway. So the Captain reckons."

She sat down. "All that about the kidnapped engineers? – it's been in the papers, everybody knows it. And Lady Kelso's mission, everyone knows that by now, too."

"Surely . . ." But they didn't know about the ransom. And neither did she, it seemed. ". . . only, what's Bertie doing, getting mixed up in it, going off down there to . . . to where it all is?"

She shrugged. "Bertie knows the Arabs – so everyone says. And the old bandit chief down there's more or less an Arab, isn't he? Perhaps Bertie put him up to the whole thing in the first place."

O'Gilroy sat very still. Then he murmured: "Jayzus 'n Mary," reverentially. He reached for his sheet of paper and began writing.

Corinna watched, amused. She couldn't see what he was writing, just that it was done in a laborious but near-perfect copperplate script. Only the educated classes, who used writing as an everyday tool, scrawled unreadably.

But O'Gilroy's runaway thoughts were outpacing his careful script. All sorts of things fell into place if he assumed Bertie had manipulated Miskal. Like where Miskal had got his repeating rifles from. And as for the ransom, it was no longer a question of whether Bertie knew about it, but whether demanding it had been his idea all along. And *then* – it was coming with a rush now – if Bertie and his bosses had actually created that "secret", Gunther could have got it from them, not the Germans. And the French, suspicious, then had Gunther killed. Certainly Bertie had been far more suspicious of them than anyone on the train.

Only . . . if he was trying to delay the Railway, he wouldn't want the ransom to work, would he? There was still something missing. His ambition to hit Monsieur Lacan with a blunt axe still held, but perhaps he'd allow himself a couple of questions first.

Corinna asked sweetly: "Do I get to mark your homework?"

"Mebbe . . . when I know ye'll give it ten out of ten." In fact, he planned to throw it into the sea . . . Oh, God, why had he remembered the heaving, churning sea?

* * *

Ranklin had no sou'wester, not even a rain-proof, so he just buttoned his overcoat to the neck. He decided against any sort of hat – it might blow off and be found on deck – and, after a little thought, shoes and socks as well. Weren't bare feet traditional for gripping a stormy deck? The bag of lead shot (which Lady Kelso didn't know about), a handkerchief to dry his hands and a dry-battery torch and he was ready to go safe-cracking.

She knocked and came quickly into his cabin. "I told the steward we were *both* getting an early night and didn't want to be disturbed. And I listened at Dr Streibl's door and he's moaning louder than the wind, so I think we're safe from him. Good luck."

Ranklin took the companion-way that led to the outside world rather than go through the saloon. The door onto the deck wasn't locked – presumably in case they had to abandon ship – and he stood outside it for a moment, rain lashing into his face like dust-shot, hoping his eyes would adjust to the darkness. They didn't much; a stormy night at sea is a very dark place, and a wet, noisy and wallowing one as well. The *Loreley* didn't just roll, she also wanted to put her nose down and whuffle along like a badger. There were long shuddering spells when he guessed the propeller had come clear out of the water.

But when he started moving forward, at least there was a rail along the deck-house wall to grip. He worked along it towards the distant light of the bridge, step by step, hand by hand.

The door of the Captain's *Büro* was unlocked, just as Ranklin had hoped and expected. Locks and bolts were civilian concepts: a senior officer's cabin was *sacred*. He pulled the door shut behind him and kept gripping the knob as a hand-hold against the wandering floor.

It was even darker in here, he'd certainly need the torch. But the cabin had windows onto the main deck and roving half-shaded torch-light would look far more suspicious than drawn curtains, so after one flash to locate himself, he staggered about in the darkness pulling them shut. Then he sat in the desk chair, which was bolted to the floor, and played the torch around.

Apart from being the Captain's office, it must be his sea cabin – where he dossed down for an hour or two between storms – because it had a bunk along one wall and a clothes cupboard next to it. That just about left room for the desk, chair and the safe. It was about twice as big as the one on the train and spattered with old-fashioned brass trimmings, and perhaps a professional safe-cracker would have rubbed his hands with glee – *if* he could have got on board a naval vessel to begin with.

Ranklin seated himself on the floor in front of it, peered at the dial – a normal numerical one – and then dug in his pocket for his diary. It had two months' of fiction about Snaipe's dinner engagements and dentist's appointments, and at the back some figures posing as expenses, bets and train times. He began decoding.

"First crack the owner of the safe," Mr Peters the locksmith had advised, and Ranklin had come as prepared as he could. So the first number to try was the Kaiser's birthday: 27–01–59. He spun the knob two full turns anti-clockwise, then onto 27. A full turn clockwise and onto 01. Then 59. If that had been right, he should have heard a small bar falling into place along the three notches on the now-aligned discs. He didn't, but there was plenty of noise from the ship and the sea, so he tugged at the handle anyway. Still nothing.

Start again with the Kaiser's accession as King of Prussia: 15–06–88. Nothing.

Then the date the German Empire was proclaimed at Versailles: 18–01–71. More nothing, and he began to doubt the Captain's patriotism.

So try his professionalism: *Grössadmiral* von Tirpitz's birthday, 19–03–49.

He couldn't remember what the remaining numbers were, though probably one was Admiral Prince Heinrich, the Kaiser's brother. And none of them worked. Just for the hell of it he tried 10–20–30 and a few like it, in the faint hope it was still at the combination the makers had set all those years ago, but somebody had gone to that small trouble.

He gave up and flashed the torch around. As Lady Kelso – and Mr Peters before her – had said, people could be stupid enough to scrawl the combination on the wall, even on the safe, but while a navy might have nothing against stupidity, it deplored such untidiness. Or they wrote it inside a desk drawer, so he returned to the chair and tried the drawers. They were locked, probably just to stop them falling out in the storm, yet he wasn't skilled enough to pick even *them*: what chance did he stand with a safe?

Outside, the sea thundered and the wind shrieked in the rigging. Overhead, he heard the clump of booted feet on the bridge and the occasional ting of the engine-room telegraph – reassuring sounds, for as long as they were there, they weren't catching him here. But it didn't advance his cause.

Nor did the photograph of, presumably, the Captain's wife on the wall. Ranklin caculated that if the combination were *her* birthday and he could guesss her age within five years, he'd have about 1800 combinations to try (even assuming the

Captain remembered his wife's birthday). He began a desultory search of the desk baskets and found plenty of figures, but all temporary ones: distances steamed, kilos of coal and other stores embarked, dates on letters and forms . . .

There was also a faded photograph of the *Loreley* itself when she had been launched in 1885 as the *Mohican*. There were a few figures in the caption, so he tried combinations of the gross and net tonnage – 53–63–64 and 36–45–36 and was left with the builders' number 90061.

Putting a zero on the front meant dialling 00, which was impossible, so he added it at the end: 90–06–10. Click.

He didn't believe it and the pull on the door was pure habit, but it opened and the torch shone on – paperwork. A mass of paperwork, and he couldn't believe that, either. As in a trance, he pulled a heavy book free and saw it was the current German Navy code. A bulky sealed envelope turned out to be instructions in case of war. Increasingly desperate, he shuffled envelopes and pamphlets all stamped GEHEIM – secret. He stared numbly as the torchlight played over a spy's treasure trove which he was totally unprepared to deal with. And not a single, solitary centime of gold in sight.

Automatically he shut the door and spun the dial to lock it, then sat back. Oh, he could see what had happened, all right. The noble military mind at work: the real treasure was codes and sealed orders, sorry, no room for mere gold, shove it in my socks drawer.

Well, *had* the bloody man shoved it in his socks drawer? Crawling as the safest way to move around, it took him under half a minute to find the four boxes in the bottom of the clothes cupboard under a collection of sea-boots.

The boxes were solidly built – they had to hold nearly a hundred pounds weight each without falling apart – but crude and unsealed apart from the nails. By now furious at the time and apprehension he'd wasted, he used his penknife to wrench one of the lids free. And there were ten bags of coin, each printed "Imperial Ottoman Bank", each drawstring sealed with red wax, but hastily and variably. Some were barely sealed at all, and he lifted each bag in turn into the torchlight to pick those out. He got two, then took a second look at the others rather than open another box.

And that bag felt odd. He squeezed it again, feeling the tiny circles of coin, but those at the bottom seemed stuck together in a lump. Gold coins sticking together? That seemed unlikely. Holding it over the box, where fragments of sealing-wax might be expected, he picked the drawstring loose, opened the bag and felt down past the loose coins on top and brought up the lump. They were certainly glued together, but holding the lump closer to the torch he saw they were blank discs daubed with gold paint. Where the paint had scratched, dull grey metal showed through.

He sat back to think – but the first thought was that this was neither time nor place for thinking. He struck a match and re-sealed the wax, reloaded the box, finding other bags with lumps at the bottom – and then realised he had nothing to hammer the lid shut with except rubber boots. He took a big metal ashtray from the desk and used it to force the nails back by silent pressure.

Then he opened the curtains, took a last think around the dark cabin, and cautiously stepped out into the storm. Before he started working his way aft, he pitched his bag of shot into the sea.

"Nobody tried to come in," Lady Kelso reported. She sounded a little disappointed. "How did you get on?" Then she realised how wet he was. "No, you go ahead and change, I'll turn my back."

Modesty wasn't Ranklin's main worry: it was the steward finding his damp clothes in the morning, since nothing would dry in that cabin overnight. Well, he'd think of something. He changed his trousers, dried his feet, and lit a cigarette.

Lady Kelso turned back. "Well?"

"I found it. It wasn't even in the safe." He frowned, trying to think one step ahead of what he was saying. But she had to know most of it: suppose she was with Miskal when the ransom was delivered and he got furious at all treacherous Europeans? She wasn't planned to be there then, but this of all plans wasn't going to go to . . . well, to plan.

"And?" she prompted.

"Somebody's salted the sugar already: some of the bags have got discs of lead in at the bottom, stuck together so they won't spill out if you just checked the coins at the top. So I left them as they were."

"Dahlmann?"

"No. It would be cutting his own throat. Most of the coins are real, so he'd still be paying a good ransom for guaranteed nothing . . . Unless he's working to some 'fiendish plan', and he doesn't seem a man to believe in fiendish plans."

She was looking calm but curious. "Then who d'you think it was?"

"I think it all happened at the Imperial Ottoman Bank. Not by them, but there. I saw Dahlmann check the coins – dammit, I *signed* that I'd witnessed that . . . Then we watched the coins being bagged and sealed and nailed into boxes . . . Then I went off to change some sovereigns." And he'd rejoined the party as they were waiting for the last box to be brought up from the vaults – so Dahlmann couldn't have been watching all four boxes all the time. "They switched a whole box. At least one."

"Yes, but *who*?"

Hardly D'Erlon, it was his – one of his – banks' reputation. So who had muddied the waters by asking a British diplomatist and an American bankeress along to sign that the whole thing had been above-board? – and been careful not to be there himself? "Did you meet a chap they call Beirut Bertie at the Embassy dinner?"

"D'you think it was him? Yes, I met him. We had a long chat about the Bedouin, he knows the tribes very well. He seems to be very much on their side."

"That's what everybody says. So perhaps nobody thinks he might be working at his real job on the French side."

"Could he have arranged it?"

"If you've been around these parts as long as he has – it must be thirty years – *and* worked for the Imp Ott at one time, I fancy you could arrange anything." Provided, of course, that you knew well in advance what the money was wanted for.

"But aren't the French supposed to be our allies nowadays?"

"Yes, but are we acting like *their* allies? On the face of it, we're helping the Germans get the Railway restarted, aren't we?"

"I suppose so," she said in a small voice.

Ranklin shook his head wearily. "Everybody's cooking to their own recipe on this one: Germans, French, ourselves, Zurga's faction of the Turkish Government. God knows what it's all going to taste like." He roused himself: "Look: this may give you an extra card. If we get into Miskal's stronghold and you're still there when the ransom looks like arriving, you can warn him in advance that he's being cheated. Just so he doesn't get angry with you."

"Thank you." She cocked her head on one side; if she'd had her fan she would have waved it slowly. "When I first met you, I thought you were a bit of a fool. Now . . ."

Ranklin groaned to himself; he'd let the Snaipe mask slip. He rammed it back in place. "Oh, well, you know . . . I mean—"

"Yes, saying things like that."

"It doesn't do in the Diplomatic to seem too bright."

"It doesn't do to *be* too bright. Remember, I was married to one once. Good night, Mr Snaipe."

20

Although he slept deeply, Ranklin must unconsciously have noticed the storm passing because he woke unsurprised that the yacht was leaning but steady. It must have sails set again, and was just pitching slowly in a long swell. Cheerful with the sense of evil safely accomplished, which was turning out to be almost as good as a clear conscience, he went to order breakfast and then up to stroll the windward deck until it was ready. The sun was bright but not yet hot; in the Mediterranean, another month would make all the difference.

When he returned to the dining-saloon, Streibl was at the table, pale and full of apologies for his weakness of last evening.

Ranklin waved them aside. "Not your fault, old boy. Why, I had an aunt who used to get sick on trains. Carriages, too. In fact, come to think of it, she got sick whenever she felt she wasn't the centre of attention. So not really relevant. Forget I spoke."

But Streibl was already quite good at forgetting Snaipe had spoken, or even still was. "The steward said we will not be at Mersina until tomorrow night. I will ask if the wireless operator can . . ."

It sounded complicated, reaching a wireless station in Constantinople or, with luck, a ship in Mersina harbour, then telegraph via the Railway HQ or sub-HQ . . . In a few years' time the world might be gossiping as between adjacent chairs in a club – that was the sort of bright future O'Gilroy believed in, anyway. Ranklin had his doubts; if it happened at all, did he really want to listen to club bores on a global scale?

* * *

Some two hundred nautical miles behind and catching up, the *Vanadis* was bouncing along through what O'Gilroy thought was a tempest and Corinna a bright, if chilly, sunny day. He spent much of the time in his cabin – being sick, Corinna suspected – but it took more than that to overcome his Army and Irish habit of taking every meal offered.

So at least they met at the dining table. "It's all in the mind, you know," she said, knowing that wouldn't help but unable not to say it.

He just grunted. Repentant, she said: "I'm sure the Captain and Chief Engineer would be happy for you to look at the engines if you liked. Shall I ask?"

It was a canny offer: Corinna, too, knew his love of machinery and belief that it would bring an earthly paradise.

"And the bridge, and the wireless office and . . . the steering gear . . ." When she repented, she didn't stint.

* * *

Perhaps it is a maritime tradition that a fine day at sea should be spent inspecting the ship's stuffiest, smelliest compartments. Or possibly this is when the officers have time to spare for the passengers. Anyway, after lunch Ranklin, Lady Kelso and Streibl were given a briefer tour of the *Loreley*, just the bridge and engine room. She was impressed by everything and charmed everybody; Streibl asked some mechanically intelligent questions about the steam engine, but what struck Ranklin was the number of stokers needed in the boiler-room. All technical matters aside, the sight of those men sweating over their shovels, and knowing that when they reached port they must go on doing so to "coal ship", made a powerful case for switching to oil fuel.

And that, after all, was why he was here. That, and the fact that the world's greatest Empire didn't include a drop of useable fuel oil.

* * *

Corinna had got O'Gilroy's lost overcoat and headgear replaced from the ship's slop chest so that he could now look like an out-of-work sailor in dark-blue pea-jacket, muffler and peaked cap. *Could* because she had only once got him to put it on and take a walk on deck; now they sat at the round table in the saloon, each with a patch of paperwork spread in front. "Just like two children doing their assignments," Corinna commented, sitting back and stretching. "When do I get to mark yours?"

O'Gilroy looked up, hesitated, then said: "One thing mebbe ye don't know 'bout this Railway business—"

"I'm sure there's a lot I don't know and I prefer it that way."

"This bit isn't our doing . . . Ye know the money, the gold, ye saw at whatever-it-was bank? S'for a ransom on these Railway fellers, if'n Lady Kelso don't get them loosed."

"You mean this bandit is demanding a ransom? Then he's not going to settle for sweet talk from Lady Kelso. Does *she* know all this?"

"Surely. But seems she gave her promise to the Foreign Secretary, so she's got to go through with it."

"Poor woman . . . Bloody *men*," she added unspecifically. She thought about it, then: "But that isn't what you want to reach Matt to tell him . . . What is it?"

"I *think* it's that the Germans'n'Turks, they're planning to take artillery up into the mountains to deal with this bandit feller."

"Artillery into the mountains? Can they do that?"

"Mountain guns, special ones made so's they break down into mebbe half a dozen loads ye pack onto mules . . ." Loads that could also be boxed up and manhandled into a luggage van, an ox-cart, a launch, a yacht. "Our Army uses 'em in India, so probly the Germans make 'em, too."

"Are you saying that they could start *bombarding* this bandit hideout when Lady Kelso and Matt are still there?"

"I wasn't saying jest that, but . . . mebbe . . ."

Corinna took a careful breath, then pushed aside her own papers and assumed a formal, almost judicial, manner. "Right. I am now in session. You may tell me everything you know's going on, or can even guess at."

"I thought there was things ye didn't want to know—"

"I've changed my mind."

"Well, setting aside what the Captain and me's supposed to be—"

"No, *not* setting that aside, because I'm sure that's fundamental to this whole damn snake-dance. I want a full confession from you, Conall, and in case it helps, I'll make the position – your position – quite clear: you are not going to get off this yacht at Mersina until you have convinced me you've told me all you know or think you know.

"And," she added, "I am going to take a lot of convincing. You may start now."

* * *

It was the steward's idea that English ladies (particularly Ladies) took tea at four o'clock, rather than any hint from Lady Kelso, that had them sipping from the German Navy's best china when Streibl came in with a handful of papers. "I have been sending and getting messages . . . One is for you, Mr Snaipe . . . Had you lost your servant?"

"*Has he been found?*"

Streibl recoiled from Ranklin's vehemence. "Er, *ja*, yes . . . The message is that he will try to catch us up."

So O'Gilroy was all right – alive, anyway. "I'm sorry I jumped at you . . . Been a bit worried, you know . . . Feel such a fool, losing a servant . . . Er, it didn't say any more? – how he's going to catch up?"

Streibl re-read the message. "Only your Embassy told the vice-consulate at Mersina, and they told the Railway company."

Anyway, O'Gilroy was alive. Lady Kelso leant forward and laid her hand on Ranklin's. "You *were* worried, weren't you?"

"Well . . . Constantinople isn't London, or Dublin."

Lady Kelso nodded sympathetically, then turned to Streibl.

"Would you like a cup of . . . well, more-or-less tea? No? And is there any news about Miskal Bey? He hasn't let the hostages go?"

Streibl looked startled. "*Was*? Er, no, not at all . . . He says, I think, that he will kill them if he does not have the ransom in two days."

"You *think?*" she demanded.

Streibl had been reading from a form; now he consulted it again. "That is what it says. In two days." He checked the paper yet again. "It is most sad. For their families . . . It is most important." He looked puzzled, then embarrassed, then hurried out.

Lady Kelso looked at Ranklin. "If he *is* threatening to kill the hostages, and the ransom is . . . spoiled, then he *may* kill them. Oh Lord."

"I thought you didn't think Miskal behaved like this."

"I still don't, but now I don't know . . ."

"But I do know that Streibl's holding something back, or lying, or both." It was an unSnaipeish comment, but it seemed more important to calm Lady Kelso's fears. "He was reading that stuff, telling us what he's been told to tell us. He's out of his depth in this business; his job's steel rails, not people."

She certainly agreed with that. "Then what do you think—?"

"Just that we should wait and see."

She thought for a moment. "Perhaps we should—"

"*Neither* of us is going to search his cabin for those telegrams. Anyway, he'll probably keep them in his pocket."

She smiled, almost impishly. "He does seem to keep everything there. All right. We'll wait and *see*."

* * *

O'Gilroy was saying: ". . . and the way I see it, in the end they know there's only one way of dealing with this feller Miskal, and that's put him out of business permanent. I'm guessing, mind, but it seems good sense, they'll wait until he's got the ransom and let go the engineers, then . . ."

"And you think this is being run by a man Matt *knows?*"

"Not knows, exactly. Not met. Ye know he was fighting on the Greek side in that war in 1912? He was up against a Turkish gunner commander they called the Tornado, and that was all the Captain knew of him. So then there was this feller Zurga coming from Germany in the train with us, an Army officer but hiding it, we couldn't reckon what he was doing. Turns out it's the same feller, the Tornado, and him a gunner. And in the luggage van all these boxes, so now I reckon that's his guns, mountain guns."

"Where are they now, those guns?"

"Went on ahead by train to t'other side of the mountains. Mebbe in place by now, I don't know how far they have to be carried by mule."

"So they won't have to go through this Railroad camp?"

"Mebbe the Captain's gone by boat so's he won't meet the guns on the train. And mebbe there's another camp on the north side—"

"There'll be one wherever the Railroad's reached on either side."

"Sure . . . But guns alone won't do it," O'Gilroy said. "Never mind what the Captain would say. If'n that monastery's like I'd think it is, thick stone, those little mountain popguns won't knock it down. Not in a month. Not in a year. The bandit fellers'll hide in the cellars – I never yet heard of a monastery didn't have cellars – all snug and sound."

"Then—"

"—*only* they can't do that if there's troops likely to come charging in the front door. So they've got to stick their heads up and start getting them blowed off. That's when ye get the difference between a monastery and a fort: a fort's built to be shooting back when it's being shot at."

Corinna nodded. "So there'll have to be troops as well. How many?"

"Dunno. Haven't seen the place. But not less'n a hundred, a half-company, anyways."

"A hundred soldiers . . . There's probably garrisons in the

towns around there, Mersina and Adana." She assembled the thoughts in her mind. "And how much of this d'you think Beirut Bertie knows?"

"I reckon he started the whole kidnap-ransom end of it . . . He didn't know 'bout Zurga, not before he left, but the woman keeps his house in Constantinople, she worked it out and was going to telegraph him. Now I wouldn't be knowing how much she can say in a telegram, with the Turks reading it—"

Corinna shook her head, dismissing the problem. "If she can go through the French Embassy they can legally use code to their vice-consulate in Mersina. They might even get direct to the ship he's on if it's a French one, and it could be. One way or another, I think we assume he knows what she knows. Did that include the artillery?"

O'Gilroy swayed his head uncertainly. "Dunno . . . I don't think she knew Zurga was a gunner, jest an officer. And anyways she'd have to guess about them boxes being mountain guns, like I did, but – begging yer pardon – it doesn't seem a thing a woman would guess at."

Normally Corinna bristled at remarks like that, but in all honesty she couldn't this time. She herself wouldn't have guessed it in a month of Sundays. "Then what d'you think Bertie will do?"

"If he's going there, it's surely to see Miskal. Now he can warn him they're setting Zurga on him, but not about the guns."

Corinna nodded. "Then – I hate to say this – doesn't that make Bertie at least temporarily a good guy and if we meet, you're going to have to postpone hitting him with an axe?"

O'Gilroy nodded – grudgingly, since Bertie's attitude to *him* wouldn't have changed.

"And what," she went on, "are you going to do?"

"Get to the Railway camp and warn the Captain – if'n he hasn't gone to see Miskal already."

She considered this. "But if he *has* gone, our Turkish chums could start bombarding the place when they're still there?"

"Like I say, I'm not thinking it's likely—"

"*How do you know?* You only have to make one wrong guess and she'll be blown to bits."

"Now jest hold on." O'Gilroy felt he had been pushed, not fallen, into a trap. "The way I see it, the whole idea's they get their own fellers away from there, that's what the ransom's for, *before* they start shooting. And getting them away means getting her'n the Captain away, too."

Corinna was silent for a while. Then she said, more gently: "I spend my life helping people put together deals – agreements. Because that's what they are, they *want* to agree because it'll be good for both of them. And these are honourable people I'm talking about, doing business in a familiar way, wanting everything clear and above-board. And have you any idea how much sweat and fine print we have to go through and *then* how often it goes wrong in some particular?

"Now, here we have a rather different situation, on account it starts with a kidnapping and shooting, which is not a normal basis for agreement. But on top of that, there's you and Matt trying to foul it up, and Bertie trying to foul it up, and now this Tornado character bringing in artillery and troops to foul it up *de luxe* and –" she threw her hands in the air "– just don't tell me this is all somehow going to go *right*. This could be a catastrophe to make Noah think he just stepped in a puddle!"

But O'Gilroy didn't seem as impressed as she'd intended him to be, and she realised how pointless it was to talk to him of agreements and above-board deals. His life simply hadn't been like that.

"All right," she said. "But can we agree there's things we can't know or guess at?"

O'Gilroy shrugged and then nodded.

"Still," she conceded, "I do know the ransom is real. So I dare say we can count on them getting that to Miskal."

"And probly getting it back again," O'Gilroy suggested. "Shells don't kill gold."

No, she thought, this is *not* my world of gentlemen's agreements.

* * *

Even with the Captain and First Officer joining them at dinner they were still a small camp-fire group eating in the wide desert of a dining-saloon that could have seated twenty easily. Watching Lady Kelso as she smiled, listened, and commented in good German, Ranklin tried to imagine her at a real camp-fire in a real desert. He couldn't, though he was sure she would have been equally at home. The calm weather, presumably why the officers were there, had also been good for the cooking and German white wine didn't suffer from storms anyway.

Streibl was nervous and self-contained throughout the meal. Ranklin left him to the First Officer opposite, who tried hard but didn't get much beyond With Survey and Shovel Through East Africa. They went up to the saloon proper for coffee, one cigarette and one glass of cognac, then the officers clicked their heels and left. Almost immediately Streibl decided he had some papers to read, and went to his cabin.

"Yes, I don't think he does want us cross-questioning him," Lady Kelso said. "What on earth does a man like that read himself to sleep with?"

"*Der Kinderbuch von* five-eighths hexagonal nuts and bolts?"

She laughed. "Of course." She looked around the big, officially comfortable, saloon. It was arranged like a club-room, for a large party that might want to split into smaller conversational groups; unfocussed. "Can't we make this place look a bit more cheerful?" She turned on the only light that wasn't on already, a standing lamp bolted to the floor near a long leather sofa. Ranklin found a panel of switches and played around with them until he had the sofa isolated in light and just a few small wall lamps glowing between the portholes.

"Well done," she pronounced, and sat at one end of the sofa. She didn't sprawl as Corinna would have done, just relaxed her neat little body. "So we'll be at the Railway camp by this time tomorrow—"

"That's the plan. And until then, we wait and see." He sat down at the other end of the sofa.

"Then let's forget it for tonight. Tell me about yourself, Patrick."

Of course, most men would jump at such an opening. But for Ranklin it meant dredging up a lot of fiction about Patrick Snaipe and being alert for errors. And Ranklin didn't want to be alert; he just wanted to slump, conscious of her as a woman just a few feet away.

You do remember she's twenty years your senior, don't you? said some small inner voice. So what? – as Corinna would say. *Ah, I'm glad you mentioned Corinna* – Corinna is going to marry this French banker, we've said our good-byes, I'll probably never see her again.

"Are you married?" she prompted.

"Me? No. I—" He was going to say something about Army officers marrying late, which was true, before he remembered he wasn't an Army officer now. "I . . . just never . . ."

"Not every marriage is the right shape for the people in it . . . Did you meet that Mrs Finn at the British Embassy?"

"Er, yes. Yes, I did."

"I believe she's a widow, but she's the kind who could make a happy marriage because I'm sure she'd stand up and say what she wants. You can only accommodate so far . . . then you begin to lose what you really are yourself. Of course, most women aren't encouraged to have real selves . . . And most men don't want them to have, either.

"Mind you," she added, reverting to Corinna, "she could also make a disastrous one, far worse than an accommodating wife."

Ranklin didn't feel comfortable talking about Corinna. He wanted her out of his mind, leaving him in the present of that (fairly) cosy saloon, glass in hand, with the ship swaying and throbbing gently around them; not intrusively, just enough to remind them their surroundings were alive.

"Was your –" he'd been going to say "second marriage", but had it been only that? Had she "married" any of the Arab sheikhs she was credited with? "– your marriage to Viscount Kelso what you hoped for?"

She smiled reminiscently. "He was a sweet old thing. And pretty shrewd, not the fool he . . . well, his family thought he was. I think his son Henry never grew out of that stage when boys think their fathers are embarrassing old dunces. He – more likely his wife – had packed James off to visit the Holy Land – that's where we met – I think hoping it would kill him. So Henry could inherit the title and get on with a political career in the Lords. Political career!" She snorted delicately. "I suppose they might have put him in charge of Dog Licences if the Liberals hadn't swept the board, I think he could just about tell the difference between a cat and a dog. Though one can never be sure, since he married a mixture of both."

Ranklin grinned, despite a warning feeling that Snaipe should have looked shocked. "And were you happy?"

She didn't answer immediately. She sipped her cognac, cocked her head, looked slowly around the saloon. At last she said: "I was content, I think. I thought all of this –" the wave of her hand might have encompassed the whole of the Near East "– was behind me. I ought to settle down to a dignified old age – as near as I could get, anyway.

"I was pretty good at being accommodating by then, too," she added. She looked at her glass. She had placed herself with the light behind her, outlining her delicate profile, putting her face in soft shadow when she looked towards him. And why not? She really was deliciously seductive in a plain blouse and skirt; she didn't need the dressiness she had favoured on the train.

"And why are you looking at me like that?" she asked.

"You're a very attractive woman."

She smiled and looked away. "A lot of men, when they know something of my past, they make certain assumptions about me and just – try to – pounce." She looked back at him. "But not you. Does that mean you're an honourable man, Patrick?"

"Perhaps they think they are." It was certainly "honourable" to categorise women in such a way; only dishonourable to get it wrong.

"But you?" she persisted.

"I think I used to be, once. I tried, anyway."

She thought about that for moment, then asked: "Could you get me just a spot more cognac, please?"

He fetched the decanter and when he had refilled her glass, she laid a hand on his wrist. "I don't think you're really what you pretend to be. No, I'm not prying; I prefer you being a bit . . . mysterious. But if you wanted to, you could take the Honourable Patrick Snaipe's clothes off, as it were, just for tonight."

He took her hand and the pull she gave was so slight it could have been ignored without offence. Accommodating.

* * *

On *Vanadis* O'Gilroy was taking an after-dinner cognac, too. Actually, he was just finishing his second, or he might have felt too circumspect to ask: "Are ye going to marry this French banker feller, then?"

Billings had laid out his saloon far more personally, and for smaller groups. They were at the far end of it; in a house it would have been around a fireplace, but here it was just an alcove of dried flowers. Corinna, stretched out on a sofa, looked up from her book. "Yes, of course I am. Have you met Edouard? – no, probably not."

"Never at all . . . Ah, 'tis a good thing." He nodded. "Ye ought to settle down."

She sat up and swung her feet to the floor. "What d'you mean, *settle down?* It's as much a merging of interests, banking interests."

"So that's the way of it, is it?" He nodded again; a marriage that blended two plots of land to form one viable farm was understandable, too.

"I'll become a full, paid-up partner in Pop's Bank *and* in the merged one, if we go ahead on that."

"Ye mean, jest the same as yer husband?"

"Of course just the same."

"If ye say so." The disbelief in his voice was tangible.

"Now look: as far as capital and clients go I'll be bringing in just as much of a stake as he will. And I've just as much experience as— Why the hell do I have to explain myself to you?"

"Ye don't. Jest, I never knew a farm that worked with two farmers on it, is all."

"We're not *talking* about farms."

"Sure. Must be different entirely."

"You think just because Edouard's a *man*— Did Matt put you up to this?"

"Himself? He never said a word, 'cept that yer marrying this feller."

"I don't believe you." But she did; she just wanted to annoy him as much as he was annoying her.

It didn't work; he only shrugged philosophically. "Anyways, I think yer doing the right thing. Ye had yer bit of fun with the Captain, and—"

"It *wasn't* just a bit of fun! I—" So now she'd got her argument firmly facing both ways. "And what *fucking* business is it of yours, anyway?"

There, she'd done it: shocked him. But only by descending to bar-room language. She felt furious, and ashamed and . . . *furious.* If she'd been shorter, she could have flounced out; with her height, she had to sweep. And if she'd gone onto the deck she'd have frozen, so it had to be down the curling steps to the cabin deck, and going *down* was ignominious. So she reached her cabin in no better temper. Even slamming the door didn't help.

Damn it, she was *going* to marry Edouard. Even if Conall O'Gilroy . . . well, even if he approved of it. What the hell did she care about his opinion? He was so *conventional*, apart from being a spy and a gunman. And that went for Matt Ranklin, too. Just let them come around and see, ten years from now, if she wasn't happily married *and* an equal partner in the merged bank.

Ten years of being married to that man?

* * *

Her body was smaller than . . . More yielding, not leading, but instantly responsive to his every move, taking and multiplying his fierce joy . . . A small voice kept asking What did he think he was doing? But he wasn't thinking now, only doing . . .

21

Ranklin woke, in his own bed, slowly, luxuriously – and a bit guiltily. But why guilt? *You know perfectly well why.* That's nonsense; it's over. She ended it, anyway. *Did I mention a name? Perhaps I was talking about being true to yourself, to your own feelings* – So my feeling is that it's over and last night proved it – *it isn't as though you've much else to be true to, in this job . . .*

Lady Kelso didn't appear until midway through the morning, and then greeted him with just a warm smile. Yet it wasn't as if she were dismissing last night; he felt she was giving *him* the chance to dismiss it. If he wanted to recall it, she'd help; if he wanted it forgotten, she'd forget.

Feeling a coward, he said nothing and the day passed calmly, quiet as the sea and its misty horizon.

The *Loreley* eased cautiously into Mersina harbour soon after dark, and anchored a couple of hundred yards off-shore. The town was no more than a long jumble of yellow lights, dimmed by a mist gathering in the still air.

But the yacht itself was brightly lit and, standing by the rail, Ranklin and Lady Kelso had a good view of Streibl as he bustled up to them. It was a remarkable sight: he was wearing a yellow-and-bright-green check shirt over faded whipcord trousers and calf-length boots, topped by a black leather coat and a stained wide-brimmed hat. Ranklin's first thought was that Streibl had got his geography wrong and dressed for some Crossing-the-Line ceremony. His second was that this was how the railwayman dressed to build railways. And for the first time, Streibl didn't look rumpled; or rather, any rumpling looked *right*, as if this was the real him.

"We go ashore to the camp soon," he announced. "Please to dress in warm and not-so-good clothes."

Lady Kelso gave him a polite but definite Look; she didn't go in for not-so-good clothes. "I shall dress *warmly*."

But Ranklin could almost match Streibl. In his cabin he stripped and threw on a flannel shirt, riding breeches, ordinary boots, a fisherman's sweater and finally his armless mountain coat, a knee-length waistcoat of patchwork sheepskin. It had tufts of wool sprouting from every join and edge and when he had bought it in Peshawar bazaar it had been off-white. Now it was much further off.

He packed a bag of shaving kit, nightshirt and riding boots and little else, and took it on deck.

One of the cutters had been lowered and was being loaded, quite openly, with the boxes of ransom money. Ranklin looked away: now he knew the ransom was flawed, he wanted no part of it. Lady Kelso reappeared in remarkably short time, but all he could see of her dress was a long blue-brown fur coat. She was an experienced traveller and he fancied it would spend the night as a counterpane on her bed.

Ashore, there were cabs waiting to take them and the ransom – guarded by a couple of sailors with rifles – to the railway station where a tank engine and single carriage were waiting. Of Mersina itself, Ranklin got very little impression; he just assumed there must be a dazed fishing village lurking somewhere behind the piles of Railway ironware and half-finished European-style houses.

The carriage was short, with platforms at both ends, as used in German mountain railways, and the train started as soon as they and the ransom were aboard. For a while they ran straight and flat on a stretch of track that joined Mersina to the regional capital of Adana, forty miles off. Roughly halfway along, the Baghdad Railway would join it from the mountains to the north, and the actual junction had already been built: a spur that wriggled and climbed through a wooded river valley and ended at the work-camp itself.

The mist was thicker here, hiding any view or sense of landscape. The camp itself was – well, "built" sounded too permanent a word – it *lay* on perhaps the last flat land at the head of the valley, and it was a shapeless mess studded with flaring hurricane lamps.

Men swarmed around them waving more lamps, grabbed their bags, and straggled off into the darkness. They followed, across temporary sidings with rows of railway wagons, past a paddock with every sort of cart, past bales of hay, heaps of broken stone and more piles of railway ironware, and reached what must be the camp's high street. This was lined with a few wooden huts and a lot of ramshackle stalls and coffee-houses built of draped tarpaulins and carpets, all crowded with dark well-wrapped figures who were squatting, sipping and haggling as in any other bazaar. Blue woodsmoke drifted through the patches of lamplight, mingling with the smells of cooking, of paraffin, of animals and latrines. The street itself was water-filled ruts and everywhere the underlying *motif* was half-frozen mud.

This didn't surprise Ranklin with his military background. He was convinced that an army could camp on the driest part of the Sahara or an Arctic ice-floe, and within hours the place would be trampled mud. It was obviously a law of nature that touched armies of workmen too.

He had taken Lady Kelso's arm as she carefully placed her button-booted feet. "Would you mind frightfully," she asked, "if I said 'bloody hell'?"

"Please do."

"Bloody hell."

Then they were ushered up wooden steps – all the huts were placed well above the mud – and into what must be the German mess hall. It was bright and functional, with some small tables and chairs, some long tables and benches, a couple of stoves and, at the far end, a half-hearted attempt to create a lounge area of padded chairs, carpets and brassware.

Streibl had undergone an odd snowball effect, gradually becoming a small crowd of men in similar hats, shirts and leather coats who hurried up to clasp his hand; in his own world, he was obviously a grand panjandrum. Now the little crowd split, pulling out chairs for Lady Kelso and Ranklin, fetching them coffee, and introducing themselves. Streibl himself had vanished.

"Is this," their self-appointed German host asked, "how you expected it to be?"

"I don't expect things," she said pleasantly. And that, Ranklin thought, is probably true: her self-sufficiency lies in her talent to go from place to place, person to person, hoping for nothing but courtesy.

"We have for sleeping," the host went on, "the huts and the new tents. Do you choose . . .?"

"You say the tents are new? – so the insects may not have moved in yet? I'll take that."

He smiled at her foresight and, when Ranklin had also chosen a tent, went off to arrange it. The mess hut was gradually filling up – it must be nearing dinnertime – with German railwaymen, most dressed in Streibl's style. For a formal people, they really let themselves rip in the back of beyond – or perhaps they were copying pictures of American railway pioneers. Masculine groups were more susceptible to that than they admitted.

Then an exception was striding towards them in a long dark coat and a semi-official-looking black lambskin cap. He looked vaguely familiar, but Ranklin would surely have remembered that long ragged scar on the left jawline.

The man smiled and said: "Good evening, Lady Kelso, Mr Snaipe." It was Zurga without his beard.

He sat down. "In Germany I got tired of always telling how I got this." He tapped the scar. "So I grew the beard."

Ranklin nodded. "Quite . . . er, how did you get it?"

Zurga smiled thinly and, now that Ranklin was noticing, slightly lopsidedly. "A shell fragment when I was too near the battle for Constantinople fifteen months ago." So he was still pretending that he wasn't an army officer and hadn't been part of that battle.

Lady Kelso said firmly: "You look much more handsome without the beard – and quite dashing, with that scar. How did you get here?"

"I have been here since two days. I came by the Railway to the far side of the mountains and by horseback from there. You go to see the bandit Miskal tomorrow?"

"I believe that we're going to see Miskal *Bey* – as you are, of course? If I fail, that is."

Zurga nodded, a quick and then prolonged affair, as if he'd forgotten he'd started his head moving. Then he said: "Do you truly think I can persuade him if you cannot?"

She barely hesitated. "Not if you regard him as a bandit, no. Nor by appealing to any Ottoman patriotism. If you want to try arguing Islam with him . . ."

Zurga smiled. "He may not see me as a True Believer . . ."

Wasn't this just what she'd said to Ranklin on the train? But she could go no further with Zurga; women had no place arguing Muslim doctrine.

He nodded again, or perhaps he'd never quite stopped. "You think so also? . . . So perhaps, to save time, it is best I do not go, we just send the ransom – *if* you should fail. I must tell Dr Streibl . . ."

When he'd gone, Lady Kelso asked: "Were you expecting him to drop out?"

"More or less. We never really believed in his mission, did we? But he's here for some purpose, and that could make it more dangerous for you." He was in trouble here; the ransom had, through no doing of his, been sabotaged. But that might no longer be enough to keep Miskal delaying the Railway, not if Zurga was plotting something dire. He wanted to meet Miskal, see the situation . . . only perhaps that meant shoving Lady Kelso's neck into the noose . . .

Damn it, what he wanted was for her to *insist* on going so that it was impossible to stop her, whatever came of it. Please, *please* insist . . .

He said: "There's still time for you to back out, not go. I'll support you, here and in London."

"That's very sweet of you to say, Patrick – but I did agree and we've come so far . . ."

"If you really want that . . ." But he had said *back out*, hadn't he? – a phrase sure to raise her hackles and make her insist. He back-pedalled: "But I still don't like the idea of Zurga coming down here ahead of us. He's not part of the Railway, so what the devil has he been arranging, the last two days?"

But suddenly the German railwaymen noticed their guests had been left alone and rushed to show hospitality, burying them with friendly small talk. The atmosphere in the hall was cheery, bubbling over into frequent laughter. He had expected them to be gloomier, but perhaps their own arrival had brought hope, an imminent end to a frustrating delay.

* * *

The *Vanadis* churned at near-top speed through the quiet dark sea – though if O'Gilroy knew anything about the sea (he didn't) hurricanes and waterspouts were waiting at the next corner. So he was back at his favourite seat, as near the centre of the ship as possible, at the big saloon table.

Corinna came in and threw a sheaf of telegraph forms on the table. "We've been wirelessing everybody and everything. We should be at Mersina by dawn tomorrow but the Railroad *says* they can't be ready for me until the day after. Sorry and all that, but pressures of work and blah-blah."

"Day after tomorrow? Reckon to have Miskal all dead and buried by then, do they?"

"It sounds like it. Damn, damn, *damn*. And there's just about nothing I can do about it. Sure, I represent an important potential investor, but they're only saying if I wait twenty-four hours they'll have the red carpet dusted off and rolled out for me."

"Can ye jest arrive there without an invitation?"

"How can I? The Railroad itself is the only route to the

camp, no road or anything—" Seeing his surprise she said: "That's normal: a railroad becomes its own road. Once you've laid a bit of track, you use it to haul up what you need for the next bit."

She ignored his affront at her knowing more than he about such a masculine thing as railway building, and laid a small map on the table. It really was small, just a cutting from a German magazine showing the progress of the Baghdad Railway.

O'Gilroy leaned over it and identified a parallel rail and road (or track) joining Mersina to Adana—

"That's about forty miles," Corinna said. "That bit of railroad was built by a French company some years ago."

—and before that, a road branching off at Tarsus—

"Tarsus?" he queried.

"Yes. Where St Paul was born, wasn't it?"

—and heading inland over the mountains. And a few miles past Tarsus a rail spur doing the same thing: turning off inland, and ending after a few miles.

"That's where the work-camp is. That spur's about ten miles long and not open to the public. We *could* hire horses in Tarsus and ride up there alongside the railroad, but what would that do except show bad manners? And I'm sorry, but I can't do that to Cornelius Billings or the House of Sherring."

"But if they're jest keeping us out while they get into a barney with a bandit—"

"Even if I were supposed to know that, what's my complaint? It's not my business how they deal with bandits. More my business if they *couldn't* deal with them and let it delay them unduly."

O'Gilroy stared gloomily at the sketch map. "We're bug—stuck, then."

"I'm not so sure about that," she said thoughtfully. "We'll have all day tomorrow from when we reach Mersina. I assume Matt and Lady K will get on out to the bandit hideout first thing in the morning, so even if we were going to the camp, we'd miss them . . . Why don't we try to catch them at the hideout ourselves?"

O'Gilroy peered at the little map, but it barely showed the mountains, let alone a monastery tucked in among them. "Pity ye couldn't get a proper map—"

"There's likely no such thing. You're spoiled: Britain's probably the best-mapped place in the world. Down here, sailors have mapped the coast and archaeologists a few sites, but the rest –" she shrugged "– it's travellers' tales."

"Then any idea where this monastery place is?"

"None at all – except it must be somewhere north of the camp, more into the mountains. And there must be another way to it: a monastery will have been there hundreds of years before the Railway."

O'Gilroy nodded, then said: "I'm wondering where Bertie is."

"Oh Lord, I'd forgotten . . . Will he go to the camp?"

"Not him," O'Gilroy said firmly. "If he's conniving with this bandit feller, it's without the Railway knowing. He'll have his own road there."

"Probably the one we're looking for." She paused, calculating. "There's an American consul in Mersina, he'll have heard of the House of Sherring . . . I'll see if I can get a telegram to him."

She saw O'Gilroy's expression and shook her head. "No, not telling him anything except when we expect to get in. You don't give consuls time to think up more reasons why you shouldn't do something."

* * *

The Railway camp's dinner was good and plentiful, but it had the bland, uncertain taste of food prepared by cooks who weren't born to that cuisine and didn't really know if they were getting it right or wrong. Streibl and the camp *Aufseher*, an elderly white-moustached man in respectable clothes and obviously ex-military, shared their table. The *Aufseher* made the conversational running, asking about the London weather, music, the comfort of their journey – topics as bland as the food.

Halfway through, a younger engineer came in to apologise and call Streibl away. Lady Kelso and Ranklin avoided catching each other's eyes and both started talking simultaneously.

After coffee, they were escorted to their tents on a side street of grass as yet not quite trampled to mud. Lady Kelso's was guarded by by a Turkish soldier in a long overcoat, a slung rifle and a lambswool cap like Zurga's.

The floor of Ranklin's tent was raised off the ground by duckboards covered in old carpets (the one thing Turkey wasn't short of: in its lifetime a carpet could go from a wall hanging to a stall awning to being cut up for saddlebags). There was also a charcoal brazier – lit – and a washbasin and jug of water. Ranklin took off a minimum of clothing, washed perfunctorily, and was trying to organise his canvas camp bed for maximum warmth when Streibl and Zurga asked permission to come in.

"We have thought about a change to the plan," Streibl began awkwardly.

"That Zurga isn't going to see Miskal? We heard about that," Ranklin said, deliberately unhelpful.

"Ah . . . no, not about that . . ." Streibl sat on a camp stool. "But . . . will Lady Kelso herself take to Miskal the ransom?"

Ranklin hadn't expected that. His instinct was to stay as far clear of the ransom as possible. And it seemed reasonable it would be Snaipe's instinct, too. "No. Most certainly not. Surely, her mission and the ransom are alternatives. If you've decided she'll fail, send the ransom up instead."

"Perhaps, but—"

"I think you are *forgetting*," Ranklin said firmly, "that Lady Kelso is on a mission for His Majesty's Secretary of State for Foreign Affairs. The ransom is nothing to do with that. I must therefore advise her not to link herself with it in any way whatsoever."

Zurga was standing at the brazier, automatically holding out his hands to it, but so detached that Ranklin sensed he was, by now, in charge. He had abandoned more than the beard: he was now a soldier in soldier's country.

Gloomily, Streibl tried one more throw: "Then would she take a message to Miskal Bey?"

"Provided it is open, and I can read it, then I may advise her—"

"But surely—"

"Lady Kelso is not a courier for the Baghdad Railway Company. She is on a mission for His Majesty's Secretary—"

"Yes, yes. You have said that." He glanced at Zurga and got heavily to his feet.

Zurga asked: "May I ask where you obtained that coat?" He indicated the sheepskin affair now spread on the camp bed.

"My brother brought it back from India. He's in America at the moment, so . . . It seemed made for this sort of country."

"Most suitable. I ask because there was an Englishman who fought with the Greeks against us in 1912, an officer of artillery, and we heard that he wore such a coat. They called him the Warrior Sheep."

"Really? The Warrior Sheep? Most amusing." Ranklin forced a laugh. *Damn it! – to risk your alias with a scruffy old coat* . . . "Was he any good – as a warrior?"

"Perhaps." He stroked his cheek past the scar. "Or lucky. It is the same thing, for warriors, I think."

"Well," Ranklin said, determinedly cheerful, "he wasn't my brother, anyway. Probably some other chap who'd served in India. I think most of our officers do, sooner or later."

"Ah, India . . . always there are Englishmen fighting in other people's countries."

"I don't think it's only Englishmen; history's full of mercenary armies . . . The Irish fighting for Napoleon, the Pope's Swiss Guard . . . Perhaps warriors just gravitate to wars."

"Perhaps so. But they cannot expect to be loved by those who fight for what they believe. Or to be trusted."

Streibl was already halfway out of the tent and looking

impatient. Zurga gave a little smile, a nod, and followed. Ranklin sat down on the bed and wished he had a drink, a proper one. Perhaps Lady Kelso . . .

Ever the Compleat Traveller – more compleat than he, anyway – she had a small silver flask of brandy. Ranklin took it almost neat.

"I've just had a visit from Streibl and Zurga . . ." He told her about Streibl's requests and his refusal.

"What was all that about?"

"I'm not sure, but perhaps they've counted the ransom and found it lacking. And—"

"Do they suspect you?"

"Not of that . . . I'd have to have known about the ransom all along and come to Constantinople with a load of lead discs. But I dare say they'd like Miskal to suspect me. Anyway, getting us to take it to him would help blur the issue for them."

She thought this over. "But we *could* have taken a message for them. Then opened it and read it and found out more of what they're planning."

He looked up in astonishment: really, women had absolutely no standards. Also, why hadn't he thought of that?

"Er . . . yes. Bit late to change our minds . . . But may I tell you what I think?"

"Please do. What do you think, Patrick?" She was suddenly a dutiful little girl at kindergarten. "Or is your name really Patrick? I suppose it might not be."

Along with the smell of the charcoal brazier, there was a feminine scent in the air and even – remarkable in this landscape – the crushed-grass smell tents *ought* to have. They were sitting decorously apart, her on a stool, he on a spare camp-bed – *not* hers – and talking in little more than whispers.

"Never mind that . . . I now think the Railway's always had a three-step plan. First comes your appeal to Miskal. Then paying the ransom; I don't believe Zurga ever intended his own visit, that was just to explain him away. But then, when they've got their engineers back, they have to make sure Miskal never tries this sort of thing again. And the surest way to do that is kill him and all his crew. I think that's Zurga's real job, as an Army officer – only I can't guess how."

"Zurga can't do much just by himself," she said slowly. "He'll need . . . well, *something*. Have we seen any sign of that?"

"We wouldn't. Think about it: Miskal must know everything that goes on in this camp. Even now there's nearly a thousand workers here, I gather, and the people running the coffee-houses and stalls, men coming and going all the time. If I were Miskal I'd have half a dozen informers here."

"Yes, I suppose so . . ."

"And the Railway must know that. So whatever they're planning they'll keep it out of the camp. If Zurga's going to attack the monastery . . ." he paused, trying for the umpteenth time to work out *how*; ". . . he'll get there by some other route."

"And you're sure that's what he's planning?"

"Why else is he here? I think he's quite capable of storming the monastery while we're there and then saying Miskal killed us – except that might kill the hostages, too. The ransom shows the Railway hasn't abandoned them . . . And in a way, they've become hostages for *our* safety, now. But," he added, "when this is over, you might try and persuade Miskal to go back to the desert or wherever."

"And I told you, he doesn't *belong* in the desert – or 'wherever'." Her dutifulness was all gone now.

Ranklin made a vague helpless gesture. "He can't win against the Railway. It's just too big a project, thirty thousand men working on it in summer, so Streibl said. Nobody really controls something that size: it has its own momentum. If Miskal stays where he is, the Railway's going to crush him."

22

The *Vanadis* crept into Mersina harbour just before dawn. Or at least, that was where everyone on board hoped she was creeping through the dark mist. It was a tense, soft-breathing time. The engines churned slowly, almost silently, so the ting of the engine-room telegraph and the shouts of the man taking depth-readings in the bows were clearly audible. Corinna and O'Gilroy were up and watching from the portside rail, and they weren't alone: a surprising number of spare crewmen were there as unofficial lookouts, *willing* the land to show itself – but not too close.

"I shall be going ashore to wake this consul," Corinna announced. She was looking warm but not elegant in a coarse fur coat down to her knees and a hat tied on with a scarf. "Are you packed?"

"I am, but I've been thinking—" O'Gilroy began.

"Always a mistake," Corinna said, and if he had been listening properly, he'd have realised that wasn't a quip but a warning.

"It could be bad country up there . . ."

"You're going to get masculine and protective; I have perfect pitch for that. So you think I'll be in the way?"

The yacht's fog-horn let off a blast that made them jump. The sound faded, echoless, into the mist and nothing answered. It had sounded not authoritative but a plea.

O'Gilroy said doggedly: "I was near ten years in the Army, South Africa and all, and we was trained for this sort of thing . . ."

"I've ridden through rough country before. D'you know what parts of the United States are like?"

"Ye know I don't," with impatient sullenness.

"And you've never heard of Isabella Bird in the Rockies? Or Gertrude Bell, for Heaven's sake, in this part of the world itself and down through Syria? And what about Lady Kelso herself? – she's literally twice my age."

"But with the bandits and all—"

"There's bandits all over the world. And women die from tripping over carpets in their own drawing-rooms. I'm not doing something stupid and I'm not doing something I haven't done before. And I'm only doing it to help Lady Kelso out—"

"And there could be nearabouts a war starting up there! A shell from a mountain gun isn't going to stop and ask whose daughter ye are!" O'Gilroy flashed, now truly angry.

"No, and it's not going to rape me or take me hostage for being what I am. So at least I'll get fair treatment from *it!*"

Then a ripple of shouts and sighs ran along the deck as an irregular line of lights showed ahead – well ahead – and the shapes of other ships and their sparks of coloured light formed in the mist. The *Vanadis*'s engines beat more confidently and she swung in a half-circle, stopped and dropped anchor a couple of lengths from the *Loreley*.

* * *

Dawn came later in the mountains. Later than Ranklin had dragged himself from his tent, anyway. Some of the lamps hung on poles and stalls were still alight, defining the line of the camp's high street, leading the way towards the mess hall and coffee.

Streibl was already there, almost alone at this time, though there was clattering and chatter from beyond the partition to the kitchen. Ranklin mumbled a greeting and poured himself coffee, then flopped into a chair. After one cup – as a guest he was doomed to a small, polite demi-tasse while Streibl drank from a big mug – he helped himself to a fresh bread roll and potted meat.

Lady Kelso came in. At the time Ranklin was in no state to realise it, but she must have thought for weeks about what to wear for the moment when she would re-meet her Arab lover. And had decided on a tricky balancing act between East and West – but done with taste and expense. She might look just a dark bundle, but Miskal would appreciate the fine wool and silk, and see that the shawl she was obviously ready to use as a Muslim head-covering was in dark blue, not black. Both her own woman and a reminder that she had been his woman seemed to be the message; God knows if she'd got it right.

"And we're off as soon as we've finished breakfast?" she asked brightly.

"When you are ready." Streibl seemed sombre, subdued. "The horses are being saddled now."

"Are you coming with us?"

Streibl seemed surprised at the idea. "No, you will have a guide . . ."

Ranklin asked: "All the way there and back?"

"I think he will not want to go into Miskal's monastery, but—"

"Then may I see a map of the countryside, please? I'm still responsible for getting Lady Kelso back safely."

It probably wasn't secrecy that bothered Streibl, just the Hon. Patrick's intelligence. "Are you . . . do you . . . understand maps well?"

Coldly polite, Ranklin asked: "How many thousands of acres does *your* family own?"

* * *

As the mist lightened, the nearby *Loreley* took on colour as well as shape. A bugle sounded and a number of sailors hurried about her deck, but they looked as if they were just being naval, not useful. And the steam launch moored at her companionway looked cold.

Another ship had been hooting invisibly for twenty minutes; now she formed in the mist as the silhouette of a small liner and slid past. Just then, Corinna came back on board; she looked grim.

"I saw the consul all right," she answered O'Gilroy's querying expression, "and got the usual sermon about a woman's place . . . But worse, there's only one automobile in town that can take that caravan road, a Ford T, and it's been booked by telegraph from guess who? Yes, Beirut Bertie."

"Probly his ship now." O'Gilroy nodded at the liner.

She nodded. "A *Messageries Maritime* from Smyrna . . . how the devil did he get there? Anyway, are you prepared to be polite to him? . . . No: you'd better stay out of sight. *I'll* be polite – to start with. After that we can descend to blackmail and threats of violence."

The ride ashore in *Vanadis*'s launch was chillier than the still March dawn itself. The yacht's Captain, foreseeing himself having to report Corinna's rape/death/disappearance to Billings, had made just as much fuss as O'Gilroy. But she didn't want to start the trek already exhausted by argument, so cut him off by demanding a parcel of food – and a rifle for O'Gilroy.

That helped keep *him* quiet, fiddling with its unfamiliar lever action. It was a Winchester repeater with a feeble-looking short cartridge. "The gun that won the West," as the Captain proudly pointed out. O'Gilroy thought the West might have been won rather quicker with a rifle that fired further than he could spit, but said nothing.

There was a small crowd waiting at the iron quay and, in the roadway behind it, the deceptively spindly-looking and dusty Ford Model T, hung with extra tyres and petrol cans. Along the wharf, bundles and boxes of freight were stacked head-high and O'Gilroy faded away among those.

Bertie was the first ashore from the liner's launch, dressed for the mountains in a shaggy goatskin coat and riding breeches and carrying a small haversack and a leather rifle case. He directed a couple of porters to take his bags into the town, then turned towards the car – and saw Corinna.

He was startled but recovered quickly and raised his shapeless mountain cap. "Mrs Finn, is it not? I am most charmed to meet you – but surprised. I had not thought—"

"Mr Billings lent me his yacht. You recall he was thinking of buying those Baghdad Railroad bonds? And he wanted someone to look over the property."

"Ah yes, it is quite logical. Then you are about to visit the camp . . ."

"Not right now. They can't receive me until tomorrow, so I reckoned today I'd take a drive up the old caravan road. Only what do I find? – that you've booked the only automobile that could tackle that road. And I wondered . . ."

There was a small frown on Bertie's forehead, and behind it his mind must have been racing, yet he kept his lazy smile. "Ah . . . I would be, of course, delighted. I myself wish to spend some hours up there . . . But perhaps the driver can take you on, show you the Cilician Gates, and while it is hardly the weather for a picnic—"

"Matter of fact, I'd like to spend a few hours myself. Rescuing Lady Kelso from the monastery, a few things like that."

Bertie seemed to relax. He abandoned the smile, and his voice got more matter-of-fact. "Ah. Yes. But this is not just a girlish adventure, I fear. There is—"

"Oh, I know that. I may know it better than you. About Zurga Bey. Or Kazurga, actually, I think – the Tornado? – is that right? And what he's up to."

Bertie cocked his head on one side and looked at her. "I did not know lady bankers were so well informed. Yes, I got a message from Theodora . . . I wonder who you spoke to, Mrs Finn?"

Corinna gave him one of her wide, bright smiles.

Bertie went on: "I admit I should have been more clever . . . But I only heard of him as a man with a beard, and Turkish officers do not have beards. So I already know Kazurga Bey will be here . . . but you say you know what he is planning?"

"The price of that is a little ride up into the hills. And some help hiring horses. But I'll throw in keeping quiet about a French diplomat consorting with Turkish bandits."

"The Quai d'Orsay allows me much freedom . . . And by now I much prefer to work alone. So I must manage with just knowing that Kazurga is here." He put on an expression of regret. "I am most sorry, Mrs Finn, but I assure you it is for your own good—"

"Tell you what else I'll do," Corinna smiled. "I'll even try and persuade my friend Mr Gorman not to shoot you for past services rendered."

Bertie turned slowly, unalarmingly, and saw O'Gilroy behind him, holding the Winchester by his side, one-handed but with his thumb on the hammer.

"Indeed you talk to the best people," Bertie said. "And do you know? – suddenly, I find I am persuaded."

* * *

It was lighter when Ranklin and Lady Kelso came out onto the camp's main road, but the mist seemed thicker than the night before. In a city, where you expected vistas of only a few hundred yards at most, it would have been unnoticeable. Here, being unable to see more than half a mile (Ranklin reckoned) was confining and, on a ride in unknown country, could be confusing. He could feel the mountains all around; he just couldn't see them.

But he could see the camp plain enough, and last night's memory of it by lamplight now seemed romantic and charming. This morning it reminded him of photographs of mining camps in the Klondike and Yukon (where on earth *were* those places?): ramshackle, damp and grey in the grey light. It was coming alive, with well-wrapped shapes at the coffee-stalls. But it didn't look like the start of a working day; the whole camp hung in suspension, like the clouds of cigarette smoke in the still damp air above the stalls.

Nothing moved on the Railway itself and there was no engine in sight. He could now see where the tracks ran on, over embankments and through cuttings across the rougher land towards the head of the valley until the mist took over.

"Do you need to go to your tent?" Streibl asked.

Ranklin had on a motoring cap with ear-flaps, leather gloves and the pockets of his "Warrior Sheep" jacket were loaded. "Riding boots?" he queried.

"The stirrups are wide, so . . ." And that suited Ranklin: he would be more versatile in his ordinary boots.

Lady Kelso reappeared from the direction of the tents. "Did you get a look at your map?"

"Yes, I think I see the lie of the land."

Streibl led them to the horse and mule paddocks, over beside the sidings. A horse-holder was waiting with three shaggy little Anatolian ponies, already saddled and with a guide wearing an elderly Martini rifle – he wasn't a soldier; modern Mausers were one thing the Turkish Army seemed to have plenty of – slung across his back already aboard one of them. A saddlebag made (of course) of carpet seemed standard issue and Streibl tucked a couple of packages into them. "Some food from the kitchens . . ."

Ranklin said: "No spare mounts? If we get these railwaymen of yours freed, d'you expect them to walk home? Or us?"

Streibl looked momentarily blank, then stammered: "I understand they had horses when they were kidnapped. And I think it is not easy to lead one of these animals. They are not . . . not castr—"

"The word is 'entire'," Lady Kelso said crisply, "so they kick each other to death if they get too close."

"Yes. And I am sorry but there is no side-saddle—"

"Never expected one." She stood with one foot in the air until he realised she expected him to make a step of his hands, then trod into it and swung into the saddle, revealing that her skirt was some sort of pantaloon. Ranklin, of course, didn't look closely.

"I've ridden these things before," she said. "They're actually quite comfortable cross-country."

They were Turkish saddles, wider and shorter in the stirrup than the European version, and with wooden bits that Ranklin foresaw would rub at the inside of his legs. He had no particular qualms about the pony itself; he neither liked nor disliked horses, they were just the way Army officers got around.

It may have been her new height, but on horseback Lady Kelso had a brisk confidence. "And suppose Miskal Bey asks about the ransom, what should I say?"

"Ah . . . Perhaps you should not know anything about it."

"That's ridiculous. I'm not going to sound like just a pawn of your Railway. I shall have to say something – What?"

"Tell him . . . It is ready." Streibl was a rotten liar. Unfortunately, that didn't tell them what the truth was. "Perhaps you will make it . . . not necessary." Then he helped Ranklin into the saddle and stood back quickly as the horse-holder let go.

They followed the line of the Railway on up the valley. Looking back after ten minutes, Ranklin could see the camp in context. It spread over what would have been a meadow, just below a sweep of fir trees coming down from the mist and drifts of vividly fresh snow where the trees petered out. And at this distance, it looked like the sodden litter of a gigantic picnic. The next time he looked, it was gone in the mist.

He was glad to see his pony keeping its head down and watching where it put its feet on the rock-strewn ground. He let it pick its own pace, and guessed it would do so no matter what he wanted; it knew who knew best. They crossed a short bridge where the river turned aside, then dismounted and walked the horses through a quarter-mile tunnel, carrying torches of tar-dipped stick. The flaring light glittered off rough-cut walls streaming with damp. This was limestone country: soft grey-white rock that was easy to tunnel through but impossible to waterproof.

The tunnel ended virtually in mid-air and actually on a short stone-built platform, guarded by two soldiers, which must be the start of a future bridge. Across the valley the real mountains began: a slope that steepened to near-vertical as it reared up and became lost in the mist or cloud. From its sheer bulk it must be miles thick at this level; a dent had been blasted out of the rock opposite, and some scaffolding erected where the far end of the bridge would rest, but that was all.

"Is this according to the map?" Lady Kelso asked.

"Yes." It had been rather a crude rough blue-print Ranklin had been shown; he had been surprised not to see a proper survey map – they must have one, to be building in that countryside – but perhaps it was too precious. Or Streibl hadn't trusted Snaipe to understand it. "They're going to put a bridge across this valley, then tunnel through the mountain on the far side."

So this, presumably, was where work had ended when the engineers got kidnapped. From here itself? The impression of a frontier was emphasised by the the clutter of brazier, coffee- and cooking-pots; this was a permanent guard-post.

"Where do we go?" she asked, as the guide doused the torches in a jar of water obviously kept there for that.

"Down there." Ranklin pointed to a fresh but already well-used path running sideways down the slope to the right. "There's a river at the bottom, you can't see it from here, and we follow it. The monastery's . . ." He gestured vaguely half-right, to the north-east.

* * *

The Ford didn't get its first puncture until they had turned off the main road just past Tarsus (whose scruffy houses and snarling dogs had disappointed O'Gilroy; he'd expected a place mentioned in the Bible to be more . . . well, at least *respectable*). They stood by the roadside while the Greek driver changed a wheel.

"Tell me something," Corinna asked. "How did you get to Mersina so fast?"

Bertie considered and decided it need be no secret. "The *Ministre de la Marine* was kind enough to have a destroyer awaiting me. At Smyrna I caught the normal steamship from Athens."

Corinna was impressed, but Bertie shook his head. "Fast, but in no way comfortable. Now please, tell me: are all American lady bankers as . . . forthright as yourself?"

"Far's I know there's only two of us. And the other, who'd

better stay nameless, does it all through her husband the bank president. On account of a little mistake he once made that she covered with her own money. She's very successful."

"Yes, I think I see a connection . . . May I also ask, have you known M'sieu Gorman for long?"

"A little longer than you."

"And you know him—?"

"Maybe a little better."

"I understand." Then he shook his head irritably. "No, I do not understand at all . . . But of more importance, you were to tell me what Colonel Kazurga Bey plans."

"Mountain artillery," O'Gilroy said.

"The Turkish Army has no mountain guns."

"Came with us from Germany in the train, in those boxes yer fellers 'n me saw loaded on the launch at Constantinople. Did they tell ye about them dropping a box and diving for cover? Reckon that was some of the ammunition."

"The boxes, *naturellement*. My men guessed only explosives. And now I remember, Kazurga is an artilleryman . . . You say it was in the train with you?"

"Joined us after Basle, before Friedrichshafen." He couldn't remember the name of the station where they'd met the second carriage.

"Bavaria – of course. One tests a mountain gun in mountain country, no? And Kazurga Bey at the same time?"

"He'd come aboard at Basle."

"Close enough. So: they were teaching the Tornado of their new mountain gun when *voilà*: a perfect opportunity comes to test it in action. And far better if it is commanded by a Turk when used against a Turkish citizen – which, however reluctantly, Miskal Bey is still.

"And after this demonstration," he went on thoughtfully, "of course the Turks must buy such a wonderful weapon. In the midst of peace we are in war, and in the midst of war we are in salesmanship. How truly wicked this world is."

* * *

After a few minutes of switchbacking along beside the river, Ranklin realised they were still on a path, but now a much older one. No particular thing told him that, it was more the ease with which they moved. As if, for centuries, people had walked and ridden this route and paused to push aside fallen rocks and trees or kick stones to fill up gulleys. So perhaps this was was an original route to the monastery. There had to be at least one.

After maybe a mile, the guide led them across a shallow patch, over a wide beach of shingle and up beside a smaller tributary flowing from the north. On its far side a slim shaft of darker rock, five or six hundred feet high, rose abruptly from wooded foothills.

The guide said something to Lady Kelso and she turned in the saddle to Ranklin. "He says that modesty forbids him to say what the locals call that peak. So now we know."

Ranklin tilted his head to squint upwards. Well, it was . . . distinctive. And would be a useful landmark in clearer weather.

After a while they turned east again, down a widish and virtually dry valley. Ranklin had a military eye for landscape – he couldn't help choosing sites for artillery wherever he went – not a geologist's understanding of how it got that way. But he knew from experience that in limestone country rivers could suddenly decide to flow underground instead, leaving dry beds above. Here "dry" was a relative term: the old stream bed was at least damp, its centre patched with grass, bushes and the occasional reeds of boggy stretches. They stayed on the firmer shoreline with its intermittent patches of shingle beach.

For nearly a mile they followed the curves of the dry stream. The left side was a bank averaging fifty feet high and dotted with thin pines; on the right steep slopes swept up to the distinctive peak. Then the left bank rose and was suddenly split by a sheer-sided ravine nearly a hundred feet high that let out only a small, apologetic stream which shuffled around fallen boulders and vanished quickly into a marshy patch. The guide stopped, pointed, said something.

"He says," Lady Kelso interpreted, "that we should climb the bank over *there*–" beyond the ravine "– and keep going for about a mile, with the ravine on our left."

"That sounds like good-bye."

"Up there counts as Miskal's land. On a clear day we'd see the monastery from the top of the bank."

* * *

Before the Ford reached the turn-off to the monastery, the caravan road had woken up and they were meeting long strings of laden mules, pack-horses and especially camels, plodding and gurgling down from a night-stop further up. It was a scene that might not have changed in over two thousand years.

"I suppose the Railroad will wipe this right out," Corinna commented.

"Perhaps." Bertie looked philosophical about it. "But on smaller roads . . . I think Turkey will never have railways like France and England."

The monastery route was just a track leading up towards a low pass on the tree-covered slope beside the road. It was marked by a small *han* – what might charitably be called a wayside inn but here a small rundown building for travellers and good, big stables with a dozen and more horses. The proprietor knew Bertie and they all sat down to tiny cups of coffee and, it seemed to Corinna, just as tiny steps in the negotiation process.

She was about to get impatient, then realised that Bertie was in just as much of a hurry, and if there were a faster way of doing things, he'd be using it. It was nearly twenty minutes before they got up and went out to choose horses.

* * *

Ranklin and Lady Kelso zigzagged the horses up the bank between the under-nourished pines and found themselves on the edge of a flat plateau of bare rock that stretched ahead, sloping sightly upwards, until the mist took over.

It was so surprisingly open and exposed after being dominated by the landscape for nearly two hours that they stopped. After a while, Ranklin unbuttoned his coat to use his field-glasses, but until he looked back at the Peak and other slopes behind them, there was virtually nothing to see. There must be mountains somewhere off in the mist ahead, but here he couldn't even feel them.

He let the glasses dangle from their strap, but Lady Kelso seemed in no hurry to get moving again. Perhaps, one short stage from the whole point of her mission, she needed time to prepare for that step.

Or just to talk. "Can they really build a railway through all this?"

"Not this bit. They're sticking to the solid mountains." He gestured backwards, west. The German taste for tunnelling made more sense now that he'd seen something of the country. It was probably simplest to say the hell with trying to follow twisting dead-end valleys and just tunnel a straight line: once you'd done that, you were at least safe from weather and landslips. Judging from the rocks around, this land didn't need much excuse to slip.

"I still wonder if the whole thing . . . it isn't that dreadful mummified little banker Dahlmann just *using* Dr Streibl to make his own dream come true."

Ranklin shrugged his eyebrows. "Well . . . perhaps no more than Streibl's using Dahlmann. He has romantic dreams of turning the golden road to Samarkand into steel rails with Dahlmann paying for it. Millions of Reichsmarks, and Streibl probably doesn't care if it makes a penny in return. And he's only romantic up to a point: he'd see Miskal Bey squashed like a fly for Standing In The Way Of Progress."

She hunched, self-protectively. "And the Kaiser's using both of them – is that what you think?"

"I don't know about the Kaiser, he sounds as much of a romantic as Streibl, but the military and the Wilhelmstrasse, yes, perhaps so."

She said nothing but didn't move, either. To seem politely

busy, he found his prismatic compass and took a sight on the Peak; although it was just a faint silhouette by now, it was still too close, filling some twenty degrees of arc.

Then she sighed and said: "Everybody *using* everybody else . . . and I suppose Sir Edward Grey's using me – and you?"

"I seem to be working to the Foreign Office which may or may not be working to Sir Edward. We're getting contradictory signals from that building."

"Oh, that's just policy as usual." She was quiet for a while, then: "And I suppose I'm using you all – or this occasion. I didn't *have* to come . . . Will you be honest with me? Am I more likely to get my foothold in English society by getting these people freed or keeping the Railway delayed? You said you'd answer honestly."

Ranklin hadn't promised any such thing, but decided to be honest anyway. "Frankly, neither, I'd say. Just Thank you and farewell."

After a time she said: "Yes. Yes, *that* sounds like policy as usual . . . I wonder if you said that to set me free?"

"Does it make you feel free?"

"A bit . . . But a bit late." She sighed and, at last, urged her pony gently forwards.

23

A few minutes up the slope from the caravan road *han*, Bertie reined in his pony and pointed to a muddy patch trampled by dozens of hoof-prints. "You see? The keeper at the *han* told me that thirty mules had come by soon after dawn. And ten or twelve soldiers, German and Turk, walking. I wonder," he smiled, "if I would have deduced for myself . . . No matter now. But how many guns on thirty mules?" he called, moving on. "Three? Four?"

"Jest two at most," O'Gilroy called back. They were on Anatolian ponies too, and keeping their distances. "Remember yer ammunition." He was trying to work it all out himself, but he'd never officially served in the Royal Artillery so his figures were distant memories or guesswork. But he knew a mule could carry around two hundred pounds, so one gun would be six or seven mule loads – probably – and each round of ammunition must be about . . . say two eight-round boxes to a load . . .

"Ye'll only have two hundred and some rounds anyways."

"That sounds *quite* enough," Corinna chipped in. But O'Gilroy's only experience of gunnery had been in war, when the gunners never had enough ammunition, and he shook his head like a sage old soldier.

* * *

The plateau Ranklin and Lady Kelso were crossing must have begun as one great sheet of rock, then cracked and weathered to look like giant light-grey cobblestones stretching up and away into the light grey mist. A few timid patches of grass grew where soil had lodged in the cracks, but not a tree in sight, just bushes sheltering in occasional deeper cracks like trenches. It was colourless, bleak and very exposed.

It was also very quiet. They had prompted a few bird-calls back among the trees, but here there was no sound but the horses' hooves and the burble of their breathing. Without mankind, and when the weather had taken the day off, the world was a pretty silent place, Ranklin reflected.

But now Lady Kelso had found an excuse to stop again and was digging in her clothing. "Would you like some chocolate?"

Ranklin dismounted rather than bring the ponies too close. "Thank you." It was a plain Swiss chocolate bar, a bit melted from her body heat.

"I bought a lot of these in Constantinople. God knows what Miskal will give us." She stared around. "Goat, probably. If you can't see anything worth eating, it's goat country."

Ranklin took the opportunity for another stare around through the field-glasses, but learnt little except that he couldn't see the monastery yet. The edge of the ravine lay a couple of hundred yards to the left, and the land beyond it looked much the same as this plateau, except that where the mist took over, it was rising into trees and rocks.

She said: "You know, Patrick, I'm very glad you're with me . . . I didn't think so to start with, but . . . Do you really belong to the Diplomatic?"

"I seem to be working for them, anyway."

"But are you really . . . ?" She left a blank for him to fill in.

But Zurga's probing about the coat had rewoken his artillery past. That, and this landscape: for him, spying had so far been a city thing.

"Right now, I'm not absolutely sure what I am. You'd better just think of me as more-or-less representing our Government." And shading towards the "less" with every step, he thought dourly. He tucked away the glasses and remounted.

A few minutes later they came to a deeper trench, a fissure that had become a natural storm drain, lying across their path so that its end spilled into the ravine. It was perhaps six feet deep and had collected enough soil to be half-full of stunted bushes. But it wasn't difficult to cross because its sides were quite gentle, if irregular, slopes.

Lady Kelso said: "Isn't that the place?"

Ranklin looked up. He'd been expecting something tall and rectangular and it wasn't, it was remarkably low, but it was an unnatural darker outline in the mist getting on for half a mile off.

"Must be." Then a glint among the rocks at the lip of the trench caught his eye. He dismounted and picked up a spent rifle cartridge case. It hadn't been there long enough for the brass to tarnish. "It looks as if the Turkish soldiers attacked up this way."

"It's probably the easiest way."

"It must be the only way." Or why advance across such open ground, visible for nearly a mile on a clear day? But they'd only expected to face old *jezeel* muskets with a range of a couple of hundred yards, and slow to reload. He could guess what had happened then: the defenders, if they knew their business (and the result suggested they did) had waited until the soldiers had got well past this trench and then opened fire. And the surviving soldiers, knowing there was cover behind them, had turned and run for this trench. Once men have run away, it is very difficult to start them forward again. The survivors would have stayed in the trench until darkness, then sneaked off.

And now it was their turn. Was anybody watching them yet? There should be, but a guard can get very bored, staring into mist. They might do better to let off a yell or a pistol shot and make sure they *didn't* surprise anyone. He had an uneasy urge to let Lady Kelso go first and, because of that, knew he must himself. He tossed the cartridge case aside and mounted.

Lady Kelso pulled her shawl over her head and threw one end over her shoulder, half-veiling herself. "I'm ready, Patrick . . . *Is* your name Patrick?"

"Matthew." Ranklin stretched in the stirrups, waved, and shouted. He realised it had been "Ahoy!" – which was a bit nautical, but what should it have been?

A few moments later there was a shot.

"It's all right, Matthew," she said. "That's a normal Arab greeting."

Ranklin swallowed. "I'm glad you can tell."

* * *

Centuries ago, the monks had tried to surround the building with gardens; probably they'd had to carry in the soil. Now there were just a few square yards of coarse grass and small bushes, but still enough to hold the thin soil in place. And the building itself had lasted even worse.

It had always been small; now time, weather and looters had worn it down to a large sheep-pen with thick, stunted walls hardly more than head-high in most places. Avalanches off the slope behind had played a part, too: embedded in the back wall was a boulder that must weigh dozens of tons and now seemed part of the structure, except that the wall was cracked and bent around it.

Inside the empty gateway all interior walls had vanished, and the floor – cracked flagstones and drifts of trampled turf – was half covered with tents that, rather refreshingly in that gloom, made it look like an Arab encampment. These weren't the European-style bell tents of the work-camp, but heavy, dark draped affairs: "houses of hair", according to Lady Kelso, so perhaps they were of woven camel hair. Carpets were spread under the raised flaps, and there was even a cooking fire burning.

After some ceremonial chatter, she with her eyes demurely downcast, the apparent leader (not, Ranklin gathered, Miskal himself) had taken Lady Kelso down stone steps to a cellar beneath – presumably where the hostages were held. Their horses had been led off to some paddock behind the building, and now Ranklin was alone with some twenty-odd dour-looking Arabs.

Travelling artists and writers are very precise about how different tribes or clans of natives dress. The problem, Ranklin had found in his own travels, was that the natives didn't always know this. Either because they couldn't afford the "proper" dress or it was in the wash or because it was just too cold, they wore whatever they'd got. There was a general tendency to baggy, very off-white trousers and turbans – not the flowing *kefiyah* desert head-dress – but the rest was a wild variety that included some Turkish Army great-coats and boots, and blankets worn like shawls.

But almost every one carried a modern Mauser rifle, as if it were part of him.

None of them said anything. He thought of offering his cigarettes, but they wouldn't go around. So in the end he just hummed to himself and wandered to the east wall in a gap between tents. In clear weather he could have seen for miles in any direction except to the north where the steep slope rapidly became sheer; it was as if the old monks had been saying Hey there, look at us being lonely. It would have been quite a good place for a fort, if there had been anything to guard except the ravine, about fifty yards off.

Then one of the Arabs came up to him and pointed towards the cellar steps. Ranklin followed obediently.

Down there was one biggish room criss-crossed with heavy arches that made it a collection of dark alcoves. Three primitive oil lamps glowed on the rough-hewn stone and flickered as people passed. Ranklin was led to where Lady Kelso was kneeling and wiping the brow of an old man wrapped in a blanket. He had a grey beard, long grey hair and the eyes in the lined, gaunt face were half-open but not seeing anything.

"Miskal?" he whispered.

She nodded. "I think he's dying. It could be cancer, I don't know."

"Is he in pain?"

"How can you tell with these people? They will be so stoical. And stuffed to the gills with opium. Thank God for that."

Ranklin looked down at the bundled figure. They seemed to have come so far, and now they had found him . . . he was just this.

She stood up. "I've told them that you are my 'brother in the book of Allah'. It means we can be alone together without it being immoral. It's more for your sake than mine: they see me as one of Miskal Bey's old whores and nothing . . ." She let her voice trail off, then rallied: "So I *was* right about the ransom demand: it wasn't his idea at all, it was his son Hakim. Oh – and they've let the Railway engineers go. A few days ago."

She had just thrown in the news as an afterthought. Ranklin stared. "They did . . . *what*?"

"Let them go. It seems that Miskal had a . . . a lucid period and asked who these captives were, and came down on Hakim like a ton of bricks for doing anything as shabby as taking hostages for ransom. And insisted they be let go. So they were."

Ranklin recovered a little from his daze. "But dammit . . . the Railway must have got them back before we got off the boat. Why did they let us come? Or go on with the ransom?" Fleeting thoughts of Dahlmann and Streibl providing fraudulently for their old age galloped through his mind – and out again. Too many people knew, or soon would.

"We-ell . . ." She hesitated. "Hakim isn't being very confiding about this; perhaps you'd do better, he speaks pretty fair French. And," she lowered her voice, "I get the impression he hasn't got a firm grip on these people. Perhaps it's his father still being alive, perhaps he just isn't the man Miskal was." She said that with feeling. "And I also have the impression he's still expecting to collect the ransom."

"For what, for Heaven's sake?"

Actual shrugging wasn't what ladies of her generation did; but she *looked* a shrug.

Ranklin felt trapped, and couldn't help looking around at the dark corners. "I don't like this at all. They knew we'd find out they'd deceived us, yet . . . I think Zurga must be close behind and I'm not sure we're supposed to come out of this alive."

She took that with complete calm. She had her job – Miskal

– and there were twenty-something men to worry about the rest.

Ranklin went back upstairs.

Hakim was standing in the gateway with another Arab, staring back along the plateau. If there was any family resemblance between him and the bundled old man downstairs, Ranklin couldn't see it, except for the large hooked nose usual among Arabs. Hakim's face was slightly chubby, and although taller than Ranklin he was shorter than most of the men around. Perhaps that didn't help his authority, and for that much Ranklin sympathised. His one badge of office seemed to be that he wore both a bandolier and a belt of cartridges – sheer unnecessary weight. That apart, he had a short beard and his age might be anything between thirty and forty; with different races you just couldn't tell.

"Hakim effendi – *je crois que vous parlez français?*"

Hakim worked out what Ranklin had said, nodded and led the way to one of the largest tents. They squatted on a carpet under a part of it held up as an awning, and Hakim called an order towards a group by a smouldering fire. Ranklin offered a cigarette and it was accepted with a grave nod.

"Your journey was good?" Hakim asked in French.

"It was not difficult. I am very sorry to learn of your father's illness . . ." The small talk went on while they attuned themselves to each other's accent. French might be beautiful, but it lacked the clarity of German when spoken in such situations.

Finally Hakim said: "You came to plead for the release of the Railway engineers."

"So we thought. The Railway forgot to tell us they had been let go. But His Majesty's Government does not mind the delay to the Railway."

Hakim thought about this. "And your country is a friend of France?"

"On most things, yes." Hakim should understand friendship being qualified at a diplomatic level – but how did France suddenly get involved? Beirut Bertie? – Ranklin began to sense his – doubtless delicate – footprints.

Hakim asked: "Is the ransom money ready to be paid?"

"I think most of it. But it is not complete. Some person has taken some of the gold and put in lead."

"Will the real gold be sent?"

"I don't know – but why should it, if the Railway engineers have been sent back?"

Hakim might have been thinking; equally, he might be deliberately but politely keeping his thoughts to himself.

Ranklin tried another approach: "They have brought in a soldier: Zurga Bey, a colonel, I think." Hakim showed no sign of recognition. "I believe they plan to kill you all. Your father, too."

"They have tried already."

"They won't make the same mistakes this time. They know about your rifles, they've had time to plan. Now they have at least a machine-gun." But without knowing just what Zurga planned, Ranklin was fencing in the dark. He wanted to be straight with Hakim – within moderation – but most of all he wanted to impress him. And had no feel for what would.

Apparently not a machine-gun. "A machine-gun is just like many rifles, no? And a hundred rifles could not capture this place. Not five hundred."

As an ex-soldier Miskal might have had a better idea of what a machine-gun could do, but Hakim did have a point: Zurga would need more than machine-guns against walls several feet thick.

A boy, perhaps a servant or slave, brought across a brass tray of small, delicate coffee cups that seemed out of place in those rough-hewn, run-down surroundings. But there was no elaborate ceremony, pouring the first cup into the ground as a libation, such as Ranklin had read about. Hakim murmured something and drank and Ranklin did the same.

"Also," Hakim said, "they will not attack while you and that woman are here."

"I think they will. Else why did they let us come when the

railwaymen had been released? So I think the Railway would rather we were all killed together. Then they could say you – your father – murdered us and they were just taking revenge to please my Government."

Hakim scowled and his brown eyes glittered. "They cannot say that!"

"When we are all dead, they can say anything they like."

Hakim went on scowling, then returned to his earlier conviction: "But they cannot kill us here."

Ranklin suppressed a sigh. People had roosted smugly in "impregnable" fortresses since time began; meanwhile even flies had learnt better than to sit around while you fetched the swatter.

Maybe he should say that, but Hakim was still no soldier. So instead he asked bluntly: "What do you still have that is worth a ransom?"

Hakim hesitated.

"The Railway already knows. Who can I tell?"

"They . . . things. To make a plan. A . . . map." Hakim was out of his depth here.

"Can I see these things?"

Another hesitation, then he called the boy and sent him into the tent. He came out laden with a plane table – just a fancy drawing-board, really – a satchel of drawing instruments, a theodolite, notebooks – and a roll of paper.

And now Ranklin understood.

He should, of course, have guessed – or deduced. Streibl, sent to take over, wasn't a mere engineer, he was a railway planner – a surveyor. As the hostages had been. The paper, once unrolled, was what he now expected: a hand-drawn but very precise survey of the whole area, with trig points, spot heights and bearings neatly enumerated in Indian ink. The notebooks seemed to be about types of rock found, cross-referenced to the map.

This was what you needed to build a railway – and if you hadn't got it, you must take weeks or perhaps months to do it again, with thousands of workmen standing idle in the building season. Certainly worth a ransom to start with, and now worth all their lives – when Zurga rescued it from among their corpses.

He looked at Hakim curiously. "You do realise that by hanging onto this stuff, you've told them you understand its value? And now they can't pay the ransom, they have to storm this place to get it back? Did you, or your father, understand all along how valuable this was, or did someone . . ." He left the question unfinished: the answer had to be Beirut Bertie. Sabotaging the ransom, probably providing the rifles, even triggering the whole kidnap from the start; the man who knew this country and its people better than any European he'd met. Yes, our Bertie would understand the value of a survey.

He rubbed a hand over his face. So they had Bertie doing his best for France, Dahlmann and Streibl their best for the Railway and Germany, Zurga for his vision of Turkey, and himself and O'Gilroy putting in their few penn'orth for Britain. None motivated by self-interest, all honourable men.

God save the world from us honourable men.

24

"Please to be quiet as we pass here," Bertie warned. "Above, there is a tunnel for the Railway, and it is guarded. But they cannot see this path, so . . ."

Soon after, an obvious path joined from that slope: the one Ranklin and Lady Kelso had descended from the tunnel a while earlier. And soon after that there was a damp, muddy patch and Bertie paused to study it. When O'Gilroy reached it, he saw that dozens of boot-prints had wiped out any mule-tracks. So now they might run up against the backside not only of mountain guns but their accompanying army.

Where the tributary joined, Bertie led across to the broad shingle beach and stopped there. "They have brought up soldiers by train," he explained. "Probably from Adana. From the tunnel to the monastery they have to march . . ." he shrugged ". . . less than two hours. They must attack from in front, there is only one way, but the guns . . . What range do they have?"

"Mountain guns? – no more'n two-three miles."

"So they may be up on the plateau or could be in the dry river before it." He gestured beyond the distinctive peak. Corinna had been looking up at it, aware of what it reminded her of, but assuming that was just her, and its real name was Flagstaff Mountain or Finger Peak or something.

"In such mist," Bertie carried on, "where would they put the guns?"

O'Gilroy knew the general principles of gunnery, and how to serve a couple of specific types, but of their tactical use . . . He shook his head. "No idea at all."

"Then we can only assume they go no further than they

must, and at any moment . . ." He got carefully off his horse, slid the hunting rifle from its scabbard – and pointed it at O'Gilroy.

"Please drop the rifle. I trust it is not cocked? Ah, thank you." O'Gilroy had had no choice. He didn't waste time saying daft things like "You wouldn't," or "What do you mean by this?" He didn't know what Bertie meant, but was sure he meant it.

Corinna, on the other hand . . . "What the blazes are you up to?"

Bertie picked up the Winchester and slid it into his empty gun case. "I am taking your horses, only for perhaps two hours, so please to remove what you may need for that time."

"Do as he says," O'Gilroy said resignedly. He dismounted and took his food package from the saddle-bag. "Got some idea ye'll be able to take on an army better by yeself, have ye?"

"Possibly. I am – forgive me – still unsure about your loyalties. But be assured that I will return."

"So after we've told you all we know," Corinna said grimly, "you abandon us in wild country."

Bertie smiled regretfully. "Only temporarily. But this matter is becoming so confused, I feel it is simpler to trust only myself. I do, you see, understand my own motives."

She took her food parcel, then wrenched her big handbag free from the saddle and stood back, clutching it in both hands.

Bertie loosed the long leading rein from O'Gilroy's mount and tied it to his own saddle, then indicated that O'Gilroy should tie Corinna's horse in procession. O'Gilroy did so, and also stood well clear.

"Thank you." Bertie lifted himself into the saddle, holding the rifle one-handed, his finger near but clear of the trigger. He kicked his horse forward, looking back to make sure the other two followed. Then he looked ahead.

Corinna took the Colt revolver from her handbag and cocked it as she strode forward. "M'sieu Lacan!"

Bertie looked round, began to swivel the rifle – and then

stopped. She was standing four-square, feet planted apart, holding the pistol two-handed at eye level.

He said: "Do lady bankers also shoot people?" He glanced at O'Gilroy, who was wearing an expectant smile. That was not reassuring.

Then the second horse, still ambling forward on the leading rein, reached the rear of Bertie's mount – which sensed this and pitched forward to lash a two-footed kick backwards. Bertie went one way, the rifle another, and both hit the shingle hard. O'Gilroy rescued the rifle first. It seemed undamaged; as for Bertie—

He raised himself carefully and painfully into a sitting position and began feeling his shoulders, elbows, ribs and ankles, swearing steadily in French.

"Really, M'sieu Lacan," Corinna said, "I don't think lady bankers should have to listen to such language."

Bertie scowled at her, debonair manner quite gone. He was just a middle-aged man who had been thrown from a horse and lost control of the situation besides.

"Any bones broken?" O'Gilroy asked.

"Every fucking one," Bertie said bilingually.

O'Gilroy nodded and went to sort out the horses, but in the end didn't. Three "entire" Anatolian ponies tied together looked like a sport the ancient Romans might have invented. Luckily they seemed as good at avoiding kicks as kicking, and there was clearly no chance of them agreeing on which way to run off, so O'Gilroy left them to tire of it.

By then Bertie was practising limping with both feet, but hadn't found any actual breaks. "Lucky yer well padded," O'Gilroy observed. "Where was yer going?"

The easy way he handled the unfamiliar weapon discouraged conversational sparring. "There is a, sort of, back way to the monastery. Not to invade, but they would let me in."

Corinna looked at O'Gilroy. "If they'd let *him* in, we could—"

"No. Bit late for that. If the guns are pretty nigh in position, the Captain'll know it before we get there." He stood looking at the landscape in front of them. "Ye say there's a dry river runs crosswise up there, and the guns could be in it? Any way we could come down at it? Like through them?" He gestured at the thinly wooded foothills of Unmentionable Peak.

* * *

The guard at the gateway thought he had heard or seen something – Ranklin couldn't make out which. Now Hakim, and Ranklin beside him, were both peering. Visibility was still only half a mile but the mist wasn't a sudden curtain, just a gradual fading out. The trench was just the faintest of dark lines where you might see a man upright and moving quickly, certainly not one lying still or crawling slowly. Ranklin could see nothing.

Hakim said: "They might be sending the ransom."

Cracks, whines and thuds shattered the air around them. Earth jumped from the patch in front of the doorway. They heard the distant rattle of a machine-gun.

Abruptly behind a nice thick wall, Ranklin growled: "*Ça, ce n'est pas une rançon.*"

Lady Kelso looked up as Ranklin came in, moving cautiously on the uneven floor in the flickering lamplight. "So it's started."

"Yes."

"Do I understand one man's been killed already?"

"Yes. They all flocked to the front wall to return fire and one got his— got shot in the head. The rest are being a little more cautious now."

"But there'll be others?"

Ranklin nodded. "I think there's worse to come."

She stood up. "Well, I didn't come here to be Florence Nightingale and I haven't any first aid kit, but I've tended a few bullet and sword wounds before. They either got better or they died," she added matter-of-factly.

Ranklin nodded without knowing why. "I came to ask if you're ready to go if we can find a way out."

"I understand there's a secret way—"

"Then for the Lord's sake—"

"No. They can't take horses that way, and Miskal can't walk. And anyway, on foot won't they hunt us all down?"

"Not if we act like brigands and not soldiers. In this country a handful of rifles could hold up a battalion. But not cooped up here."

She said: "If you can get Hakim to go, I'll stay here with Miskal."

"For God's sake—"

"I don't think they'd harm us. Not if you're free to spread the word."

She wasn't being brave. Not what men usually call brave. Just . . . matter-of-fact, perhaps. Making the best of each moment that arrived.

Hakim came up to them. He glanced at his father, ignored Lady Kelso, spoke to Ranklin. "Snaipe effendi, do you claim to understand machine-guns? Why does it shoot so well at such range?"

Ranklin was about to start on the merits of a heavy tripod well embedded, then realised that wasn't the point. He took his big field-glasses from inside his coat. "Someone out there has a pair of these. Give these to one man with good eyesight, and I suggest you appoint *one* sharpshooter to fire back. Do you know the range to the trench?"

"Six hundred and eighty-five metres," Hakim said with a hint of a smile. "We paced it when we got the new rifles." His people might not be much help around the house, but they were very practical when it came to weapons.

Then, very faintly, came the sound of a bugle call. He and Hakim looked at each other, then ran for the stairs. The call itself was unintelligible, but it had to signal something. They had reached the open air when there was a distant *thud* and, a few seconds later, an explosion out to the east.

Ranklin made it to that wall in time to see a whiff of smoke dissolving in the air perhaps a hundred yards off. After a while, the bugle called again.

"Artillery," he told Hakim. "Controlled by that bugle. You must get your men into the cellar." And when Hakim hesitated: "They can't shoot back at something they can't see. And they'll be bursting shells right overhead in a minute."

Perhaps the simple, practical gesture of lending the field-glasses had been crucial in getting Hakim to listen to him; it may also have helped Hakim's authority. Now he herded his reluctant warriors downstairs. Ranklin stayed where he was; despite what he'd said, it would take several more shots to get the range.

The bugle sounded again, a long, unmusical message. About a minute later there was another *thud* and explosion, much louder, but this time to the west where a cloud of dust was settling beyond the edge of the ravine; the shell had fallen short, hitting the rock face a few feet down. And that had been "common shell", high explosive, not shrapnel like the first. Two guns? – and firing different types of shell to make observing the results easier? The guns must be spaced well apart . . .

Hakim, standing a few steps down towards the cellar, had said something. Ranklin waved him quiet. "It's all right, I'm an Army officer. *Artilleur*." Was that the right word? Never mind. They had to be dismountable mountain guns – brought in those boxes from Germany? Probably a bit lighter shell than the French 75's he'd commanded for the Greeks, say ten or twelve pounds. And low velocity, so that if you stayed alert, you'd always hear the gun before the shell arrived. Moreover, on this rocky ground, he'd have used only common shell, with its all-round effect; shrapnel was dangerous in only one direction, bursting in the air and spraying its bullets forwards like a flying shotgun. And air bursts were notoriously difficult to judge for range.

Was he just impressing himself with his own knowledgeable deductions? At least he felt more on a par with the enemy commander – Zurga, presumably – but the big difference remained: Zurga had two guns and he had none. And Zurga wasn't hurrying, with minutes between each shot. Unfamiliar gun crews, perhaps, and taking time to get troops forward into that trench to mount the final assault. But they still had half the day.

The next shrapnel shell seemed to explode with just a large *pop*, right against the front wall. Ah! – he'd been hoping that would happen before they got the range right. He peeked around the gateway, saw smoke eddying at the base of the wall, and crawled towards it.

Firing shrapnel, you got a number of "grazes", shells that hit the ground before the time-fuse burst them. Indeed, some gunners claimed you hadn't got the right range (given the variations in the fuses) unless there was one graze in every five shots. And there it was: a score mark ripped across the rock and earth before the wall. He took out the compass and sighted carefully back along it . . .

Machine-gun bullets clattered into the wall behind him. He cringed as flat as he could, and glanced back – and there was Hakim and another, standing in the gateway, laughing unconcernedly. If the Englishman could show his disdain for shot and shell by taking bearings on shell scrapes, then by God they weren't going to be outdone.

He screamed: "Get back!" and grabbed Hakim in a rugby tackle and tried to fling him through the gateway. The second burst of machine-gun fire arrived – accurately – and they all three collapsed inside amid screeching ricochets and stone fragments.

Once they had sorted themselves out, the other Arab lay groaning with a bullet through the stomach. In a good field hospital he might – *might* – survive. Out here it was a slow death in a lot of pain.

When he had been carried to the cellar and Hakim had been persuaded to order all the others back down, Ranklin turned on him. "D'you want these Ottoman conscripts to defeat *your father*? D'you *want* him tried for treason? Or more likely, just executed here, like a dog, to be rid of him?" He over-rode the indignant protests. "You've lost two men already and not caused the enemy a single casualty! Is that good? You have to be a great –" perhaps *soldat* wasn't much of a compliment: try "warrior" "– *guerrier* like your father, and you will defeat those *farmers* out there. But by being better *guerriers* than they. Now, let me see the map."

It had got left upstairs but there were plenty of volunteers; Ranklin made them wait until the next shell had burst. With the map spread on the floor, he used the surveyors' own instruments to plot the bearing: 155 degrees. The gun could be on the edge of the plateau or down in the dry riverbed, further along than they'd had to go. His bet was the riverbed: up on rock, the gun would hop around with the recoil, needing elaborate relaying after each shot.

But to hit the wall of the ravine, the other gun must be on the far side of it, again in the riverbed but half a mile or more from the first – probably well out of sight of it. Dividing your guns was unconventional, but being able to fire on both sides of the monastery as well as the front was sensible. Zurga was no fool.

Perhaps Hakim was beginning to realise that now, and see the future as Zurga planned it: more casualties if he exposed his men, being overwhelmed by attacking troops if he didn't. The men crowding the cellar stared at him openly, waiting to see if their enemy or their leader was in control. This was where you needed discipline, not courage: even in an army the situation would be bad, but this brave mob could fall completely apart.

"*I* would post one man upstairs to watch," Ranklin said conversationally. "A sensible one. Have him shout down that he's all right after every shell-burst. You'll know when they're going to attack: the bugle calls will stop, both guns will fire together – as fast as they can. The machine-gun, too."

In a lamplit corner, Lady Kelso was carefully tearing the clothing from the newly wounded Arab's body. He screamed as the air reached the wound.

Perhaps the scream helped. Hakim gave out authoritative orders – and was obeyed. Lady Kelso came past to rinse her hands in a brass bowl, leaving the water rust-red in the lamplight. "Is this the 'worse' you expected?"

"Artillery. Mountain guns. I should have thought of them."

"There's nothing to be done about them, I assume."

"There *might* be . . ." Only two guns, too far apart to support each other if attacked . . .

She waited, but he was silent, thinking. She turned away. "It's all right. Not asking questions is one of the things I'm best at."

"Just providing answers."

She paused, then said: "I suppose so . . . Too often, the answer used to be just me. But now . . ."

She went back to the wounded Arab as Hakim returned to ask: "And is that all we can do?"

"No. If you've really got a secret back way out, let me take half a dozen men and I might capture one of those guns for you."

25

The pass that O'Gilroy found between the foothills and the Peak existed, but nobody had used it before because it was an unnecessary loop, the route up the tributary and then along the dry riverbed being flatter and easier. This way meant weaving around rocks and ducking under tree branches, but on the far side it could also mean the advantage of the high ground and O'Gilroy did know infantry tactics. Anybody who had fought the Boers, and lived, had learnt more than the Army taught.

They had barely started upwards when a faint noise brought their heads up. Bertie listened, then called: "Was that a Maxim gun?"

"Probly. They've got one."

They plodded on, and were still below the crest when they heard the bugle sound, and the first gun went off. All seemed well distant and O'Gilroy scowled to himself; the detour seemed to have been a waste of time.

The bugle called again and a second gun fired – far closer. In fact, just over the crest. He dismounted, tied his horse to a tree, and went forward on foot. By the time he was over the crest, he had guessed at a pattern. The machine-gun had no part in it: it was firing random short bursts, probably replying to the single shots which must come from the monastery. But the bugle calls – from somewhere in sight of the monastery – were controlling the fire of the guns, themselves with no sight of the target.

The first gun was far off to his right. But the second was in the riverbed almost directly below him. It fired again and he placed it exactly. Looking down on it from behind, he was in an infantryman's dream and a gunner's nightmare.

* * *

The secret way started by going out of the back of the monastery by the rough-fenced paddock. The dozen horses there – nothing like enough for the whole band – were frightened by the explosions and would soon be hit by them. But what could anybody do? The next step, it seemed, was to climb down a well, an idea which didn't appeal to Ranklin at all. But it appeared that the wide, irregular-shaped shaft had been hacked down, centuries before, to intercept a small underground stream. So it led to a tunnel rather than just plunged below the local water table.

They swarmed down a knotted rope, sometimes crawling backwards down a slope of rock, sometimes dangling free and going hand over hand. It was perhaps thirty feet in all, one of those distances that doesn't sound much but is *enormous* when you're lowering yourself into increasing darkness and damp. And then he was standing calf-deep in freezing gushing water waiting for the last two men to come down and for one already there to get a storm lantern lit.

In fact they moved off before the last man was down, a devil-take-the-hindmost attitude that assumed each man could keep up and nobody was really in command. For the moment nobody needed to be: they were simply following the tunnel, stumbling and slipping on a downward path. But if any decisions came to be made, Ranklin realised he would have to start imposing his will. Without a common language that could be tricky, particularly if you were to do it in wheezes and grunts from the back of the queue.

Then he realised he could see – vaguely – where he was putting his feet, and another turn brought dull green light ahead: green because the outside world was blocked by a scrawny bush, perhaps growing naturally in the dampness, perhaps planted to hide the fissure through which the stream spilled down into the ravine.

They were still fifty feet up, but away from the spattering water there was enough fallen rock to make it relatively easy to scramble down. Or up, Ranklin reflected, but no invader could count on climbing that well.

With the monastery out of sight above, and the end of the machine-gun trench hidden behind a bend in the ravine, they splashed up it through a small stream to a smaller, steeper ravine in the opposite wall, spilling out a yet smaller stream. The Arabs went light-footed up it, making no pretence of slowing to his panting, puffing pace. And once they reached the top they would have to run perhaps a mile in a wide half-circle beyond sight of the machine-gun, to reach the dry riverbed and the gun.

Already he was breathing through his mouth; God knows what he'd be trying to breathe through in twenty minutes.

* * *

To O'Gilroy the firing seemed spaced-out and leisurely. But with nearly six hours of daylight left, Zurga could take his time and get it right. When O'Gilroy got back to Corinna and Bertie he had a firm plan in mind.

"Yeself, ye stay here with the horses," he told Corinna. "Don't argue: we've only the two rifles so ye'd jest be a target up forward." He turned to Bertie. "Would I be right in thinking ye'd rather shoot the fellers working that gun'n me?"

Bertie nodded docilely. "I feel much remorse that—"

"Forget that, feel like killing someone." O'Gilroy took a handful of cartridges from his pocket; Bertie had been carrying his own rifle again, but empty. "Have ye ever shot a man before?"

"In thirty years of the East and deserts—" Bertie was quite incapable of answering Yes or No, and O'Gilroy cut him off. "The feller ye spare, he's the one'll kill ye."

* * *

Trotting across a rock-strewn slope just below a line of trees, Ranklin had heard through the surf-like roaring from his lungs the occasional thuds of gunfire and chirruping of the bugle.

Now it seemed to have stopped and, thinking back, he realised the last bugle call had been different. A few short notes and one long one. It sounded like the "still".

Oh God: the guns had ranged. That had been the signal to stop, to stack ammunition to hand, and be ready for the final uncorrected bombardment of the attack – and they were still hundreds of yards short. He was too late for anything but revenge.

* * *

O'Gilroy chose two positions a few yards apart, each shielded by a tree or bushes rather than rock. Rock was a snare and delusion. It was solid enough, but you couldn't peek through it as you could a bush, and it produced ricochets, giving bullets a second bite at you.

Bertie had wanted to get closer, but O'Gilroy refused. He'd accept the longer range – it was only just over three hundred yards anyway, he judged – and an easier retreat in cover back over the crest. That was the old soldier showing through.

And whatever they did would cause trouble enough, ambushing the gun from above and behind. It was sited on the near side of the dry riverbed, where the pass opened to form ground as near flat as could probably be found. It was important, O'Gilroy remembered, to have both wheels level if possible. You *could* fire with one wheel high, but had to add in a correction, firing slightly off to the one side. High side or low? He couldn't remember.

The gun itself was surprisingly small, dwarfed by the four men tending it: two seated either side of the breech, two fetching rounds from boxes set back to the side. They all wore light khaki; Turkish uniform, presumably. A fifth man – the gun captain – wore grey and stood off to the left: O'Gilroy thought he recognised Albrecht, the portly Bavarian. Hard luck, him being on the other side. That was the only way to think of it.

And he was Bertie's target anyway. "Ye take the one sitting

at the gun on the *left*," O'Gilroy whispered, emphasising with his left hand, "and then next left. I'll get the feller sitting on the *right* and work right. Ye got that?"

It should be easy – to start with. The tricky bit might come when the defensive picket came to hunt them down. He couldn't see such a picket, but they had to be there; probably up among the trees on the far side of the riverbed, guarding against attack from the direction of the target. He'd send Bertie back, and perhaps stay long enough himself to knock off one of them, to blunt their enthusiasm, but after that the old soldier in him could take over.

"Would it not be better to shoot at the ammunition boxes?" Bertie whispered.

"No. Might not go off and the men'd scatter. They're what matters. Watch me and I'll signal ye."

Bertie nodded and crawled away to his position. The bugle called, a twiddly bit and then one long note.

Albrecht blew a whistle, the little group around the gun relaxed and broke up. The seated men, numbers two and three in the crew, stood up, stretched and lit cigarettes. The loading detail began stacking rounds on a coat laid over the damp, gritty ground beside the gun, and Albrecht bustled. He interfered with the placing of the ammunition, checked the firmness of the trail spade, peered into but didn't touch the sight. He was the picture of a man with nothing to do, whose job was done. The gun was on target.

When the bugle sounded again, he whistled and the crew closed up, crouching or sitting. O'Gilroy lifted the Winchester, took a sight, then nodded across to Bertie who snuggled down competently behind his own rifle. Still, it wasn't the man's competence O'Gilroy mistrusted. Oh well . . . He sighted, took and let out a breath, then squeezed the trigger.

* * *

Ranklin's group heard the firing and went to ground immediately. He crawled to the cover of a rock and began remembering and analysing what he had heard. No bullets had come past, and two different rifles had fired. Odd. He looked across to the nearest Arab and he seemed puzzled, too.

The firing stopped. One Arab rose cautiously to his feet, and of course all the rest did. So Ranklin had to. They moved forward in a crouching unsoldierly trot, perhaps three hundred yards from the line of treetops growing on the bank below the rim of the plateau.

They heard shouts and more shots, and the Arabs threw themselves down and this time fired back. Back? – Ranklin wasn't sure anybody had shot at them yet. But this was a sure way to make them do so.

* * *

The loader just stood there, a shell in his hands, as the numbers two and three slumped off the gun's seats. He must have heard the shots, he could see the results, he simply didn't believe it. He was just beginning to turn when O'Gilroy's second shot took him in the side and he staggered. O'Gilroy was just aware of Albrecht running towards them, for the cover at the bottom of the slope, then sprawling as Bertie fired. His doubts about Bertie's willingness to kill in cold blood had, O'Gilroy realised, been misplaced.

He himself swung and shot at the second loader, who was heading down-stream at an astonishing pace, perhaps even faster than the Winchester's low-powered bullet, because it missed. He re-aimed at the first loader just as Bertie finished him off. Then there was no-one left to shoot at.

O'Gilroy waved Bertie back, as planned, before the picket could scramble down from the wooded bank opposite. But Bertie knew just how well he had done with his familiar and high-powered rifle and pretended to be busy reloading. O'Gilroy cursed him and the Winchester both and worked the action. The lever was simple and fast, but by God it cut into his knuckles.

As the ringing of the shots faded, he realised several voices were shouting – questions and orders, it sounded like. Then a Turkish soldier lost his footing and slid out from under the trees onto the open riverbed; O'Gilroy let Bertie slaughter that one while he himself fired three quick shots at a movement among the trees higher up. There was a yelp.

Then, for the first time, several rifles fired in their direction – certainly a bullet howled off a rock nearby. But the shooting had sounded distant. They were high enough to see over the treetops of the bank opposite to the flat, misty rockiness beyond. There O'Gilroy saw the wink of a rifle flash.

"Jest left of front, beyond the trees, on the top, 'bout five-six hundred yards—"

"Do not shoot," Bertie said. "They may be friends."

"Hey?"

"That is the back way to the monastery, up there. It may be Hakim's men."

"Whose?"

But Bertie had rolled on his side to give his lungs room, and bellowed in Arabic.

* * *

Abruptly the Arabs around Ranklin had stopped firing and begun listening, but the distant shouts meant nothing to Ranklin. The Arabs explained it to him – but again in Arabic. Then he thought he heard ". . . O'*Gilroy* . . ."

He yelled: "Is . . . that . . . you?"

"*Yes . . . move . . . right*."

The Arabs already were, and Ranklin followed before he realised why: their two groups were almost opposite each other, sandwiching an enemy, and O'Gilroy wanted to send them around the flank to attack down the line of the riverbed . . .

They ended up with four more Turkish dead – two of whom, Ranklin suspected, *could* have been taken prisoner, if it wasn't for old scores he preferred not to know about. At the cost of one rashly brave Arab shot clean through the heart. But with the Arabic-speaking Bertie now on hand, he left them to chatter while he listened to O'Gilroy's news and inspected the gun.

He walked slowly around it, working out where it must break down into mule loads and giving those junctions a good kick or shake to make sure they were locked tight. Meanwhile, O'Gilroy was saying: "The feller Zurga, his real name's *Kazurga*, and that means 'Tornado' in Turk, which makes him yer old mate from the war, don't it?"

Well, well, well, Ranklin thought. So I'm up against my old enemy; no wonder he brought up the "Warrior Sheep" when he saw this jacket – could he suspect? And I bet he got that scar from *my* guns, before Salonika. Quite a coincidence – except that he would be sent here because he's their artillery hero, and I got involved mainly because of my experience in that war . . . What a peaceful world we must live in when so few of us are accustomed to action that we all know each other.

O'Gilroy, who was routing in the pile of captured weapons to replace the Winchester with a proper bolt-action Mauser, suddenly stood up. "Oh shit. I'd best be telling Mrs Finn. Getting her down here."

"You brought *Corinna*?"

"She brought me, more like. Ye know how she is," O'Gilroy protested.

Ranklin let his fury subside and nodded. He knew. "Get her, then."

And now he could look at the gun properly.

It had no shield, but he guessed why: it would just be a metal plate about a yard square, an awkward load and dispensable if you didn't expect to come under small-arms fire. That apart, it was small, no higher than its wheels which were about three feet diameter. It looked like a toy – no, crouching with its squat nose slightly raised, it looked like an ugly metal toad. Yet it was beautiful. The Devil may have invented artillery but it took man, created in God's image, to make guns such lovely things.

He ran his hand lovingly over the breech, warm from the shooting, noted the position of the breech-handle on the right of the horizontal sliding block, the elevating and traversing wheels and dial sight to the left. Very simple, merely the reverse of most British gun layouts.

And the love for such weapons, built up over twenty years and which he thought he had set aside, came back with a rush. Suddenly the knowledge he had acquired as a spy, the tricks of disguise and pretence and mistrust, all became a handful of pennies beside the fortune of understanding he had amassed in the Guns. He had never seen this type before, yet already he knew it, it was part of him, stretching his reach to miles and giving him the power of legions. Alexander, Caesar, even Napoleon, had never known such power. Give me a lever and I will move the world? Hah! Give me a gun and start looking for a new world!

If, in that mist, he could work out which direction to fire the bloody thing.

The Arabs were standing around, chatting to Bertie but all eyeing the gun eagerly. Absently, Ranklin picked up the shell the dead loader had dropped, noted the safety pin had already gone, and began wiping it clean of grit on his sweater sleeve while he worked out what to do.

Zurga would be forward in the trench with the machine-gun, bugler and all: a commander wanted to see the enemy, not his own guns. So now what would he be thinking? He must have heard the firing from where there should be none, would guess his second gun had been attacked yet not know if the attack had been beaten off. And you hadn't worked out a bugle call to answer *that* question, had you?

Still, he'd know this gun hadn't fired recently, and that itself must have postponed the attack – there had been no shooting, no bugle calls, for minutes now. Zurga wouldn't launch an attack covered by just one gun and with his rear in doubt. So he'd want to know the situation. Would he send a runner back? Come himself? Wait for the crew of the other gun, which must be closer to here, to investigate? . . . *Oh damn*: that escaped loader that O'Gilroy had reported, he'd probably have reached that gun and be pouring out the sad tale . . .

. . . And if *that* gun had protecting troops to spare, they might even now be charging up the riverbed towards him.

"M'sieu Lacan?"

Bertie turned from the Arabs. "Do I still have the pleasure of addressing the Honourable Patrick Snaipe?"

"You don't, actually, but—"

Bertie shook his head sadly. "*Hélas* – I made a mistake, so many mistakes . . . You have seen Hakim?"

"Yes. They let the hostages go –" Bertie's half-closed eyes flicked open "– but Hakim kept the survey map. I've got it." He took it out and shook it open.

Very still now, Bertie stared at it and said: "I hope it will not go back to the Railway."

"Right now, I need it myself. The problem is . . ." But Bertie understood immediately ". . . so would you take three men forward to give us warning and try to delay an attack? If you can get up on the high ground *here*, opposite where the dry ravine comes in, you can't be flanked . . . Don't be heroic, but send a man back to say when you're retreating."

Bertie nodded at the gun. "And will you shoot that?"

"Probably."

"And you know how?"

"It's my work."

Bertie smiled. "*Not* the Honourable Snaipe." He turned back to the Arabs. None of them wanted to go with him. They wanted to shoot Turks, yes, but that was old hat; right now they wanted to see this gun fired, maybe even help. But Bertie knew his business: he chose three of them, then trotted off. Reluctantly, they followed.

Ranklin turned to the ammunition boxes, a dozen of them with eight rounds to a box. He hadn't time to fathom the abbreviated German on each shell that told what it was, but could identify two boxes of shrapnel by the time-fuse bands on their noses. He didn't want to fool with unfamiliar time-fuses and was relieved that the rest had pull-ring safety pins so must be common shell.

O'Gilroy and Corinna tacked down the slope from the pass, each leading a pony and keeping them well apart.

Ranklin went towards them. "I think—"

"Captain Ranklin of the Artillery, I presume? Well, looks like you've got yourself a gun again."

"I *think*," Ranklin said firmly, "you should get on that horse and get back to . . . wherever. Somewhere safer."

Corinna just slapped the leading rein into the hand of the nearest, and rather astonished, Arab. "I've been stuck out of sight being a *horse-holder* the last half-hour. So who are you going to fire it at? And why are those guys sleeping on – oh."

She realised she was looking at a row of bodies, collected against the bank.

"You heard shooting," Ranklin growled. "That's what it causes. *Now* will you get on that horse?"

She may have looked a little paler, but: "I'd be more scared on my own in this country. I'll stick with you, so give me something to do. Who *are* you going to shoot at?"

"I'm not sure." He waved to O'Gilroy. "Tie up the horses upstream, away from the mules." Those, more than a dozen of them, were tethered a hundred yards down the riverbed. They should be closer, but these were civilian animals, not accustomed to gunfire.

He went on: "It might be better to blow this gun up than actually fire it at anyone—"

"Oh, you'll fire it at someone, all right."

Ranklin clenched his teeth. *Of course* he wanted to shoot this gun, as much as any of the Arabs, but he needed a sensible target. Or to persuade himself he had one.

He reopened the survey map. He couldn't be sure of his exact position, but the map showed the line of the riverbed well enough that he could guess within a few yards. Measuring with the boxwood protractor he reckoned the gun had been firing at nineteen degrees magnetic, and the attackers' trench lay at about forty-three – "about" because it was a linear target. But he'd need to be pretty exact about the range, always the most difficult. Or maybe not: the important thing might be to let the Turkish troops know *they* were now under fire, give their morale a jolt. Or would that just be confirming to Zurga that the gun had been captured?

Damn it, *fire* the thing and you may be lucky, even hit Zurga. You won't if you don't.

He had O'Gilroy, Corinna and two Arabs as his crew.

"Hoick up the trail and swing her round . . . No! Wait!" He stooped to the sight and squinted; it was focussed on a dead pine standing out on the bank two hundred yards upstream. He might as well keep that as the aiming point; it was meaningless in itself, just a reference point from which you measured the angles of targets. "All right, move her now . . . point about *here* . . ." He adjusted the sight to show the aiming point again and found they had moved only fifteen degrees. "Bit further round . . . stop! . . . back a fraction . . ." With O'Gilroy translating orders into action, the Arabs jostled each other to help. They were willing slaves if he proved master of this weapon.

He checked the clinometer and set O'Gilroy to digging in the slightly high right wheel with an empty shell-case, then indicated he needed the trail spade shoved firmly into the earth. The Arabs took a moment to get the point of this – keeping the gun as firm as possible against the recoil – then began stamping the spade down to China.

The elevating wheel was set to 1950 metres; that didn't mean it was actually that far to the monastery – the map made it 1800 – just that that setting was right for this wind (there was none, thank God), temperature, pressure and the fact that the monastery was perhaps two hundred feet higher. Which meant that, to fire at the trench . . . Figures jostled in his head and he organised and related them, if this then that, a familiar routine that boiled down to microscopic twiddles on the two aiming wheels. *This was home* . . .

He straightened up. O'Gilroy was already in the right-hand seat, finding out how the breech-lever and firing lanyard worked. "Right," Ranklin ordered. "You be number two: Corinna, you load." He handed her the round: it was about the diameter of a wine bottle but far heavier and rather longer, almost half being the brass case that held the charge. "Lay it over your right forearm and push it firmly home with your left palm – and get that damned coat off, it'll catch in everything."

She gave him a sharp look but said nothing and tossed the expensive fur coat aside.

"Load."

She had to kneel on the shingle and damp sand, leaning in to her left behind O'Gilroy's back. It was not dignified, and if Ranklin had been less preoccupied he might have overheard what she was muttering. O'Gilroy did hear and turned his head, startled.

He recovered himself to report: "Ready!"

"Put your hands over your ears," Ranklin instructed – but he was talking about the noise to come, and demonstrating to the Arabs. "Fire!"

26

Corinna balanced the fourth shell on her forearm and rammed it home savagely. It slid more easily now that the grease from previous shells was building up nicely on her jumper sleeve.

"When does –" she clapped her greasy hands briefly to her greasy ears "– the utter fascination –" she took the fifth shell "– of artillery—"

"Fire!"

"—set in?"

"Stop. That'll do. What did you say?"

"No matter."

Ranklin had no idea whether they'd hit anything, all he could tell was that the shells had exploded. And nearer the trench than the monastery.

Anyway, there was no point in going on firing into the mist. Better to switch aim and try to hit the second gun. He laid out the survey map and fell comfortably into the world of figures and calculations again. But this was a trickier problem, since the only idea he had about that gun's position was the rough bearing he'd taken from the shell-scrape at the monastery, and an assumption that it, too, must be in this dry riverbed. Moreover, now he was trying to hit a small target, not just pass a message to a big one.

Then he realised he'd sent a message to Zurga, too. He'd hardly believe the Hon. Patrick or the Arabs could have laid and fired this gun, so probably he'd guessed that the man in the sheepskin waistcoat really was the Warrior Sheep. Which evened things up, you might say. But what would Zurga now do?

And the answer to that was very easy: he was a gunner, so

he'd rush back to direct the one gun he still had. Someone else could bring back the troops from the trench if need be (and the ravine would stop them from attacking this gun from where they were; they must come down into the stream bed and then past Bertie's outpost, so he was safe from surprise).

Then he remembered that Zurga had probably spent the last two days scouting this area: measuring and taking bearings, picking the gun positions . . . Damn it! – he'd know to a yard just where this gun was!

"We've got to move!" He peered desperately up and down the riverbed. Now it didn't matter being close to the far bank, he wouldn't be trying to shoot over it. What he needed was any scant cover . . . *there*, a clutter of rocks tumbled from the opposite bank a couple of hundred yards down-stream . . . "Swing her right around! And *HAUL*!"

With the two Arabs carrying the trail, O'Gilroy pushing the barrel and he and Corinna at each wheel, a thousand pounds of gun began to trundle, horribly slowly and reluctantly, across shingle, obstinate rocks and grasping patches of wet sand, down the riverbed beach.

Keeping the momentum, they covered fifty yards, then a hundred . . . There was a distant fusillade of rifle fire: Bertie's men were in action. Mentally, Ranklin patted himself on the back for his foresight in sending them forward – then knew that God would punish his *hubris* by bogging down the gun in the soft centre of the riverbed. They still had to swing across that.

"All right, hold it, take a breather." They had come nearly level with his chosen rocks on the far side.

"Ammunition?" O'Gilroy suggested.

"Fetch it later." Ranklin was choosing the least-soft place to cross. "O'Gilroy, you take the trail—"

BANG – a shrapnel shell had exploded behind them, more-or-less over their old position. So Zurga was back: nobody else would know so precisely where they were supposed to be. In a way, he welcomed that: he'd rather have Zurga firing accurately at the wrong place than someone else dropping shells all over the shop.

"The rest of us take the wheels. Grab the spokes and just *keep it moving* – never give it a chance to sink in." The Arabs nodded, following his demonstration, then both attached themselves to one wheel. He'd rather have had their wiry strength evenly distributed, but neither wanted to share a wheel with a woman, so he had to.

Another shell burst back up the stream bed. They weren't hearing Zurga's gun fire; distance, and the solid ground in between, mopped up the sound. "Go!"

They made five yards in an accelerating rush, then slewed to a near-halt in a marshy patch. "*Heave!*" Ranklin pushed at the metal spoke, hands sweating and slipping, moving it by millimetres, then centimetres, everyone gasping, grunting, the gun twisting with the Arabs' strength, O'Gilroy trying to wrench it straight . . . Then they bumped over a rock and rolled free on shingle.

Despite their breathlessness, it seemed easy to twitch the gun into line behind the rocks. These weren't much protection, not as much as the missing shield would have been, but what mattered most was being in a new, unknown, position. Shrapnel shells still burst over the old one – where the ammunition still was.

"Ye want me to go back?" O'Gilroy asked.

"Wait. He won't go on for ever. If we don't fire, he may think he's got us."

"Mebbe Bertie'll be thinking the same," O'Gilroy pointed out. "Mebbe his fellers'll get a bit down-hearted, thinking we're dead like. Difficult to keep them in line . . ."

"Just *wait*," Ranklin said angrily. Even if he had something to fire, he would still be guessing at his target. Whereas Zurga, once they fired and so told him they had moved, could fire a pattern to seek them out, knowing where to start and that they couldn't have gone far. He needed an advantage before he fired again . . .

"Can't wait for ever," O'Gilroy said remorselessly. "T'other soldiers'll be coming back, likely, and we'll have a hundred of 'em coming up this valley. Bertie can't hold off *that*."

"What we need," Ranklin said, "is an observer up there—"

O'Gilroy said: "I'll do that."

"—if we had a way of signalling. By sound."

"A whistle do?"

"Have you got one?"

O'Gilroy took it from his pea-jacket pocket. "Took it off Albrecht, he was captain of this gun . . ." He sounded a little sheepish – perhaps it had been a sentimental souvenir – but Ranklin hadn't time to bother.

He decided quickly: "One blast for over, then clockwise: two for right, three for short, four for left. On target, continuous short blasts."

O'Gilroy nodded, snatched up a rifle and ran off downstream.

Corinna was looking back towards the cluster of ammunition boxes. "They seem to have stopped. Let's get some ammunition."

"Not *you*—" Ranklin began.

"You get the gun nicely pointed. None of us can do that." She scooped up her skirts and trotted off. Startled, the two Arabs looked at Ranklin. He gestured and they rushed away, overtaking her.

Cursing to himself, Ranklin turned to the gun. She was right, damn her. So at least he'd better get this right . . . By moving, he'd lost the aiming point; he had to choose another – he picked a tree on the opposite bank – and start again from the map. Call the range now 1040 metres, bearing eighty-two degrees, and—

BANG.

He jerked around. Smoke was melting in the air – but, thank God, off to the left.

"Get among the trees!" he yelled. "Get behind them!" Zurga had fooled him. Guessing they might have temporarily abandoned the gun – artillery steel wouldn't be harmed by lead shrapnel balls – he had just paused until they were lulled into going back to it. Wrong in theory, but horribly right in practice . . .

Corinna scurried across to the trees on the bank, but the two Arabs had already started back with a box between them, and they staggered on. The second shell burst on graze – right in front of one of them. He must have taken almost all of its hundred-odd balls, and what was left was just a scatter of meat and clothing on the shingle. The other Arab reeled out of the dissolving smoke, dragging the box by one rope handle. Then, dazed, he sank to his knees.

Ranklin began to run.

But he had gone only a few yards when a shell burst over the ammunition boxes, safely behind the Arab and his box. Immediately, Corinna charged out of the trees, almost tumbled as she caught a foot on his skirts, recovered, grabbed up one handle and pulled. The Arab scrambled to his feet, seized the other handle and together they *sprinted* twenty-five yards as if they were carrying a feather pillow.

Ranklin ran, too, with the number thirteen in his head. Instinctively, he'd been counting the seconds between the bursts, and now it was ten . . . eleven—

"Get *down*!"

They flopped on the wet shingle and this time the shell didn't burst at all, just clanged off a rock and tumbled away, a dud.

"*Now move*!"

He ran on. Now halfway home, they were theoretically safe; only bad luck would pitch a shell short enough to catch them, and it didn't happen. They got back to their gun carrying the box between the three of them, gasping and panting.

Corinna flopped to her knees and then her hands, her long and now-tangled dark hair dangling almost to the shingle. "I'm not . . ." she gasped, ". . . going to . . . marry Edouard . . . on account . . . life with you . . . is so much more . . . Goddamn *fun*."

Ranklin had nothing to say. She was on the edge of hysteria, where each new death or horror would be hilarious, because her mind had realised that was the only way to keep going. Maybe the Arab, splattered with the blood of his colleague, felt the same way. But Ranklin could only treat them as gun crew, try to sustain the high fever, because the alternative was the common sense of running away.

He lifted a shell from the box and pulled the safety pin.

Corinna said: "Here, that's my job," and scrambled to her feet. The Arab slid onto the number two seat, grasped the lever and whipped the breech open. Of course, he'd studied just how O'Gilroy had done it; this was a weapon, wasn't it?

The breech whanged shut, the Arab pulled the lanyard taut and shouted: "Ret-ti!" which was a good enough imitation of O'Gilroy's call.

Ranklin hesitated. Had O'Gilroy had time to get into position yet? They had only eight shells, little over two minutes' firing time, they couldn't afford to waste . . . Yet he had to keep up the pace, not give his amateur crew time for common sense to set in . . .

The devil with it: "Fire."

The Arab opened the breech, the hot shell-case clattered off the trail and Corinna kicked it aside.

"Quiet!" Ranklin ordered, listening. He heard the distant *crump*, then nothing. Damn. One wasted, with nobody seeing where it had fallen. Then blessedly, a single faint whistle. "Over." *Peep-peep-peep-peep*. "And to the left. Load."

He made the corrections as they reloaded. Zurga had stopped firing – it was well over thirteen seconds since the last shrapnel burst – so he must know they had moved their gun. And he would have heard the whistle, so guessed he was under observed fire. What would he do now?

It was absurd how this thing had become a duel.

He was about to give the fire order when there was the bang of shrapnel. But distant, in front.

He frowned, then realised: if O'Gilroy could see Zurga's gun, then vice versa. And instead of firing blindly at where Ranklin might or might not be, Zurga was trying to destroy O'Gilroy so as to blind Ranklin as well. Now it wasn't a duel, it was a race.

27

The *bang* of the bursting shell was followed by the rattle of shrapnel balls among the trees and rocks and then the crackle of falling branches.

Bertie raised his head, frowned, then said: "Quite logical. Our good colonel shoots at the target he can see, not the one he cannot. But does he really see us, or only guess from the noise of your whistle?"

O'Gilroy crinkled his eyes with peering. Zurga's gun was just a darkish blob near the misty edge of vision, an amoebic shape that seemed to wriggle as the crew moved, fetching and loading shells. "If'n he's got good enough field-glasses – and he should have, being a Gunner – mebbe he can. We'd best move . . . split up, anyways, so one shell don't get us both. Hold on."

They had heard the *thud* of Ranklin's gun firing, now both fixed their stare on the far-off blob. A flash and a cloud of smoke and dust jumped from the slope to its right.

"A *droit* – to the right now. And perhaps beyond still?"

"I think so." O'Gilroy slid down and turned his back to the tree-trunk, then blew a single *peep* and a double one. "*Now* let's move."

Only it wasn't that simple. Bertie's diplomatic training had obviously been pretty comprehensive, for apart from being skilful and calm about shooting fellow human beings, he had picked good defensive positions on both sides of the riverbed. Two Arabs were up among the rocks on the Peak side, but the one who had come with him on the plateau side had been unlucky. O'Gilroy had passed him, seemingly having bled to death propped against a tree, as he climbed up to join Bertie among the trees just below the plateau. The ravine leading towards the monastery lay perhaps 150 yards ahead, and somewhere in its mouth were a handful of Turkish soldiers. The first encounter had left two of them dead in the dry bed itself; the rest were firing a shot every so often but clearly waiting for their comrades to get back from the trench and join in before they did anything else.

But it was only from this one position, at the top of the slope, that O'Gilroy and Bertie could see round the curve of the bed to Zurga's gun. Moving down would unsight them, and they couldn't go higher, only out onto the open plateau.

"I'll go *forward*," O'Gilroy said. "Jest ten yards – metres – should be enough. After this," he added, as Zurga fired.

The rocks up here were few and small, so they crushed themselves into the pine needles and unyielding soil behind inadequate tree-trunks, feeling horribly naked.

Shrapnel tore through the branches overhead, thudded into O'Gilroy's tree and kicked up earth a few inches from his cowering nose.

"Are you unhurt?" Bertie called.

"That and moving both." O'Gilroy began a snake-like crawl forward, zigzagging around tree-trunks and their bulging, clutching roots. At least with his age, shape and infantry training he should be better than Bertie at this. He had thought of leaving his rifle behind, but to let go of it was a form of surrender. That was why men threw away their weapons when they panicked and ran.

The *thud* of Ranklin's gun made him stop and, cautiously, slowly – it was movement that caught the eye – raise his head to watch the shell burst.

Zero the gun on the aiming point, pull pin, load, close breech, "*Retti!*" – and wait impatiently for the whistle and its corrections . . . They were down to five shells now, and perhaps even when they were on target, the high explosive would bury itself in soft sand and burst like a damp firecracker . . .

Such waiting gave you too much time to think . . . Then

peep-peep-peep: on line but too short. He corrected up twenty-five metres. "Fire!"

O'Gilroy had gone at least ten yards, finding a good position behind a fallen tree, but slightly down slope so that he had to half-stand to see. Only he wasn't going to stand until he heard Ranklin fire. Before then, Zurga was due to fire at him – only he seemed to be taking his time.

Thud-thud – an echo? Or Zurga trying to time his own shell to reach O'Gilroy at the one moment he must be watching? Whatever it was, he *had* to stand now – but as he stretched up the shrapnel banged almost overhead, and the upright tree beside him exploded splinters in his face. Blinded, he ducked instinctively for cover, hearing dimly the unseen *crump* of Ranklin's shell, but muddled by the memory of another sound, a shot, nearby . . .

"Did ye see where that one went?"

Silence.

"Are ye hit?"

More silence, while O'Gilroy found his left cheek was grazed and bleeding, but his eyes unhurt. He rolled cautiously to look back.

A rifle cracked, someone gave a choked yell from up on the plateau, and Bertie called: "A Turk had come up the cliff. I am sorry, he distracted me. He will not distract me again."

So it *had* been a rifle shot that filled his face with splinters. Pretty adventurous of an ordinary soldier to have scaled the wall of the ravine to out-flank them. But all he'd achieved was making them miss one shell-burst. Ranklin would just have to fire another.

Wait a minute: an ordinary soldier would never be adventurous alone, it wasn't what he was trained or allowed to do. O'Gilroy opened his mouth to shout a warning.

Every battery commander knew this impatience: *are you blind or just asleep up there in the observation post?*

Or, in this case, of course, just dead?

They heard the second rifle shot, but intermittent shots had been coming from along the riverbed all the time.

"Devil with it," Ranklin said. "We'll have to stick on the same aim." Which would bring them down to four shells. "Fire!"

The second Turk's shot and the firing of Ranklin's gun were almost simultaneous. O'Gilroy saw Bertie sprawl out from behind his tree, was aware of where the rifle flash had come from, but then had, *had* to turn away to watch Ranklin's fall of shot. A second rifle bullet slammed into the trunk of the tree he was sheltering behind, and instinctively he sucked in his belly to make himself even thinner . . .

A flash winked behind the gun, blotted out immediately by erupting earth and dust. If that was over, it was only by mere feet, not worth bothering with. He flopped back behind his fallen trunk, dragged in breath, and began blowing *peep-peep-peep-peep-peep-peep* . . .

Then he reached for his rifle and started crawling. And now we'll see how Turkish Army training fits you to meet a *real* soldier . . .

Exultantly, Ranklin lost count of the *peeps*. "We're on! Ready? Fire!"

The breech slammed open, the empty case clanged fuming off the trail, a new shell slid home, the breech slammed shut – "Fire!" They were breathing the pure reek of cordite fumes now, but they had become a team, automatic and unthinking, *relay*, *close*, *fire*, *open*, *load*, *relay* . . .

"Fire!"

The explosion was stunning. Distant, yet far larger than a shell-burst should be.

Corinna looked at him, wide-eyed with hope. "What was—?"

"I'm not sure . . ." But as the silence spun on, as Zurga's gun didn't fire, he became sure. "I think we hit their ammunition."

Her face was stained with powder-smoke, streaked with grease where she'd rubbed it. "Then have we won?"

Have we just torn Zurga and half a dozen men – anybody within a dozen yards of that gun – to pieces with red-hot fragments of metal? But she and the Arab were mere gun crew, obeying his orders; it was childish, selfish, to infect them with his own post-action tristesse.

"Yes, we've won. Well done, *bloody* well done." He hugged her, pumped the Arab's hand – that might not be the correct thing to do, but his wide, if forced, grin made the gesture clear. Then he took the last unfired shell from the breech, not wanting it to cook in the hot gun, and rested it carefully on the ground. Then, with the Arab helping, he relaid the gun to point straight along the riverbed, just in case, and sent him back for a couple more shells.

O'Gilroy and two Arabs came around the bend in the riverbed where the gun was now aimed, a quarter of a mile ahead. Their own Arab came back with two more shells, Ranklin directed him where to put them, then offered him a cigarette and lit one for himself. When O'Gilroy came up, he passed it across and asked: "Bertie?"

O'Gilroy took the cigarette with a hand that shivered slightly. He took a deep drag, blew smoke, and said slowly, "Coupla fellers – Turk soldiers – tried to flank us, coming up the cliff. Near got me, 'n' Bertie got that one, then t'other got him. Then I got t'other." Maybe, by tactful questioning – and half a bottle of whisky – Ranklin would one day learn what had really happened. If it mattered.

"T'other Arab got himself killed 'fore I got there," O'Gilroy added. He sucked on the cigarette.

"Well done, anyhow."

"I'd probly have killed Bertie meself anyways," O'Gilroy said. "Him being a bastard." Ranklin nodded. You didn't want to like, even to know, the ones who died. You wanted them just to be things. He looked around. The scattered shell-cases, the dead Arab on the beach, more shell-cases and boxes and the little line of bodies . . . There were plenty of things.

Oh God, why did You make courage so damned *normal*? We know You're on the side of the big battalions – but are You also on the side of the men who send out the battalions? – who use men's courage to plug the gaps in their own stupidity? Surely You aren't another of those who believe the more terrible war becomes, the more likely men are to give it up? You're supposed to *know* about us! Have You forgotten so much since You last visited us 1900 years ago? *Oh God, just stop men being brave!*

Corinna was looking at him. The streaks on her face were now further streaked with tears. Reaction. But she'd want him not to notice. She asked: "Are you all right?"

"Just praying. I think." He threw his cigarette on the ground and got brisk. "There's still getting on for a hundred soldiers up there somewhere. They won't attack the monastery now but we're on their line of retreat even if they don't want to catch us. So you and O'Gilroy get on horses – if there's any still alive – and get back past the Railway tunnel and up to . . . your caravan road."

"And you?"

"I'll disable this gun and go back with . . ." He waved at the three remaining Arabs. "Through the back way to the monastery. And get Lady Kelso out somehow . . ." At least they could now put Miskal on a horse (if *they* had any left alive) and move off to . . . their village? Or haul him down to Mersina and a doctor? Somewhere, somehow; he was too drained to worry. "I don't think we'd better go back through the Railway camp, so if you can get something to meet us on the road . . . And after that, we'd appreciate the hospitality of your – Mr Billings's – yacht."

"Of course." She looked up the riverbed. "Aren't we going to . . . bury them?"

"Digging even one grave takes an age."

She turned away and then half-turned back. "Did you hear what I said about Edouard?"

"I heard. I think it's . . . just . . . Oh hell. I'm very glad." They smiled at each other; the past seemed very past.

28

The Foreign Office had been built over fifty years later than the Admiralty, so Corbin's room was more grand than elegant. They sat near the window, just out of the slant of the afternoon sun, the Commander, Ranklin and Corbin himself, nobody from the Admiralty or India Office. Ranklin had asked about this and been told, politely, that it wasn't his concern.

Now Corbin was asking: "And this survey map is definitely destroyed?"

"I burned it myself," Ranklin said firmly.

"And you believe that will delay the Baghdad Railway for . . . weeks? Months?"

"I think you'd have to ask an experienced railway surveyor that."

"Umm. I think we'd prefer to go on not having heard of it," Corbin said. "But we – somebody – is going to have to talk to the French. After all, they have lost a diplomatist. You say he was more, or less, than that – which seems borne out by their rather guarded manner in making enquiries about him – but nevertheless *prima facie* a diplomatist, so something has to be said. Would it be best if you – " his look switched between the Commander and Ranklin "– had a word with your French counterparts and left them to tell the Quai d'Orsay as much as seemed appropriate?"

"We will if you like," the Commander said without enthusiasm.

"I think it would be best. They may settle for an assurance that he died bravely. I trust that he did?"

"I don't know," Ranklin said. "I was half a mile away."

Corbin looked irritated, so Ranklin shrugged. "I expect so. Men usually do."

Satisfied, Corbin nodded. "Which seems only to leave the matter of Lady Kelso . . . What do you suggest we should do to express our thanks to her? Bearing in mind that any *public* acknowledgement of her contribution might bring the whole . . . complex story into the open." He'd probably been going to say "shabby", not "complex".

Ranklin had known this must come, but that had been no help. "I'm afraid there's not much I can suggest, except—"

"She does rather seem to have everything already," Corbin mused. "The title, the house in the Italian lakes . . ."

"I think she'd rather like an introduction to English society – at a level suitable to her rank."

There was a moment of rather surprised silence. Then Corbin said: "Society . . . Yes, odd how people value that . . . But although, at the Foreign Office, we have to deal with some strange and even weird races, the upper reaches of English society are, thank God, not within our remit. So I'm afraid . . . A warm letter of appreciation from Sir Edward himself, perhaps?"

It was, as Ranklin had expected, the best they could do. On the way out, he asked: "Will you be letting the Admiralty and India Office know whatever's 'appropriate'? Or do they expect us to report to them separately?"

This time Corbin looked vexed. "The Admiralty will be informed. But the India Office . . . They may have started this thing, but it isn't any risk to India that concerns us, it's the Gulf and oil."

As they reached the pavement of King Charles Street, the Commander demanded: "What was that about the *India* Office? We don't have any dealings with them."

"Spying," Ranklin said cheerfully. "Corbin said the India Office started it. So now we know Gunther sold his secret to Hapgood, not the FO or the Admiralty. I suppose foreigners do tend to overrate our concern for India."

"Are you still worrying about van der Brock?"

"Wouldn't we like to re-establish good commercial relations with that firm? Their terms seem to be strictly eye-for-an-eye: one of Gunther's partners wanted to balance their books by killing me. May still want to, for all I know."

"We can't have *that*," the Commander frowned. "Could you suggest to them that it was the late Monsieur Bertrand Lacan who had Gunther killed? – he was in Paris, just a telephone call away at the time, wasn't he?"

Ranklin nodded. "Actually, I think it really *was* him – or his department or whatever. I think Gunther got his information from an informant in Paris, not Berlin. And from what they said, or didn't say, to O'Gilroy at Constantinople, I think Gunther's partners know that."

"Fine," the Commander said cheerfully. "So all you have to do is persuade them that Bertie found out, and Bob's your uncle."

"Suppose," Ranklin said cautiously, "they ask *how* Bertie found out?"

But the Commander refused to be uncheered. "They probably won't. Anyway, loose ends add veracity. It's only lies that explain every last detail."

"How very true," Ranklin murmured.

* * *

"I believe," Ranklin said, "that you're an expert on the rupee?"

"Oh no, just an amateur, a pure dabbler on the fringes." Hapgood, the outsider, had picked up the self-deprecation of the genuine insider. Only perhaps he overdid it.

"But you've never seen it in its native habitat? Never visited India?"

"No-o." Hapgood was puzzled but kept a smile on his honest, open face.

"Now might be a good time."

"Really? Why?"

"Because I'm going to have to tell Gunther van der Brock's partner that you betrayed Gunther to the French, had him killed."

"I did nothing of the—"

"Perhaps for what you saw as the best of motives: so that, once Gunther had sold his secret to you, he couldn't sell it to anyone else. Only – I suppose you had the sense to make it an anonymous message? – you'd have to pretend that he was *coming* to this Office, not that he'd already been."

"I tell you this is abso—!"

"I suppose you thought that was what a real born-to-rule insider would have done. Charming but ruthless. But you overdid it: more royal than royalty sort of thing. It can be tricky, knowing what to be true to, I know . . . And incidentally, you were wrong about Gunther. He would never have sold the same secret twice. He was, in his way, an honourable man – for purely commercial reasons, no doubt, but in these lax times . . ."

Hapgood had gone red-faced under his curly fair hair. "I had nothing to do with it . . . And why are you making a fuss about some damned little informer, anyway?"

"He was a *spy* – just like me. He spent his life risking his neck and being despised by people like you, and he'd learned to expect that, we all do. That doesn't leave us much to cling to. But one thing is not being betrayed by the people we work for: we don't have to stand for *that* – is that quite clear?"

Hapgood stared at him, truly bewildered. "But you can't compare yourself with *him* . . . You work for—"

"You don't understand." Ranklin nodded to himself and stood up. Hapgood rose, too, towering over him. "And if you don't understand, don't *meddle* . . . I'm serious about visiting India."